Sugar Rush

BELLE AURORA

Sugar Rush

BELLE AURORA

Published by Belle Aurora
Copyright © 2014 Belle Aurora

Editing by Hot Tree Editing

Cover designer by Cover It Designs
Internal formatting by

3

Sugar Rush

PROLOGUE

Helena

I weep openly. A high-pitched whimper leaves my mouth that is so high, I think I hear a dog howl somewhere in the distance. I alternate whimpering and bawling, snorting every now and again. Tears drench my cheeks. Boogers almost run into my mouth. I'm a hot mess.

When the celebrant smiles happily and utters, "I now pronounce you man and wife. You may kiss the bride," my sister, Natalie, throws her bouquet behind her. Without flinching, Mimi snatches up the flowers mid-air before winking to the crowd. Nat stands on her tiptoes and kisses her husband, Asher, through a smile. He gently hooks a hand around the back of her neck and holds her close, deepening the kiss and refusing to let her end it. They smile lip-to-lip.

It's beautiful. And so I howl. I look across to the middle-aged man sitting next to me. He watches me with a mixture of concern and fear, backing up just a little. I try to speak through my hitching breaths and sobbing, "Izz juzz so beautafoo." *Hitch*. "*So beautafoo*."

I break down again, louder this time. Sinking down into my chair in the most unladylike way, I let out a long, keening cry. I hear someone say an annoyed, "Will someone please get her out of here?"

Wet mascara makes my eyelashes stick together. When I realize the annoyed person is my sister, I lift my face heavenward and cry harder. Nat glares at me and hisses only loud enough for me to hear, "Seriously, shut the eff up and stop with the crying. You're bringing everyone down, skank!"

I weakly reach a hand out to her, body shaking with silent sobs and try to speak. "I lubb ewe. Ewe look beautafoo. *So* beautafoo." I sit up and wail, "I'm juzz happy. So *happy*."

My sister. She speaks my language. So when I see her eyes fill with tears and her lip quivers, I know it's not long before this solo turns into a duet. She looks at me and whispers, "Aww." The first of her tears fall, and before I know it, we're clutching each other and sobbing openly, wailing, sounding something like a couple of chimps fighting in a turf war.

If you couldn't tell, I don't do weddings well. They get me. They *always* get me. It's the same thing every time. I give myself a firm pep talk. I don't bother packing tissues, as if somehow that'll stop the tears, and usually, before the cake is even cut, my makeup is all over my face and my eyes are swollen shut.

But today is worse. Today, it's my sister's special day. Well, my sister's *second* special day. She and Asher eloped. They got hitched in Vegas, married by Elvis. They said at the time it felt right, but when they got home, it felt wrong, that it felt like something was missing. And what was missing was family.

They organized another small celebration to be held in the best man, Nik, and maid of honor, Tina's, backyard. I have known Tina Tomic all my life. She grew up with us. Her parents and mine were the best of friends, meaning, naturally, we all developed a special bond. Not quite close enough to be sisters, but too close to be called just friends.

We became soul sisters.

When Tina lost her mom and daughter, she left California and moved to New York. She opened a very successful boutique called Safira's, and Nat followed closely behind. Nik and Tina met, developed a friendship and fell in love. A special kind of love. One for the ages. The type of love poets write about.

Nik owns the club across the street from Safira, The White Rabbit. And with Nik comes his posse—his younger brother, Max, his best friend, Asher or Ghost, as the boys call him, and their cousin, Trick. Tina, having her own posse, her worker girls, Mimi and Lola, and my sister, Nat, decided to merge the two groups to form one. And they did.

They formed a family.

Not all families are bonded through blood. Some have been sewn together by love and laughter.

Now, Nat and Asher, they didn't always like each other. In fact, they despised one another. They fought their attraction to each other for a long time...until it became unavoidable. When they finally came together, they collided with a bang. Literally. Heads were butted. Hooves were bucked. It wasn't pretty. Not your typical romance, for sure. They fought until it hurt to fight anymore. You know the saying, *'There's a thin line between love and hate'*? Well, they severed the line and the emotions merged. They realized their love for each other was too strong to ignore.

And here they are, happily married. I smile shakily.

I can't believe it.

My sister is married.

Someone pries my Kung-Fu death grip off Nat and ushers my sobbing ass away. I peer out of a swollen eye to find my older sister, Nina, shushing me and rubbing my back soothingly. She tries not to make eye contact, knowing it'll only make things worse, but in a moment of confusion, her eye meets mine.

We both still.

Her eyes widen.

So do mine.

Her wide-set gaze darts from side-to-side in panic, looking for a quick out. But it's too late. My lip quivers. I lift my face and I let out a wail so strong it sounds like an animal has made it—namely, a moose—and etiquette tells me that alarming noise has no place at a wedding.

But I just *can't* stop it!

Nina's steps quicken, in turn, quickening my own. She pulls me along, and then we're inside. "Jesus C, kid. Buck the fuck up," she utters in exasperation. "I seriously don't know how we're related sometimes. It's a wedding, not a funeral! No more tears. *Capisce*?"

My breathing hitches so much that my face jerks to the side with every heavy breath. "I." *Hitch*. "Can't." *Hitch*. "Help." *Hitch*. "It."

She takes some tissue and wipes my face gently. "God, you've made a mess. C'mon. I have to redo your face. You look like a bee stung you. And the bee was on crack."

Away from the music and sounds of the wedding, Nina leads me into the bathroom, carrying her makeup kit. She sits me on the edge of the tub while she sits on the closed lid of the toilet. She attacks me with a powder brush. It tickles my nose and I want to sneeze and laugh all at once, but I don't dare interrupt Nina while she does her thing. I take a moment to slow my breathing and calm my erratic emotions.

Being a hairdresser, Nina has been assigned hair and makeup duties today. She really did an amazing job. Nat looks stunning. Nina was careful with her, took her time, and her time paid off. Nat looks like an angel.

When we arrived last week, Nat shocked us all by making an announcement. Flicking her fire-engine red hair, she admitted, "I'm done with this color." Smiling at Nina, she asked, "Feel like making me a brunette?" It had been years since I had seen Nat in her natural shade of chocolate brown, and honestly, I wasn't sure how Ash would take it. It's not like she warned him or anything. In typical Nat style, she cornered him.

Nina had just finished styling the newly dyed hair when Ash came home. Nat stood with her cape still on and strode over to him. Once she was toe-to-toe with him, she placed her hands on her hips, widened her eyes, shook her head lightly and asked expectantly, "Well?"

But the tall, strapping, ash-blond didn't move. He just looked down at his wife, his warm brown eyes following the length of her now-brown hair. I could tell the exact moment Nat went into panic mode. I knew this because she started rambling, "It's just that I'm not getting any younger and I wanted you to see me. You know, *me* me. Not hiding-behind-bright-hair-and-boobs Nat. But I can change it—"

Her words were cut short when she was tugged into his arms. Legs splayed, Ash held Nat tightly in his hold, lightly rocking her. I don't know what he said to her because his words were whispered, but as his lips met her ear and started moving, I caught her expression. Her eyes closed slowly and her mouth parted in relief before she smiled softly.

Asher is not a man of many words, but he's getting better. The thing with men who don't talk much is they make the words they say count.

Poor guy never stood a chance.

You can't exactly stay quiet in our family. In order to be heard, you need to yell over the other four people talking.

Nina applies more powder. "So, you seeing anyone, kid?"

Eyes closed, I respond quietly, "Nah." I gesture weakly to my body. "Who could handle all this?"

She huffs out a laugh through her nose. She remains silent a moment, but I can feel it. She wants to say something. And before I know it, she does. Nina is not the type to hold back. She liked to speak what's on her mind, but she doesn't talk about herself. Her private life has always been just that—private. Her tone is gentle, but serious. "Take it from me; don't wait too long." My eyes open at the wistful note in her voice. She smiles sadly. "Don't want you to regret putting it off."

I understand what she's saying, but it doesn't change the way things are. "It's a little hard dating right now, you know? I just finished my studies, and I'm about to be offered a placement God knows where. I think I need to concentrate on my career. The thought of having a boyfriend right now," I cringe, "it's exhausting."

Firm fingers grip my chin. Blazing eyes meet mine. "Excuses."

"What?"

Nina loosens her grip on me and applies a little blush. "You're making excuses." Her voice gentles once more. "What if you found the person who's right for you and you turned them away because of your so-called career? Then, when it came time to settle down, you realize that person didn't wait for you. And they shouldn't have, because you were selfish. That career you did it all for, you'll resent. They'll always be the one who got away, and those kinds of things play on your mind."

I take my sister's hand, pausing her mid-brushstroke and ask gently, "Who was yours?"

Her face voids of expression. She quickly dips her chin and clears her throat. When she looks up again, all I see is sadness. Sadness so cutting, my chest aches. She mutters a hoarse, "Doesn't matter. They'll always be one who got away, and I can only blame myself."

Nina carefully adds the last of the makeup, restoring my puffy eyes and tear-stained cheeks to near perfection. I stand and pull her close. Her arms wrap around me and hold me tightly, and for the first time in forever, I think Nina needs this hug more than I do. "Thank you, Neens. I love you."

She responds on a squeeze. "Love you, too. Now, go talk up some guys. There're some real Johnny's out there." When my sisters and I talk about guys, the hotter they are, the more Johnny-like they are. In fact, I *still* have a Johnny Depp poster in my room. He sets a high standard.

I love you, Johnny. They'll never be you!

Pulling apart, I smirk. "Are you telling me I should hook up or somethin'?"

Nina smirks right back. "No harm in a little diddle here and there."

I chuckle and shake my head, but she's right. I mentally roll my eyes at myself. Here I am, crying and pouting, when I could be talking to a Johnny. And Lord knows, I haven't diddled in a while.

Where are my priorities?

I leave Nina to pack away her things and head back outside into the open courtyard. As soon as the fresh air hits me, I close my eyes and breathe it in. When I open my eyes, I smile.

The courtyard looks stunning. Nat hadn't wanted anything too complicated, going for the less-is-more approach. Always a win, if you ask me. All she wanted was white and apricot sheeting gathered and lining the inner border of the yard. The only extra she asked for was color coordinated Chinese lanterns that will be lit after dark. Finger food was indeed a better choice in this warmer weather, and with no need for tables, people are up talking and laughing together, while the hired waiters bring around trays of food.

My eyes scan everything around me. I look to the left to see a pregnant Tina holding hands with her husband, Nik. A waiter passes them, and Tina's eyes follow the tray of food. Nik, being Nik, follows her gaze to the retreating waiter's back before letting go of her hand and walking away. Not ten seconds later, Nik returns with the entire tray of hors d'oeuvres, smiling down at her. Tina looks from the tray to Nik. She takes a tiny morsel from the tray he holds for her, her face turns soft, and with a gentle smile, I see her mouth form the words 'I love you'. Nik doesn't respond, but wraps his free arm around her and leans down to kiss her forehead. As his lips touch her, his eyes close and he allows his kiss to linger.

My heart aches, and that bitch Jealousy rears her head for a single second. I want a love like that. One day, hopefully I'll have it.

Nat and Ash come to stand by Nik and Tina. A smiling Nat hands Tina a small bottle of apple juice before she lowers herself to a crouch in front of Tina's belly.

I feel a pang in my chest.

Nat splays her hands on the protruding melon that is Tina's baby bump as she talks to it. Ash reaches over to squeeze Tina's shoulder. With an understanding smile, Tina smiles before lifting her hand to rest on his. It takes true friends to do what Tina and Nik are doing for Nat and Ash.

You see, Tina is pregnant, but the babies aren't hers. They're Nat and Ash's babies. Tina is acting as a surrogate for them, because Nat can't carry babies to full term, and that's just the kind of person she is. To see people unhappy makes her unhappy. She would do anything for the people she cares about. We recently found out there are two babies, but don't yet know the sexes. Truthfully, Nat doesn't care what the babies are, as long as they're healthy.

Holding hands, Lola and Trick make their way over to the group closely followed by a severe Johnny. A Johnny I have never been able to take my eyes off for more than a minute, because he's *so* Johnny that my Johnny poster weeps at night, struck by jealousy. Max Leokov slides up behind Nat, smiling a dangerously naughty smile. Without warning, he pulls her up from her kneeling position by her underarms and turns her to face Ash. I can't help but chuckle at the look and Asher's face. His jaw tics, any ounce of friendliness quickly replaced by anger.

But Max doesn't care. He wraps his arms around Nat's middle in an intimate embrace, lowers his face to her neck, and begins to pepper her with kisses. Ash steps forward, scowling, jaw tight, but Max simply steps back with Nat in his hold. I can't hear what's being said from here, but from the sly smile on Max's face as he speaks and the way the others start laughing, I can tell he's being a smartass and clearly has a death-wish for winding Ash up the way he is.

Clearly.

I've seen what Ash can do when he's pushed. It's not pretty.

Ash leaps forward, and like a coward, Max releases Nat, but quickly moves in front of Tina, arms open expectantly. Tina, being the sucker she is, moves into his embrace, laughing while he smacks wet kisses on her cheek.

A split second before Nik's fist moves to punch him, Max dodges it, reaches out, and takes Lola's hand. He pulls her to him, and rolling her eyes, she smiles, allows him to hold her close—almost too close—and dances a slow dance in the middle of their circle of friends. Trick, not liking this, pulls her away from him and tucks her close to his side. She sighs and happily wraps an arm around him.

Max opens his arms to his friends and shakes his head slowly. I see him mouth, 'You're no fun'. As he walks over to the bar and finds Mimi, he wraps his arms around her from behind. She stiffens a moment, turns, then relaxes back into him. He whispers something into her ear, and swatting him away, she laughs loudly. He holds a hand to his heart, wearing a mock-wounded expression.

And for a moment, I'm jealous. They truly are a family. A part of me craves to be a part of it. I feel like a geek looking into the cool group at school. Still, I look around for a Johnny I like, and there are more than a few hotties in the crowd, but my eyes keep moving toward the tall, dark, and handsome man with golden eyes and the magic dimple.

Max.

I've lost count of the amount of women I have seen him flirting with, and—let's face it—he's almost as Johnny as the man himself.

Dare I say, he's *more* Johnny than Johnny?

Sacrilege!

If there ever was a Johnny I'd want for the night, it'd be him. He meets all the check boxes. Gorgeous. Funny. Intelligent. Sweet. And from the way he's been throwing himself around, he's a sure thing.

I spend the next ten minutes watching Max flirt with every woman within arm's reach, including my mom, before I pep myself up enough to talk to him. I don't really like men who flirt, but I like that he's an equal opportunity flirt. No woman is safe from him. Old, young, thick and thin, he's all over it, and I see he's moved on to Nina, who isn't left unaffected. As he takes her hand and kisses it over and over again, she lifts her free hand to cover her mouth as she fights a smile.

This is my chance. I've found my in.

As I approach, Nina removes herself from his wandering arms—the fool—and moves on to chat with Mimi by the bar. With no new potential victims near, Max pulls his phone out of his pocket and begins to scroll.

You like to flirt, Max? Get ready to meet your match.

With every step closer I take to him, my stomach flips and flops around in anticipation. I'm excited! Finally, I reach his side and gently clear my throat. He glances up at me with his brows raised before looking back down at his phone. "Hey, Helen. How you doin'?"

My smile falters.

Helen? *Really*?

Well...not a good start.

He continues to play around on his phone, brows drawn as I speak, "Uh, it's Helen*a*, actually. Anyways, I was wondering if you'd like to have a drink with m—"

Before I can get another word in, he mutters, "Cool. Nice to see you again, Helen," then he walks away, never taking his face from his phone, leaving me standing in the middle of the courtyard, mouth gaping. I blink as a frown overtakes my face. I try to make sense of what happened here. The serial flirt, the man who flirts with anything with a pulse, anything that moves, did not flirt with me.

Hmmm. If my calculations are correct, that would deem me undesirable.

Embarrassment flows through me, heating my cheeks. My embarrassment quickly turns to forced disinterest. I turn my nose up and stand taller. That's fine. He doesn't have to like me. Sometimes people just don't like other people. It happens. It's all good. *And, hey, this is a good thing*, I think. I mean, I sure as hell don't hold a candle for Max Leokov.

Not anymore.

CHAPTER ONE

Helena

"Helena, mail!" my father shouts from the kitchen.

I jump up from my laying position and bounce off my bed. My feet try to move quicker than physically possible, causing my sock covered tootsies to slip and slide on the floorboards. A casualty is made quickly. My knee slams into my nightstand so hard the photo frames on the top fall over and the half-full glass of water topples, spilling aqua all over my open textbook.

Gasping with wide eyes, I clutch at it, willing the pain away, but the agony continues, stronger than before, and in a moment of clarity, I think to myself, *This is it...this is how it all ends*.

Okay, so maybe I'm a little dramatic, but *damn*, that hurts!

Oh, dear God. Will the pain never *end?*

My throbbing knee numbs, and I know it'll have to go. I'll likely be the only nightstand amputee. Just another statistic. I crawl over to my bedroom door and lie dying in the open doorway. I call out to the only person who can save me. "Ta, help!"

There's a moment of silence before my father's heavily accented voice calls back, "No."

I'd like to say he's a terrible father and he wants me to die, but he's a great dad. Maybe a tad dramatic (hence my own dramatics), but a great dad. And I may have claimed death being on my door a few times before. Once or twice. But this time, it's *actually* happening. My vision starts to darken. I see the light. "Ta, help me! I'm fading fast!"

My father sighs long and hard. "What happen this time? You get a paper cut, or plug your toe?"

A disgruntled expression crosses my face, and I use my elbows to elevate my body into a semi-sitting position. "Firstly, old man, it's *stub* your toe, not *plug* your toe. You need English lessons. Secondly, I stubbed it really bad that time. It was hanging by a thread! If I didn't use the Band-Aid when I did, not even a plastic surgeon would have been able to save my pinkie toe."

My father's chortle fills the kitchen. "Yes, my English is no good, but you, my sweet, are a hurt in my butt."

I try really hard not to laugh, but he's adorable sometimes. "It's pain in the ass, Ta! *God!*"

Flipping over, injury forgotten, I calculate this being the three-hundred-and-twelfth time I've cheated death by injuries caused by my clumsiness. I use the term clumsiness loosely. Sometimes my body just thinks it knows what its doing, brain be damned. My body seems to come with an auto-pilot function other bodies don't have. As far as I'm concerned, it's just an added extra.

I stand, and using the wall for stability, I limp into the kitchen, where my father doesn't even look up from the newspaper he's reading to see if I'm okay from my near-fatal fall. Scowling, I say way too loudly, "I'm fine, thanks! No, I'm okay; I don't need an ice-pack. God, you're such a great dad, though. Father of the year strikes again."

Dad closes his eyes, sighs, and then looks heavenward, thanking God for such an awesome daughter, I'm sure. He *should* be thankful.

I'm the shit.

My limp suddenly gone, I move behind him and wrap my arms around his neck, resting my chin on his balding head. "One day, I'm actually going to die from a stubbed toe, and when I do, you're going to have to explain to the doctors who run my autopsy why there were so many prior stubbed-toe incidents you never reported. You'll probably get grilled for it, or even go to jail for neglect."

My father wheezes out a heavy laugh, and kissing his cheek, I take the letter on the table and open it. Leaving it folded, I make my way to the fridge and pull out a bottle of apple juice.

As I sit at the table, my father asks, "How is Natalia?"

I shrug. "I don't know. She's been busy lately. No time to talk, really."

He frowns. "Find time. Nina calls every day. You call her. Today."

I unfold the letter and begin to read. The more I read, the more my heart races. My eyes widen. I read faster. As I reach the end of the letter, a smile spreads across my face. "I don't think you'll have to worry about Nat." I slide over the letter. His eyes skim the contents, face devoid of expression. I add, "She'll have company soon enough."

My father reads aloud, "Center of Physical Therapy. New York."

Throwing up my hands, I whoop and yell out an excited, "Yeah, baby! I'm going to New York!"

He slumps back in his chair and mumbles sadly, "Why you all leave me?"

Reaching across the table, I take his big hands in mine and rein in my excitement. "It's not like I won't ever come home, Ta. This is a great opportunity. We talked about this."

"I know." Sitting straighter in his chair, he utters confidently, "You will learn, and work, and you will someday win a big award because you are so smart."

For a man who doesn't speak English well, that compliment hits me hard. I blink away tears and mutter softly, "Thanks, Dad."

The back sliding door opens and my mother walks inside holding a bag full of groceries. As soon as she sees my father and me together, she looks down at my hands covering his, our faces sad, and she drops the bag of groceries with a gasp. "Someone died?!"

Okay, so maybe dramatics come from both sides of the family.

I release my father's hand, stand, and make my way over to my mother with the letter. I hold it out for her to read. She takes it with shaking hands, expression petrified, before she reads it over. She whispers, "New York." Then she cries. And laughs. And cries again.

She pulls me into a firm hug and rocks me. "Oh, baby. This is wonderful. This is exciting!" My throat tightens with emotion and I close my eyes, just letting my mom hold me, 'cause sometimes, the warmth of a mother's hug is all a person needs. She kisses my temple. "You're going to do great. Now, call them and accept the position before they give it to someone else." I open my eyes to look at my miserable father and hesitate. Mom whispers, "He'll be fine. I promise."

My mother has always been my biggest fan, a number one fan to all us girls. She is a firm believer of following your dreams, wherever they might be. She kisses my head once more before releasing me, turning me, and slapping my butt to get me on my way. I chuckle, take the letter, and make it back to my room without any toe or knee casualties. I pick up my cell from my desk and dial the number on the letter. "Hi, I'd like to speak to a..." I quickly scan the bottom of the letter for a signature. "...James Whittaker."

A mature voice answers, "What was your name, ma'am?"

"Helena Kovac. He'll be expecting my call."

"I'll just put you on hold a moment and make sure he's in."

"No problem."

I'm put on hold. I close my eyes and nod to the song playing, and just as I'm about to belt out the chorus to the power ballad, the line clicks over. A deep but kind voice greets me, "Miss Kovac. James Whittaker here. Please tell me you have some good news for me."

A wide smile spread across my face. "Thank you for the opportunity."

He chuckles. "Top student in your class. I should be thanking you for the opportunity. But please, the suspense is killing me." I like this man already. "Will you accept the position? I know it's a move for you, but we'll be happy to help with moving costs and such, as well as temporary housing."

That's definitely good to know. "I want this position, Mr. Whittaker. My sister actually lives in New York, so I don't think housing will be necessary."

The smile in his voice makes me smile harder. "Please, call me James. And this is great. I'm so glad to have you on-board. As soon as you email through your acceptance of the job offer, we can get moving." He pauses a moment before asking cautiously, "How soon can you start?"

Today is Tuesday. I think for a second.

How long will it take to pack up my life and start over?

"Is Monday too soon?"

James lets out a chuckle. "Heck no."

This is happening. It's *really* happening. "I can't wait." I really can't.

He responds, "You just get yourself down here. We'll take it easy that first week, ease you in, then schedule in some clients for you. How does that sound?"

I near whisper, "Amazing."

"Well, if you need anything, anything at all, just call. I'll give you my private extension, as well as my cell number." He rattles of his private numbers before speaking quietly, "I know what it's like to be new in town. Five years ago, that was me, so I'm going to make sure your transition is as painless as it can be."

Wow. That's so nice. I love my new boss! "Thank you, Mr. Whitt—" I quickly catch myself. "Thank you, James. I'm looking forward to a change in scenery."

"See you Monday."

I hang up and thank God my new boss isn't a mean old asshole. Still holding my cell in my hand, I press number 2 on my speed-dial. She answers within seconds, "Hey, bitch, I was just thinking of you."

I snort. "Oh yeah? Let me guess...you saw a woman with a beard and it reminded you of me?"

"Moldy cheese, actually."

I laugh before sobering. "Nat, the reason I called—"

She gasps, *"Someone died?!"*

I shout an exasperated, "No one's dead! Jesus C! What is it with this morbid family?"

Nat returns, "You went all serious on me. What was I supposed to think? You scared the crap out of me."

"Sorry. I just need to ask you a favor is all."

Silence...then suspicion lines her voice. "Which is?"

I try to keep the smile out of my own. "I need you to find me an apartment."

I can almost see the confusion on her face. "Um, sweetie, wouldn't that be easier for you to do, seeing as I don't live in California anymore?"

I sigh. "I suppose so." I pause a moment. "Of course, I don't need an apartment in California. I need an apartment in New York. My new job is in New York, so finding an apartment in California would just be silly." I grin. "Howdy, neighbor!"

A gasp, then a quiet, "Shut. Up."

"I will not."

Then louder, "You shut your lying whore mouth, right now!"

A startled laugh bursts out of me. "Well, that got serious fast! No, no joke. I'm moving to New York and I need a place to stay. Like, soon...ish."

I hear the shock in her voice. "How soon?"

"Like, Monday-soon."

Another gasp. I hear slapping and a male voice mutter 'Ouch', and I just know she's got the excitement slaps, Asher being the likely victim of the assault. "Oh, my God, this is so awesome! I can't believe you never told me you applied here, you lying sack of shit!"

We both laugh. My sisters and I talk to each other as if we hate each other, but the truth is, we love each other very much. We just have a weird way of showing it.

Excitement takes over. "We never found someone to take over the lease from my old apartment, so I guess we're actually going to be neighbors. Real neighbors! Oh, my God, we're going to have so much fun! You can come here all the time, and we'll eat together and cook

together, and have sleepovers!" She gasps, then shouts,
"*We are gonna have so much fun!*"

   I bite my lip over my smile.

   Monday can't come soon enough.

CHAPTER TWO

Helena

Four days later

Taping up the last of the boxes, I look around my room. It looks so…bare. The walls are bare. The floor is bare. The bookshelves are bare.

My room is naked.

I don't know how I feel about that.

If the pang in my chest is anything to go by, I'd say it makes me sad. This room has been mine from the day I was born. I played in this room, grew up in it, sought comfort, and hid away from the world in here.

This room has been good to me. I'm going to miss it.

Now, all that's left of it are the eight boxes on the floor. I've organized for movers to come this afternoon. I was pleasantly surprised when I found out my new workplace would cover the entire expense. Asher called yesterday to let me know the apartment was getting a spring clean by all the girls and would be ready by Monday. Nat also let me know it had most of the furniture still in it from when she lived there, so I won't need to spend a lot to set myself up.

I offered to pay for the extras in the apartment, but Nat refused while using a ton of cuss words. But, of course, I argued, which made Nat use some nastier words. Suddenly, Ash took the phone and simply said, "You aren't paying for shit, girl. You just get your ass down here. You wanna thank me? Feed me."

There really is no arguing with Asher. He's firm like that.

A final sweep of my room reveals one last thing I need to do, but I'm torn. My Johnny poster still hangs behind the door.

It's time.

But I'm not ready.

It's time. He's had a good life. Let go.

Brain is right. It's time. I need to let him go.

Walking to the door, I stare into Johnny Depp's eyes and my gut sinks. "I'm sorry. You've been a good imaginary boyfriend, but I'm a grown-up now. There's no room in my life for a boyfriend. Not even an imaginary one." But he just stares at me. "Don't look at me like that." But he does. He's torturing me.

I sigh tiredly and rub at my forehead. "Don't make this any harder than it has to be. Please, Johnny. It's over." I'm getting a headache. I take my time pulling him down with the utmost care, rolling him up and putting a rubber band around him. I hold him in my hands and walk him over to the recycling bin. I lift the lid and put him in. I slowly close the lid and turn around.

My mother stands there, looking from me to the bin. I nod solemnly and whisper, "It was time."

She smiles and shakes her head, and with a heavy heart, I let my first love go.

Ten minutes later…

My sock-covered feet slip around on the kitchen tiles. Hyperventilating, I open the cupboard under the sink and dig through the recycling 'til I find him. I clutch Johnny to my heaving chest and turn to find both my parents having coffee at the dining table. They eye me with worry.

"I thought I could do it." I clutch Johnny harder. "I can't do it. He's coming with me."

As I walk back to my room with Johnny in hand, I breathe a sigh of relief.

I'm sorry, Johnny. Let's never fight again.

CHAPTER THREE

MAX

My leg bounces hard and fast under the dining table.

I'm nervous.

I sip at my coffee as my eyes dart from Nik to Tina. I watch them eat their breakfast, wondering how the hell I broach this subject. Tina eats her oatmeal; she must feel my eyes on her, because she looks up at me mid-bite. Her eyes widen and she mutters slowly, "What?"

I quickly avoid her gaze and shake my head. "Nothin'."

Sip your damn coffee and keep your eyes down.

And that's what I do. I avert my gaze so much that I look directly down into my coffee cup.

Nik's foot nudges me under the table. Brows raised, I look up at him. He carefully folds the newspaper before putting it down, eyes narrowing at me.

Uh oh.

Nik leans back in his chair, when suddenly, he starts to smirk, his dimple, almost identical to mine, cuts into his cheek.

And I sweat. "*What*?"

He jerks his chin at me. "You're acting weird. I mean, you always act weird, but now you're acting *weirder*." Tina looks over at me and nods gently.

"Am not."

"Are too," my brother argues.

"You're going senile in your old age."

Nik's eyes widen. He's a little sensitive about his age ever since he found a grey hair. I know it's not a big deal. It's natural. People eventually go grey. But the hair...

It wasn't on his head.

He leans over and snarls, "Yo' mama."

I grin. "She's *yo' mama* too, and I'm telling her you said that."

He opens up his arms, taunting me, "Do it. I'll tell her the real story about the dried basil leaves in your sock drawer."

The motherfucker. "It was yours! I was hiding it for you!"

He shrugs. "She don't know that."

I reach over the table to slap him—he hates that shit—when Tina speaks up. "Nik, stop it."

My bird flips him a hello, then Tina's on my ass. Gently, of course. "Max, honey, do that again and I promise you won't get any cupcakes for a year."

I gasp. She wouldn't! But the look on her face says she would. I sink back into my chair. "Holy shit, you're mean when you're breeding."

She smiles sweetly then rubs her rounded belly. "I guess I do get a little cranky nowadays."

I add, "And emotional."

Nik grins. "And horny."

Tina yells, "Nik!" at the same time I screw up my face and yell, "Dude!"

I love Tina, and she's a total fox, but I don't want to think about her in the sack. Especially not with Old Man River over there. I can't help myself. I turn to Nik and smile cruelly. "So, how's your grey pube? Lonely?"

A chair screeches, then I'm on the floor with two hands wrapped firmly around my neck, choking the shit out of me. *"Shut your mouth, punk!"*

I gasp, *"Never!"*

Tina chuckles sweetly, completely ignoring the fact her husband is roughly feeling me up. "Oh, honey, it's not that bad. Just pluck it out. It's okay. I love you *and* your grey pube."

Nik's hands still as he looks up at her. "If you pluck them, more come!"

She shrugs. "So more will come. I'll love those grey pubes too."

Looking at her, he roughly shakes me, choking me and making a point at the same time. Nik is a multitasker. "No you won't! No one loves grey pubes!" he exclaims.

She looks him dead in the eye then smiles softly. "I will." And she means it too.

Tina seriously is the shit.

Nik throws me down. My head hits the floor with a dull thud. Panting, I rub the back of my head and mumble, "That hurt, fucker."

He stands, then holds a hand out to me. I take it, but before I can get him into a headlock and show him how you choke like a man, my reason for living comes out from the hall.

"Daddy, I can't find my school bag."

I smile, even though she sounds frustrated, and turn to her. Her long, reddish-brown hair has been brushed and tied already. "You did you hair," I frown, "on your own." I'm sulking; I know it, but I don't get to do a lot for my little girl anymore. And I like doing shit for my little girl. I'm her daddy. I'm allowed to like being useful. Tina clears her throat, and I'm sure if I were close enough, she'd kick me. I quickly change my pout for a proud, fatherly smile. "Which is great. Good for you, baby."

Ceecee looks down into her lap, hiding her blush. My baby gets embarrassed easily. She doesn't take compliments well. It sucks for her that I compliment her all the damn time.

My daughter's name is Cecilia. Since that she's named for her grandma, we like to call her Ceecee. She was born a healthy baby. She wasn't planned or nothin', and I gotta admit, finding out Maddy was pregnant was one of the scariest things ever, but I soon got used to the idea of being a young dad. In fact, soon, I loved the idea, and I couldn't wait to hold my baby in my arms. Maddy, Ceecee's mom, was very much the same.

But once we brought Ceecee home, things changed.

Maddy was constantly unhappy, getting annoyed at Ceecee for crying, not wanting to hold her, feed her, or change her. It didn't take a genius to figure out my Maddy was not bonding with Ceecee, and not long after, she was diagnosed with postpartum depression.

I didn't really know what to do, but that was okay. My family decided for me. Mom moved us into her house. I always felt like a burden there, taking up her space, but I had to work to make money to clothe my woman and baby, so while I worked my ass off, Mom and my sisters kept an eye on my girls, helping out where they could. More like where Maddy would let them.

I don't pretend to be a saint in all this. I was young and on-edge myself. I can remember getting angry and yelling at my girl to get the fuck out of bed and look after our child. I remember throwing her in a cold shower after spending days in bed. I remember crying from confusion, frustration, and helplessness. I just couldn't understand why she hated our kid. I couldn't understand why she couldn't see the beauty that was our baby girl.

Truth is, depression looks black and white, but depression is a fuck load of grey. It's so easy to think things like, *Why can't she just…* or *She should just…*, but it's not that simple. I spent all my free time researching the causes of depression, 'cause if I found the source, I could fix it. Turns out, the triggers are different for each person.

Depression doesn't make a person weak. People with depression live their lives. Some live in pain, and not the type of pain you can see, but pain of the heart, and pain of the mind. They walk on while it feels like their world is breaking up around them. If you ask me, people fighting depression are some of the strongest people out there.

Living with Mom seemed to be working. My mom is one hell of a woman. Regardless of how frustrating it was to live together, Mom showered Maddy with love and affection, always telling her we'd get through it as a family. And, wouldn't you know it, Maddy started to smile again. Then she started to hold Ceecee, feed her, change her, and bathe her. She was doing it. She was fighting it.

Maddy was healing.

Mom and I were both confident Maddy was beating the depression. She was a different person from the months prior, and I started to see the woman I fell in love with again. Life was lookin' up.

But it lasted about a second.

I remember the phone call. I remember listening to what my mom was saying, but not really hearing at all. I remember my heart dying a slow, painful death. I remember hospitals. I remember scrubs. I remember looking at my little girl and wondering what size casket I would have to get for her. I remember choosing the pink one, because she was my little princess, and princesses always wore pink. I remember Maddy just...disappearing.

Here's what I don't remember...

I don't remember hating someone as much in my life than I hated Maddy. And I still hate her.

As far as everyone else knew, it was an accident. Maddy was preparing lunch for Ceecee, who was just over a year old, and put her to sit on the counter while she was getting the things she needed from the refrigerator. As far as everyone else knew, Ceecee fell off the counter and hit a stool on the way down, severing her spinal cord. Yes, that did happen.

What the others don't know is that Ceecee had been fussy that morning. Maddy had placed her on the counter, frustrated with dealing with a whining Ceecee, and turned her back. What the others don't know is when Ceecee started to cry, Maddy got angry. She got so angry she turned from the refrigerator, fuming, and yelled at my baby. She yelled hard.

Ceecee got spooked. Her little body stiffened, and that's when she fell.

As far as everyone else knows, that never happened. How do I know that happened? Maddy sent me a letter after disappearing, a letter I still have to this day. I received it four days after she left. Turns out, she went and turned herself in to the police. She had been under suicide watch. Part of me was so angry with her that I wished she would kill herself.

A lot happened in the meantime. Ceecee had surgeries upon surgeries. She was either doped up or screaming in agony. She cried a lot in that time, and I cried with her. I didn't understand what I had done for this to happen. But the answer is simple:

Shit happens.

You find a way to cope and you roll with it. You can be the stiff branch that breaks, or the tree that bends with the wind. It's up to you.

Ceecee had already lost her mom. She wasn't about to lose me. Not then, not ever. We spent so much time in the hospital that we were on first name basis with all the doctors and nurses in the children's ward. My mom fed the staff. We exchanged Christmas gifts. They quickly became an extension of our already large family. They were awesome. I don't know what I would've done without them. Regardless of how sour I was, or how frustrated I was, they always took care of us. And they did it with a smile. Doctors, nurses, hospital staff...they were amazing.

Ceecee's spine is severed. There's no fixing that. We just had to learn to deal.

"Have you checked your room?"

Ceecee stares at me, eyes narrowed, shaking her head slightly. "Uh, yes. Yes, I have."

I throw up my hands. "Then I'm stumped."

She wheels her chair into the dining area, close enough to Tina to get assaulted with hugs and kisses. She huffs a frustrated, "I just don't know where I left it."

And I grin. My God, she is adorable.

Nik rolls up his newspaper and playfully smacks Ceecee over the head with it. "I don't think my Cricket said good morning to me yet, Tina."

Tina hugs her closer and looks over at her husband, love in her eyes. "I think you're right, but I don't think the princess is in the mood for your games, sweetie."

Ceecee is almost thirteen years old. Not quite a child, not yet a teenager, stuck somewhere in between. I can see her changing every day. Every single day. I'm torn. I wish there was some way to stop her growing, but at the same time, I can't wait to see my daughter bloom into the good woman I know she'll be. But Tina is right, Ceecee has been frustrated a lot lately. I know this has to do with growing up. Hell, I've been dreading the hormonal changes that are coming.

Luckilyy for me, I have my sisters, my mom, Tina, Nat, Lola, and Mimi to help me out with *those* talks when they come. I mean, *c'mon*! Talking to my little girl about her period and what to expect when I don't have a fucking clue about it is just ridiculous.

Ceecee's face softens. With a small sigh, she wheels herself around to Nik's side, and smiling, he leans over, pulling her into a deep hug. Her eyes close as she rests her head on his shoulder. He whispers something to her I can't quite here. I only hear her hushed response. "I know. Love you, Uncle Nik."

He kisses her forehead, stands, then claps his hands together like he means business. "Right, school bag. You check the kitchen, and I'll check everywhere else."

Ceecee moves into the kitchen, and Nik searches the rest of the house. It takes me a little while before I realize I'm still standing in the middle of the dining area, watching them.

I don't know what I would've done without Nik when Ceecee came home from the hospital. He moved us into his home and spent as much time as I did tending to her, and he worked full time while I took time off. But he worked as hard as I did, maybe harder, at making sure not only Ceecee was taken care of, but that I got as much sleep as I needed and was fed.

He is my hero. I have never told him that. He is a good man. He deserves a good life, a life invested in his family. His new family, not the one he was born into. Which is part of what makes this so hard. I don't actually want to do what I'm doing, but I feel he needs it. The time is right.

Nik calls out, "Found it!"

Ceecee calls back, "Where did I leave it?"

As Ceecee comes out of the kitchen, Nik walks down the hall entrance with her school bag on his back. He hooks it over her chair and responds an amused, "By the front door, princess."

Ceecee shakes her head, but a small smile appears on her face. Her cheeks color and she mumbles a sheepish, "Sorry."

A horn honks from the front of the house and Ceecee makes a move to the school bus. As she passes me, she wraps her arm around my legs. I lean down to kiss her hair. "Have fun!"

She wrinkles her nose. "It's school, Daddy."

I shoot her my best teasing grin. "I know. *Suffer*."

She punches my thigh while trying to suppress her smile and I mock jump. "Ouch, girl. We need to enroll you in boxing classes."

I watch her make her way down the hall. As the front door opens, she yells out, "Bye! Love you!"

We all call back in unison, *"Love you."*

My heart aches. I'm going to miss this. The front door closes and I turn to Nik and Tina. They both smile up at me. But what I say makes their smiles fade fast.

"So," I start, "we're moving out."

CHAPTER FOUR

MAX

Nik and Tina blink up at me, Nik's face full of confusion, whereas Tina's mouth gapes. And I just stand here, nowhere near embracing the awkward silence, wishing I were the invisible man so I could lose my sweats and boxers, and hightail it out of here.

My brother's accent thickens in frustration or anger. So, right now, when he says, "What the fuck are you talking about, man?" it actually comes out, *"Tha fuck you tawkin' 'bout, man?"*

Tina's eyes lose focus. She shakes her head, trying to comprehend what I've just said before lifting her saddened gaze to me. "Honey, what on earth are you saying? You can't move out. This is Ceecee's home. *Your* home."

I dip my chin, place my hands on my hips, and bounce one leg. I think of what to say without sounding like an asshole. "No. This is *your* home. You have two little girls and a growing family. Yeah, Ceecee was brought up in this house, but it isn't ours." I dare to look at Nik. "Never was."

He shrugs lightly. "I don't get where this is coming from. What happened?"

I breathe deeply, raise my arms, rest my wrists on my head, and reply on an exhale, "Nothing happened. It's not like that. This isn't a decision made out of anger or anything."

But Nik doesn't hear it. He immediately stands and moves in front of me. "Whatever it is, we'll fix it. Tell me what's goin' on."

"It's nothing. I swear…"

"It must be somethin'. Tell me what I need to do to get you to change your mind."

"You don't get what I'm sayin'."

Tina stands from the table, approaching me, but I back up, hands out in warning. When Tina hugs you, there's not a lot you wouldn't do for her. I hold my arms out. "Don't, Tina, not right now. I need my head clear."

Nik quickly becomes pissed. "Don't fuck me around, Max. Tell me what the issue is."

Frustration erupts inside of me, and molten-hot anger spews out of my mouth. "Fuck, *man*, not everything is about you! It's about me! It's about Ceecee! It's not about you, or Tina, or the girls! It's about me and my girl. That's it."

Tina's quiet voice breaks through my anger, taking me down a peg. Or six. "You're not happy here?"

There's not a sadder sight you'll see than Tina upset. That shit stings. I quickly reach out and take hold of her hand. "No, sweetheart. That's not it." I run a hand through my hair. "I'm not explaining this how I should be."

Nik folds his arms across his chest, looking agitated, but sounding patient. "Take your time."

I release my hold on Tina's hand and move to sit on the back of the sofa. I remain quiet a moment, thinking up what I should be saying, not what my mouth seems to want to say. "Okay. So, we've been here forever, right?" Nik nods. "We've been real happy here, Nik. You helped us out when I needed you, and I look at Ceecee and what a great little lady she's becoming," my throat thickens, "and it's because of you."

Nik's harsh features soften with his eyes. I avoid his stare and move on, "But I stayed too long. I stayed when I should have left. I kept this going, and now it's hard. I should've left when it was easy, because the thought of moving out now," I look up at Tina, "it gives me heart palpitations."

Tina quickly pleads, "Then don't go! We love you. We want you here. There's plenty of room for all of us; just *don't go*."

I smile sadly at the both of them and drop a bomb. "Already bought a place."

Nik runs his hands across his face and whispers, "Fuck me."

"Listen, it's time. We've been here ten years too long."

Nik interjects heatedly, "I wanted you here." He pauses, his eyes pleading. "I *want* you here, man."

I shake my head and gently but firmly tell him, "I love you for that," and I mean it, "but I need to start living again. I need to move on. Maddy..." I breathe in a ragged breath, "...she fucked me, and I was broken for a long time. But I'm not broken anymore. *We're* not broken anymore. I gotta do what I should've done years ago. I need to take charge of my life," I look up to meet Nik's eyes, "and I'm finally ready for it."

"Well, this fucking sucks."

Nik and I both turn in shock to stare at Tina. Tina never swears. Not ever.

She watches us watching her, sniffles, and pouts, "Well, it does."

We stand there, not sure what to say to each other, basking in an awkward, question-filled silence. It's not a nice feeling. Sorta like heartburn. Nik nods. "I s'pose it was going to happen eventually. I mean, it's not like I pictured Ceecee leaving for college from here." But the tone of his voice and the look in his eyes say he did.

Tina asks quietly, "Does she know yet?" I shake my head, because words fail me.

Nik asks, "Where's the house?"

That, at least, makes some of the tension ease.

I point to the east, hiding my smile and waving my hand around. "That way."

Nik's face turns stoic. "Where?"

I point again, this time with feeling. My smile breaks through.

Nik's lips tilt upwards. "You didn't."

Tina asks, "Did what?"

"I did," I respond smartly.

Tina repeats, louder, "Did what?"

Nik covers his face with his hand as his body shakes in silent laughter. "You sneaky son of a bitch."

Tina's voice borders hysterical. "*I'm freaking out*! Someone tell me what the hell is going on!"

I grin down at her. Nik shakes his head and breaks the good news. "Looks like we've got a new neighbor."

She gasps, her body shaking in a fit of excitement. "Shut *up*!" She jumps up and down on the spot, then squeals, "Oh, thank God!" Not able to lose the smile on her face, she giggles then asks, "Where's the house? Can we see it?"

"Sure. Let's go."

Tina all but runs down the hall, her belly bouncing along the way. "Come *on*, you guys!"

Nik and I walk behind closely. He chuckles. "She has no idea. She's gonna freak."

I smirk. "Oh, I know."

As we exit the house, Tina stands by the car, waiting for Nik to open it. As he walks by her, he hooks an arm around her waist. "No use wasting gas."

Tina allows him to lead her away, but her eyes narrow at me in suspicion. I move to her free side to walk with them. We walk up the driveway, and when he reach the sidewalk, Tina squints into the sunlight, turning left then right. "Which way?"

I move to stand behind her, gently grasp her hips in my hands, and move her body to face the street. I can feel the confusion coming off her, but she doesn't say a word. I know the exact moment it clicks. She gasps, and then covers her mouth with both hands. Her body turns to face me very, very slowly.

Wide eyes meet mine. She whispers, "You're moving across the street?" I grin so hard my dimple cuts into my cheek. Tina squeaks, then launches herself into my arms, laughing. "You're a sneaky, sneaky man, Max Leokov. And I love you to death." She yells through her laughter, "*I love you!*"

Tina refuses to release her monkey grip on me, and that's all right with me. I hold her while my gaze moves to my new house across the street. Nik's hand squeezing my shoulder brings me back to reality. I look over at him, a question in my eyes. His face beams with pride, and although I don't *need* it, it feels good to have it, especially coming from Nik.

My throat thickens. I clear it and announce, "We'll tell Ceecee tonight."

Tina moves back from me, and she looks nervous for me. She takes my hand in hers and utters, "Yeah. We'll tell her as a family." She smiles big, although it doesn't reach her eyes. "I'm sure everything will be just fine."

I nod. Yeah. I'm sure it will.

Ceecee's tear-stained face breaks my heart. "Why? Did I do something wrong?"

This is not how I expected things to go. It happened so differently in my head. In my stupid, stupid head. I move to hug her, but she backs away from me. Tina and

Nik immediately start trying to explain. "No, Angel! Most definitely not. We love you!"

"Aww, Cricket. You know that's not it."

Her breath hitches from crying. She whispers a mournful, "I don't want to leave. I love it here."

I try to be the voice of reason. "Baby, we can't live here forever."

She looks up at me and snuffles, "I don't want to be alone."

I smile down at her, although my heart has effectively been ripped from my chest. "It's not like we're going to be far. We're just across the street. You can come here anytime you like."

I'm not prepared for her anger. "Then you go!" She turns and wheels away from me. Just as she hits the hall, she calls out, "Go, if you want! I don't care!" Her killer blow makes me wheeze out a breath. "I don't need you anyway."

Nik moves toward me, his face full of sympathy. I hold my hands up in warning. I don't want anyone near me right now. I look down to the floor and make an escape to the courtyard. I walk halfway down the steps and take a seat, closing my eyes, taking in the evening breeze. A sigh escapes me.

'Have a kid,' they said. 'It'll be fun,' they said.

A humorless chuckle rumbles deep in my throat. I stay on the steps for a long time, hours even, and I still can't figure out what the fuck I can do or say to comfort my baby.

Sometimes, life is hard.

CHAPTER FIVE

Helena

This morning was as uneventful as originally planned. And by uneventful, I mean crying relatives, rushing to the airport, and an awkward goodbye to my eldest sister.

I woke at five am, had a shower, and ate a small breakfast of toast and coffee. My bags, already packed, stood by the front door ready to go. The boxes of my things had left a week ago, and Nat called to tell me they had been received already. I thanked the gods of shipment for that. It really would've sucked to not have my things when I got there. Nat asked me if I wanted her to unpack the boxes, and I quickly yelped a no. Truth is, I didn't leave my vibrator at home. For two reasons.

Reason one: my parents likely would have found it.

Ewww.

Reason two: I need it. It's a part of my pre-bedtime ritual. It wears me out and helps me sleep. And while I have no boyfriend, or even a bed buddy, it's coming with me. And I don't need my sister seeing that shit.

Don't misunderstand me. My sisters and I talk about sex, and we talk about it openly, but it's one thing to talk about sex, and another thing to actually see a long, thick, purple glitter jelly dildo vibrator that your sister named Sir Squeal-A-Lot.

She doesn't need to see that. No one needs to see that. *I* don't need to see that. Why do you think I find my happy place in the dark before bedtime?

We rushed to the airport, where I lined up with the ten thousand other people who were travelling at the butt crack of dawn. I all but threw my suitcases at the poor attendant. I just wanted to get to New York already. I was excited. This was going to be a huge change for me. A good one, I could feel it. *But,* I may have left a small detail out when I spoke to Nat.

I may have told her I was arriving at six pm. Not midday. I'll tell you why I did this. Firstly, Nat would've left work early to come get me, which would've been an inconvenience. Secondly, she would not have come alone. She would've brought all the girls and their guys, and it would've been made an event—something I don't like at all. Thirdly, it may sound strange, but the first time in my new apartment, I'd like to be alone to get better acquainted with my new surroundings. And yes, I have visited Nat before, so I've seen the apartment, but I didn't go through all of Nat's drawers and cupboards.

I need a little me time.

As I said goodbye to my parents and held them tightly, trying to memorize their smells, I was shocked to find I wasn't even sad about leaving. I would've thought I'd have shed a tear or two, but no. After my parents, I stood in front of Nina. She placed her hands in her pockets and looked down at the floor, avoiding my eyes. Nina is never emotional.

Never.

Not. Ever.

It should've had me worried, but it might make me a shitty sister to say it made me happy. I think I melted the ice queen. She cleared her throat. "You got everything you need?"

I patted my hand luggage. "Everything. I'm all good."

She peeked up at me. "You're coming home for Christmas, right?"

I opened my mouth to say yes, but then I thought about it. I shrugged lightly. "If I get time off, definitely."

This answer did not placate her. At all. She scowled. "You better come visit."

I glared right back. "Why don't *you* come visit *me*?"

She made a face. "Because I have a salon to run and it would be easier for you to visit us here."

I placed a hand on my hip. Oh, yeah, she knew she just threw down. "Well, you have two sisters in New York now. Get off your *fat ass* and come vacay with us sometime."

She folded her arms across her chest. "Why should I? You're the assholes who left!"

I continued to glare while she scowled. "Fine."

"*Fine.*"

We stood there another minute or so before I caved. I'd miss my sister. I love my sister. Even if she is a total fucknut.

With a sigh and roll of my eyes, I rushed over to her and wrapped her in a tight hug. The bitch didn't hug me back for a full minute, but then her hands gently gripped the back of my jacket and she pushed her head into my shoulder. I felt wetness there. I kissed her cheek and whispered, "I'll come home for Christmas."

She sniffled and choked out, "And I'll come visit. I promise."

We held each other tightly until an overhead announcement aired. My flight was boarding. I waved goodbye to my forlorn family and boarded a flight to my new life.

Nat told me she'd left a key with the little old lady in apartment 309, the apartment across from mine. As soon as I landed, I gathered my suitcases and caught a cab over to the apartment complex. When it came into view, I broke out into a huge smile as butterflies flew around in my stomach, a mixture of nervousness and excitement flowing through me.

The cab driver is sweet enough to help me with my suitcases. We walk them up the stairs to my apartment on the first floor. I pay him, and then I knock on apartment 309. Not a second passes before it opens with a jarring bang as the security chain stops it from extending all the way. I jump and hold a hand up to my heaving chest. She scared the crap out of me.

A wrinkly face appears in the gap, covered by thick coke-bottle glasses. I force a smile. "Hello. I'm Helena

Kovac. My sister Natalie told me she left a key with you for me."

The tiny woman's face wrinkles in confusion. She yells, "*What?*"

I blink.

Are you fucking kidding me, Nat?

I clear my throat and speak louder. "My sister Natalie says you have a key for me." But the lady just blinks. I dip my chin to stop myself from laughing. After I get myself under control, I lift my face and smile. I point to my own ear and say, "Can you hear me?"

But the woman just frowns at me. "You'll have to speak up. My hearin' isn't what it used to be."

I nod sympathetically and near-shout, "*My sister Natalie says you have a key for me. I'm Helena.*"

The woman scowls. "No need to holler, young lady. I hear just fine, thank you very much."

What the fucktruck?

She heads inside and locks the door. I wait patiently, but nothing happens.

She's abandoned me.

I knock again. The door opens and the little old lady looks up at me through her glasses expectantly. I'm not sure what's happening here, so I go on and just stare back. When she attempts to close the door in my face, I quickly say, "I need the key Natalie left you to get into my new apartment."

The woman blinks. "You'll have to speak up. My hearin' isn't what it used to be."

Oh, for the love of cake.

I dip my chin and my body shakes in silent laughter. New York, I like you already. I lift my face and ask slowly, clearly, and loudly, "Do you know Natalie in 306?" I point at Nat's apartment door to help her along.

The woman looks over at Nat's apartment, then back up at me. "She's not home. She works."

I explain *again*, "I'm her sister. I just came from California." I point to my suitcases next to me. "I need the key to my apartment." I point to my new apartment before making a key-unlocking-a-door motion.

The little old lady's face beams in recognition. She smiles. "You're the sister!"

I beam right back at her. "I'm the sister!"

She laughs. "You need the key."

I chuckle and confirm, "Yes! I need the key! The key, please."

She nods and steps back into her apartment. "Just a second, sweetie."

She closes the door and I sigh in relief. I wait. And wait. And wait some more.

Nothing.

I knock once more. Maybe she needs help finding the key. The door opens, and the little old lady looks up at me through her glasses like she's seeing me for the first time.

Part of me wants to laugh, but another part of me wants to knock her over the head with something so I can find the damn key myself. I smile sweetly. "Do you have the key yet? I really need to get inside."

The woman blinks. "You'll have to speak up. My hearin' isn't what it used to be."

I run a hand down my face.
Oy vey.

It takes me a whole forty-five minutes to get Mrs. Crandle to give me the fracking key. Turns out she's not only hard of hearing and forgetful, but she has a thousand cats, all of which she wanted to introduce me to. By name.

She made me promise to come drink tea with her sometime, and I promised I would.

As I put the key into the lock and open the door, I laugh in relief. Relief that this *is* actually the key and I won't have to word battle Mrs. Crandle again. I open the door and shuffle my suitcases inside. Pulling the door closed, I look around. My boxes are stacked nice and neatly by the right-hand wall.

A sudden thought comes to mind. *You could pack your entire life into eight boxes?*

That's kind of sad. They aren't even extra-large or large boxes; they're medium sized boxes, full of crap. Yes, crap, but all of that crap, I love. Pushing the thought aside, I pull my phone out of my purse and text Nat.

Me: I'm at the apartment. Don't be pissy. I didn't want to bother you. The place looks amazing!

Approximately thirty seconds later, my phone pings.

Nat: YOU DIRTY TOERAG! I KNEW YOU WERE LYING. YOU ALWAYS LIE! WHY DO YOU LIE?

I snicker.

Me: Whatevs, bro. I'll see you after work.

Nat: I'm going to tear you a new asshole. But I'll bring cupcakes.

My eyes widen at the last part. I salivate. I freaking love cupcakes.

Me: Oh Em Gee! Pls pls pls get the salted caramel ones. And the choc fudge brownie. And maybe vanilla creme. You know what? I don't even care which ones, because CUPCAKES!

Nat: Now you get none.

Me: You're a rugmuncher.

Nat: And you have a hairy asshole.

I burst into laughter. My sister is so vulgar. I love it.

Me: Love you x

Nat: LY2. Can't wait to see you. Even though you're a lying sack of shit x

Ahh, feel the love?

I take my suitcases and roll them over to the bedroom. And I stop dead in my tracks. I blink, then back away into the hall. Shaking my head, I tiptoe over to my bedroom.

There's a man on the bed. A man spread-eagle, face-down, right on my bed.

My heart races.

By the way his back moves up and down in an even motion, I know he's asleep. My head tells me to call the cops, but if I do that, I need to be sure I'm in danger. A sleeping man on my bed doesn't seem like much of a threat right now. I think hard for a moment before quietly moving back into the kitchen and going through my purse. I take out my pocket mace and my cell phone, and walk back to my room.

It takes me a full minute for me to realize I have the mace to my ear and my phone held out as a weapon. *Genius.* I quickly switch them around and enter my bedroom. The man's sock-covered feet hang over the foot of the bed. Lifting my own foot, I nudge his calf. He grumbles, but doesn't wake. I nudge him again, harder this time.

A sleepy, "Nik, fuck off," comes out of the man, and my body goes rigid.

I know that voice.

I *really* like that voice. Why the hell is he in my apartment? In my *bedroom*? I lower my mace and clear my throat.

"Fuck off, man. Not kidding."

I don't bother with niceties. "*You* fuck off. This is *my* apartment."

His body stiffens. Without another word, he turns over, tilting his head up, blinking up at me. "Helen?"

Oh, man, you're on a roll, asshole.

I glare. "It's Helen*a*! *Not* Helen!"

He looks adorably mussed. His dark brown hair sticks up in the back and he blinks his sleepy golden eyes. His *red-rimmed* golden eyes. I don't like that. I frown as I speak, "Are you drunk?"

A look of confusion passes him. "What? No, I'm not drunk."

"Then why are you here?"

He looks around the room, gathering his bearings before his body slumps. "Oh, shit. I was supposed to be fixing a leaking faucet, but I guess, I...uh..." He scratches at his chin—his amazing, strong, manly chin—and finishes, "...fell asleep."

My brows rise in disbelief. He watches me closely. We don't say a word.

I take in a deep breath and respond on an exhale, "Well, if you're done, I need to move my stuff in...without anyone sleeping on my bed," I look down at my pillow and accuse, "or drooling on my pillows."

He quickly opens his mouth to defend himself, but turns around to look for himself. "I didn't drool..." He trails off as he sees the wet spot on my pillow. At least he has the grace to look sheepish. "I can wash that."

I scoff. "Yeah, right."

He stands and stretches, but as he lifts his arms over his head, extending his muscular arms as far as they can go, his tee lifts over the waistband of his jeans to reveal low-rise jeans, boxer elastic, and a well sculpted *V*.

The dark blue jeans he wears encase his strong legs. The plain black tee is nice and fitted over his muscular arms, but looks well worn. His feet are covered in white socks. A very obviously child-made, bright yellow, purple, and blue elastic loom bracelet rests around his right wrist.

He looks delicious.

Warmth hits my dipping belly and works its way down. I squeeze my leg together tightly, holding the doorframe for support. *Holy shit.* I'm suddenly hyper-aware I have on no makeup and am wearing grey sweats with my white stay-at-home tank. It's a stay-at-home tank because it's ratty. *So* extremely comfortable, but ratty.

Okay, it's more like a rag. Somehow, this only makes me angrier. "You can't just come into people's homes when they aren't there."

Max rubs a hand over his face. Mid-yawn, he utters, "Sure I can."

My blood begins to boil. "No, you can't."

He lowers his hand from his face and smiles at me. All I see are full lips, white teeth, and that magical dimple.

That *fucking* dimple.

He takes a step toward me, eyes trained on mine. His voice is still sleep-husky when he drawls, "I'm here, aren't I?" He looks over my face then mutters distractedly, "A face like this should not be frowning."

My cheeks heat. I choke out, "What?"

He says louder, more confidently, "I said a face like yours should never frown."

I flush and mumble, "What's wrong with my face?"

Max looks me over, slowly, meaningfully, "Absolutely nothing, from what I can see." He smirks. "I'll just use my imagination for the things I can't." Then he winks.

He *winks*.

I take a shaking hand and point to the door, hard. "You need to leave."

He sighs. "Yeah, yeah, I heard you the first time." I watch him sit on the edge of my bed and slip his shoes on. Then he walks out to the kitchen. I follow. He lazily walks around my kitchen to the refrigerator. He opens it and scowls at the almost bare interior.

I ask heatedly, "Can I help you there?"

He continues to search the refrigerator while absently scratching his belly. "I'm hungry." He straightens. "Are you hungry? We should go get something to eat."

My mouth gapes. Boy, he works fast. I laugh humorlessly. "I'm not going anywhere with you."

His brow furrows. "Why not? You're hungry, I'm hungry. Let's eat."

This man is exasperating. "I'm not hungry!"

He looks into the refrigerator one last time. "Sure you are. You said, 'Max, I'm starving and would love to eat with you'. You said that. Just now. You don't remember? I think you should see a doctor about that."

Damn him for being funny. I bite my lip to stop my shocked laughter. In this moment, I can see why so many women like being fawned over. Despite my dislike of flirting, it does make a woman feel good to be fawned over. But I'd prefer real words to pretty lies any day. I'm suddenly very tired. I close my eyes and lean against the wall. "Listen, Mack…"

I hear his frown. "It's Max."

Yeah, don't feel so nice, does it?

Yes, I can be a complete child sometimes. But that felt good.

"Max, I'm tired. My flight wasn't great. The guy I sat next to was…ugh, and I'm stinky. All I want to do is wash the fat guy sweat-stink off me and sleep for a little while before Nat comes over."

I feel the warmth of his body in front of me. I quickly stand up straight and open my eyes. He looks down at me in concern. "You okay, cupcake?"

Oh, my God. He's *killing* me.

Trying to ignore the angry swarm of killer bees in my belly, I whisper, "Fine. I just need you to go."

Much to my surprise, he doesn't take offense. He simply nods once and heads for the door. As he opens the door, he announces, "See you tonight." He winks once more, then he's gone.

All before I can ask, 'Tonight?'

I move to the door and attach the chain lock. I hear a door open in the hall.

Max yells from the hall, "Hey, Mrs. Crandle. What's shaking?"

"You'll have to speak up. My hearin' isn't what it used to be."

I cover my mouth with my hand and burst into laughter.

CHAPTER SIX

Helena

I've been sleeping for almost an hour, and by sleeping, I mean tossing and turning, thinking about Max in my bed, and secretly wanting to lick his drool spot.

After he left, I managed to shower, eat some cereal (because it was all there really was to eat), and tried in vain to catch some Zs. And sleep, in my family, is sacred. We sleep when we can. We get excited about catnaps. But it's just not happening.

And I blame Max. Max and his sexiness. And his dimple. And his funniness. And his being sweet. I mean, c'mon! I bet he's like that with all the girls, flirting and charming-like. I bet there isn't a genuine bone in his body.

I scoff aloud. "Stupid, sexy Max."

Not a second later, the front door opens. "Hello? Anybody home?"

I smile into the pillow at the familiar voice and bury myself deeper into the covers. Footsteps make their way into the hall, then into my bedroom. She spots me. "*Arrrggghhh!*" Next thing I know, I'm attacked. Nat jumps on me. "You're a shithead!" But she says this with so much love that I decide not to punch her in the nose.

She bounces on top of me, forcing my breath out in sporadic wheezes before wrapping her arms around my waist and snuggling into the bed with me. She holds me silently for a long while before I turn over to face her. As soon as she sees my face, we both break out in wide smiles. Then she says, "You're a liar. Always lying."

I nod. "I know."

"But even though I want to shave your head, I still love ya."

"Good to know."

"Did you get in all right?"

I lean back into my pillow. "Fine, but when I got here, I almost sucker-punched poor Mrs. Crandle for the key."

The bed shakes with her silent laughter. "Damn, I would've paid to see your face when she opened the door."

I choke on a laugh. "I'm not even kidding when I say I had to play a fucking weird game of charades with her, three times, for the damn key. Then she tried to lure me inside with candy, tea, and promises of playing with her thousand cats. I yelled, '*Stranger danger!*' and got the heck out of there."

Nat laughs so hard tears leak out of her eyes.

"Then, when I finally get inside, there's a dude sleeping on the bed."

Nat straightens immediately and shouts, "*What*?"

I snort. "Oh, yeah, Max was sleeping on the bed when I arrived."

She cocks her head to the side. "That is weird. Not like him at all." She watches me closely. "Doesn't sound like you enjoyed that."

"I didn't."

She sits up on the bed. "Sorry, kid. Almost everyone has a key to this place. I asked for all the spares back and they all told me to shove it." She chuckles. "The only one half-willing to give you your privacy was Tina. And when she saw no one else was giving in, she jumped on the bandwagon."

I shake my head. "You got some weird friends."

She smiles and sighs happily. "I know, right?"

Suddenly, she gasps in shock. I still. "What?"

Her eyes water. "It just hit me, you know? That you're actually here. *Living* here." She sniffs and whispers, "That's awesome."

I grin. "Now we just have to find a way to get Nina to open a salon up here too."

Nat's face turns dreamy. "That would be amazing." Standing, she claps. "Right! Well, I was going to tell the guys to come here tonight, but I thought I better not. So they're next-door at ours. That way, when you get tired, you can just leave and not have to worry about offending anyone by kicking them out."

Wow. She's gone and surprised me.

My brow creases as I respond quietly, "Um, thanks, dude."

But she's already out the door. She yells back, "Come on over when you're ready. No one will care if you're wearing pajamas!"

I think about going there in my PJs. With a sigh, I slide out of my flannel pants and shirt, and change into jeans and a plain white tee. I quickly slip on some white flip-flops, grab my key, and head next-door.

As soon as I open the door, a cheer sounds. My eyes widen and my heart races. The entire gang is here, as well as Nik and Max's sisters, Leti, Maria, and Isa, including the two little pugs sleeping in their little beds by the sofa. No kids tonight though. They all look extremely happy to see me. I've only met the sisters a couple of times, but they're a hoot. I like them a lot.

Asher, being the closest to me, comes forward wearing a small smile. Before I know it, I'm wrapped in a brotherly hug. I bury my nose into his collar and breathe him in. I whisper against his tee, "Hey."

He pulls back and beams down at me. "Fuckin' great to have you here."

That's, like, the most words I've ever heard Ash use in one sentence. I grin, and being the honorary little sister, I yank his chain. I imitate him as best I can. "Nice to *fuckin'* be here."

He catches me in a headlock and I choke on my laughter. When he lets me go and playfully pushes me away, I turn to see everyone staring at us. They all look shocked. Nat is the only one smiling softly. I suppose there are not a lot of people who can act this way with

Ash. But he and I…we get each other. We have a bond, formed even before Nat and Ash were a thing.

"Um…hi," I say nervously.

The rest of the guys jump into greetings, hugs, and kisses. Tina almost smothers me. I spend a little time holding her belly, getting down on my knees and kissing the current home of my nieces or nephews. Nik simply smiles down at me and kisses my forehead. Lola jumps on me and we squeeze each other a long time. Lola and I are closest in age; we have the most in common. Trick punches my arm a little too hard. Mimi smirks as she pulls me into a hug. Her hands drift down to my ass and I chuckle. Mimi's always said I have a nice ass. Leti, Maria, and Isa all give me love, hugs, and kisses. Then finally comes Max.

Grinning like the fool he is, he steps forward with open arms, and my heart races. I quickly step away. "You already saw me today."

Asher's face turns harsh as he mutters, "The fuck is that meant to mean?"

Max doesn't even look at Ash; he just keeps grinning at me. "I never got to hug you though."

I take another step back. "I don't need another hug. I'm all hugged out. Besides, I feel like we've bonded enough with your drool stain on my pillow."

Ash's face turns bright red. He moves over to Max and grips the front of his shirt. "You better start talkin', or I'm gonna start maulin'."

Max just chuckles. "Relax, Ghost." His face suddenly turns dreamy. "Her bed smells like vanilla. And she smells like cupcakes."

My stomach flip-flops. Damn him! Damn him and his words to heck!

But Ash is too busy focusing on the prior remark. "When the fuck were you near her bed?"

Max, having no idea how close he is to being pummeled, shrugs. "Today, when she arrived."

Ash's face turns deadly. He lunges for Max, but I quickly step between them. "It's not what you think! He was asleep on my bed when I first came into the apartment."

Maria snorts. "My brother—the classiest guy in New York," she remarks, and then raises her glass in a silent toast before drinking the entire contents in one hit.

Mental note: don't ever go drinking with Maria.

Max looks over at his sister then flips her the bird. He quickly defends himself. "It's not like she was actually living there when I fell asleep." His eyes narrow at me. "So, *really*, you owe me an apology for cutting my nap short."

Is...is he being serious?

His eyes remain narrowed, and I soon realize he isn't joking. I bark out a shocked, humorless laugh. "In your dreams! I am not apologizing to you. Not now, not ever. For *anything*. Besides, you were basically squatting!"

Although his narrowed eyes don't ease, his lips twitch. It's then I notice how everyone around us is listening in on our non-argument.

They're all grinning.

All of them.

Nat quickly excuses herself, claiming the need to organize things in the kitchen, and pulls me along with her. She drags me so fast I'm all but running. As soon as we hit the kitchen, she whisper hisses, "What the heck was that about?"

Searching the cupboards, I take out the dinner plates and set them on the counter. I answer quietly, "I don't know what you're talking about."

She moves to stand in front of me. "No. You don't get to cut me out. Why are you so angry at Max?"

My shoulders lift in a casual *it's-not-a-big-deal* shrug. "I just don't really like him, is all."

A look of shock settles over her features. "What? Why?"

I move to open the napkins. "He's a total flirt. I hate that."

She watches me closely for a moment before responding, "He's a single guy. A *good* guy. And an even better dad. He's allowed to flirt, Lena."

Folding napkins and placing them on each plate, I mutter, "I bet he's got a string of women he's leading on right now." The more I think about it, the testier I become. I start slapping folded napkins onto plates. Nat makes a choked noise and I look up to see her wide-eyed but tight-lipped. My brows bunch. "He does, doesn't he?"

Those poor, stupid, defenseless women. Stupid, stupid women.

Her face turns expressionless. "It's not your business, and not my business to tell." To me, that automatically confirms my suspicions. But Nat quickly adds, "You think a man like him—the man you're insinuating he is—

could raise a beautiful little girl like Ceecee by being such a jerk?"

I pause mid-step. I hadn't really thought of Max as a dad in my vendetta against him. And Ceecee is truly a remarkable young woman. Part of me wants to believe he's a good guy. I mean, I used to think he was a good guy, but I was clearly blinded by my being smitten with him. Now those feelings are gone.

And you're bitter.

Am not.

Yeah, ya are.

Suddenly, I feel a bit like a hole—of the ass variety.

"I'm not saying he's not a good dad…"

Nat quickly returns, "Just not a good guy."

Well, when you put it like that, of course it's going to sound dickish.

She takes the plates and napkins, and moves to stand directly in front of me. "Listen, I don't know what's going on with you, but Max is one my best friends. If you got issues with him, ones that aren't even issues at all, you got issues with me." My cheeks heat at her firm telling off. She goes on, "I know he's a little flirty, but he's a great guy. He's generous, and funny, and kind, and thoughtful. He's one of the good guys." She looks me in the eye. "*Shit*, he'd give the shirt off his back for someone who needed it!"

I roll my eyes at the clear over-exaggeration, and she begins to walk away. Leaving the kitchen, she turns back around to me. My heart clenches when I spot disappointment in her eyes. Lowering her voice, she utters, "I've seen him do it."

My throat thickens in shame. Sometimes it's hard to swallow your own bullshit. My heart sinks, and I suddenly wish I could go home. Before I can think too hard about what Nat said, I step back into the living area, wringing my hands together. "Guys, I'm so sorry, but I'm suddenly not feeling the best."

To my absolute horror, Max is the first to approach me. He stands a foot away from me, searching my face. He mutters, "Lookin' a bit pale there." As if there is no other option in his mind, he places his hand on my shoulder and says, "C'mon. I'll walk you home."

That shame I felt before? It floods my system.

Oh, God. You're an asshole. It's a little too much at this moment. I step away and look to the ground. "No, stay. It's just next-door. I'll be fine."

Nat comes at me from the side and lies for me. "Oh, honey, you said you weren't feeling great before, but I didn't think it was that bad." She hugs me and whispers, "It's okay. Go home and rest up."

I mumble back, "I'm sorry I'm being a dickhead tonight. I think I'm just overwhelmed."

She nods into my shoulder. "S'okay. I know how that feels."

We separate and she smiles at me. A real smile. I don't realize how much I need that smile until I see it and it eases my soul. As I walk to the door, I turn halfway and mutter a poor excuse for a goodbye. "See ya, guys. Sorry."

Tina quickly calls out, "Take a cupcake with you!"

Oh, my gads! That's exactly what I need. I shoot her a smile before heading over to the bright purple box of cupcakes. Normally, Tina would make them, but being she was at work, they bought some from a bakery close to work. Nat says they're almost as good as Tina's.

I don't think anything could be as good as Tina's baking. When I open the box, I suppress a gasp. *So pretty!* There are three different kinds. I smile to myself. All the cupcakes I asked for are there. Which one to take though? This is a tough decision. The caramel ones are delicious, but so are the vanilla cream. The choc fudge is a given. But should I take just one? I don't know what New York cupcake etiquette is! At home, it was first come, first serve, and you were lucky if you got one at all, because, let's be honest here...who ever eats *one* cupcake? Doesn't happen.

I reach for a caramel one, but pull back.

Okay. The vanilla cream. Yes, I'll go with the vanilla.

I reach for it, but pull back again. Geez, I'm in bad shape over here. Is cupcake anxiety a thing? The choc fudge is always delicious. I reach for one of those and hesitate. I swoop up the box and look over to the gang. "I'm taking this."

Before anyone can say a thing, I'm out the door with my plunder. When I close the door behind me, I reach into the box, take a caramel cupcake, take off the wrapper, and shove the whole thing into my mouth. The sweet saltiness rolls around in my mouth, I feel the thick frosting on my lips, and I slump in what I know is a sugar rush.

I live for this.

Speaking to myself, I lean against the wall and garble, "Oh, sweet Jesus. *Yes.*" I swallow, sigh, and make my way back to the apartment feeling a little bit better about myself.

Or, at least, I pretend to.

MAX

Poor Helena.

She didn't look too good. I mean, she looked *good*, but she seemed a little off. Even a blind person could see how pretty she is. That thick, brown hair almost touching her waist. Bright green eyes that are even brighter than Nat's. Those long black lashes making her eyes look huge. Those perky tits, and best of all...

That ass.

Motherfuck me straight to hell.

The girl's feeling like shit, and I'm checking out her firm, round peach. I'm a bad, bad man.

Now that I think about it, pretty isn't a strong enough word for her. Stunning might be close, but even that sounds too flat to use for someone who has a light around her. She literally glows when she smiles. Makes me wonder why I never noticed her before.

Pizza arrives not long after she leaves, and I need a beer. I call out, "Beer?"

All the guys raise their hands. I head into the kitchen where Nat is preparing a salad to go with the pizza. I open the fridge and fish out four beers. When I straighten, I tell her, "I'm going next-door, see if Helena wants a slice."

Nat stiffens. She doesn't talk for a long while. Finally, she utters, "Yeah, I wouldn't do that."

I shrug. "Why? She's your sister and she's not feeling great." I pause before adding, "She's cool."

She makes a choking noise before trying to string her words together. "Well, it's just that she...uh...she, well..." She cringes before explaining very, very slowly, "She's not your biggest fan, Max."

My breath leaves me in a whoosh. I don't understand. This has never happened to me before. I blink at her before shouting a high-pitched, "*What*?"

Nat continues to putter around the kitchen. "I know, right? So weird. I can't believe we're related sometimes."

I'm still in shock. I ask a panicked, "Why?"

She lifts a shoulder. "Well, she says you're a flirt."

What the hell? My defenses at an all-time high, and I sputter, "I'm a single man! I'm allowed to flirt!"

"Preaching to the choir, babe."

My mouth gapes. I can't comprehend what I'm being told. "But *why*?"

Nat turns and comes at me, wearing a face full of sympathy. She cups my cheek and speaks gently, "Sometimes people don't like other people, and sometimes they don't need a reason at all. It happens, honey."

Now I'm just sad. "But everyone loves me. I'm adorable."

She pulls my face down to her and kisses my forehead. "If it means anything, I think you're the best thing since sliced bread."

I try not to pout, but it's hard. Really hard. "Why doesn't she like me? I like her."

"Leave it alone."

"No way!" Determination pulses through my veins. "Only one thing to do now."

Nat eyes me suspiciously. "I'm almost scared to ask."

I stride to the door. "I'm going to make her like me."

She calls out after me, "It doesn't work that way, Max. You can't *make* her do anything!"

"Watch me!"

Challenge accepted.

CHAPTER SEVEN

Just before I make my exit, I pick up my plate of pizza and take it with me. Truthfully, I'm a little pissed I'm having to prove I'm a good guy to some chick I don't even know.

At least, I think I'm a good guy.

My stomach twists in knots.

Great. Now she's got you questioning yourself. What a bitch.

Hey now, brain. Don't you talk about her like that. I'd hate to have to kick your ass.

My brain smiles and nods in approval.

See? Good guy.

Knowing somebody doesn't like you for such a weak reason sucks hairy balls. But it quickly makes me wonder if some asshole ex-boyfriend of hers was a flirt, someone who flirted with women in front of her. I shake my head at the thought of wanting to break

Helena's non-existent ex-boyfriend's nose. No way would anyone who had a woman like that risk losing her over somethin' so stupid.

It don't matter. I'm determined to win her over. Mark my words; we are going to be friends. If I could just get her to see what a nice guy I am…

Standing in front of her door, I hold my plate in one hand and raise the other to knock. A few seconds later, Helena answers the door wearing the ugliest navy flannel pajamas I have ever seen. I have no idea how she's pulling off looking sexy in 'em. Her hair in a messy knot at the very top of her head, and I smile at how adorable she looks.

Brows bunched in confusion, she begins to ask, "What are you—" but as I move to step inside, I trip over my untied shoelace. The plate in my hand is projected forward, and in slow motion, I watch as the three pieces of pizza fly through the air and splatter across the front of her sleep-shirt.

Her mouth gaping and body rigid, she stands there wide-eyed, in shock. A whimper leaves her mouth. I stare at the tomato sauce marking her and I can't help it.

I snort.

My laughter subsides when I see her face flush bright red. Her bottom lip quivers and her eyes brighten with tears. She nods once in resignation, then closes the door in my face.

Shit!

"Helena, please open the door. I'm an ass. I shouldn't have laughed, but you got to admit...it was kinda funny."

My chest tightens as I hear a sniffle from the other side of the door. *Oh, man.* I run a hand through my hair in helplessness. This went a whole other way in my head. She would open the door, see the pizza in my hands, and smile at me. She'd tell me she was starving and that I was her hero. We'd go inside, talk and bond over pizza, and then every time we'd eat pizza together, we'd smile at each other knowing our entire friendship began with our favorite savory baked good.

Really, universe, would it kill ya to make to me her pizza hero? I'm not asking a lot here.

I hear her shuffle away from the door and I quickly knock again. "Helena, cupcake, I really am sorry. Please, open the door. At least let me help clean up." My forehead hits the door with a dull thud. I close my eyes and hear another sniffle. "Please, don't cry. You're breakin' my heart over here."

I wait a little while longer, but she's gone. Probably to shower.

Helena's hot little body in the shower. Soaking wet. Droplets sluicing down her body. Her nipples beaded, and...

Fuck, brain, you dirty fucker.

I know.

I mentally high-five my brain. So does my semi.

My mind works overtime thinking of ways I can fix what I just messed up with Helena. If we're going to be a part of the same friendship group, for the sake of everyone else, we need to find a way to get along. If it were up to me, we would get along, but I have a feeling Helena is the type to put up a fight.

I smirk. She won't win, however hard she fights. But something tells me she's worth the battle.

Max walks back into the apartment with an empty plate and looking mad.

Uh oh.

I stand and walk over to him. "What did she do?" I'm going to bitch slap her. Seriously.

He open his mouth to speak, then closes it. He makes another attempt, then another. Finally, with a sigh, he asks, "If Helena were mad at a guy," he cringes, "what would said guy have to do to get in her good book?"

My eyes narrow dangerously. My teeth gritted, I hiss, "What did *you* do?"

He chuckles nervously and rubs the back of his neck.

I'm going to bitch slap him.

Seriously.

Helena

I can't stop laughing at the look on Max's face when the pizza splattered all over me.

Tears prickled my eyes and I thought about crying, but when he snorted, it was hard to not laugh. But I hid it. I had to shut the door that very second, because if I didn't, I would've lost it in a fit of hilarity. I couldn't let him see me laugh. That would not flatter my stone-cold bitch act.

And the way he calls me cupcake...*Gah!*

I snuggle into the covers...the covers Max had been sleeping on not hours ago. "The guy sure is something else," I whisper into the dark.

My brow furrows as a thought crosses my mind.

Why is he trying so hard?

I ponder this a long while before my eyes get heavy. Soon, I'm drifting off. And I do it thinking about Max's dimple.

MAX

"If I wanted to impress a woman, what would I do?"

Nik grins. "If you were me and wanted to impress a woman, you'd just be alive."

Trick guffaws. "Whoa. Someone get a wheelbarrow for the douche's head."

Ghost bites into his sandwich, shoulders shaking in silent laughter. I look to my brother and throw a balled up napkin at his head. "You're so funny. Asshole."

The guys laugh, but I'm frustrated. "I'm bein' serious. It's been a long time since I've had to do any of this shit."

Suddenly, Ghost narrows his eyes at me. Swallowing his food, he asks, "Who is it you're trying to impress?"

I don't know why it makes me nervous, but Ash just has that effect on people. I laugh it off. "None of your business, *Asher*." When I put emphasis on his real name, his jaw tightens. Not a lot of people out there can get away with calling Ghost by his given name. As far as I know, he only gives women he loves the honor. I clear my throat. "It's no one." Then I lie through my teeth. "I'm thinkin' about dating."

I feel their eyes on me. Quiet overcomes the table.

Nik's the first to speak. "Seriously?"

I shrug, not sure what to say. Dating has never been an option before, but the older Ceecee gets, I guess I can start meeting women. There's only one problem. I don't want to meet women. I'm done with women. I had a woman—a woman I thought was a good woman—and it got me nothing but heartbreak. I loved Maddy. Loved her so much I would've done anything for her. But she changed. Soon after Ceecee was born, she wasn't the woman I fell in love with.

But I stuck by her, and I would've stuck by her 'til death if she had let me. I'm dedicated that way. And what was I rewarded with?

Attitude and ugly-ass words.

If you're thinking I'm bitter from one bad relationship, you're right. Just thinking about dating has my stomach coiled tight.

I clear my throat and straighten in my chair. "Maybe."

Nik smiles down at the table. Looking back up, he nods. "I think that would be cool."

Trick nudges my shoulder and jokes, "You can't have Lola."

I grin and poke the bear. "Nah, I want Nat."

Ash stands suddenly, his chair squealing behind him. He points at me, jaw rigid. "Lucky I love ya, bro."

Nik asks, "Got anyone in mind? Anyone in particular?"

I'm honest when I say, "Not really, I'm just takin' it as it comes."

My brother slaps a hand on my shoulder and responds, "Sometimes the best things are unplanned."

The guys make their leave and get back to work, leaving me sitting in the chill-out room with my own thoughts for company. My thoughts consist of green eyes and attitude.

I stand, shake my head to clear it, and head back to my office. Once inside, I take my cell out of my pocket and dial the number I was given the night before. It rings, and rings, and rings some more.

"Hi, you have reached Helena Kovac. I'm unable to take your call. Please leave your name and your number, and I'll get back to you as soon as I can." *Beep.*

I'm suddenly panicked. "Um...Helena. Hi, it's Max. Nik's brother. The guy you found sleeping in your bed. The same guy who threw pizza at you last night." *Oh, my God. Shut your mouth, idiot!* "Anyways, I just wanted to see if you were free tonight. I mean, I know it's Saturday and you're probably going to the club tonight with the girls, but—"

Beep.

Fuck. I must've reached the message time limit.

I call again. The voicemail message sounds out again. I wait patiently for the beep.

I lean back in my chair, getting comfortable to talk to Helena. "Sorry, I've been told I talk a lot. Anyways, I was saying if you'd let me, I'd like to take you to an early dinner to apologize for being, well, stupid last night." I sit up. "You know, I think I already feel so comfortable with you, because you're Nat's sister, and I love Nat. I mean, I know you don't like me, but if you—"

Beep.

Motherfucker!

I quickly redial and cover my face with a hand as I cringe at myself. "The fuck am I doing?"

Beep.

I sigh into the phone. "You know what? Don't worry about it. I...uh...I just realized I'm busy today anyways. So, um...yeah. Just...just don't worry about it. Sorry for spilling pizza on you. If you need a new pair a pajamas, let me know and I'll pay for 'em. And sorry for making you cry." I pause. "Never meant to hurt you, cupcake."

The message still recording, I tap my phone against my temple then end the call.

Well, that wasn't half-awkward.

I sink into my chair and wallow in self-pity.

Helena

Having just woken, I sit cross-legged on my bed in my spare set of pajamas, seeing as my favorite ones are still covered in tomato sauce. I listen to the three new voicemails.

"Um...Helena. Hi, it's Max. Nik's brother. The guy you found sleeping in your bed. The same guy who threw pizza at you last night. Anyways, I just wanted to see if you were free tonight. I mean, I know it's Saturday and you're probably going to the club tonight with the girls, but—"

I smile to myself then listen to the next message.

"Sorry, I've been told I talk a lot." I chuckle and listen on. *"Anyways, I was saying if you'd let me, I'd like to take you to an early dinner to apologize for being, well, stupid last night. You know, I think I already feel so comfortable with you, because you're Nat's sister, and I love Nat. I mean, I know you don't like me, but if you—"*

My face flushes bright red. Oh, dear God. Nat *told* him I don't like him? I'll cut a bitch!

But he called anyways to apologize and *ask you to dinner.*

My brows rise as I ponder this. This is true. What do I do now?

Go out with him. Let him buy you dinner. Talk to him. Get to know him a little.

Yeah. I straighten on my bed. *Yeah.* That's exactly what I'm going to do. My stomach flutters in excitement. I listen to the third message.

He sighs. "*You know what? Don't worry about it.*" My face falls. My heart sinks. "*I...uh...I just realized I'm busy today anyways. So, um...yeah. Just...just don't worry about it. Sorry for spilling pizza on you. If you need a new pair a pajamas, let me know and I'll pay for 'em. And sorry for making you cry.*" A slight pause, then a quiet, "*Never meant to hurt you, cupcake.*"

A sudden rush of anger flows through me. I delete the messages. "Fuck him."

He's right. I am going to the club tonight. My determination steeled, I get out of bed and head for the shower. I am going to the club, and I'm not coming home alone.

CHAPTER EIGHT

MAX

I can't shake it, this feeling I have just sitting like a rock in the pit of my stomach.

Why did I do that?

Stepping out of the shower, I wipe down my body and stand in front of the fogged mirror. I use my hand to wipe at it to look at my reflection. Yep, that's me. I mean, it looks like me, but I don't feel like me. Not today. In sixteen hours, I've thrown pizza at a girl, a girl who doesn't even like me, asked her out, and then cancelled. I'm normally a confident guy. What is it about this broad that's fucking with me? I'm sure there are people who don't like me. I know how I can get. Sometimes, I'm not very likeable. But I always try. Always.

I slip my boxers on, head out of the bathroom, and look at my room. This is my last day in this room. I try hard not to think about it, or look at the boxes scattered across the floor. Tomorrow is moving day. Ceecee is thrilled...and by thrilled, I mean still not talking to me.

I slip on my black jeans and White Rabbit tee. It has my name on it. Under my name, it says 'I'm here to serve you'. I grin. It always goes down well with the ladies. My black belt goes on next. I had a special buckle made for it that reads 'Follow the white rabbit'. I like it because it's big and silver, and a lot of women think *white rabbit* is a euphemism for my dick.

My sneakers are hiding somewhere around here. Just as I look under my bed, my mom sticks her head in and informs me, "We're leaving."

Got 'em. Always under the bed. I fish my sneakers out and stand. "Okay, Mom. Thanks again."

She smiles. "It's no problem." Her smile wanes. "She's still angry."

I pretend not to hear her and slip my shoes on. She steps forward and turns on her mom voice. "Don't you think about ignoring me, Maximillian."

God, she's might be small, but my mother is a scary woman when she wants to be. I grin up at her. "I would never ignore you, Mama. Never." She glares at me and I sigh. "I know she's angry, Ma. What do you want me to do? I'm not changing my mind just because she's pissed. We're moving. She's got to get used to that."

Mom's face softens. "Don't be upset at her for being scared to leave the only place she's ever known."

Well, when she puts it like that...

"I'm just upset that she's upset. I wish I could do something to make it easier for her."

Mom comes forward and hugs me. "Just show her you love her. That nothing will change that. That you will love her, even if she's angry at you. Be firm with your love and her heart will gentle."

I squeeze her back. "Okay. I will."

Stepping back, she smiles. "Good. Now go say goodnight to her."

I wink at my mom before I step out of my room. Just as I exit, I almost run over two little fairies with golden eyes and dark hair. They gasp when they see me. Then it's on.

"Uccle Max!"

"Mak!"

Tatiana and Ava, Nik and Tina's daughters, attach themselves to my legs. "Oh, my God, I'm being attacked! I thought fairies were the good guys!"

Tina steps into the hall, looks down at her babies, and rubs absently at her stomach. Geez, her belly just gets bigger and bigger. Two times the fun with twins. I mentally cringe.

Good luck Ghost and Nat.

Tina asks the little girls blinking up at her. "Grandma's ready to go, girls. Why are you running away?"

Tatiana looks around before leaning forward and answering, "There's a monster in our room."

Tina widens her eyes in shock. "Well, why didn't you say so?" She walks toward the girls' bedroom door and knocks. "Um, excuse me? Monster? You need to leave now. We're running late."

Nik calls from the other side of the door. "No can do, Mommy. I need food. I hear little girls are tasty," then he smacks his lips loudly.

Tatiana giggles, but Ava grips my legs tighter, not quite old enough to get that the monster is actually her dad trying to make a funny. Tina sighs dramatically. "Can't I just get you some bread, or cereal, or something?"

Nik responds, "Nope. I need little girl and I need it now."

Tina looks over at the girls. "You heard him. He's hungry. Which one of you wants to be munched up?" Tatiana nods while Ava shakes her head emphatically. Tina crooks a finger at Tatiana. "You better get in there. Sounds like he's *starving*."

As soon as Tatiana takes off down the hall, Ava wails, "*No!*"

I pick up my tater tot, hug her close and whisper, "It's okay, baby. It's only pretend." She sniffles into my neck. Tatiana creeps up to the door, and as soon as she puts her hand on the knob, the door flies open and out comes the monster.

Nik steps out and I gasp. "Oh, my God, it's hideous!"

Ava's smiles and kicks her little legs. Otherwise known as *let me down now*.

I let her down, and Nik chases his babies down the hall and into his bedroom. Not a minute later, growls, roars, laughter, and baby squeals let us know they've been caught.

Tina laughs softly then turns to me. "Where's Ceecee?"

My smile falls. My stomach drops. "I thought she was with you."

Tina's smile fades quickly. She calls out, "Ceecee? Honey, where are you?"

No answer.

My pulse spikes. "Ceecee, baby?"

Nothing.

Fuck.

Tina rushes to Ceecee's room and throws open the door. She turns to me, eyes wide. "She's not in here."

I don't wait to consult with anyone. My feet move of their own accord. I quickly check the kitchen, living area, and all the bedrooms.

Empty.

My heart races as I check the backyard. "*Ceecee!*"

My mom rushes out of my room. "What's going on?"

I snatch my car keys off the table and tell her, "Can't find Ceecee. She's gone."

Fear fills me as I run down the hall and see the front door open. I whisper to myself, "Please God, no."

I run as fast as I can, hearing Nik's heavy footfalls behind me. On the front porch, Nik bellows, "*Ceecee!*"

My feet don't stop. I run to my truck and jump in. I start it up and Nik jumps in the passenger seat. The tires screech as I take off down the driveway. Just as I'm about to hit road, Nik calls out, "Wait. Stop! Over there." He points out the window on his side.

My racing heart slows. I see her. She sits there, at the front gate, staring over at our new house. I grip the steering wheel and lower my head onto it, hyperventilating.

Fuck. Shit. Fuck.

Nik pats my back. "It's okay. She's okay."

So many thoughts go through my head. Ugly, disturbing thoughts.

What if she wasn't okay?

I feel tears prickle my eyes, but I hold them back. I step out of the car, not bothering to turn it off. As I walk toward her on Jell-O legs, I hear Nik exit the car and get into the driver's side. The car reverses away, leaving me with my daughter. I move to stand behind her, and I equally want to hug the shit out of her and beat her ass for scaring the crap out of me. I settle with resting my hand on her shoulder. She looks up at me, golden eyes sad, then looks back across the street. We stand there a while, and I'm glad for it. I need a moment to get my shit together.

Another five minutes or so, and Ceecee mutters, "We're not very far, are we?"

My throat is thick with emotion from the ordeal I've been put through, so I clear it. "No, honey. We're not far."

She takes a moment to process this, then asks quietly, "And I can come here whenever I like?"

I reply on a squeeze of her shoulder, "Of course, baby."

Another moment, and then she nods once, firmly. "Then...then I guess moving won't be so bad."

My eyes widen in surprise.

What did she just say?

I stop myself from jumping in the air and kicking my heels together. Instead, I kiss the top of her head and hug her around the shoulders. "It won't be bad. It'll be fun. We're having an adventure, me and you."

Her small hand comes up to rest on mine and she utters a shaky, "I'm sorry, Daddy. I haven't been very nice to you."

I don't bother accepting her apology. It's been, it's done, and it's over. "Love you."

I feel a tear drip from her cheek onto my forearm. She sniffles, "I love you, too."

My heart lightens. I take hold of the handles of her chair and start wheeling her back to the house. As soon as we get through the front door, I tell her, "You want to get your things ready?"

She smiles up at me and nods. Then she's gone. I find myself on the arm of the sofa, biting my lip, looking into nothingness. Nik startles me when his hand comes down on my shoulder. I jump, but when I see it's just him, I breathe deep. "Fuck, man."

"I know."

I exhale shakily. "No, really."

He squeezes my shoulder. "I know."

My hand comes up to pinch the bridge of my nose. I look up at him. "I don't think..." I shrug.

He shakes his head. "You're not workin' tonight. Not after that. Go and take your girl out. Get ice cream. Have some fun."

It takes me a moment to respond. Even then, it's quiet. Too quiet. "Thanks, man."

Ceecee comes out of her room with her backpack over the side of her chair. She wheels herself over to me and narrows her eyes at my smile. She asks a long and drawn out, "What?"

I pick up my car keys. "Change of plan." I jiggle the keys. "How about dinner and a movie?"

Her face morphs into shock. She asks on a whisper, "Really?"

I shoot her a *well, duh* look. "Uh, yeah."

She sputters, "But...but why?"

I shrug. "I need a reason?"

She looks left, then right, then nods.

Leaning back against the dining table, I stroke my chin. "I see. Then I would like to take my girl out for the following reasons." I count them on my fingers. "Number one, you're my daughter and I love you. Number two, you're the only person in the world who can out-eat me in ice cream. Number three," I lean closer and mock whisper, "you're much better company than all those *old* people."

Nik calls out, "I heard that!"

Tina adds, "I did too!"

Mom returns, "We'll see who's old next time you come over begging me to feed you!"

I mutter, "Whoops." Ceecee giggles. I smile down at her and hold my hand out. "Now, can I take you out?"

Smiling big, she responds, "I'd like that, Daddy." Then I proceed to take my little one out for pizza, a movie, and ice cream.

And we have a blast.

MAX

As I lie in bed at the end of a great night out with my daughter, it hits me what happened tonight. It hits me hard. That I may not have found her. That she could've been gone. Forever. My eyes sting beneath my closed lids. I cry silently under the covers for a long time.

No one said being a parent was easy.

Helena

The White Rabbit is just how I remembered it. I'm glad to be back.

I spent the afternoon getting ready with Nat, seeing as she had the afternoon off. Most of the afternoon was spent eating, bitching at each other, Nat throwing clothes at me excitedly, and me kicking clothes away, wearing a look of disgust.

No offence to my sister, but she's much more open about her body than I am. I don't like to show a lot of skin, but if I do show skin, it's likely to be my back and shoulders, rather than my legs. We spent over an hour getting ready. We made up our faces, Nat did my hair, and I ended up wearing one of my own dresses. I look over at Nat and my inner self sighs in jealousy. She always was the fox of the family.

Take what she's wearing right now: a simple cut, bright mustard-yellow dress hitting high up on her thighs with tan heels. That's it. Her now brown hair is worn straight with minimal makeup as she glosses her lips and smiles at me. I smile back, but there's a shitload of envy in that smile.

My Grecian-style, white floor-length dress is twisted at the shoulders, and although simple, is one of my favorite dresses. I've worn it a heap of times, and when I find a new place to go, it's always the first thing I go for. This is for a number of reasons. Firstly, it's comfortable. Secondly, it's flattering to my curvy body. Thirdly, it's quaint and charming. All I have to do is slip on a pair of flat gold sandals, add a few big gold bangles, and top it off with a pair of dangly earrings. I wanted to leave my hair up, but Nat wasn't having it. She made me wear it down, gently adding loose curls in my already wavy hair.

She dusted my cheeks with gold shimmer, lined my eyes, and put a crap-ton of mascara on me. I don't know how she did it, but I sort of look ethereal, like a goddess...in a very human kind of way. Either way, I feel good going out tonight. I want to look my best. After all, I'm on the prowl. Max can eat a dick.

Ash comes in without knocking. I mean, why would he knock while breaking in through the back sliding door? He just strides on in like he owns the place. Might have something to do with the fact he bought the apartment building last year. He jerks his chin at me and states, "Nice." Then he spots his wife. His eyes glaze over at the sight of Nat's ass as she checks herself in the mirror. She spots him in the reflection and winks at him. He mutters, "Nic*er*."

I'm offended. Well, no, I'm not. Mock-offended, really. I scoff and throw one of my many stuffed toys at his head. "Thanks, bonehead."

He sheepishly rubs at the back of his neck. "You look hot too. In a sisterly way." We both stiffen and recoil at the off-key statement. He points a finger at me. "Don't repeat that. That was sick." Closing my eyes, my body shakes in silent laughter. For a man who looks like he's the epitome of cool, Ash is just...not.

Nat graces us with her presence. "Ready to go, kids?" She smacks a kiss on Ash's cheek, leaving behind a glossy mess. He doesn't even wipe it away, just snags her around the waist and pulls her close. In a dance they choreographed long ago, she comes willingly, moving to his front. He bands both arms around her middle, resting his chin on her head. This pose they're in, I can't remember seeing anything that looked more natural in the world. This pose...it's just *them*. I love it. It makes me happy.

I'm ready. "Hell yeah. Watch out New York; I'm about to tear shit up." Ash shoots me a warning look. I quickly amend, "Yeah, New York, you better watch it, 'cause I am going to tear your shit up in a moderately and unobtrusive way, ya hear?"

Nat bursts into laughter and calls out a high-pitched, "Holla!"

I pick up my bag and purse my lips. "That's just how I roll, yo."

CHAPTER NINE

Helena

We arrive to The White Rabbit long before anyone has even lined up to get in, even though it opens at eight. But, really, who starts their clubbing journey at eight? None of the cool kids, that's who. I'm actually glad for it though. Being that all the gang are here, I can catch up with them without being interrupted or being knocked down by drunken fools.

Last year, Nik axed the VIP area of the club. The area is still there and it still gets used, but now it's strictly reserved for family and friends. And being the cool brother he is, he even reserved a booth for his newly legal little sister, Isa, who turned twenty-one just months before. He said this was because she'd earned it, being that she'd always been a sweet kid and had kept up her grades. But we all knew it was just a way for Nik, Max, and Ash to keep a close eye on her and who she is hanging out with, without outright asking.

Stupid men. They think she doesn't know. She knows, all right.

Nat and I sit at the booth with our cocktails and talk. Soon after, Tina arrives with Lola and Mimi in tow. By nine, we're laughing and talking up a storm. Lola nudges my shoulder. "So, you leave a guy back home sobbing his little heart out?"

I roll my eyes. "No, dorkette," I wiggle my brows, "I left about ten. And they all cried. One proposed."

Nat almost loses her drink. She snort-coughs, then asks through a wheeze, "Is that shit true?" I throw her a deadpanned look. Her shoulders slump. "That's what I thought. I mean," she looks me up and down, "who'd be stupid enough to want to marry *you*?"

I glower and pull her hair. She yelps then reaches over to pinch my arm. I squeak. We both mutter at the same time, "Bitch."

Mimi cuts in with, "Ya know, I never thought of you as a one-night stand sort of chick." She looks me dead in the eye. "You ever had one before?"

I sip my drink and shake my head at the same time.

Nat scoffs. "They're messy."

Tina nods emphatically and adds, "And awkward." Everyone stares at her. Tina's only ever slept with two men in her life. She quickly utters with a small shrug, "Or so I hear."

Lola chirps in, "But they can be fun."

Mimi runs her finger down her beer suggestively and snarks, "If they're not just a bratwurst with shit for brains."

Well, these bitches sure are putting a damper on my sexy mood. I quickly ask, "Surely, one of you have had a good one-night stand." I expect one of them to answer with an 'Of course', but they all seem busy in other things right now. Mimi sips her beer. Tina checks her phone. Lola coughs and blinks as if fighting through a really bad memory. Nat just looks up, lost in thought. I nudge Nat. "Well?"

She shushes me. "I'm thinkin', all right?"

Steely determination runs through me. I sip my drink 'til it's finished and announce, "I'm going to be the one to prove y'all wrong." I shuffle out of the booth and stand. "I'm going to have the best one-night stand ever. It's going to be hot, and not messy. We'll shake hands afterwards and it won't be weird. At all. The guy will have a ten-inch cock, and well," I concede with a shrug, "probably shit for brains, but his dick will make up for it." I smile a small smile as I describe what I'm looking for. "He'll be tall and built, and have dark hair and smiling eyes. And a dimple."

Crap, you just described Max! Take flight!

I fight the flush with all I have. "I'm just going to go find him. Right now." My dress swishes around my legs as I walk away.

Probably shouldn't have worn a thong tonight.

Oh, my God, I *know*! It's so uncomfortable. I have to force myself not to try to pick out this never-ending wedgie. Instead, I think of other things, like dogs riding skateboards and chipmunks eating things with their widdle teethies.

I make my way downstairs to the bar. I spot him immediately, and I sigh. "There should be a warning sign above this bar."

He grins. "Oh, yeah. And what would it say?"

"Something about eye candy and killer smiles, I'm sure."

Sherriff chuckles. "You flatter me, Lena." He reaches over the bar and slowly and leisurely kisses my cheek. "How you doin', beautiful?"

The last few times I've come to The White Rabbit, I've spent more time than I should have at the bar. Truth is, I have a teensy crush of Stefan the Sherriff, the barman. And it all started at Nik and Tina's wedding. What can I say? He's just something else—dirty blond hair worn at a length that borderlines too long, sexy, warm brown eyes, a body I like to watch work the bar, and an easy smile. But best of all, he's easy to talk to. He listens intently and shows it by asking questions and getting involved in what you're saying.

He's super sweet. Any woman would be thrilled to call him hers. I sit at the bar talking to Sherriff and drinking the drinks he makes me. I can taste less and less alcohol in my cocktails, but smile knowing he's trying to look after me. Before I know it, it's ten thirty and I still haven't seen Max.

My head feeling light from the countless drinks I've had, I ask, "Where's Max?"

Sherriff answers on a shrug. "No idea. He should be here."

My haunches rise as I add another dot point on my shit list against Max. *Point five: slacker.*

Whatever. I move off my stool, and just as I'm about to say goodbye to Sherriff, a hand on my forearm stops me. I look up, and all I see are green eyes.

"Helena? Helena Kovac?"

I frown. How the hell would someone know who I am in New York? I step back and assess the situation. The man standing in front of me wears a gorgeous, wide smile. He's at least a foot taller than me. *Not as tall as Max.* Shut up, brain. He's extremely fit and has no hair—as in, Baldy McGee—but it looks good on him.

He holds a hand out to me. "I know you don't know me, but you will."

Okay. Officially freaked out now. Holding a hand up, palm out, I step away again. "Don't. Stay where you are."

He looks down at me in confusion before realization crosses his face. He laughs aloud. "I'm sorry; I shouldn't laugh, but...but I just realized how that sounded. Okay, let's try this again." He straightens, holding his hand out once more. "Hi, Helena, I'm James Whittaker."

My mouth rounds into an *O. This* is my new boss? *Schwing!*

Still holding out his hand, he explains, "I recognized you from the photo you sent for your identification tag, which I actually have in my car." I bite my lip to hold in my laugh and look anywhere but at him. He cringes. "Yeah, okay, I heard it that time too. Creepy as hell."

I laugh and step forward. "I'm sorry for freaking out, but you sounded a little stalkerish. Sorry."

I place my hand in his and we shake, smiling all the while. He releases my hand then puffs out a breath. "I probably should've just let you be. I'm sorry if I made our first meeting awkward."

"No, it's fine. My friend owns this club, so I was just catching up with people."

His brows rise. "You know the Leokovs?"

My nose wrinkles in an attempt to be cute. "Yeah, Nik married a close family friend, Tina. My sister Nat is married to their adoptive brother, Asher. So we're all a tight knit little family of sorts."

James smiles warmly. "That's really cool. So you know Max Leokov then?"

Before I can stop myself, I sniff. "Yeah. Him, I've met."

James's smile declines. "You don't like him then?"

I don't answer. Instead, I ask, "How do you know him?"

He leans on the bar and explains, "His daughter Ceecee is a client of mine."

Fuck. Of course she is. I'm such a dick.

I smile genuinely. "I love Ceecee. And Max is okay, I guess, when he's not sleeping in my bed or throwing pizza at me."

Oh, *noooooo*! *Why did you say that, you social disgrace of a homo sapien?*

James's eyes widen. My entire body heats in embarrassment. I sputter, "Oh—oh, no! It's not like that, I swear. He sleeps in my bed when I'm not in it, is all." *Yeah, that wasn't any better. Try again.* "What I meant to say is that Max…he's…I mean—" I suddenly blurt, "I don't know how to make this better!"

To my absolute surprise, James tilts his head back and roars with laughter. He laughs 'til he's hoarse. "Oh, man, I thought I was bad. Why don't you just leave it there?"

Biting my lip, cheeks flaming, I nod once.

He smirks at me. "I think we're going to get along just fine."

Holy shit, that was brutal. My shoulders slump in relief. I clear my throat and change the subject. "How often does Ceecee do PT?"

He nurses then sips on his beer. "Depends, you know? Sometimes, she's okay to go without it for weeks, because she's doing her exercises at home, but sometimes she needs a session or two a week. She doesn't exactly like her exercise program. She says it's boring, and because she doesn't like doing it, she pays for it with spasms and aches."

My face softens. It must be hard for her. "She probably just needs the right motivation."

James looks me in the eye. "Max...he's tried everything short of forcing her. She listens sometimes, but not often enough."

A sudden thought floods my mind. "Has Ceecee ever had a say in her exercise program?"

His eyes narrow in confusion. "How do you mean?"

I step forward and sit on the stool in front of him. "I mean, she's a teenage girl. I know there are exercises she'll *need* to do, but has anyone asked her what she *likes* to do?"

James open his mouth to respond, but he pauses. His mouth snaps shut. "No. I...um—I don't think I have asked her." I raise a brow. He grins in response. "I like it."

I return his grin. "She's a young woman who's been told all her life what she has to do. It must be tiring."

Suddenly, his brows bunch. He mutters, "Yeah, it must be."

A wild hair reaches into my brain, and before I can stop myself, I ask, "Would you like to come upstairs and meet my sister?"

A look of surprise flitters across his face before he beams. "Yeah. I'd love to."

Oh, this is so crazy awkward. I have no idea what I'm doing. "Cool. Come on up."

As soon as we reach the top of the stairs, Nik calls out, "Whit! What's up, man?"

James takes his hand in a rough, competitive man-shake that looks more like an assault. "Not much, Nik. Just met Helena here."

Nik looks down at me. He loses his smile. Throwing James an acid look, he states, "She's off limits."

James looks over at me, trying to hide his smile. I roll my eyes and shove Nik in the gut. "He's my new boss, Niki. Ease up."

Nik looks over at me, smiling a brotherly smile full of pride. "Seriously? You're working at the center? That's awesome, kid."

I blush. "I know. I worked my butt off for it."

Nik wraps his arm around me and pulls me close. He says to James, "She's family, ya know, so you better treat her good."

Oh, God, no.

I shrug Nik's arm off and tug James by the wrist toward the stairs. "This was *so* not a good idea. I'm sorry. We should go back down."

But James just grins. "Are you kidding? This is the highlight of my night!"

Oh, he's pushing it. I lean in and hiss, "At my expense!"

He leans in closer to me. "Just go with the flow, Helena. It's never as bad as you think it is."

That's when Nat calls out, "I remember when Helena was three and took off her diaper. She peed on the furniture 'cause she wanted to be like our dog."

Holy mother of God!

I cover my face with my hands and mock-sob. "It's *always* as bad as I think it is." James turns away from me, but I see his back shake in silent laughter. I narrow my eyes at him and whisper, "It's not true, you know. What she said, I mean." It's a poor attempt at saving my honor, but it's worth a shot.

He faces me, eyes smiling. "Yeah. Yeah, it is." My face flames, but he just bumps my shoulder. "It's okay, Helena. You were three. If you did that last week, then yeah, I'd be a bit worried."

My pride already out the window, I sigh dramatically. "I guess I shouldn't tell you about last week's incident then."

Suddenly, he's in my face. A dangerous smile on that gorgeous face, he whispers, "I'm all ears, babe."

I think that's the exact moment we both realize this conversation is extremely inappropriate. My eyes widen. So do his. We start at the same time.

"Oh, my gosh, *James*!"

"*Crap*. I'm so sorry, Helena."

"That was…"

"….really not cool. I-uh…I don't know what I was thinking. *Shoot*."

Laughter lines my voice. "It's okay. You're funny. I think you're a hoot." I dip my chin and laugh quietly. I am not offended; I'm amused. Really damn amused. I like him! But he doesn't laugh in return as expected. I look up to find him incensed. I quickly put my hand on his forearm. "Hey."

He pulls away from my touch. "Uh, it's probably best if that didn't happen again. I've never acted that way in my life. I am—" he coughs, "so sorry. I'm usually quite professional. It's not like me to flirt with an employee." His eyes hold a clear apology. "I should go."

I can't believe this is the same man I was laughing with a few minutes ago. Where did he go and who is this stiff? I reach out a second time and wrap a hand around his wrist tightly. "Hey, don't leave. I'm just as much to blame. I'm sorry." His body loses some of its tenseness. I add slowly, "I thought you were funny. I mean, I don't offend *that* easily. And just for your information, I'm not your employee." He raises a brow in my direction. I lift my shoulder. "Not yet. Not for another two days."

His other brow rises to join the first. A low chuckle escapes him, and I smile knowing I've eased the tension. Shaking his head, he lets out a long sigh. "I can say this has been a very interesting evening." He stills and his eyes dart from side to side. "I should probably mention I don't date employees." A sudden rush of embarrassment disguised as anger clenches my gut. I'm just about to lie through my teeth and tell him I wasn't coming onto him, when he adds, "I'm screwing this up again. Sorry."

My middle unclenches with a slow exhale. I reply, "I don't date, James. I'm just looking for a friend."

With an easy smile, he utters, "That, I can do."

CHAPTER TEN

Helena

Safely seated two booths away from my sister and the rest of the guys, James and I sit, drink, and get to know each other in our comfortable surroundings. "So you've got two sisters. One is the loud-mouthed brunette over there, and the other is a hairdresser back home. Both of your parents are still alive and kicking, and are still together after twenty-five years." He squints. "Did I get that right?" I nod with smiling eyes.

He tells me, "Well, my family really only consists of two people. It's just me and my brother, Trent. Both our parents have passed on. Dad, when Trent was a baby, and Mom just last year." Just as I'm about to offer my condolences, he mutters, "You really weren't kidding when you said you guys are like a family."

Fiddling with my straw, I smile warmly. "I was never really part of the family myself until recently. *Very* recently. Tina was, and my sister was, so I guess when they told the guys I was going to be living here," I shrug, "they just sort of included me."

James responds to me, but looks over at the booth filled with laughing women and their men. "Must be nice." I look over at the booth myself and smile at the scene they don't even know they're making. He adds, "To be included just as you are."

I turn back to him. "May I be frank?" He nods, lifting his beer to his mouth. I mutter, "It's fucking awesome."

He chokes on his beer and I laugh. He bangs on his chest with a closed fist and wheezes out, "Potty mouth." Then shoots me a thumbs up. "Nice."

Still laughing, I cringe at myself. Who the heck did I think I was having drinks with? "I'm sorry. I'm not exactly making the best first impression. Especially since I'm supposed to be making a good impression. I just...I guess you just make me feel like I can talk freely with you, you know?" I look down at the table. My cheeks heat as I mumble, "I already feel very comfortable with you."

A warm hand covers mine. I peek up at him. He confides, "The feeling's mutual. And as far as I'm concerned, as long as we're off the clock, you can cuss like a damn sailor and pour rum down your throat. It's all good."

Eyes full of awe, I confess, "I think I just fell in love with you a little."

He suavely leans back in the booth and shoots me with a finger gun. "It happens."

I couldn't get the damn smile off my face if I wanted to. Not that I want to.

I think working with James Whittaker will be a treat.

MAX

The sound of vibrating wakes me. I squint over at the clock. 1:14 am. What the fuck? I open the message sent from Nik.

Nik: Not that you care or anything.

Attached is a photo. The hairs stand up on the back of my neck. Well, she didn't waste any time, did she? Helena, looking something like an angel, leans over a booth, laughing. Her hand rests on the man's forearm. He's smiling down at her, looking at her like she's the most beautiful girl in the world.

Wait. Is that…?

My gut knots in what I refuse to believe is jealousy. That's Whit, Ceecee's PT, and she's looking up at him like he's a God. My chest aches. I quickly type a response.

Me: Glad she's having fun.

I switch off my phone and try to get back to sleep. But sleep doesn't come. Instead, I wonder what it'll take to get the green-eyed hothead to smile at me like that.

Helena

It's close to two am, and now James has left, I'm moving back over to the booth with everyone else. As soon as I get into hearing distance, my sister calls out, "So how big is his cock?"

I shoot her daggers. "Shut your whore mouth. He was a gentleman."

She smirks. "So you tried and he pleaded innocence?"

Nik cuts in with a curious, "You tryin' to bake cookies with Whit?"

I wave a hand in his direction to shut him up, and get back to bickering with my sister. "No, dumbass. He's my boss. I wouldn't do anything with my boss. That's just stupid. He's my *boss*." Her eyes narrow at me in a *bullshit* gesture. I point a finger at her. "Thinking about it is not the same as doing it!"

She chuckles. "You're fucked. You got a crush on your boss. And the way he was looking at you all night..." She fans herself. "Holy shit. This is not going to end well. I can see it already."

I bunch my nose. "Looking at me like what? He was uber-friendly."

Ash chokes on a laugh. "Uh, no. No. That wasn't friendly." He wraps an arm around Nat. "That's how I look at your sister. And trust me," his brow tilts upward, "I don't want to be her friend."

This can't be. I have a great read on people. How could I have missed this? I only picked up friendship vibes. There were definitely no *wanna-play-hide-the-bratwurst* vibes thrown in there. My face must convey my confusion, because suddenly I'm being harassed in the form of twenty questions.

Trick starts. "Did he flirt with you?" I begin to shake my head, then memories of the beginning of our conversation come flooding back. I nod. He jerks his chin at me in response.

Nik asks, "Did he make excuses to touch you?" Wide-eyed, my head jerks up and down. Nik sighs. "Yep. That ain't friendly."

Mimi sighs too, saying, "I think your boss has a thing for you, sugar."

I shake my head. "No, he said he doesn't date employees."

Everything screeches to a halt. Lola tilts her head to the side. "He had to make that clear? Like he was thinking about it?"

"No, no. We might've play-flirted when we first met. And it may have gotten a little serious."

My sister wraps a hand around me and hisses in a breath. "Oh, bitch, please. You know he's gone home and played *Slickin' Willie* to the memory of your thong through that flimsy white drape you call a dress."

I stiffen, then squeak, "You can see my thong?"

Everyone at the table nods. Oh, will you just fuck my life already and be done with it! My mouth rounds in shock. I can't believe this shit. Why does everyone always wait until afterwards to tell you these kinds of things? It doesn't matter though. I decide to clarify why James and I would never be a possibility. With a gentle shake of my head, I explain, "Well, nothing's going to happen, so you all can just take a chill pill. I don't date."

At the very same time, Nik asks, "Why?" while Asher utters, "Good." Both sets of eyes snap to each other. They have a silent conversation. Ash's eyes narrow dangerously. He shakes his head discreetly. Nik's brow rises. He nods even more discreetly, eyes firm on Ash. Not discreet enough. Ash stares down his best friend. Nik's lip twitches.

After a moment, Ash sinks into the booth, a look of annoyance plastered on his face. He mutters, "You've got to be kidding me with this shit." Nik just grins, and it almost looks victorious, his dimple making an appearance. Everyone at the booth seems to be smiling. All except Ash.

I can't handle it! It's like I'm not the only one not in on the joke. I like jokes! I want in! "What?" I ask, a small smile playing at my lips.

Nik just smiles harder. "Nothing, sweetheart. We're just glad you're here."

A warm smile spreads across my face. I reach over to pat his hand. "I'm glad to be here. You guys make it too easy to fit in. It's like I'm part of your little family."

Nik mutters, "I have a feeling if you weren't now, somehow, you always would've been."

I don't even pretend to mask my confusion, but Tina just giggles. "Don't even try to decipher the Mister Miyagi remarks he makes. You'll waste hours of your life."

Nat nudges my shoulder. "C'mon, kid. Let's get you home."

A yawn escapes me just as I state, "But I'm not even tired."

She shuffles out of the booth and pulls me along with her, wrapping an arm around my waist as I stand. Pouting her lips, she coos, "Oh, come on, sweepy baby. I know yo' a sweepy widdle baby. You can't wait to get to sweep, can you?"

I hate her for making me actually feel like a sweepy widdle baby. And I do like sweep. I yawn a second time, leaning my head on her shoulder "Okay. Let's go."

Trick calls out, "You're coming back to the club, right?"

I lift my head and jerk my chin toward him. "Bet your ass I will."

After saying our goodbyes, Nat leads me to her car. I get in and lean my forehead on the window. The last thing I think about before I fall asleep is a laughing dimple.

But it's not Nik's.

MAX

"Come on, baby. One more set."

Panting, she hisses through clenched teeth, "I can't."

Don't give me that shit. "Yes, you can. One more set."

Her hands shake in the handles of the pulley as she lowers herself back down to the padded mat. "No more."

I push harder. "One more. It's one more. You can do it. Show me how strong you are."

But she's had it. Frustrated and annoyed, she throws down the handles of the pulley and yells, "I'm done. God, stop yelling at me!"

I wasn't yelling at her. Even so, I lower my voice a little. "I wasn't yelling at you, baby. I was motivating you."

She pulls herself toward the edge of the mat, over to her chair. Sweaty and panting, she lowers herself into her chair, and without another word, she wheels herself away. Fast. I look around the room I had converted into a makeshift gym for me and my girl, and sigh. "Fuck."

Just another day. It's getting harder and harder to motivate Ceecee. She's becoming a woman; her attitude is changing. She's not as compliant as she used to be. She's becoming her own person. Which is great. Which also sucks. For me. I'm thinking the only thing I can do right now is ask Whit to take her on full-time again. If he doesn't, I don't know what I'll do.

CHAPTER ELEVEN

Helena

I wake around noon on Sunday. And when I say I wake, I mean I'm woken by loud ass banging coming through the wall.

At first, I thought it was maintenance working on the building, but with a cringe to end all cringes, I quickly work out what the noise is.

"Oh, God, baby! Yes, Ash. Do it just like—*Yes*! Keep going. I'm almost there. Almost there. Almost—" A long, drawn out female moan has me jumping out of bed.

"Oh, my freaking *God*! Dude!" Covering my ears, I chant, "Ew. Ew. Ew. Ew. Ew," as I run into the bathroom.

I change into sweats and a loose tee, pull my hair into a high ponytail, and throw in my headphones, quickly blasting some random song on my MP3 player that I don't really hear at all. I'm just glad it's blocking out my sister's sexcapades. Not knowing or caring if the main event is over, I walk back into my room, snatch up my cell, and type out a heated text.

Me: Dude! The walls are paper thin. SERIOUSLY! Keep the moaning to a minimum. Pretty fucking please!!!

After a second, I quickly type again.

Me: You know what? Moan all you like. I'm out. Peace, bruh.

I walk out the apartment, and just as I'm about to close the door behind me, I spot something out the corner of my eye. Faster than I thought possible, I spin on my heel and rush back inside, shutting the door behind me as quietly as possible.

My chest heaving, I lift my wide eyes to the peephole and peek out. I see nothing, but I hear something. I pull out my headphones and listen intently.

"Why, hello, dear." That's Mrs. Crandle.

I hear no one respond.

Mrs. Crandle mutters, "I'm well, thank you." She sounds happy. "What's your name, sweetie?" Silence, then she speaks again. "Very nice to meet you. Won't you come in?" A moment's quiet before I hear her speak softly. "That would be very nice. Thank you." Her voice turns to a morose hush. "I don't get much company." And even though I'm not sure who she's talking to, or if she's talking to anyone at all, I feel shame course through me. Mrs. Crandle is my neighbor. I should be more neighborly. I had no idea she was lonely. "Okay, dear. Come around for tea sometime. I'll introduce you to my cats."

A low, masculine chuckle sounds before his face is right in my vision. My heart skips a beat. I place a hand over my mouth to stop the squeak from escaping.

Knock knock knock

I hold my breath. If he thinks I'm not home, he's bound to leave. Ten seconds pass. I'm about to pass out if I don't breathe again soon.

Knock knock knock

My face is surely turning purple. My lungs burn. I see the light. *Need. Air. To. Live.*

Knock knock knock

He sighs. "Helena, I know you're in there. I can see the shadow of your feet from under the door."

I huff in a much-needed breath. Panting, I glower at him through the door. There's only one thing to do now. I turn the volume up on my MP3 player to an ear-splitting level. I open the door as if I hadn't known he was there all along. I fake a look of surprise. "Max. I didn't hear you there." I point to the earphones and hope he can't see the blood leaking down the sides of my face from the loud screeching currently being projected into my ears. I turn it down and remove the earphones. All I hear is ringing. It's quite possible I have caused permanent damage.

He grins down at me. His dimple is so awesome that I think there should be a shrine somewhere in the world dedicated to it. He shakes his head at me. "Liar."

I feel a flush creep up from my neck. I fight the urge to be a bitch. I really do. "What can I do for you?"

Without waiting for an invitation, he slides past me and into my apartment. Stuck in the doorway, I try with all my might not to think about how his body felt sliding next to mine.

Sweet Jesus on a platter! He's toned.

He moves across the room, over to the kitchen. He opens my fridge and sighs. "I'm hungry." He looks up at me. "Are you hungry? We should get something to eat."

I dip my chin. Why must he be so…Max?

"Max, we've been here before. Dude, focus. Why are you here?"

He checks my fridge again, as if food will magically appear if he looks hard enough. "What are you living on? There's nothin' in here. You gotta eat." He peeks up at me, his golden eyes watching me closely. "You eaten?"

Rather than answering, I dodge the question like a pro. "I just woke up."

His face bunches. "It's past noon."

I don't have to explain myself to you.

My mind pokes its tongue out at him. "I had a late night."

Until now, I hadn't realized what he's holding in his hand. He rubs absently at his belly. "I'm in bad shape over here. I need food and you have…" he winces, "milk." His nose bunches adorably. "Milk is not food, Helena. I'm a growing boy. I can't survive on milk. I need solids."

Still eyeing the item in his hand, I ask quietly, "Why do you have a mini whiteboard in your hand?"

He looks down at it, then back up at me. "To talk to Mrs. Crandle."

I don't get it. "Why did you need to speak to Crandle?"

He shrugs. "I didn't."

Everything screeches to a halt. *Hold the phone.* My brows knotted, deep in thought, I place the fingertips of one hand over my mouth. Having gotten my thoughts together, I ask quietly, "You went out...out of your way...to buy a mini whiteboard to communicate with a deaf old lady for no good reason at all?"

His eyes narrow as he looks up in thought as if processing what I just asked. He nods quickly. "Yep."

The complete selflessness of this single act has my mind at war with my heart. My mind, still bitter and hurt over something Max likely doesn't even remember, rolls its eyes. My heart has tears in its eyes, sniffling and muttering, 'I love him. Can we keep him?' Warmth spreads through me from my belly out. "You know what? I am hungry after all."

Max's eyes widen in surprise before he beams. "Great! Let's go."

Suddenly shy, I avoid his gaze and tuck a stray hair behind my ear. I stop short. "I should probably change."

Warmth on my lower back has me swallowing hard. Max gently coaxes me with his hand. "Don't change, cupcake. You look good enough to eat."

My smart mouth opens and shoots out, "Well, I'm not on the menu."

Pew, pew, pew!

I thank God he's behind me, because he can't see the look of absolute horror on my face.

Who's the real flirt here?

119

He leads me out of my apartment, his voice no louder than a hush as he responds, "That's a damn shame."

Helena

I'm not at all surprised when we end up only a block away from the apartment at a diner. A diner where the staff know Max. They're on a first name basis, of course. What I am surprised at is that he drove us here. When he parked the car, I let out a stunned laugh. "Why didn't we just walk?"

He looked up and uttered, "It's grey out. I didn't know if the weather would turn." He smiled at me, warm and sweet. "Didn't want you getting wet."

Too late.

I mentally shook my head. Oh, brain. You dirty, dirty effer.

Seriously. Does he have to be all cool and suave and thoughtful and stuff? I totally wish he were a dirt-bag. It would be so much easier to dislike him. I don't know how much longer I can keep this up. He's making it very hard on me, the inconsiderate boob.

On the street, he ran around the car and opened the door for me, even though I had already pressed the latch. He held out a hand and I took it, only because he'd parked away from the gutter and I needed a hand to not step in a heap of street crud. Two ladies passed us, both with strollers, wearing sports gear. They smiled at him and all but fluttered their lashes.

Max didn't waste any time. He threw them a panty-dropping smile I wished was aimed at me. He tipped his head slightly. "Ladies. How you doin' today?"

They both answered on a sigh, "Fine."

My jaw tightened.

Inside, he helped me into the booth and I snapped at him, "I can sit all on my own." I threw him a deadpanned look. "I'm a big girl, Max."

Completely oblivious to my bitchiness, he smiled. "I know, cupcake. I guess it's in my nature, ya know, to help out."

Harsh reality sinks in. I'm suddenly reminded he's a dad, and a full-time caregiver to a child with a spinal cord injury. What the hell is wrong with me? I've never—not *ever*—had a man wind me up so much before in my life. I don't like it. I'm acting out of sorts. I'm a decent person, dammit! I may not be nice all the time, but I always make an effort. I'm a people person. I always give people a chance, sometimes more than they deserve. I know Max is a good guy. I feel ashamed for treating him the way I have been. I don't think he hurt me on purpose. He's just kind of...unmindful. Sort of like a male version of a ditz.

Our waitress arrives as we're looking over the menu. She's a middle-aged woman with blonde hair and blue eyes. She also has junk in her trunk. *My sistah.* I like her immediately. I feel as though we're bonded through booty.

Sugar Rush

She spots Max and rolls her eyes. Max grins up at her. "Shelly, babe, it's been a while."

She scribbles something onto her notepad. "Max, sweetie. Don't lie to me. I know you're cheating on me."

He holds a hand up to his heart. "They all have eggs and bacon, but I swear it, Shell. It's only yours I love." He winks and I fight a smile. He's such a dork. Such a sexy dork.

She harrumphs. "Yeah, yeah. You all stray, but you all find your way back to Shelly." She looks over at me and smiles warmly. "Hi there. I'm Shelly."

I smile back. "Helena. Nice to meet you. I have a feeling you'll be seeing me a bit. I just moved down the street."

Her smile intensifies. "That's great, honey. I definitely hope to see you here. And often."

It's almost as if he can't help himself. Max must feel left out of the conversation, because he announces, "We'll come back next weekend. Same time. I'll bring Ceecee."

We what now?

Shelly's smile softens at the mention of Ceecee. "It's a date. Now, what can I get you?"

I order granola and orange juice. Max orders a banana smoothie and 'The Big Breakfast'. I have no idea what that is, but it sounds, well, big. Shelly takes our menus and we're left on opposite sides of a booth that somehow feels way too small right now. Max eyes me intently.

"What?"

122

He opens his mouth to speak but nothing comes out. He snaps his mouth shut. Relief flows through me. That was close. I'm happy to sit here in complete silence. Really.

Shelly returns with our drinks. She sets them down on the table. "Food is just around the corner, guys." She walks away and I sip at my orange juice.

"Why don't you like me?"

My single sip turns into two. Into three. More juice. Juice is so yummy right now. I'm suddenly so thirsty that I sip and sip and sip 'til I sip in air.

Holy crap. I drank the whole thing.

He pushes gently. "I've got all day, girl. We're gonna get this out of the way." I really need to pee now. His eyes train on me. He's not going to let me go without an answer.

I sigh and lean back into the bench. "It's not that I don't like you. I don't know you, Max. You just do things I generally don't like in a guy." I fiddle with the straw in my now-empty glass. "It's not you. It's me."

"I don't believe that."

My head snaps up. "What?"

His golden eyes trained on me, he responds in all seriousness. "A girl like you...she's not a problem. She's cool. I mean, I think you're cool, which makes me think I did something to piss you off."

I'm cool? My heart flutters and leans against the closest wall while letting out a dreamy sigh. My cheek tics at how right his stab in the dark is. "You did nothing." The lie sounds as weak as the person making it.

He taps a finger on the table and avoids my eyes. When he speaks again, it's quiet and meaningful. "I don't know what I did. Chances are, I didn't mean to. So maybe...I mean, I hope I can just say sorry now and we can be friends, because," his expression earnest, he utters, "I could use another friend." He looks up, nothing but sincerity in his eyes. "I could always use another friend."

It almost sounds like plea. One I refuse to ignore. "We can be friends, Max. I'm sorry for being a judgey shrew. Like I said, I don't know you."

He smiles. "Give me a chance and I'll make sure you never regret it." Not a plea. A vow.

I can't stop myself. I roll my eyes and tease, "Would it kill you to stop the flirting?"

He actually looks confused. "What flirting?"

I smile harder, waiting for him to laugh, but his brow creases further. Oh Lord...he doesn't *know*. How do I broach this delicate subject? "Well, in the half-hour we've been together today, you've flirted...a lot."

He looks at me like I'm clearly seeing things. "What? No I haven't."

My smile falls away. "Yeah, you have."

"Nuh uh."

"Yah huh."

He sits straighter on the bench and holds his arms out in question. "When, huh?"

I return, quick as lightning, "First, with me in my kitchen, second, with the ladies on the street, and now, with Shelly." He snorts and I feel the need to add, "Hell, I don't even know what you said to her, but I can pretty much guarantee you were flirting with old lady Crandle too!"

He wears a look that says *bless your heart little one* and chuckles. "That's not flirting. That's being friendly."

Is he for real? I scoff. "No it isn't, Max! That's ridiculous."

He waves a hand in my direction dismissively. "That's just me being friendly. I'm a friendly guy, Lena."

I like that he called me Lena. A little too much. Which, of course, adds fuel to my fire. Invisible steam pours from my ears. My cheeks heat in frustration. "You're not friendly; you're a horn dog!"

Shelly comes by with our food and he gestures to her. "Perhaps we'll ask someone else, shall we?"

I nod. "By all means."

He asks Shelly, "Helena here thinks I'm a serial flirt. I'm trying to explain to her that I'm just being friendly, but she doesn't get it. What do you think, Shell?"

He lays on a million dollar smile and she looks at him a moment before her eyes narrow. She turns to me with a look that questions his sanity and whispers, "He doesn't even know, does he?" I shake my head, fighting a smile.

Max's smile fades. "What? Don't know what?"

Shelly places a hand on his shoulder in consolation and hits him with it. "Honey, she's right. You're a flirt." Shocked, he opens his mouth to protest, but she cuts him off. "That's not a bad thing, Max. You're good at making people feel comfortable with you, but I think if you'll look back, you'll find the majority of the people you befriend are, well, women." Shelly leaves us alone to eat our late breakfast. She squeezes Max's shoulder as she goes.

I don't feel very hungry. Victory leaves a sour taste in my mouth. "You okay?"

He nods, picking at his food. "I'm good." But it's a lie.

I don't know where the urge to make him feel better comes from, but I suddenly announce, "You know, I'm a terrible flirt." Max looks up at me, his face questioning. I nod. "Yeah. I'm not very good at it. At least, not when I try. When I don't try to flirt, I'm pretty damn good at it." I nibble at my granola. "Maybe that's what's happening with you. Your subconscious is probably just a really good flirt, with mad skills it feels it needs to use, like, all the time."

He doesn't look placated, but his lip tilts up at the corner. "Mad skills, huh?"

I confirm, "Mad skills."

Then he smiles, obviously impressed with my efforts to cheer him up. "Maybe."

I smile in return and eat my granola.

"Helena."

Chewing, I look over at him.

He nudges my foot under the table. "Thanks."

I have no idea why I'm being thanked, but I'll take it. "You're welcome."

CHAPTER TWELEVE

MAX

When I was in high school, I met Madeline Connolly. I was sixteen, stupid, and horny. Most girls, back then, would try to get close to me to get to Nik. I could smell 'em a mile away. Honey-sweet voices and sticky fingers. But they normally had big tits and red, glossy lips. My sixteen-year-old self didn't give a shit if they wanted Nik, as long as they'd put out.

See? Stupid.

One girl—I can't even remember her name—told me she was pregnant with my kid. She was my age. I remember laughing my ass off...so hard I cried. With a stern face, she asked me why I was laughing, told me this was serious. She knew I had money. Everyone knew we had money. She told me to talk to my brother, and if I didn't want to marry her and take care of our kid, then Nik better, 'cause her baby needed a father.

A dangerous smile crossed my face. I stepped toward whatever-her-name-was and warned her, "I don't care what you do to me, but," my fists balled in anger as I snarled, "don't ever, *ever*, fuck with my brother." A look of fear crossed her face. I shook my head in disgust and started to walk away. A fair distance away, I called back, "Besides, sweetheart, you can't get pregnant from a blow job."

This was a lesson to me. A harsh one, but a good one. That was the point I realized what lengths women could and would go to in order to tie a man down.

So one day, I'm at the library after school, working on fuck knows what. It was pretty much deserted, but I spotted this girl sitting at a desk with a shitload of books in front of her. She looked panicked, overwhelmed by her workload. Dressed in a white tee and blue jeans, she stood in a huff and started stacking her books, slamming them one on top of the other. She was beautiful in a very tame way. With long, reddish-brown hair down to her waist and no makeup in sight, her cheeks flamed red, her blue eyes blazing. As she picked up her stack of books and turned, the top two books slid off.

I smirked. That was my cue. I rushed forward, picked up the books, and held onto them. The girl stood there, waiting for me to hand them to her, but I held them tight in my grip.

She huffed, "You can put them on the top."

I shook my head. "Nah, think I better walk you to your locker. In fact, I think I should carry all those books.

You're a safety hazard, an accident waiting to happen." I ended on a grin.

Most girls would have laughed and let me carry their books, would've thanked me. They would've told me how funny I was and asked if I had a girlfriend. They would have flirted with me and given me an inch. Not this girl. Her cheeks turned even redder. She gritted her teeth. "Put the books on the top. Please."

But I didn't listen. I reached forward and tried to take her books. I grabbed them from one side, and she held firm on the other. I tugged; she tugged. She wasn't letting go, but neither was I. I pulled too hard, and her pile of books came crashing down.

I laughed. She did not. I felt the need to speak. "Shit, sorry. I'm Max. Max Leokov."

Eyes filling with tears, she knelt down on the ground and let me have it. "I know who you are. Why are you even here? I'm sure you could pay the teachers to pass you."

I tried to say sorry. "Let me carry your books as an apology. C'mon."

She stepped back, out of reach. "The pickings must be slim if you're coming on to me." She lifted her nose. "I've heard all about you, *Max*." She said my name like it tasted awful. "I'll tell you this once. I am not a bedpost notch. I am not a giggling idiot. I'm not one of the hundreds of girls at this school who want you."

She looked me up and down and shook her head in disappointment. Then she turned on her heel and walked out, leaving me standing in the library on my own looking like an asshole. Which was fitting, considering I felt like an asshole. Truth was, I hadn't even known who she was, and she was right. I had expected her to be a giggling idiot. I'd expected flirting, conversation, and maybe a blowjob too, if I was lucky.

I grin. I was *always* lucky.

When I got home that night, I scanned a yearbook. I searched for over an hour until I found her smiling face looking back at me. I smiled right back at her. She was even more beautiful when she smiled. So I made it my mission. I would do what it took to make her smile, because I needed to see it in person.

It took weeks for this to happen. I stopped hooking up and made her my priority. There was just something about her, something that told me she would be worth it. The first thing I did was find out where her locker was. I had to follow her around all morning. She took her books out as the bell rang, and she headed off to class. I could afford to skip. No one really knew it, but I was up-to-date with all my work and held an average grade of A-minus.

When the hall was clear, I got to work. Smiling like an idiot, I waited for the bell then hid behind a pillar, quietly watching. When she approached her locker, she paused mid-step. Placing a hand to her chest, she approached with caution. Students began to whisper and point, and I was glad for it. She would get the attention she deserved.

As she read the message, her eyes narrowed. She searched the crowd for a hint of who had done this. I stepped out of my hiding spot, leaning against the pillar with my hands in my pockets. Our eyes met. I smiled and lifted a brow. A look of surprise crossed her face, and her lips parted slightly. All I wanted to do was kiss those pink lips with a gentleness I had never shown a girl. I ached for her.

She looked back at her locker, uncertainty in her eyes. She read the message again.

Smart is sexy.

Painted in yellow and lined with black, I hoped the message would stay up there forever as a reminder to her that she was exactly right. I was the asshole, and she deserved better. So I would try to be better for her. I would be the person she deserved.

My sixteen-year-old self was in love. I felt it like a punch to the gut. It was love at first sight. I was sure of that. I had to have her.

The next day, I had a flower arrangement delivered to the school's office. I had Nik choose it for me. I was clueless that way. He said tulips were always good, but if I didn't want to scare her off, to get every color but pink and red. When I heard her name being called over the PA system, my hands started to sweat. I was nervous.

My nerves were eased when I saw her walking down the hall, smiling into her bouquet of tulips. Nik was right about the color thing. He chose yellow, white, orange, and purple tulips, and from the way she was smiling at them, I wish I'd done some research and picked them myself. I wouldn't make the same mistake twice.

I wanted to talk to her, but she was suddenly swarmed with a dozen whispering girls.

"Who are they from?"

"They're so beautiful!"

"Oh, man, you're so lucky!"

"Maddy, they're gorgeous!"

She lifted her head and looked right at me. A gorgeous smile crossed her face and she mouthed, 'thank you'.

My gut clenched from the beauty of that smile. I knew I was in deep shit.

Later that night, she called. To say I was surprised was an understatement, because our number wasn't listed and I had no idea how she managed to get it. I was surprised, but overjoyed. We started talking every night, but avoided each other at school. She was still unsure of me. I would give her as much time as she needed. I lived to make her laugh, and I did. A lot.

We got to know each other and talked up until the early hours of the morning, or until one of us fell asleep. One night, about four weeks into our secret friendship, I went out on a limb. Lying in my bed, I whispered into the phone, "I would give anything to be your guy. I want you to be my girl, Maddy."

She hesitated. "What if it doesn't work out?"

I countered, "What if it does?" She remained silent. I all but begged, "Gimme a chance. One chance." Without answering me, she pleaded a headache so I let her go.

The next morning, I walked down the hall toward my locker. I was in a mood. I couldn't understand what more I could do to prove to Maddy I was serious about her. But I wouldn't give up. I packed my books inside and closed the door. As I turned, I stilled. There she was, right in front of me.

She looked scared. "Hi."

A small smile tilted my lips. "Hey. You okay?"

Breathing deeply, she exhaled slowly, stepped forward, and placed her hand in mine. Our fingers entwined. I looked down at our intertwined hands and beamed. She answered with a shy smile, "Perfect. Everything's perfect."

Three weeks later, we shared our first kiss.

A year later, we made love.

Three years after that, Maddy told me I was going to be a daddy. It was love in its purest form.

Nine months later, I met the second love of my life. She came wrapped in a pink blanket. She had my eyes, but she was all Maddy. I named her for my mother.

In five years, my life was turned on its head. I would've done anything for Maddy, but she didn't feel the same. And that's why I don't ever want to fall in love again.

Love hurts.

MAX

I stroll across the street, making my way toward Safira. Doesn't matter how old I get, I'll still be Nik's little brother...and his lackey. Tina hates when Nik does this, but I come bearing gifts, so she'll get over it. It's Monday. Tina shouldn't be working at all. She's on maternity leave. I use that term loosely, because Tina's been on maternity leave for a month, but still goes to work every day.

Nik tells her to take it easy. She smiles sweetly up at him and tells him she will. He leaves for work, and she throws on a sassy outfit and heads over to her store. She's lucky she's hot.

I open the door and hold it open to let out a couple of young women. I smile hard. "Ladies, how you doing today? Looking good."

There you go again.

That wasn't flirting. It was being a gentleman.

...seriously?

Shut up, brain.

I back through the door, balancing the loot, and call out, "Good morning."

In unison, they all call back, "Morning!"

I place the stuff on the front counter and turn to find Tina waddling out of her office. Her eyes are narrowed and she has her cell to her ear. I grin. *Ha-ha! Nik's gonna get it.*

He must've answered, because she immediately starts, "Nik, baby, you want to tell me why I have a delivery here this morning, with Max being the deliveryman?" And even though she's pissed at him, she takes a second to smile at me and mouth, 'hi'. That's just how she rolls. Tina is the shit.

I don't hear what he says, but she responds an annoyed, "I don't need food. It's ten am, for Pete's sake! What are you trying to do, honey? Turn me into a whale?" I know the exact moment he gets sweet on her. Her shoulders slump and she sighs. "I know you want to take care of me. I love you, too." She pauses, then lifts a hand to cup my cheek. "Yeah. I love Max, too."

I lean down and kiss the top of her head. She wraps an arm around me and squeezes, then she's waddling back into the office.

Mimi appears behind me. She jerks a chin to the box on the counter. "More food?"

I grin. "Yep."

She shrugs then lifts the lid of the box, picking up a sandwich. "Don't mind if I do."

Lola walks down from the back of the shop, eyes wide in delight. "Are those free sandwiches?" Mimi chews while nodding. Lola makes a *score* motion in the air. "I love free sandwiches!"

Nat comes through the office door, her cell on her ear. "Lena, I love you. Really, I do, but this isn't up for discussion. You're going to have to learn to deal with it." My brows bunch. This sounds serious. She walks toward me, spots the sandwiches, and does a little dance. She utters into the phone, "I'm turning you on speaker now. Because…sandwiches."

I whisper, "What's up with Helena?"

Nat, not caring Helena will hear, takes a bite of a sandwich and explains a garbled, "My sister has a problem with hearing me have sex."

Helena gasps, "Oh, God, you have *no* shame, you ho! And by the way, you moan so loud it sounds like I'm in the room with you. Yuck!"

Nat swallows and rolls her eyes. "Dramatic much? It's sex! It's normal! I'm married, for Christ's sake! It won't be long before I have two babies to look after. I have to get the sex in now!"

Helena responds, "La-la-la-la-la!"

Nat turns to me. "Shouldn't you be at work?"

Helena answers with what sounds like a pout. "I am at work. No one's here yet. Well, people are here, but James isn't here."

James, is it? He always introduces himself as Whit. Why is Helena allowed to call him James?

Nat chuckles. "I was talking to Max, doofus."

Silence, then Helena asks, "What is *he* doing there? Doesn't he work?"

I sulk at her tone. "I work, thank you very much. I'm doing a delivery right now."

At least she has the grace to sound apologetic. "Oh, right. Sorry."

While I have her on the phone, I need to ask her to check Whit's schedule for me, so I can come have a chat to him. "Hey, cupcake, you're at the center, right?"

Her response is suspicious and drawn out. "Yeah. Why?"

"I need you to check Whit's schedule for me."

Confusion lines her voice. "I don't have it."

Having been at the center about a thousand times, I'm familiar with the surroundings. Very familiar. "That's cool. You need to...wait. Where are you right now?"

"I'm in the admin lunchroom."

I nod. I know where that is. "Okay, you need to head out of there, then turn right. Once you reach a wall of photographs, you keep going forward 'til you reach the children's playroom. You'll see a giant whiteboard with everyone's schedules on it. I need you to tell me if Whit has any time-blocks free."

She utters an amused, "There are photos of Ceecee on here."

I smile. "I know. Look for the one where she's a pilot."

Helena laughs softly. "Turning her chair into a plane…" She utters an awe-filled, "*Genius*." A pause, then, "God, she's grown."

"I know. Like a mushroom."

I hear the sounds of footsteps echo through the phone. "Okay, I'm almost there. Ah, yes! I see it."

"Is he free today?"

"He's got one pm free and two pm free."

Cool. "Take a marker and put me in at two pm, will ya?"

Rustling, then, "Done. You're booked in."

"Thanks, cupcake."

She responds quietly, "You're welcome, Max."

And that's my cue to leave. "Okay. I'm out of here. Take it easy, ladies."

As I walk away, they call out in unison, "Bye!"

CHAPTER THIRTEEN

Helena

I hate myself for watching the clock. Two pm is getting closer and closer, and I'm having real problems with my reaction to seeing Max. More specifically, to my *wanting* to see Max. It's one fifty-three and the tummy flutters have started. I bounce my knee and tap my pen on the desk. Actually, I don't have my own office right now, so really, I bounce the pen off James' desk. He looks up from his paperwork and down at the pen, raises a brow, and looks up at me.

I drop the pen with a noisy clatter and whisper, "Sorry."

I'll be shadowing my boss for the next few days. I've already met the three other PTs on regular rotation. The only other man on the team is a guy named Kerr. He's not very tall, but super muscular. He almost looks as if he's a popped kernel of corn with all his bulging muscles. He's got dark hair and eyes to match, and he's so very gay.

How do I know this? I know this because when Felicity—the token blonde bombshell of our team, with Restylane lips and the body of a salsa dancer—bent over to stretch, he did not look at her perfectly toned ass.

I know what you're going to say: that means nothing. Right?

Wrong!

Exhibit B: When James took on the same pose, Kerr did not just look at James's ass; he *devoured* it! Mentally, of course.

It was uncomfortable to watch. Really, it was. What was frightening was the thought of James and Kerr together rolling around in the sack turned me on. *A lot*. Embarrassingly so. So when James caught me looking like I was about to swallow my tongue from my impure thoughts and narrowed his brows at me, asking cautiously, "You okay?" I all but yelled a panicked, "Nothing!"

So there you have it. Kerr likes sausage, and I like man-on-man fantasies.

Who knew?

Felicity is tall, blonde, and has fantastic perky boobs that match her ass. And, of course, me being me, I assumed she'd be a complete ditz. Felicity...is not. She is smart, and funny, and super sweet. I like her. The first thing she said to me was, "You look like a garden nymph." That was it. *So* random. I was sold.

The third member of our team is shy, quiet Willa. She is tall and willowy, graceful, and extremely pretty. But shy. Painfully shy. She has gorgeous hazel eyes, light brown hair, and a smatter of freckles across her nose. She is, for lack of a better term, geek chic. Oh, and she loves James.

So there you have it. Two team members want James 'Whit' Whittaker. No wonder he told me he doesn't date employees. They all want to tear off a piece of him. I don't blame them. He's a special type of fine, but I wasn't lying when I told James I don't date.

I've worked too damn long, too damn hard, to date then fall in love with a guy who'll likely resent me for working my dream job. Call me selfish, but I'm doing me right now. When I'm at a good point in my career, I'll consider dating again.

The last date I went on was my first year of college. I cancelled...five minutes after the date had commenced. Brad, or Bob, or Brett, or whatever the heck his name was told me I couldn't cancel *after* the date had already begun. I simply said, "Watch me," then handed him back his cheap bouquet of carnations and walked back to my dorm room.

You would not be wrong if you guessed dating scares me. I'm just so worried about meeting a guy who becomes my everything, only to have to sacrifice my career for him. I mean, why must I sacrifice *anything*? Why can't I have the whole enchilada? Alas, it doesn't work that way most of the time. My job is demanding, but the fruits of the labor are rewarding. So rewarding, I don't think given an ultimatum I would make love my choice.

I haven't noticed James has finished his paperwork until he coughs. My face snaps to his. A small smile spreads across his face. "Where'd you go?"

Shaking my head, I sigh. "I don't even know. I checked out. Sorry."

He shrugs. "It's cool. Today's a slow day anyway. I wish I could show you more, but I need clients to do that. Sorry it's been a boring day. I wish it were more entertaining." He grins. "Maybe I could twerk on a table for you or something."

I snort. "*That* I would pay to see, sir."

He winces. "Aw man. You seriously just *sir*'d me? I feel so old."

I chuckle. He's adorable. "You're not old. If you're old, then I'm old, and if you call me old, you might just catch a shoe to the head, because I am *not* old."

His small grin intensifies. "I like a woman who's willing to throw a shoe every now and again."

I nod regally. "It's so uncommon these days. Such a shame." He smiles at me. And smiles. And smiles some more. I'm suddenly nervous. My eyes widen. "Why are you looking at me like that?"

After a moment, his smile loses some of its strength and he utters, "I like you."

A look of surprise crosses my face. It's quickly replaced by a blush. I mutter quietly, "I like you, too."

A knock at the door snags my attention. Max pops his head in and spots me sitting behind James' desk. He throws a thumb behind him and states, "I can come back."

I quickly stand. "No. We were just talking. You sit."

I move to leave, but James stops me by lifting a palm. "Actually, Max, I completely understand if you say no, given your families are intertwined, but I need to ask. Would you mind if Helena sat in today? She's going to be shadowing me for a little while, just until she gets the hang of how we run things around here."

Max doesn't hesitate. "I don't mind."

Ahhh, Max. Understanding, thoughtful Max. Annoyingly perfect Max.

Shooting me a small smile, he moves to sit beside me and winks. "How you doing, cupcake?"

My brows about hit my hairline. I lean forward and whisper, "You can't call me that here. I mean, I told you to stop calling me that. You can't call me that."

He whispers back, "Sure I can."

My nose bunches. I whisper back heatedly, "I'm not a cupcake."

Leaning closer, our noses almost touch. His warm eyes look directly into mine. "But you smell like one."

James' eyes dart back and forth between us. "Maybe this isn't such a good idea."

But Max waves a hand at him. "It's fine. I'm totally cool with it. She needs to learn, and she knows Ceecee, so let's do it."

James looks uncertain. "Well, if you're sure..." He looks over at me.

I concede with a nod. "Yeah, everything's fine."

James smiles. "Okay then. What did you need to see me about, Max?"

Max gets right to the point. "I need help with Ceecee. She's not exercising, not stretching. She keeps getting cramps and spasms, and she tries to hide them from me. I mean, I'm not stupid, ya know? I know what pain looks like. I don't know what to do anymore, Whit." He bites the inside of his lip in a childlike gesture. His tone makes my chest pang. "She's breakin' my heart, man."

James' face immediately shows concern. "She's not doing her stretches?"

Max shakes his head slowly. "Last time I saw her initiate any form of exercise was about four weeks ago, so I've been trying to get involved, ya know? Like, I try to make it daddy/daughter time, something we can do together, but ninety percent of the time, she ends up angry with me. She'll leave in a huff. She barely talks to me anymore."

James takes a moment to process this, then nods. "Okay. We need to get her moving again or she's just going to keep cramping, and that kind of discomfort is bound to make anyone cranky. How about we get her back here twice a week until I see some improvement?"

Max lifts his arms to rest them on top of his head. His eyes close in relief. "Yes. Yes, please. She's driving me nuts. She knows what she needs to do, I just…" Surprisingly, he looks over to me. "I just don't know what to do anymore. She's shutting me out."

I feel the pain in his voice. Part of me wishes I could wrap my arms around him and hug him until the pain melts away with my warm embrace. But that would be insane, so I'll just sit here, staring back at him with a blank expression on my face.

Nice.

James pulls up his schedule. "I had a cancellation this morning. I can get her in as early as tomorrow afternoon, right after school."

Max quickly stands and reaches over the desk to take James' hand in an enthusiastic shake. "I owe you, man. Thanks. We'll be here tomorrow around three."

I don't even think he realizes he does it, but Max turns, leans down, kisses me on top of my head, and then leaves. The place where he kissed me warms, and I want to feel that warmth on my lips.

As soon as he leaves, James asks me, "You sure this isn't going to be uncomfortable for you?"

I lie through my teeth. "Not at all."

Helena

Max was on my mind all afternoon. I saved his phone number from the voicemails he left me. I was so tempted to call, or message, or *something*. I heard his voice when he spoke about Ceecee. He looked right at me. *In*to me. If I hadn't seen it with my own eyes, I wouldn't have believe someone like the flirty, carefree Max I had built up in my mind was capable of such deep emotion. And it seriously rocked something inside of me.

I'm a judgey bitch. That's what it comes down to. I want to change. I made a vow to myself today. I would stop judging and start accepting. What happened with Max at Nat's wedding happened. I'm willing to accept I was bitter. My bitterness was caused by rejection, whether he knew it or not. But he was right. Our friends and families are interwoven, and to hold a grudge over something so stupid is, well, stupid.

We can be friends. I can do this. It won't be hard. Not at all. So what if he looks like a God and smells like the tears of Jesus? *Pffft!* No problem. We got this. I just have to make sure he never knows I considered him my fantasy fling for a long, *long* time. And that will be a cinch. I never told my sisters. Hell, I never told anyone!

Speaking of dream guys…

Stepping out of the shower, I wrap a towel around my hair, and then myself. I throw open the door and head over to my hand luggage. The zip comes open with a sharp tug and I see him. I breathe, "Johnny."

My hands are gentle as I undo the rubber band securing my main man. As soon as I see his face, I break into a smile. But his face is not impressed. My stomach muscles clench. "Don't look at me like that. I've been busy." I swear, his brow rises, marginally. I *swear* it. I huff out an annoyed, "Yeah, well, some of us have jobs, Johnny." I don't like the attitude I'm being given. "You wanna stay in the freaking luggage?" If he could roll his eyes, he would.

I unravel him and lay him on my bed. I towel myself off. My gaze veers to the bed to find the upper-half of the poster curls up, so he's looking at my naked body. My nose bunches. "Perv."

I dress in jeans and a black tee that reads 'Classy, sassy, and smart assy', which was a gag gift from Nina for my last birthday. Being that I'm actually wearing it would bring her to tears. I was mean to be offended. I love it!

Slipping on my white sneakers and placing my phone in my back pocket, I'm just about to head out the door when I spot the mini whiteboard Max left on my kitchen counter. And my heart sinks. It takes me no more than a second before I pick up the whiteboard and head out of my apartment. I ring the bell at apartment 309.

Mrs. Crandle opens the door, dressed in a robe with her thick coke-bottle glasses sitting on the bridge of her nose. Confusion crosses her face. "Yes, dear?"

Taking the whiteboard marker, I quickly write, 'Am I still invited to tea?'

I hold up the whiteboard and her face morphs into stunned disbelief. A surprised smile tilts her lips. "Of course! Come on in. I'll get the water boiling." She disappears down the hall. For a little woman, she's quick. I let myself in and close the door behind me. When I turn, it takes me a moment to wrap my head around what I'm seeing. My feet are glued to the spot. I'm so shocked my mouth gapes.

Three large black and white photographs hang side-by-side on the living room wall. The first is a portrait of a young woman in her twenties, sporting pin-up curls, a lithe body in a revealing but tasteful leotard, and she wears a smile so pretty I have to smile in return.

The second image is a group shot with approximately thirty people in it. I'm quickly drawn to the third image.

The man in the photograph doesn't smile. Looking to be in his thirties, he scowls into the camera, looking fierce and angry. He wears a crew cut, and the muscles he flexes are bulging ridiculously. He is a *tank*.

"Don't let his expression fool you. He was an absolute teddy bear," Mrs. Crandle utters from behind me. I almost jump out of my skin. My heart racing, with a squeak, I lift a hand to my heaving chest. She laughs softly. "I didn't mean to scare you."

A sheepish expression crosses my face. I write, 'That's okay. I scare easily.' After another peek at the photographs, I write, 'Your husband?'

She looks up at the photo and nods. "Yes. That's my Chester." She mutters, "He wasn't just my husband though." She looks up at me, wistfully. "He was my whole world. I would've followed him anywhere." She shakes her head and chuckles. "In fact, I did."

Wiping away my previous writing, I pen with a disbelieving smile, 'You were carnies?'

Without answering, she reaches over to gently take my arm. "Come sit, dear. Tea will be ready in just a moment." As we reach the sofa, she shakes her head in confusion. "I'm sorry, I must have forgotten your name."

I shake my head. 'I don't think you heard me when I told you. My name is Helena.'

She reads quickly and smiles. "My, what a pretty name." Her little feet lead her away, and she calls out, "Tea should be done by now."

Cups rattle, cutlery clinks and finally, Mrs. Crandle returns with a teapot and teacups on a serving tray with cookies. I have to admit, the tea smells lovely, and the cookies look divine. My stomach rumbles.

Down, girl.

As I reach forward to pour, Mrs. Crandle intervenes. "I may be a dinosaur, but I can still pour tea, Helena." She ends on a wink, and I thank God I didn't make this spontaneous visit awkward.

My phone buzzes in my pocket. I take it out and check the display.

Nat: Dinner's almost ready.

Crap.

Mrs. Crandle pauses her pouring when she spots my phone. Her face falls. "Leaving so soon?"

I quickly reply to the text.

Me: I'm running late. Save a plate for me. x

Then I switch off my phone and put it back into my pocket. 'Sorry about that. Not leaving. I would love some tea, please.'

Happiness replaces her expression. She passes me a teacup and the sugar, as well as the cookies. "I'm so glad for the company. I don't have much of an excuse to entertain these days."

I sip at my tea while looking around her living room. That's when I hear it.

Meow

My brow furrows as I look down at my feet. I gasp. "Oh, my God!"

I reach down to pick up the little grey kitten and hold it up high. "Hi there, sweet thing!"

Mrs. Crandle chuckles. "Oh, dear, how did he get out? He's a little escape artist, that one. And he shouldn't be away from his mama right now, but he always finds a way."

Holding the little guy on my lap, I write, 'He's adorable! I love him!'

Mrs. Crandle grins. "Then he's yours."

My face voids. "What?"

She must catch what I say, because she shrugs. "I can't keep any more of them. He and his brothers and sisters will likely go to a pet store in a few days' time. If you want him, he's yours."

Stunned, I look down at the sweet little kitten with green eyes.

Meow

Writing so fast, I'm sure it's barely comprehensible, I scribble, 'Yes, I want him! Thank you! Thank you so much!'

She nods, a shy smile appearing on her face. "You're welcome. What are you going to name him?"

I cuddle my kitten close. 'I like Ted. But I like Woody too.'

Mrs. Crandle lifts her face in thought. "How about Tedwood?"

I say it aloud. "Tedwood. Sort of like Edward, but not." Nodding, I write, 'I like it. That's it!'

She sips her tea then nibbles at a cookie. "I have everything you need for him right here. You can take him home tonight if you like."

I smile down at my kitty. He gently bats at my chin. Oh, my gosh, I love him already. He's so damn cute. Smiling up at Mrs. Crandle, I mouth, 'Thank you.'

She returns my smile. "I hope you get as much joy out of him as I get from his mama."

I know I will. I just know it.

CHAPTER FOURTEEN

Helena

"Where are you, you little psycho?" I hiss, crouching on top of the kitchen counter, feet safely off the ground. Why did no one tell me what little jerks cats can be? We never had a cat growing up. We never even had goldfish, dammit! "Teddy?" I call out hopefully. The little worm is somewhere around here, but he's hiding well. I coax in a false calm, "Come out, honey. I'll give you a nice little treat if you just come *out*."

Slowly sitting on the countertop, I put one foot down on the ground in perfect silence. Thank God for socks. The other foot comes down to meet the floor. I quietly tiptoe from the counter to the doorway of my room. I peek in. There's nothing there. *Where is he?*

I have so many scratches on my feet and ankles. Over the last day and a half, my toes have become chew toys for my new roommate. I am not enjoying this. I thought having a kitten would be ninety percent cuddles and ten percent making cat-shenanigans—

equaling making videos to post on the Internet. This has not been the case.

What's worse is Tedwood likes to hide, and then reappear when you least expect it. My heart begins to race. I swallow hard. "Teddy? Baby? Momma would really like for you to show yourself now." I start to hyperventilate, grip the doorframe, and whisper in a singsong voice, "Momma's freakin' out, dude."

Oh, my God, it's morning and I am too tired to deal with this shit. I need a shower, stat. I find courage from somewhere deep inside of me. I straighten and roll my shoulders as I storm into my bedroom. "You know what, Ted? I need a shower, and I'm having a freaking shower. Hide all damn day if you want to. I don't care." Opening drawers with a racket, gathering my work wear and closing the drawers with a bang, I stomp over to the bathroom, muttering, "I'm not scared of a little cat. That's all a kitten is. A little cat. Not even scared." I drag my feet into the bathroom and turn on the light.

"Mother*fucker*!" I jump in shock as I'm attacked from behind. Even though I'm wearing thick socks, I still feel his needle-sharp teeth in my ankle and his claws firmly wrapped around my foot. "*Arrrrgggh*! Get off me, you psychotic feline *freak*!" I shriek.

With my kitten still attached to my foot, I lift it high and commence project *shake it off*. I shake gently at first, but he's holding on tightly, his beady eyes all-pupil right now. That can't be good.

I shake harder and harder 'til I wobble on the spot. I lose my balance. I'm falling backward. My back hits the bathroom sink and I feel the breath leave my body in a whoosh. Throbbing pain blooms from my middle as I land onto the tiled floor with a bounce.

Shit. That hurt! Lying on my bathroom floor with a kitten attached to my foot by its teeth and claws, I burst into tears. "Jesus C, I sure as shit was wrong about you."

As if feeling my pain, Tedwood appears by my face. If a cat could look concerned, he would. Still crying, I sniffle, "You're a bad kitty." He licks my nose, as if taunting me. Slamming my balled fists on the hard tiles, I lift my face and wail, "Oh, God, I fucking hate you."

He climbs on top of me and sits on my chest.

Meow

My body shakes in silent sobs. "Why are you doing this to me? I just wanted to give you a nice home. And you looked cute, like a normal cat that does normal cat things. I didn't know you were mental." I look up at him and plead, "Please stop trying to kill me!"

Over the last twelve hours, Tedwood has *quote* accidentally *unquote* knocked over a candle and set part of my bed on fire, chewed open live wires, which I have almost touched with my bare hands, and has hidden in every spot possible, attacking me whenever I least expect it. I have a theory. Don't quote me on it, but...

I think my cat is the devil.

I'm not an expert on the matter, and I will consult with a veterinarian, but I don't think it's normal for a cat to try to assassinate its owner. Repeatedly. I close my eyes and cry as I wait for my back to stop aching, but it's futile. It'll be aching all day. It's bruised. I know it. A little rough tongue licks my nose. I push him away gently. "Dude, stop licking my boogers."

He purrs and rubs his head against my chin. I still and ask hopefully, "So, we're friends now? No more funny business, right?" He settles in the crevice between my neck and chin, purring all the while, and I sigh in relief. "Thank you, Lord." Okay. If he's cute like this most of the time, I won't have to find a new home for him.

Reaching up, I pat his little back. His purr deepens. I lie back, savoring the sweet-kitty side of Tedwood I know won't last. "This is the calm before the storm, isn't it?" I ask him. His back arches and he hisses in response.

Yep. That's what I thought.

Helena

As I walk down the block to work, I call Nat. She answers on the first ring. "Sup, dawg?"

Sounding more like a junkie than intended, I whine, "I need you to hook me up. I need a fix, and I need it soon."

Silence, then, "And what will you do for me?"

I think hard. I shrug, even though she can't see it. "I don't know. I'll cook for you."

She scoffs. "Bitch, please. I cook better than you do."

Damn. She doesn't lie. I'm getting desperate. I all but shout into the cell, "I'll do anything! What do you want?"

She grumbles into the phone and I know she's thinking. After a moment's thought, she answers, "Clean my place."

I blink. Is she fucking serious? I am *nobody's* maid! I respond louder than expected, "Fuck you, bitch!" The man walking next to me glares at me. I cover the bottom-half of the cell and mutter, "Oh, don't worry. It's just my sister." I didn't realize it was possible, but he actually looks more disgusted as he walks away. Offended at his misplaced revulsion, I call out to him, "Well, fuck you too!"

Nat chuckles. "Ah, New York." Then she bursts into song, "It's a hell of a towwwwwnnnn!"

I can't help but laugh with her. "I probably shouldn't have done that."

"Meh. He'll get over it." She allows a moment's pause before trying again. "So you cleaning my place, or what?"

I sneer. "Hell to the no. I've heard you and Ash in action. No way I'm cleaning up after that. I'd require a hazmat kit!"

She sniffs. "You act like you've never come into contact with jizz before. Since when are you a prude?"

Since college.

I laugh humorlessly. "I am not a prude. Never was."

She returns with, "When's the last time you got laid?"

July 4th, 2010. It was a Sunday. The weather was superb; the sun shone all day long. "I don't know the exact date!"

"If you're talking the date, it was longer than a year ago."

My nose bunches. "You're way off."

She lets out a sound of exasperation. "Okay, whatever, you don't have to clean the whole place, just the bathroom."

"Yeah, I'm hanging up now."

My finger is just about to hit the end button, when she sighs. "Fine. You get a free pass. This time. I'll send you the details."

Happiness fills me, warming me. I smile brightly. "You're amazing. A goddess. I love you like a siste—"

Beep. I check the display. And scowl. *Bitch hung up on me.* My phone beeps. It's a text from Nat. I almost squeal in delight. It's the address to Icing on the Cake Bakery, and it isn't far from my work. Using the internet map on my phone, I can see it's four blocks away from me. And five blocks in the opposite direction is Safira and The White Rabbit. Not exactly around the corner, but not far either.

I need a car. As soon as I make some money, that's the first thing on my to-buy list. Just as I approach the block my work is on, I shoot out a quick text.

Me: I hate you.

A few seconds pass before I get a reply.

Nina: Hate you more, turd. x

I walk into work smiling, knowing today will be a good day.

Helena

James leads me into a large room filled with workout equipment. He waves out a hand. "You've probably seen most of this stuff before, but if you see anything unfamiliar, let me know and we'll go over what it is and how it's used."

After a quick scan of the equipment, I shake my head. "I've used it all before, but if I see anything that looks new to me, I'll tell ya."

He claps his hands together and smiles. "Great! This is great. You're the easiest person I've had to train. I feel like it should be harder than this, but you're making it too easy for me."

I mock an apologetic, "Sorry."

Laughing, he shakes his head at me. "I've never met a small girl with so much attitude before."

I walk over to him and playfully push him away. "It's not attitude. It's spunk."

He nods in agreement. "Yeah. Your pep."

I laugh at his choice of word. "You could even say I have moxie."

He shudders. "I don't even think my grandma used the word moxie. And she died at ninety."

My face bunches. "You callin' me old, boss?"

"Nah. Just an old soul, I think." For a reason unknown to me, his words make my chest pang. My smile slides off my face. I suddenly feel very awkward. James is by my side in an instant. "Hey. I'm sorry."

I paste on a small smile. "No, don't be sorry. You're right on the money." He looks down at me expectantly. "Really, it's not what you said, more of me not being happy with how I've been doing things lately."

Without a word, he walks across the room and picks up two chairs. He brings them over to me and places them facing each other. I sit in one while he sits opposite me. "Talk to me, Helena."

James is a friendly guy. I can talk to him. At least, I feel like I can talk to him. It would be nice to cement a friendship here in New York. Opening up to him may be the way to do that. We've already spoken about so much already. I open my mouth to speak, but nothing comes out. I try again. Nothing. Finally, I swallow and start, "Why is it that the reason I started to like a person is also the same reason I started to dislike that very person?"

It's true. The reason I started to like Max was for his flirty, lighthearted ways. So it doesn't make sense for me to dislike him being flirty now, does it?

James's lips purse in thought as he thinks on his answer. "Maybe you saw something in that person that you wished you had in yourself. And maybe, because you're very different from that person, you started to develop a jealousy toward them for not being able to adapt that trait to your life."

A sad smile tugs at my lips. "He rejected me." I watch James wince and quickly add, "But I don't think he evens knows it."

He shrugs. "Lena, from what I know about guys, being that I am one, is...we can be very stupid sometimes."

I chuckle, but cover my face with my hands in embarrassment over having this conversation with my boss. "It's just that I've seen him recently, and he's been sweet. Like, too sweet. Annoyingly funny too. It's really pissing me off."

"Oh, yeah. Sweet, funny guys totally suck," he deadpans.

I laugh-cry, "See what I mean? I'm an ass!"

When he reaches over to take my hand, I look up at him in surprise. He responds gently, "You're not an ass. I don't think you've been an ass a day in your life."

"I told my sister to fuck off this morning, and when the guy next to me looked at me funny, I told him to fuck off too. Then I sent my other sister a text telling her I hate her."

He blinks.

And blinks.

And blinks again.

He shrugs. "Yeah, I got nothin'."

We laugh together. "I'm sorry. I don't even know why I brought this up."

"You brought it up 'cause it's bothering you and you needed to talk to someone." He smiles. "I'm actually happily surprised you talked to me about it. Thank you for trusting me."

I roll my eyes. "Oh, please. You know you're awesome."

He tilts his head slightly and deliberates, "I do. I really do." He winces when I play punch his arm. "*Ouch!* Okay, okay, I'm joking! But thanks."

We stand and I ask, "Have you been to Icing on the Cake? It's a bakery somewhere around here."

He exaggerates heavy breathing. "Uh, yeah. It only has the best cakes, cupcakes, and pie in New York."

I'm overcome with jealousy. I scratch at my arm like a junkie needing her next fix. "I need a cupcake, James. I need it soon. I'm a once-a-day kind of girl. It keeps me sane. I've already been a day without one; I can't go another."

He grins. "Sweet tooth?"

I breathe, "You have no idea."

"I can take you there after work, show you where it is."

Relief flows through me at knowing I'll have delicious baked goods soon enough. "Thank you. I just need you to show me once and I'll be set."

He smiles. "No problem. We've got Ceecee in at three o'clock. We don't have any other afternoon appointments. We can go after that."

Can this guy be any more awesome? Really? "You're my hero."

He winks at me, and then walks out of the room. All I'm left asking myself is why I'm so unaffected by that wink. My brain answers for me.

It's not the wrong wink.

It's the wrong guy.

Helena

James and I stretch before Ceecee gets in. Honestly, I can't wait to see her. I haven't seen her since Nat's wedding, and even then, I didn't get a chance to speak to her before Nik and Max's mom, Cecilia, took all the kids for a sleepover so the adults could party on. I wonder what James will do about her derision to exercise. After all, if a teenager doesn't want to do something, it doesn't matter about the reasoning; they aren't going to do it.

A knock at the door sounds, and James and I both lift our heads.

Max pops his head inside the room. "Hey, I thought you'd be in here." He walks over to us, and in comes Ceecee right behind him.

My smile fades when I see she looks about ready to spit fire. Her auburn hair is braided, and she wears a loose tee and sweats. She's grown since I last saw her. She's stuck somewhere between a child and a woman, in that awkward stage when your body is changing. You start to get boobs, and suddenly, there's hair where there wasn't before. Being a teenager sucked. I feel for her.

James smiles down at her. "Hey, C. How you doing?" She shrugs with a face of stone, not willing to look up at him.

I try. "Hey Ceecee, remember me?" She nods once without looking up. My bravado fails, but I fake it. "You've grown so much. You're becoming a fine young woman." I look over at Max. "I can see why your dad is so proud."

He smiles at me. A warm smile I hadn't yet seen before. It almost knocks me on my ass. She looks up at me cautiously before lowering her gaze again. Her jaw steels.

Max looks down at his daughter, eyes narrowed. "Don't be rude."

Ceecee mutters through gritted teeth, "Hi."

Damn. We've got our work cut out today.

James looks to Max, then jerks his chin toward the door. "Mind if I have a word outside?"

My eyes widen as panic settles over me.

No! Don't leave me alone with the broody teenager!

Max nods, but looks over at me. "You gonna be okay?"

The concern on his face is palpable. No way am I telling him his daughter is a little scary. I wave him off. "Go. We'll be fine. Won't we, Ceecee?"

She sighs, long and drawn out, resting her chin on her balled fist. He hesitates.

I mouth, 'Go.'

He does, but he does it reluctantly. James follows him out the door and I'm left here, alone with Ceecee. She's a completely different girl to the happy one I remember.

"How was school?" I ask with interest.

"Fine."

Form a connection. "What's your favorite subject? I loved art."

"I hate art."

Of course you do. "Do you like to read?"

She looks around the room, eyes trained on the equipment in the far corner. "Not really."

Okay. This isn't working. *Be blunt.* "Ceecee?" She looks up at me. "Honey, you look a little tense. Is something wrong?"

Her eyes blaze at my question. "I don't want to be here. The only reason I came was because my dad brought me. If I had a choice, I wouldn't have come."

Okay. Fair enough. "Is the exercise so bad?"

Sweet, little Ceecee long gone, she rolls her eyes at me and turns her chair around. "You don't get it. You don't understa—" A sharp yelp has me kneeling by her side in an instant. Her face screwed up with pain, her body is so stiff the tendons in her neck bulge. This is a spasm. A bad one.

"Breathe, honey. *Breathe.*"

Her mouth parted, she huffs in short, jerky breaths. I see the pain in her tear-filled eyes, and I finally understand a small portion of what Max goes through every single time this happens. "Look at me, Ceecee." Her eyes meet mine. She's panicking. "Breathe with me." I reach out to hold her hands tightly. "Breathe in deeply, and release slowly."

I show her exactly what I want her to do, and I'm relieved when she takes in a long albeit jerky breath. "Good. Again." The second time around, she manages a smoother inhale and a longer exhale. "Excellent, Ceecee."

Her tightly strung body begins to loosen. Sweat beads on her forehead. We breathe together for another thirty seconds, and when I move to release her hands, she grips mine, not quite ready to do this alone. Eventually, her body relaxes completely and she sighs. She looks exhausted.

I move to the water cooler and fill a glass of cold water. I hand it to Ceecee and rub her back as she drinks. "Good job. You handled that really well. I'm impressed."

She looks up at me, eyes filling with tears. Her bottom lip trembles as she mumbles, "It hurts."

I nod in agreement and respond in the gentlest tone I can muster, "Yeah. That's bound to happen though when you stop exercising, honey. Your body is really tightly strung. You need to help loosen it."

She looks down at her now-empty cup. "Thank you. For helping me."

I smile at the uncertainty in her voice. "You're so welcome."

CHAPTER FIFTEEN

I watch from the door as Helena talks Ceecee through the spasm. Part of me told myself I should step in, the other part was curious to see what she would do. She handled it like a pro. Even though the pain has ebbed, they continue to breathe together, long and slow. And it might sound cruel, but I'm glad Helena got to witness this. Maybe I can ask her for advice. Whit is great and all, but he isn't a woman. I need to talk to a woman about this, a woman who has experience with people having a spinal cord injury.

Helena walks to the back of the room to get Ceecee a glass of water. She's so focused on my little girl she still doesn't see me. Ceecee drinks the water in one gulp. Helena rubs her back, still looking mildly concerned. It's probably going to sound stupid, but she's never looked sexier to me than she does right now. If it weren't completely inappropriate, I'd lay one on her, nice and slow, kissing those full, pouty lips.

Ceecee looks down at her hands. "Thank you...for helping me."

Helena smiles down at my baby. "You're so welcome."

In that moment, a decision is made. What's that saying?

Oh, yeah.

Desperate times call for desperate measures.

Helena

"Sweet baby Jesus," I breathe.

James replies, "I know."

I'm awestruck. "It's just so..." I can't even finish my sentence.

He nods next to me. "I know."

"Is this heaven?"

He snorts. "It may as well be." He moves forward in the line, but I'm so busy looking at the list above the counter that I don't see it. A hand attached to my wrist pulls me forward. He laughs when I don't even stop to look at him. "You weren't kidding, were you?"

"Sshhhh. You're ruining the moment," I whisper. Every time the line moves forward, James has to tug me along with him. I'm like a kid in a candy store. Or, more accurately, an adult in a cake store.

Before I know it, we're at the beginning of the line. The woman in her fifties with kind eyes smiles and says, "Hi there. Welcome to Icing on the Cake. What can I get you today?"

I still. My breathing heavies. I'm in a panic. "I don't know! I want it all!"

She smiles harder. "That can be arranged. We have a sampler box option for cakes and cupcakes. It comes with one of everything."

My eyes widen and my mouth gapes. I'm pretty sure my heart stops. "You're shitting me."

She chuckles. "I assure you I'm not."

I look up at James with a goofy smile on my face. He shakes his head at me, lip twitching. "We'll take two sampler boxes, one cake, one cupcake. One for you and one for me."

I should get a box for the ho I call a sister. After all, she did lead me here. "Make that two cupcake boxes." James looks at me funny. I promise him, "For my sister."

He mutters, "Sure it is."

I kick at his leg and he dodges it with a chuckle.

Another woman appears by my side. In front of her, she holds a tray of white cupcakes. They look incredible. She smiles from me to James and asks, "Would you like to try our newest flavor combination?"

My brain can't form words to answer this question. I look back up at James with a smile that is so goofy it borderlines special. His shoulders shake in silent laughter. "Yes, please."

We both take a cupcake, and without thinking, I remove the wrapper and shove the entire thing in my mouth. As soon as the sweetness hits my tongue, I have a mouthgasm. My eyes roll into the back of my head as I garble, "Holy shit, that's amazing." James nods in agreement, biting into his cupcake like a normal person.

The older woman tells us, "This one's a light vanilla base with white choc macadamia ganache."

But I physically can't right now. I lean back into my boss and rest my head on his shoulder. "Jesus C. I can't even. That was just...I'm not even...so, so good. So damn good." His shoulder bobs and I know he's laughing at me again, but I don't even care.

The woman smiles at me. "You like?"

Prying my now-sleepy eyes open, I respond through a sigh, "I love."

Her nose wrinkles with amusement. She turns to her co-worker. "Verna, add one of these to this young lady's sample boxes."

My eyes snap open. "No way."

Behind the counter, an amused Verna replies with a soft shoulder shrug, "Way."

I turn to James, bottom lip trembling with emotion. "Best day ever."

I'm not surprised when he wraps an arm around my shoulder and squeezes. But I am surprised when he lowers his lips to my ear and whispers, "You're adorable." I'm surprised, because James ticks all the boxes for me. He's attractive, tall, and sweet as sugar, but the spark...it's missing.

Stupid son of a spark bitch. Show yourself! I know he said he doesn't date employees, but he didn't mention anything about having sex with them. I mean, I'm *due*, for crying out loud! It's been forever since I've had sex, and right now, James is looking like a mighty fine contender. He's also been giving all the go-ahead signs. Or, at least, I think he has. Maybe I'm just hoping he's sending those signs, and because I'm horny, the horniness is fogging my intentions radar.

What's worse is that my once-a-night happy time has come to a halt. Imagine my surprise when my first night in New York, I settle into bed and reach for Mr. Squeal-A-Lot, only to be reminded I removed the batteries before I packed it. If I had gone to Nat's at eleven pm and asked her for batteries, the skank would've given me that look. The one that says 'I know what you need these for, you dirty Gertie'. Not to mention, she probably would've told Ash. Screw that.

Mental note: buy a pack of batteries.

On second thought...

Revised mental note: buy a bulk *pack of batteries.*

Maybe James can be my very own personal happy time friend. I must look into this, but not too far. I don't want to end up being *that* girl. Or better yet, that employee.

Mental shudder.

Testing the waters, I wrap my arm around his waist and squeeze back, smiling up at him. "Back at ya." I allow my arm to linger around his solid body, liking the feel of him very much. I expect a reaction of some sort, a change in demeanor even, maybe for him to stiffen in uncertainty or for him to give me sexy eyes, but I'm shafted. I get nothing.

Friendly James is just that. Friendly. So friendly that as I reach into my pocket to get money to pay for my cupcakes, James reaches over and pays for all three boxes without ever releasing his hold on me. I'm speechless, and quite frankly, I feel slightly uncomfortable about it. That is until he pulls me closer to him and utters, "Don't be pissy. It's just a welcoming gift." Nose bunched in annoyance, I glare at him. He just smirks. "Welcome to New York."

I take our bags full of cake and allow James to lead me out of the bakery. It's close to six pm now, and I reach into my pocket to check the subway schedule. We walk in silence until I realize I've just missed my way home. "Crap. I gotta call my sister to come get me."

"I can take you home." I look up at him with a tentative look on my face. He drawls, "That is, if it's not weird for you."

Dude, he already knows where you live from your paperwork. What gives?

I guess so. But something feels off. My silence is making this awkward. "Um, sure. Only if it's not out of your way."

He asks, "Where do you live?" I prattle off the address and he assures me, "That's actually on my way, so no biggie." We walk down the street to the center's parking lot. He walks over to red family sedan and unlocks it. I smile to myself. This is not the car I envisioned him having. When we're both seated, he catches my smile. "What?"

I shake my head. "I thought you'd have a truck, or something manly."

He shrugs. "This was my mom's car." Then he grins sheepishly. "My truck's at home."

"I knew it!" I clap my hands together and whoop.

We drive out of the parking lot. "Yeah, yeah. You win at life. Congratulations."

I laugh aloud. "Oh, my God, you're, like, *so* funny." As he drives, we talk about work. James explains tomorrow will be a busy day, as Wednesdays usually are. We talk, laugh, and joke, and it feels like only minutes before we're at my apartment building.

He pulls into one of the free spaces and I free myself from the seatbelt. I smile over at him. "Thank you so much. I had so much fun this afternoon." I think a moment, and admit reluctantly, "I have a lot of fun with you, James."

"You're welcome. Anytime you need help with something or don't know where something is, let me know. I'm volunteering to show you around." He pauses a moment before adding, "I have a lot of fun with you too. I didn't know when I hired you I'd be making a friend."

My heart swells. Before I have a chance to think on it, I lean forward and throw my arms around him. I hug him hard. "Me too. And you don't know how much I needed a friend, so thank you."

I feel him hesitate, but his arms slowly come around me. I rest my chin on his shoulder as he mutters, "You're welcome."

And that's about the time a harsh knock sounds at my door. My heart jumps in time with my body. I squeak and turn around to see Ash staring into the car window. I wave and smile. He doesn't smile back.

Oh, hell. He's pissed.

The car door opens, and my cupcakes and I are pulled outside. He growls, "Get inside. Now."

What the hell? Where is this coming from?

James's eyes fixate on Ash. He glowers at him and utters in false calm, "I wouldn't do that again if I were you." I'm so confused right now.

Asher stands just outside of the open car door. "Mind your own fucking business, jerkoff. You make a fucking habit of driving home your employees and getting touchy with 'em in dark parking lots?"

Oh no. *No, no, no, no, no, no, no!* My eyes widen. I tug on Asher's arm. "It wasn't like that, Ash. God! You don't even know him!"

But he doesn't even hear me. He grins cruelly toward James. "I think you just lost your job, *boss*." He points upward toward the security camera pointed directly at the car.

Fuck! He would dare!

...would he?

Panic turns me into a crazy woman. I pull Asher back by his arm enough to get him away from the car, and then I push at his chest with all my might. He finally looks down at me with a scowl. I push him again and snarl, "I am *not* my sister. You don't have the right to pull shit like this! Get out of here, Ash! Just leave!"

Ash just blinks at me. "You serious? He's fucking playing you, Lena!"

My body shakes with anger. I hiss through gritted teeth, "Not everyone is like you used to be, *Ghost*."

The shot hits its target. His eyes widen a moment. He looks ready to attack me, but then a bored look replaces Asher's concern. "You know what?" He starts to walk away. "Forget about it."

I quickly look toward James. "I'm so sorry. He's not usually like that. He was way off. I promise you you're not going to lose your job."

James doesn't look at me. Jaw steeled, he looks down at the steering wheel and mutters, "He's right."

"What?" I'm shocked.

He looks over at me. "I said he's right. I shouldn't be treating you the way I am. I shouldn't have put my arm around you today, and I definitely shouldn't have put my arms around you just then. If anyone had seen us, I'd have been in deep shit. I'm sorry, Helena, for being so inappropriate with you."

His change of demeanor is making my heart hurt. Have I just lost my friend? "But I liked it," I assure him wholeheartedly.

He smiles sadly at me. "That's the problem." He starts the car. "I did too."

He reaches over and closes the car door before driving away, leaving me standing in the middle of the parking lot, wondering if I just lost my job as well as my friend.

I don't know how much time passes before I hear a car beep behind me. I turn to see Nat smiling and waving at me through her car windshield. As soon as she sees my expression, her face falls. She quickly occupies the parking spot James had used and jumps out of the car. "Okay. Whose ass do I need to kick?"

I'm still in shock. I can't believe that just happened. Shaking my head, I tell her, "No one's. Just a shitty day."

She wraps an arm around me and coos, "Naw, cheer up, glum chum. We're going to Tina's for dinner!" She shakes me back and forth in a silly dance, and cheers, "Yay! Free dinner! Poor people love free dinner! You should be ecstatic!"

Stupid sister, making me laugh when I really want to cry. "You're a dork."

She bunches up her nose. "Yeah, well, you smell bad. And that's not even a joke. Get upstairs and wash your stinky butt." We make our way upstairs together while I half-listen to Nat tell me about her day. When we reach our apartments, she pushes me to my door. "You got a half-hour to get ready. And by half-hour, I really mean twenty minutes."

As soon as I unlock my apartment door, I fish my wallet and work ID out of my pocket and throw them onto the counter. Holding my cell in my hand, I quickly type out a text.

Me: I'm so sorry, James. I understand you'll probably want to stay away from me, but I need to know. Are we still friends?

A minute passes before my cell pings.

James 'The Boss' Whittaker: Of course.

My gut clenches. Great. From hugging and joking, to a two-word response. Talk about being demoted. I walk from the kitchen into the bathroom. I throw on the light and step inside. "Mother*fucker*!" I shriek as I'm attacked from behind. Needle sharp teeth bite into my ankle and teeny claws firmly wrap around my foot. As I lift my foot high in the air and shake it, kitten securely attached, I wonder if today can possibly get any worse.

Surely not.

At least, I hope not.

CHAPTER SIXTEEN

Helena

"I mean, I just don't see the need for them, is all. They look so poofy and stupid. Who the hell uses them these days anyways?" questions Nat. I've only been half-listening to her as we drive from the apartments to Nik and Tina's house. "Hello? Earth to Helen!"

That catches my attention. "Don't call me Helen, bitch."

She turns in her seat to look at me in the back seat while Ash drives. "We're discussing something serious here. I need you to tell me I'm right."

Looking out the car window, I rest my chin on my balled fit and sigh. "Sorry. What are we discussing?"

"The banning of the cravat worldwide."

I bunch my nose. "We're Croatian. Croatians invented the cravat. In fact, cravat is a French term meaning 'in the style of the Croat'. I don't want to ban the cravat. Ties exist because of the cravat. I like the cravat. I like ties too."

This has peaked her interest. Her brows rise. "No shit?"

I nod. "No shit."

She turns in her seat. Then she announces, "I say we get the cravat back into fashion. I'll discuss with Tina." Smirking, I look into the rearview mirror to find Asher looking at me. My smile falls and I quickly look away. Stupid man. Stupid, nosey man. Ruining my life and such.

Finally, we arrive at Tina's house. As soon as we're parked, Nat jumps out and heads toward the front door. I move to follow, but a hand at my elbow stops me. "Wait."

My shoulders stiffen at Asher's urgent tone. "What?"

"We need to talk."

Snatching my elbow from his grip, I walk away from him. "No. We most certainly do not."

When I walk inside, I find Tina there rubbing her swollen belly. She smiles at me. "Hey, sweetie!"

I hug her tightly. "Hey, sexy mama."

She squeezes me. "I feel so bad for not having you over earlier, but with the kids, and work, and everything in between," she frowns, "I really don't have a good excuse other than I've been busy."

We pull away from each other and I reach for her hand. "You're busy incubating my nieces or nephews. You're forgiven. A thousand times over."

It's almost as if she can't help herself. She grips my cheeks and kisses them both. "I love you."

"Love you more, Teeny."

Mimi spots me and winks. "Shake that ass, baby."

I grin at her and add a little sway to my step. When I reach her, I turn. She places both hands on my butt cheeks and squeezes. A silence encompasses the room. I look around to find all the men in the room looking down at Mimi's hands. Trick, Nik, and Max have an identical dreamy look on their faces, while Asher's lips twitch. Trick suddenly announces, "I have to use the bathroom," at the same time Max states, "I'm needed in the kitchen."

They both scatter, and Mimi cackles. "Fucking amateurs," she taunts, then she kisses my cheek. "How you doing, babe?"

Thoughts of this afternoon swarm my head. I force a smile. "Fine. Just fine."

A look of confusion crosses her face. She sniffs the air and utters, "I smell bullshit."

I roll my eyes. "It's nothing."

Before she can dig, I move over to Lola and wrap my arms around her from behind. "Lola, why are men dicks?"

She pats my arm, leans back into me, and laughs through her nose. "I realize I should have the answer to this question, being that Trick is Trick, but I don't," she pouts. "Sorry."

Speak of the Devil. Trick appears in front of us. He looks up and spots me. He fakes offence, "Did you sneak in here without saying hello to me? What kind of monster are you?"

I play insulted. "I would never!"

He takes a finger and taps his cheek. "Pucker up, sister."

I reach over to kiss his cheek, but at the very last second, he moves and I kiss his lips. I squeak and slap at him while Lola laughs out loud. "Get out of here, you little shit!" Both laughing, Lola looks to me and says, "I'd apologize for him, but," she shrugs, "you totally fell for it."

A chuckling Trick runs away, then he bursts into song. "*You make it hard to be faithful, with lips of an angel.*"

Nik comes out of the kitchen holding an oven tray full of ribs. He places them on the dining room table before engulfing me in a bear hug. He holds onto me, rocking me back and forth. "Hey, little one. How's work?"

"It's great. I love it. I'm so glad I took a chance."

His dimple makes an appearance, and although it's a nice dimple, it doesn't make my belly turn like Max's does. "I'm glad you took a chance too. Now I get to see you *and* all my girls happy. And seeing my girls happy...well...that makes me happy."

I tut. "You need to stop with all the sweet. I can't fall in love with a married man, Niki." I lean forward, take his oven mitt-covered hands in mine, and whisper with regret, "It would never work out."

He chuckles and leans down to kiss my forehead. "Goofball."

Arguing from the front door has all our heads turning. "Don't you turn away from me." But she does. Ceecee comes down the hall and into the living area, and without greeting a soul, she wheels past us all and down the hall leading to the kids' bedrooms. "Ceecee, get back here. I'm not done talking to you!"

Whoa. I've never heard Max talk to his daughter that way. I'm guessing whatever happened it wasn't something small.

Nik mutters, "Excuse me," then joins his brother down the hall.

I move over to where Nat stands and try to ignore the heated exchange between the brothers, but it's not easy. Also, I'm nosey. I whisper to Nat, "What do you think's happened?"

She responds quietly, "Who the heck knows? She probably disappeared again."

Wha—? I whisper shout, "What? When did she disappear?"

Geez, Louise, my sister loves gossip. She discreetly looks around before leading me a few steps away from everyone and explaining, "You know the weekend you arrived and we all went to The White Rabbit?" I nod, so she continues, "Well, the kids were getting packed up and ready to go, but no one could find Ceecee. They looked everywhere in the house for her, and Max was just about to head out onto the streets looking for her, when Nik spotted her at the front of the yard." Nat's face turns annoyed. "She had to have heard them all calling her, but she didn't call back to let anyone know she was okay. Max was so shaken over it he skipped work. And he *never* skips work."

Mouth parted, I swallow hard and mutter, "I thought he was just a slacker."

Nat snorts. "Max? You're kidding, right? The guy is seriously ambitious. And he's a good guy, and a great dad too."

I'm beginning to see that. Also, I'm a judgey bitch. Shame makes my middle tense. Shaking my head at myself, I sigh. "God, can I be more wrong about a person?"

Nat bumps her shoulder into mine. "I really wish you would give him a chance."

"I am." I look over at her and promise, "I will."

Noise from the hallway calls for my attention. Max walks over to me, smiling a totally fake smile. I'm immediately wary. He starts, "Hey, cupcake, you got a sec?"

My eyes search his face. He looks drawn and tired. I respond, "Sure, what's up?"

He quickly looks around before leaning down to ask quietly, "Can we talk in private?"

Nodding once, I follow him down the hall. He talks as we walk. "Let's go to my place." Nat told me Max recently moved across the street. He opens the door for me, and we walk down the driveway. Sounding strained, he apologizes, "Sorry for making you walk like this." He stops suddenly, turns to me, and in all seriousness, he asks, "You want a piggyback ride?" I'm not sure if he's serious or not. He adds, "I can carry you. You weigh what? One hundred and twenty-five pounds?"

One hundred and forty-nine-point-seven, actually.

Bless his heart.

I'm still blinking at him when he turns his back to me. He pats his lower back. "Jump on."

That snaps me out of it. "Max, I'm not jumping on your back."

"Why not?" He actually sounds perplexed.

I snort a little. "Because I'm a grown-ass woman and I can walk."

He turns to face me, and replies, "I know. But why would you, when you can ride me?"

Oh, dear Lord. The images. Make them stop. Sweet Jesus, make them *stop*!

I look up into his bright amber eyes and swallow hard. I whisper, "I'm not going to ride you, Max."

He nods. "Okay. Suit yourself."

Not a second passes before I'm swooped up bridal-style and being walked down the driveway. I yelp and wrap my arms around his neck. He smiles down at me with his gleaming, straight teeth. "There. See? You weigh about as much as a pillow."

I glare at him. "Put me down. You know as well as I do that I do not weigh as much as a pillow."

He concedes with a tilt of his head. "Okay, four pillows, then. Happy?"

With his strong arms around my back and under my knees, wetness seeps from where wetness should *not* be seeping right now. His rock-hard chest and abs feel warm against me. He smells amazing too. All it would take for me to kiss him is to lean up a little. "Please put me down."

He purses his lips. "Nah." He looks down at me and grins. "I like you in my arms."

Those words both annoy and excite me. "Why don't you ever listen?"

He pauses a moment to throw me up in his arms a little, then shrugs. "Because I like getting my way." The honesty of that answer makes me pause before I laugh. He utters, "Good answer, right?"

Realizing I won't be getting my way, I settle in his arms and allow him to carry me. "Yeah, it was."

At the end of the driveway, he settles me on my feet, but reaches down to entwine our fingers. "We're just across the street here."

The house is amazing. It's just as big as Nik and Tina's. I had no idea Max had this kind of dough. I hate to say it, but it's kind of a turnoff. He unlocks the front door and ushers me in. Everything is perfect. Paintings hang on almost every wall, and the smell of fresh paint assaults me. The deep apricot color of the walls is intimate and inviting. Picture frames are scattered everywhere, but mostly things are still in boxes. "Max, this place is amazing."

His reaction earns him serious points with me, even if he didn't know I was scoring him. With a shrug, he walks deeper into the house. "It's just a house." My heart smiles that he's not all about money. It's a relief. He turns on a light and I follow him into the kitchen. He pulls out a stool for me to sit on, then walks to stand on the opposite side of the counter. He paces, looking unsure of himself. "Okay. So, you know I've been having issues with getting Ceecee to work out. Well, today she's stepped up the rebellion." He looks me in the eye and reveals, "She skipped class today. Not one. *All* of them."

Damn. That's a shame. I slowly drawl, "Okay? I'm not sure where I come into this."

He holds up a palm. "Getting to that." He paces some more. "I know you didn't see me, but I saw you with Ceecee today. I saw you help her."

Oh. I see. Here it comes.

"I was hoping you'd be able to do a session or two a week with Ceecee. I know you're not her PT. I mean, I still want her to have Whit, but she needs more than him. I want to do this privately, away from the center."

I start, "Max, I don't know. I don't think I can."

His face falls. "Why not? I'd pay you, of course. And because it would be after hours, I'd pay bonus rates." His eyes plead with me. "She needs help, Lena."

But I'm already shaking my head. "I'm too close to the situation. It would be a conflict of interest. I know you. Our families are all twisted together. I see Ceecee as more than just a client."

He raises his arms to say *what's the problem*? "That's great! You'd be awesome!"

I bite my lip. I hate this so much. "I'm sorry, Max. I have to decline." The sincerity in my voice must alert him to the fact I mean it. His shoulders slump and he looks down at the counter. I tell him, "There are other trainers at the center. We'll find another—"

He looks into my eyes and cuts me off with, "You're the first person I've seen her react to in a positive way in over a year." Neither of us looks away. It's becoming awkward, quickly. He straightens with a nod. "You're right. We'll find someone. I'm sorry I dragged you into this. I never wanted to force you into anything. I'm just worried about my girl."

I stand. "I know." I feel he needs something right now, something I can provide. Moving slowly, I walk around the counter toward him. He looks down at me questionably. Swallowing hard, I step closer, wrapping my arms around his waist. He doesn't wait to respond; his arms wrap around my shoulders, holding me tight. I breathe him in and mumble, "You're a good dad, Max. I'm sorry I can't help."

He kisses the top of my head. "Thanks, cupcake." He releases his hold on me. My hold on him lingers a second longer before I let him go. He smiles down at me. "Let's get back. Dinners probably gone by now."

We leave his house and head back across the street.

After we eat our weight in BBQ ribs, Tina takes the little ones for a bath while Ash and I glare holes into each other's heads. Before I snap at him again, I take it upon myself to clear the dishes and load the dishwasher. Mimi helps. We get the job done in less than five minutes and make our way back to the living area to find everyone has moved over to the three three-seater sofas surrounding the TV in a *U*-shape. The only two seats free are the ones next to Nik and Max. I have a feeling Nik will want to sit with his wife, so I seat myself next to Max.

Nik puts on a DVD, and soon Tina joins us, baby monitor in hand. She tells us, "Okay, the kids are sleeping and Ceecee is playing her Gameboy."

Max chuckles. "Her 3DS, babe."

Tina sighs. "Whatever."

Ash looks over at me and utters, "Pass the popcorn, Lena."

But I lean back into the sofa. "Get it yourself."

Nat looks between us before laughing uncertainly. "What's going on, you two?"

We stare, and glare, and glower, and stare some more before I lose my shit. It all comes out with a bang. "He attacked my boss!"

Ash sits taller and returns, "Yeah, well, the guy was feeling her up in the parking lot in his car."

All the guys growl, the women gasp in shock, and Nat yells happily, clapping, "Oh, yeah, baby!"

"It was just a hug!" I quickly explain.

Tina asks giddily with a smile, "He hugged you?" while Max asks in disbelief, "He hugged you?"

A whole explosion of conversation breaks out, and while this is happening, I quickly realize I'm done. I slip out the back door onto the patio. Silence is bliss.

The back sliding door opens and I close my eyes with a sigh. I feel someone standing by my side. Nik rests his arms on the balcony and mutters, "I gotta admit, Lena. I don't like that. Doesn't sound good."

I'm officially exasperated. "It was just a hug, Niki. I like him. He's my friend." I add quietly through the thickness in my throat, "Sometimes you just need a hug, you know?"

Without a word, Nik leaves. I turn back to the yard, taking in the stillness. The door slides open again. Arms wrap around my middle, pulling my back into their front. I know that scent. "What are you doing?"

Max responds a hushed, "I don't know. Nik came inside and said you needed a hug. I figured, I can do that." Ridiculously sweet Max.

I turn and wrap my arms around his middle, burying my nose into his throat. I mumble, "Stop doing that."

"Doing what?"

I whisper, "Winning me over."

CHAPTER SEVENTEEN

MAX

I wish I could let it go. But I can't. As I sit behind my desk, I think hard before making a decision, reaching into my pocket, and pulling out my cell phone. I dial the number. It rings only a moment before someone answers. "Good morning, Icing on the Cake Bakery. How can I help you?"

I smile. "Verna. How're you doing? It's Max."

Her smile can be heard from the other end. "Max, sweetie, I'm good. How are you?"

"I'm great. Listen, I need you to do me a favor."

She doesn't need time to think about this. "Anything for you. What do you need?"

A smile tilts my lips.

I never said I wouldn't fight dirty.

Helena

The wrapper peels away easily, unveiling the vanilla crème cupcake. I salivate and say a hushed, "Oh, God. I need you." I propel it into my mouth and chew, shaking my head in ultimate satisfaction. "Sweet Jesus, that's good." Standing from my position at the breakfast bar, I walk over to the trash to dump the empty wrapper and now-empty sample box.

I ate eight cupcakes.

I ate eight cupcakes in one day.

Am I ashamed of myself? Nope. Not even a little.

This is one of the reasons Nat bought me a baby pink tee with *The Cupcakeinator* written across the front. It was my workout tee for a long time. It has since been retired to be one of my bedtime tees.

I sit on the sofa, where Tedwood sleeps rolled up into a little fuzzy ball. I've come to find that when he's sleeping, he doesn't mind being cuddled. Lowering my face to his head, I nuzzle him with my nose. His purring exaggerates and I smile. I reach down to slide on my sneakers when someone knocks at the door.

Ted and I both look up at the door, then at each other. I mutter under my breath, "I wonder who that could be." When I move to pat Ted on the rump, he hisses. And I mock-cower. "Ooooh, sorry, your highness. I forgot; you're awake and that shit doesn't fly." I stand and walk over to the door, still talking to my cat. "God forbid someone would show you some love." I throw my hands in the air and exclaim, "The absolute horror!"

I chuckle and answer the door. My lips thin. "What?"

Ash stands in the doorway, leaning on the frame, looking freshly showered. "C'mon. I'm taking you to work."

I roll my eyes. "No. You aren't. Don't you think you've caused enough trouble?"

His jaw tics and he swallows hard. He speaks through gritted teeth. "I would really like to take you to work, Helena."

My arms lift to cross over my chest. "Why?"

Avoiding my eyes, he scratches his chin and utters a bored, "So I can apologize to your asshole boss."

My eyes narrow at him. "Nat put you up to this, didn't she?"

He sighs in exasperation. "You want me to apologize to the douchebag or not?"

My head tilts slightly. I consider this. I walk over to the breakfast bar to grab my purse, work ID, and cell phone. I shove them in my pockets and walk past Ash through the open door. "Let's go."

"Fuck," he mutters as he follows behind me.

Just as we enter the center, Ash opens his mouth. But I'm quicker than he is. I raise my hand, palm up, and shake my head slowly. "Nuh uh. Don't you say a damn thing to me. I'm still pissed at you. You save your words, buddy. You save 'em for James."

He follows me down to reception, where I make him sign in and wear a stupid-looking visitor's badge. He pulls at his shirt and grumbles, "Woman, if I didn't love you..."

I screech to a halt and spin to face him. "You love me?" He makes a face. One of torture. As though I'm pulling teeth. My feet still firmly attached to the ground, I put a hand to my chest as warmth fills me. "Nawww, Ash."

"You know what? Fuck this. I'm leaving."

Poor Ash. I should let him leave. I mean, I won't. But I should.

He turns and takes a single step away from me before I snag the back of his shirt and pull him backward. Smiling, I link my arm through his and drag him down the hall toward my office. "Don't be so dramatic. There's no shame in loving family. I love you, too, by the way. I've just never heard you say it. It shocked me."

He lifts his head heavenward and mumbles, "Hold it together, man."

Grinning, I utter, "Drama queen."

As I reach my desk, I sit quickly to log into my computer, when Felicity approaches, quiet as a cat. I don't even look up when she says, "I thought you said you didn't have a boyfriend."

I just know she's got a firm eye on Asher. "I don't," I tell her distractedly, keying in my passwords and opening up the programs I need for the day.

Her tone changes immediately. It becomes deeper, smoother, and sultrier. "Well, hi there, friend of Helena. I'm Felicity."

Still not looking up, I snort. "Yeah, he's married. To my sister."

Exasperation lines her voice. She huffs out, "Well, shit. Figures. All the hot ones are taken, stupid, or gay." That's when I look up.

Ash looks so uncomfortable it makes me chuckle. "Felicity, stop eyeing the man like a piece of meat. He's going to get hives any second now."

She pauses, looks him up and down, and then breaks out into a million-dollar smile. "Sorry. A girl's gotta do what a girl's gotta do. I'm not getting any younger now."

A *pffft* noise leaves my mouth. "Oh, puh-leeze. How old are you? W about my spelling THRITY-nine or something."

Suddenly, I'm being wrapped in a warm hug with plenty of boobage. Felicity states on a squeeze, "God, I *love* you." As she releases me, she asks Ash, "Don't you just love her?" Before he can answer, she tells me, "I'm thirty-five, sweetie."

I open my mouth to tell her I never would've guessed, when James walks toward us from down the hall. He looks to be in bad shape. Firstly, he hasn't shaved. Secondly, he has bags under his eyes. When he spots Ash, he stops in the middle of the hall. I look up at Felicity. "Mind if I catch up with you later?"

She smiles warmly. "Of course," she says, and then leaves the three of us to talk.

James approaches slowly, head lowered. When he reaches us, he utters quietly, "I'm resigning this morning. You don't need to file the complaint. I've put all the reasons in my resignation letter."

My mouth gapes a second before it snaps shut. My jaw sets. I nudge Ash with my shoulder. He steps forward. "You got an office?" James still won't look up. It's breaking my heart. But he nods. Ash asks, "You got a second? I gotta get to work."

James sighs, running a hand over his bald head. "I don't need a lecture—"

I see the moment when Ash has had enough of tiptoeing around. "Fuck. Stop feeling sorry for yourself and take me to your fuckin' office, man."

James finally looks up. At me. "You okay?"

Oh, man. I could totally fall in love with this man. Thinking his world is falling apart around him, thinking he is about to lose his job, he looks over at the cause of all of his problems and asks if she is okay. I could *so* totally fall in love with this man. My smile is small, but genuine. "I think you should talk to Asher."

Half-turning, he says, "If you say so."

He starts to walk to his office, Asher in tow, and I wonder if—and hope that—James and I will be friends again before the day is out.

ASHER

The guy looks ready to throw in the towel. I wish I felt bad about what I did and said yesterday, but I don't.

I got my reasons. He walks me into his office and sits, throwing out a hand in invitation to also sit. I do. We stare at each other for a minute. My eyes narrow. His don't, he just blinks at me, looking like a man who's accepted the worst. I should tell him now that I'm not filing anything. Instead, I tell him a little about myself.

"My name is Asher Collins. Most people call me Ghost. The only people who call me Ash are my mom, my wife, and her sisters. Natalie, Helena's sister, is my wife, and that makes Helena one of my sisters. That makes her my responsibility." I have his attention. He gives me all of it.

I can sort of see why Lena likes this guy. Even though he thinks I'm about to fuck him over, he's showing me respect. I continue, "I have a mother, three brothers, and nine sisters." I pause to let that sink in before I reveal, "None of them are blood relatives."

He looks confused. I don't give him anymore about me. I'd rather tell him why I did what I did. "This isn't my story to tell, but I know my wife won't mind." Leaning back in my chair, I look him in the eye. "You got siblings?"

He nods. "Yeah."

I look to the ceiling. "Make you want to rip your fuckin' hair out sometimes, right?"

He huffs out a quiet laugh. "Yeah. Sometimes."

My eyes meet his. "But you'd do anything to keep 'em safe, yeah?"

He's quiet a moment before he reveals, "Fuck yeah."

"You have no idea." I look at him and shrug. "Or maybe you do. I don't know you." I start again, "You have no idea what it's like to see the battered face of a loved one. More accurately, of the woman you love, knowing a man put his hands on her. I do. I saw bruises, a black eye, and handprints on my woman's body, put there by the guy she was dating at the time. True, if he didn't do what he did, I'd probably not have her right now, but I'd sacrifice everything to make sure she'd be safe from anything and anyone."

James nods in agreement, and I realize I'm warming up to him.

"I've got a lot of sisters, but Helena..." I look toward the open door, my voice quiet. "Helena is special. So when I thought some asshole was taking advantage of her, I did what I needed to do. I will always do what I need to do to keep my girls safe. Understand?"

He utters, "Yeah, man. I get that. But I swear, it was nothing. She hugged me. I hugged her back. That was it."

I huff out a laugh. "Hard to say no to her, ain't it?"

A small smile tugs at his lips. "She's something else."

I smile at that. "She is, and that's why I need to protect her. She's got something good inside of her. Something trusting and pure. If I ever saw that broken, I'd fuckin' kill the person who stole that from her." Not allowing him to respond, I stand. "Listen, I know she's not a kid, but she's family. Time's gonna come when she meets a guy and falls in love." I tell him honestly, "I don't know if I'm ready for that to happen, but I know I have to trust her to make her own decisions."

I walk toward the door. He looks at me in confusion. "Wait. What does this mean?"

"It means your job is safe. And I'm sorry for calling you a jerkoff, even though you probably are a jerkoff. As long as you're good to Lena, we're okay." I turn the knob, opening the door. I pause a moment and tell him seriously, "But if you hurt her, in any way, I will tie cement blocks to your legs and throw you in a river. Oh, and I'll make it look like an accident."

His face loses a bit of color. I smirk. "See ya around, *boss*."

As I leave, I jerk my chin to Helena with a small smile. She smiles back and waves enthusiastically, not caring who sees.

Just another reason to love the dipshit.

Helena

The second Ash leaves, I make my way over to James' office and knock gently. "Come in," is called out, and I can hear relief sound out through his voice. That makes me happy. I smile and poke my head in. "Mind if I have a word?"

His eyes soften. "Sure, of course. Come on in."

As I sit in the visitor chair, I wring my hands together. "I'm hoping you're going to say you aren't going to hand in that resignation letter today."

He rubs at his naked scalp, looking sheepish. "No. Not today anyways."

My shoulders slump in relief. "Thank *God*. James, I am so sorry. So sorry."

He waves a hand out at me. "No, don't be. I caused this, not you. And I understand why Asher did what he did. If it were my sister, I would've done it too. Maybe worse."

I nod and bite my lip. "Does that mean…I mean…are we still friends?"

He looks into my eyes. "You couldn't get rid of me if you tried."

Dipping my chin to hide my smile, I breathe, "Cool."

When I raise my head, he looks like he wants to say something, but he's hesitating. I tell him honestly, "I would feel so much better if you'd just tell me what's on your mind."

He nods. "Okay, I just don't want you to get offended or anything." I raise my brows expectantly. He starts, "I don't think it's a good idea for us to hug or anything anymore."

Quite frankly, I am a little offended. Or is that embarrassed? Maybe it's shame. But I don't let it show. "I agree. I'd hate for someone to cause problems like this again." I shoot him a smile and stand. "I'm so glad things are back to normal."

"Yeah, and you've only be here a week. I can only see good things for the future." He deadpans, "Yippee."

I laugh in relief more than anything. "Oh God, you're an ass."

We laugh together and I feel peace ease into my bones. I stand to leave when he says, "You know, we can still hang out and do things. I'll be at The White

Rabbit this Saturday again, so if you're there, we can have drinks. I don't want things to turn awkward."

He didn't have to say that, but he did. Not out of obligation, just 'cause he wanted to. I smile. "I'd like that."

Decision made, I will definitely be at The White Rabbit this Saturday.

CHAPTER EIGHTEEN

Helena

My lunch break is an hour long. If I quicken my pace, I'll be back in forty-five. Thank God for sneakers. I breathe deeply, exhale slowly, and speed-walk down the sidewalk in the sunshine. The city doesn't smell too good, but I smile regardless, knowing I'll be there soon. Panting a little, I slow when I reach the entrance. It's busy, but I think I'll make it back in time.

Five minutes pass, and finally, I reach the front of the line.

Verna smiles. "Welcome to Icing on the Cake. What can I get you?"

All but beaming, I place my order. "I'll take a cupcake sampler box, please." Just as she moves to get me one, I ask, "Can I freeze them?"

Verna nods. "Sure are, hon."

I mentally squeal, jump, and clap, then adjust my order. "Make it two boxes, please."

4*4*4*4*4*4*4*4*4*4*4*

She places the boxes on the counter. "That comes to forty-six even."

Yeesh! This habit is going to burn a hole in my pocket.

I mentally shrug. *Meh.* I'm so totally okay with that.

I hand over the money with a smile and reach for the boxes, when the other mature worker lady runs out of the kitchen and whispers something into Verna's ear. As I reach for the boxes, Verna pulls them away. Her eyes apologetic, she asks, "Are you Helena Kovac?"

My eyes widen. I respond a slow and drawn out, "Yes."

The other worker whispers loud enough for me to hear, "I told you so!"

Verna snaps at her. "How was I meant to know, Tammy? She looks different in the picture!"

Tammy argues quietly, "You old bat, wear your damn glasses."

Verna squabbles some more. "You're older than me! You're the dinosaur!"

But I just want my cupcakes. "Excuse me," I cut in. "Can I have my cupcakes now? I have to get back to work."

Verna shakes her head, handing me back my money. "I'm sorry, dear. I can't serve you."

My heart speeds up and is soon racing. I'm confused. "What? Why?"

Tammy leans forward over the counter, and whispers loudly, "You're banned!"

My mouth gapes. I sputter, "B-but why? What did I do?"

Verna's shoulder jerks. "Not sure. But Max said we weren't to serve you until he says so, and we look after our stockholders. If it weren't for them, we'd never have opened this place."

Tammy adds on a nod, "We owe them so much."

My eyes narrow. "Who?"

Tammy and Verna look at each other a long moment before turning back to me. They say in unison, "The Leokovs."

Sweet baby Jesus.

I'll kill him.

I run back to the office, and panting, I sit at my desk and reach into my top drawer for my cell. The message is written so fast that I can't help but be proud of my nimble fingers.

Me: Oh my God. You are dead. DEAD! Not just dead…dead meat! Don't talk to me ever again. EVER!

I slam the phone down on my desk, fuming, and log back in to my computer. A few seconds pass before my cell chimes.

Max: Cupcake, don't say things you can't take back. I mean, ouch. You're killing me with your words, babe.

Then,

Max: I'm guessing this has something to do with you being blacklisted at a certain bakery.

My eyes narrow at the screen. How dare he be cute? How *dare* he? I stomp my feet and whimper. *Asshole!*

Me: What do you want?

He must have been waiting by his phone, because only seconds later, my phone vibrates in my hand.

Max: For you to train with Ceecee.

I shake my head enthusiastically as I write.

Me: We've talked about this! I can't! It would be a conflict of interest. Please understand, Max.

Max: You're perfect.

I roll my eyes and growl, trying to ignore the fluttering in my stomach from that statement, then resume texting.

Me: I could get into a lot of trouble for training her. I could lose my job.

Max: No, you won't. Besides, I can keep a secret. I won't tell if you don't.

I'm beginning to feel bad. The guy clearly wants to help his daughter. My gut coils in regret.

Me: Max, honey...I can't do it.

Max: Name your price. I'll pay anything. I'll do anything, Lena. Name it and you got it.

He just won't take no for an answer. I place my phone back in the top drawer and get ready to sit in on another session. It's my last session of the day, as well as my last session assisting. Tomorrow, I'm on my own. I'm anxious, but eager.

From behind me, someone leans down to my ear and whispers, "I'll do anything. Please." My entire body jumps in fright. My hand flies up to my heaving chest and I turn to face a restless looking Max. "Please."

Jesus C, he's breaking my heart. I step closer to him and whisper, "I gave you my answer, Max. Give up."

His eyes close. He shakes his head. "Never. I mean it. I won't give up. I'll wear you down. I won't stop."

My shoulders slump. "Max—"

My entire body stiffens when he pulls something from behind his back.

I hope that's not what I think it is.

MAX

Her eyes narrow down at the little white box. She places a hand on her hip and points at it with the other. Feigning boredom, she asks, "What's that?"

I grin. "A cupcake."

Her eyes flash. She quickly masks her excitement and shrugs dismissively. "And?"

I hold it in one hand and tap my fingers on the top of the box that holds the delicious treat. I tilt my head. "Well, if you don't want it…" I open the box to reveal the most decadent looking double fudge brownie cupcake in the history of man.

Helena gasps.

I lift the cupcake out of the box. Her eyes narrow and her jaw sets. Slowly, I bring it to my opening mouth. She clenches her hands so tightly that her knuckles turn white. Just as the baked sweet touches my lips, she launches forward, snatches it out of my hand, and shoves the entire thing into her mouth.

Chewing animatedly, her eyes close in bliss. She moans long and low. And my dick hardens. Hey eyes flutter open. She glares at me and utters a garbled, "Do that? again and I will cut you. Hard." She turns and walks away.

I call out after her, "Does that mean you'll do it?"

Her response comes in the form of her middle finger saluting me high up over her head, her round ass swaying seductively with every heated step.

Fuck me.

I'm in love.

"Max. What are you doing here, man? I didn't think we had an appointment today," states James from somewhere behind me.

I watch Helena walk away until she disappears down the hall. I turn to James. "We didn't, but I figured if you had a second free that we could talk about something that's bothering me."

James checks his watch then smiles. "I've got time."

I fight my grin.

She's going to kill me.

Helena

There's still time before the next appointment. I decide to get some time in doing some research about the client and his injury. Engrossed in my reading, I don't look up when James calls out, "Helena, you got a sec?"

I call back, "Sure do."

I make my way to his office, but when I reach the door, I screech to a halt.

What the fuck?

James smiles up at me. "You should have told me."

Wide-eyed, I look over at James before turning my sights on a smirking Max. I croak, "What?"

James motions for me to sit. I do, next to Max. He looks to Max. "Max was just telling me about how you want to do some private sessions with Ceecee."

I glare at Max and mutter through gritted teeth. "He did, did he?"

Max shrugs, smiling. "I did."

James starts again, "You're sweet, Helena. Really. But you shouldn't have worried."

My brow creases. "What?"

Max explains, "I told him about how you said you wanted to do the sessions, but didn't want to step on anyone's toes. Especially James', being that he's Ceecee's PT and all." Max reaches over to squeeze my thigh. "I was going to let this go. Really, I was." *The lying sack of shit!* "But I know how much you wanted to do this and how you thought it would help Ceecee so," he looks over at me with fake regret, "I had to tell him, Lena."

I'm stunned. I lift my panicked gaze to James and ask a shrill, "And you're for it?"

James beams. "Of course I am. I'd do anything to help Ceecee, and I'm glad you would too. As far as I'm concerned, we're a team, Helena. You're not stepping on my toes. I love the idea of the two of us working with Ceecee."

I slump in my seat and utter a quietly hoarse, "Okay." I quickly remember to ask, "You don't think this is a conflict of interest, do you?"

James' face falls. I side-eye Max to see his smile fall along with James'. James scratches at his chin. "Hmmm. I'm not sure, really. I mean, I know your families are twisted in together. That could be a problem." I turn to Max and silently gloat. I hate myself almost immediately when I see the dejected look on his face.

James asks Max, "You didn't really know Helena before now, did you?"

Max responds through a sigh, "No, sir."

James looks over at me. "And you said yourself that you don't know Max all that well, right?"

I said that? When the heck did I say that? Stupid mouth with the saying things and such! I think about lying, but instead mumble sorely, "Yeah."

James smiles once again. "Then I don't see a problem here."

Max stands, raises his arms in the air high above his head, and hisses out, "Yes!"

I'm suddenly yanked into a tight hug. Max lifts me so my tiptoes barely touch the ground, his cheek pressed firmly against mine. The light scent of his cologne wafts up gently, just enough to silently tempt me. He sways me excitedly from side to side, the tips of my sneakers making squeezing noises as they're dragged along the ground, then he utters into my hair, "See? I told you he wouldn't mind. I knew it would work out."

My arms limp by my sides, I whisper hiss into Max's ear, "I am going to cut off your balls then feed them to you, one testicle at a time."

Max sighs happily, pulls back, and rubs my arms, beaming, "I know. I'm happy too!"

Forcing a smile, I puff out, "Hooray."

James smiles up at the two of us. "I'm so glad it worked out."

Max wraps an arm around my shoulders, pulling me close. "We are too."

As my head touches his shoulder, I again breathe in the woodsy scent of him and wonder if he's worth five-to-ten in a maximum-security prison.

MAX

The look on her face. I chuckle to myself as I walk through my house. I know I shouldn't laugh, but, shit, it was funny. My mama taught me better than to poke a bear, but here I am, poking away.

Me: Come have dinner with us tonight at home. We have to work out a schedule.

Nik asked if I was coming back to work this afternoon. I wasn't sure what time my impromptu meeting would end, so I told him I wasn't. Now, at home alone, I think of what to cook. What would Helena eat? My phone pings.

Helena: Eat shit, asshole.

I tilt my head back and burst into laughter. I really like this girl.

Me: Pan-fried shit with roasted potatoes and salad. We're all set. Luckily, I have all those things at home :)

Shaking my head, I reach into the fridge and pull out the steaks I had marinating from the night before. She looks like a woman who would eat a steak. Her ass looks like she's a woman who likes steak.

That ass.

Fuck *me*, that ass.

My forehead hits the fridge with a thump. My hand slides down to cup my semi-hard dick and squeezes it tight. I can't stop thinking about her. Her damn body looks like it was made to fit mine. It's teasing me, taunting me every time I see her. Toned and firm, thick in the places it should be, a smart, kissable mouth, those sexy pouting lips, tits that would fit nicely in my palms, long, wavy, dark hair, green cats eyes, and long lashes.

All I want to do is bend her over and let my hands roam. I want to feel her body, hold her hips tight, her ass pressing back against me as I grind into her, her looking back at me through hooded lids, cheeks flushed pink, lips parted, breathing erratic.

I bite my lip. My eyes shut in a mixture of pleasure and pain. I can't deny it. I want her in my bed. But she's a lady, not the type to fuck around. I won't lie. That just makes me want her more. Broads are broads. I've never wanted a broad for anything more than to warm my bed. Helena's a lady. That's a whole different story. My mind wanders. Is she quiet in bed, or does she moan loudly? I bet she's a quiet one. I'd also bet I could make her scream.

Stop it, moron. My hand squeezes my cock harder. I groan, then whimper.

Shit.

I need to get laid.

Helena

Why must he taunt me? As if it's not bad enough that he's gorgeous and his body is something out of Men's Health magazine, he's funny when I don't want him to be. And that sucks! It's true I didn't want this private training position, but I have to admit I spent the afternoon researching things I can do with Ceecee, and I've got to say I'm excited about it. If she knocks back the things I've found, I'll just search and search 'til I find something that suits her.

It won't be easy, but I have to try. I hate to see her so miserable, and I don't like seeing normally happy Max so sad. He annoys me, but I don't want him unhappy. Being happy is in his nature. To take away something from a person that is a natural reaction is cruel. As much as I want Ceecee healthy, I want Max content.

I slip out of my work clothes and make my way to the bathroom, and just as I switch on the bathroom light, I lean down and hiss at Tedwood a split second before he gets to me. He scrambles in the opposite direction and I chuckle quietly. He's not such a bad cat once you get to know him. A little broody, sure, but a complete coward.

Just as I place one foot into the warm spray of the shower, claws and teeth attach themselves to my leg. "Mother*fucker*!" I shake my leg in the air, Tedwood firmly attached, and yell, "Stop being an asshole, asshole!"

Why won't this day end already?

CHAPTER NINETEEN

Helena

How great are showers? Not only are they a pretty decent way to wash off stank, they're also relaxing as heck. I spend a good half-hour letting the borderline boiling water wash away the day's frustration. For some time, I simply stand under the spray and bask in the feeling of being submersed in my own little bubble of tranquility.

Today not being a hair-washing day, I turn off the shower and step out. With the bathroom door wide open, I towel myself off before slipping on a white t-shirt bra and light blue boy-leg panties. Just as I'm about to step out of the door, a loud crash sounds in the kitchen.

I jump as the crash reverberates through my ears, but quickly sigh, "Ted*dy*. Goddamn it, cat!" My feet are dragged from the bathroom to the hall. I squeak, then squawk, "What the hell are you doing here?"

Max doesn't look up. Instead, he finishes plating up steak, potatoes, and salad onto plates. "Don't you use that tone with me, cupcake. Here I am slaving away over a hot stove all afternoon so we can eat together, and you stiff me. So I bring you dinner after a long day's work, and you use that tone?" He straightens, then tuts, "Working girls."

His eyes move to mine, widen, and then slide over my body. I'm not one hundred percent sure, but I think he drools a little. When his stunned expression is replaced by a leisurely grin, dimple flashing, he drawls, "I wasn't expecting dinner and a show."

That's when I'm reminded I'm standing in the hall in my underwear. Not even my good underwear, but my *Helena's-sleeping-alone-again* underwear. My mouth wants to gape, but I stop myself. Instead, I decide to play it cool. Heart racing, I fake poise and murmur, "I'm going to change."

Max grins harder, placing a hand to his chest. "Please, don't dress on my behalf." I walk to my room, acting as normal as possible, but cringe when he calls out from behind me, "I like your undies. They're not the usual type I see women wear. They say, 'I'm cool and I don't care what you think'. That's cool. I mean—"

I can't take his incessant rambling right now. "Max, shut *up*!" I shriek.

His booming laughter fills my kitchen, and although I could die from embarrassment, I like the sound of his unrestrained hilarity. My lips twitch when I realize he baited me...and I fell for it. I mutter under my breath, "Ass."

I quickly change into black yoga pants and a loose yellow tee and join him in the kitchen. He's already placed the plates and cutlery down on opposite sides of my small dining table. It smells amazing, but we'll be sitting so close together our knees will touch. It seems far too intimate.

My favorite yellow vase lies in the sink in pieces, and I'm reminded of the crash I heard. I narrow my gaze at Max. His eyes dart from side to side, clearly panicked. He suddenly blurts out, "Someone broke that."

Standing a foot away from the table, my body slumps in restlessness. "Why are you doing this?"

Without skipping a beat, he walks around the breakfast bar with two glasses of soda, and answers, "Because I like you, and I want you to like me too."

That statement does something to me. My stomach clenches. Heat blooms in my middle.

If you only knew how much I liked you…

"I do like you," I answer weakly and unconvincingly.

He stills mid-step and grins. "No. You don't," he throws me a wink, "but I'm working on that."

Oh man, you aren't the sharpest tool in the shed, are you, Max?

He pulls my chair out and motions for me to sit. I hesitate a moment before allowing his assistance. He gently pushes my chair in like a gentleman, then sits himself down opposite me. I look down at my heaped plate, and then look up at him. He shoots me a panty-dropping smile and a sudden thought rushes through my mind:

I could get used to looking up at that smile.

He works on cutting a piece of steak, and by how quickly he does it, I know it's butter soft. He lifts his fork to his mouth, but holds it mid-air. "Why don't you like me again?"

I sigh exaggeratingly long. Can't we move past this already? "We've been through this before, Max. I like you fine."

He smiles, chews, and then swallows. "You don't treat me like you treat Nik, Ash, or Trick. You treat me different."

That's 'cause you're so gorgeous you literally make my eyes water.

I pick at my food and mumble, "I never really noticed. Sorry." Desperate to change the subject, I ask, "Where is Ceecee tonight?"

Max chews his food carefully. When he swallows, his eyes meet mine. So much sadness there. "She's at my mom's. She wanted to sleep over there tonight, and she wants to sleep at Nik's tomorrow. The next day, she'll tell me she wants to stay at Mom's again. I just..." He shrugs, helpless.

"She's avoiding you." A statement. A sad one.

His low voice stabs me directly in the heart. "She doesn't like me much right now."

As I cut into my steak—my butter soft steak, damn him—he starts, "I know I haven't given you much of a choice with training Ceecee, but I meant what I said. I would do anything for her. I don't mind stepping on toes to do that. She's my everything, ya know?"

I take a moment to digest those words.

Would I do the same for my own children? Absolutely.

His eyes meet mine. I watch him closely a moment before I smile. "I know. Besides, I actually found some things I think might suit her." I lift the fork to my mouth. The moment the steak hits my tongue, I groan, "Oh, my God, this is *awesome*." I moan and groan some more before asking, "What did you use to marinade this?"

His brows rise in surprise. "Yeah?" He looks down at his steak, and for a moment, I think he's embarrassed. "It's a family recipe." His trademark grin appears. "If I told you, I'd have to kiss you."

I pause mid-chew. "You mean you'd have to kill me."

His grin grows. His eyes train on my lips. "Nope, I'd have to kiss you."

Ignoring my racing heart's '*yes, please!*' and tummy's flutters, I roll my eyes and chuckle. "You're a dork." Thinking more about Ceecee, I nod and state confidently, "I'm excited to try something new with Ceecee. And if those things don't work, I'll keep looking. There are a lot of options out there. There's bound to be at least one thing she'll take to. If it's out there, I'll find it."

The sound of a chair screeching makes my ears bleed. Suddenly, I'm lifted out of my chair and off the ground. His arms wrap tightly around me and pull me close. Chest to stomach, I breathe him in. I lightly snake my arms around his toned middle and rub his back. He breathes into my ear, "You're amazing."

My light squeeze becomes firm. This should feel awkward, but it doesn't. Not at all. I love the feel of him, the smell of him. Just him. I tell him honestly, "We'll figure this out. Together."

He holds me a long moment before he responds a hesitant and quiet, "Good, 'cause I don't know what the fuck I'm doing."

My arms squeeze, offering him comfort and support. I pull away and smile up at him. "I'm starved."

His eyes warm. "Let's eat."

Helena

Growing up with two older sisters was hell some days. If we weren't fighting over makeup and clothes, Nat and I were fighting over boys and friends. My parents never stepped in until we were tearing each other's hair out, literally. Nina acted as judge and jury, and Nat acted as executioner. Being the youngest meant I was always blamed for things at home. This was because my parents could never stand to be mad at me.

I was the baby. And cute as hell. But even though my sisters got me into trouble, we were a team. I'd take the blame for something one of my sisters did, and then later that night, I'd get three times the dessert in thank you. We sure weren't the Brady Bunch, but we had a lot of fun tearing into each other. We laughed a lot in our house. Although all three of us girls are hot-headed, we got over things quickly and always made time to laugh with each other. We gave affection freely amongst each other, mostly in private.

If you messed with my sisters, you messed with me. I was never afraid to get physical to avenge my sisters in one way or another. I remember one day, Nina, Nat, and I all came home from school late. We were all bleeding from a fist fight after school involving the girlfriend of a football player who kissed Nat over the weekend. The girl was devastated. She was in love. I get it; I do. Nat stayed after school to talk to her about it, to ease the tension. The douche had told Nat he'd broken up with his girlfriend. He knew Nat liked him, so he played her like a violin.

It was only on Monday when Nat got to school and everyone was whispering and giggling behind her back. She knew something was up. Amanda Adelaide Christiansen, head cheerleader and blonde bimbo, was waiting for her by her locker. She greeted Nat with a smirk. When she stepped forward and slapped Nat across the face, Nat didn't flinch.

Come on. Seriously? It was on. Like Donkey Kong.

Nevertheless, Nat still wanted to talk to the girl, but when she showed up and six members of the cheer squad were waiting for her, we knew where it was heading. Nina and I stepped in. Nat followed suit.

We knocked 'em on their asses.

Of course, we were all suspended but it was totally worth it. We walked home laughing and smiling, bonding over our bruised faces and split lips. As soon as we came home, Mom lost it. She grounded us and we accepted our fate. There was no point in arguing. Later that night, Mom sent Dad in to talk to us. He was pissed. We were petrified. My dad never got angry. As in, *never*. So when he shut the door behind him and searched our faces, we knew we were in deep shit.

"The others...they look like you?"

Nina choked on a laugh. "Much worse."

Nat and I bit our lips to stop our own laughter from joining hers. But Nina quickly straightened, remembering we were in deep doo-doo.

But Dad asked, "You punch like I show you?" We all nodded, confused, not knowing what the hell was going on. Dad smiled and lowered his heavily accented voice. "Mama send me in here to scare you, you know? She is very upset. Girls should no come home bloody."

We all nodded. "Yes, Tata."

He shook his head, chuckling to himself. When he reached the door, he turned and spoke softly, "You must block better." He smiled then added, "I show you how. Tomorrow."

There sure never was a dull moment at our house. I never realized living the way I did, with two older sisters, gave me a life skill I never knew I'd need. I have an insane ability to take and dish attitude without blinking an eye. Who knew I'd need that ability to deal with a thirteen-year-old paraplegic? I really should thank them. My sisters, that is.

Nah. Fuck 'em.

Today was my first day of unassisted work. Just because it was unassisted, it didn't mean I wasn't supervised. For the next week, James will watch over me to make sure I'm doing everything I should be, but then it's all me.

After today's sessions were over, James pulled me aside to tell me how much of a great job I was doing. Personally, I felt like I was doing okay. Not great, but okay. Having him tell me how impressed he is with me was definitely something I needed. And although I wanted to hug him, instead, I rubbed his bald head for luck. He laughed and playfully shoved me away. My heart warmed. It was nice to have my friend back.

Felicity took me out to lunch and tried to get Willa to come along too, but she kindly refused. I told Felicity about The White Rabbit. She told me she'd always wanted to go, and invited herself along this Saturday. Somehow, I don't think Felicity is the type of person who needs an invitation.

I asked Nat to pick me up after work. As we reach our destination, I punch her arm. "Thanks for picking me up."

Flinching, she rubs her arm and responds, "No problem, bitch. And *ouch*!"

I grin and murmur, "Oh, toughen up, princess."

Nat pulls over in front of the house. "You know what you're doing?"

I shake my head. "Nope, but I think Ceecee will help me figure it out."

She leans over and kisses my cheek. "Good luck. I'll be at Tina's. Come get me when you're ready to go."

Shame fills me, hard and sudden. I look up at my sister and promise, "I'm going to get a car soon. I swear. As soon as I've got the money."

She lifts her arm and punches me in the same spot I got her. I flinch, "*Ouch.*"

Her brows rise. "See? Told ya it hurts. And seriously, I don't mind driving you around. Neither does Ash. Take your time sorting things. We got your back."

The bridge of my nose stings. Nat has been an absolute godsend. A pillar of support. My voice cracks as I tell her, "Thanks. I love you."

As soon as she spots my tears, she shoves me out the door. "Nope! We're not doing this right now! You need to work. Vamoose!"

Sniffling, I step out of the car and chuckle. "Yeah, yeah. I'm gone."

I walk up the long driveway, my duffle bag by my side. When I reach the front door, I ring the bell and wait. A minute passes before the door opens. I smile and look down at my new client. "Hey, Ceecee. How're you doing, sweetie?"

Today is no different from the other days I've seen her. She all but rolls her eyes and mumbles, "Fine."

An awkward silence follows. My smile falls. I clear my throat and force a smile so hard my cheeks hurt. "Is your dad home?" She nods and rolls her chair back out of the doorway in silent invitation. I step inside and ask, "So how are you liking this place? It looks amazing."

Her eyes reach mine. Her answer is quick, but harsh. "I hate it."

"Why is that?" I ask gently.

Her gaze flickers to the floor before she murmurs, "It's empty. And cold."

Doth my ears mishear, or is that the bitter sound of loneliness?

My chest aches for her. I wish I could bend down and hug her without having my head bitten off. Before I can think better of it, I step forward, lean down, and wrap my arms around her. She doesn't hug me back, but she doesn't stiffen either. I hold her a long while before she asks quietly, "Why are you hugging me?"

She asks this question in a soft way, a sweet way, so I know this is not a warning to never do it again. As I separate from her, I answer her just as quietly, "Because hugs are free and you looked like you needed one."

The squeak of a door opening snags my attention. Max steps out of what I can see is the bathroom. How do I know this? I know this, because as he opens the door, steam follows him out. That, and he is dressed in a towel.

Only a towel.

Holy Mary, mother of God. He is magnificent.

I've seen men and I've seen their bodies. I've been to the beach a thousand times before. So I can say with absolute confidence, using my mental guide of comparison, this body is ridiculous. Ridiculously hot.

My body's reaction is just as ridiculous. My tongue swells. I begin salivating. My nipples bead and warmth hits my belly, hard. All I can do is watch in awe as he walks into the hallway. Water beads all over his olive skin and I silently wish to lick it off. With abs of steel and not an ounce of fat on him, my eyes follow his strong body as it moves gracefully down the hall.

With a towel around his waist and one in his hands, he wipes at his face before calling out, "Baby girl, someone here?"

I watch Ceecee smirk. "Yep."

Oh, man. This is not good. This is not a playful smirk. This smirk is spiteful and nasty. What on earth is going on here? Why is this normally sweet girl hating on her dad? I don't understand, but I vow to find out.

When Max looks up and sees me, his slow smile has my stomach flipping around like fish out of water. "Cupcake. What are you doing here? I thought we had an appointment tomorrow sometime?"

My heart smiles at the fact he's not mad about me showing up uninvited. "I-uh...I just wanted to—uh..." My mind is finding it hard to concentrate when we're trying to picture what's underneath that towel. "Do you want to get changed, and then we'll talk?"

Ceecee starts to move away, when Max calls out, "Don't go far, baby."

She doesn't answer, just moves faster, and his smile fades. I would hug him if he were dressed...and if it weren't completely inappropriate right now. Instead, he looks back at me and points to his towel. "Changing."

I nod dumbly, staring down at the towel. Unable to look away, the towel comes closer and closer 'til my head snaps up. I find Max in my face, grinning like the fool he is. He lifts a hand and runs it through his wet hair, and then leans into me and whispers, "I guess we're even."

My mind—now comatose from copious amounts of sexy—flat-lines. "Huh?"

He looks down at my cleavage and tugs at the bottom of my tank. "I've seen you. Now you've seen me." He smirks. "Even."

My brain-to-mouth filter sparks and I blurt out, "Technically, you'd have to lose the towel and put on undies. And a bra."

His laughter is loud and so happy-sounding that my moment of regret is replaced by tummy flutters and a small smile. He walks away, leaving me in the hall. Just before he enters his room, he looks back at me, smiling, and drops the towel a second before he walks through the door, giving me a heart attack, as well as a nice view of his taut butt.

The door closes and I can only think of one thing.

Dat ass.

CHAPTER TWENTY

Helena

I was told to make myself at home, so that's exactly what I do. Hell, if it were Max being told to do it, he'd do it. I'm just returning the favor. When I step into the kitchen, I look through cupboards until I find the glasses, take one out, and then open the fridge. I hear footsteps come into the kitchen and I ask, "Don't you have anything to drink in this place?"

I look up from the fridge door to find Max standing there in black sweats, a navy skintight tank, and white sneakers. I look down at myself then back up at him. I ask through a laugh, "Did you color coordinate yourself to look like me?"

He shrugs, a smile playing at his lips. "I thought we could play 'who wore it better?'"

Not thinking at that moment, I respond immediately, "You. Definitely you." Closing my eyes, I slap a hand across my mouth and giggle nervously. "Oh, shit. That was stupid."

Max comes up behind me, leaning over me to view the sad state of his fridge. His body molds to mine, his front pressing into my back. As my minds squeals then faints dead away, he murmurs as he pulls away, "This is worse than I thought. Come on. Let's go to the grocery store."

I shake my head. "No, I just came to talk. Nat's waiting at Tina's for me."

His eyes narrow as he shrugs. "So? Tell her I'll take you home."

I sigh through my response, "That's not an option."

He pokes me in the rib. "Why?"

I have no idea. My brain has farted so hard it might've pooped a little. "I...uh—she's waiting for me, is why. She's across the street, waiting for me. She's waiting so I-um...can't do that right now." I think I should get an award for getting through that sounding only half-special.

His eyes on me, he lifts his cell to his ear and waits. "Yo." He smirks at something the person on the other end has said. "No, I haven't killed her. Yet." He rolls his eyes. "Or seduced her." He looks at me and winks. "Yet." He pauses to listen, then speaks into the receiver, "We're going grocery shopping. I'll bring her home later. You need anything?"

The little shit. My face heats and I hiss, "*Will you stop doing that*?"

Placing a hand over the cell, he asks a confused, "Doing what?"

My mouth gapes. I near-shriek, "Making me do what I don't want to!"

He doesn't answer me, just shakes his head as he speaks into the phone. "Okay, babe. No problem. And you tell that husband of yours he better watch his back. The second he fucks up, I'm all over you like stink on shit."

My eyes narrow.

Of course he flirts with my sister. Of course he does. He doesn't flirt with me, but he flirts with her.

He takes in my murderous glare then grins, "Okay, I have to go before your sister cuts my balls off. Love you."

He places his cell in his pocket and smiles. "See? No problem." Before I can get a word in, he calls out, "Yo, baby girl. Let's go."

She calls back, "Where are we going?"

"Grocery shopping."

It takes a moment before Ceecee comes out of her room and into the kitchen. She mutters, "Thank God, I'm starving." She looks up at me and asks hesitantly, "Are you coming?"

I don't get to answer. I don't get to answer, because Max throws his arm around my shoulders, pulling me close. "Of course she's coming. We need to feed her too."

And for the first time since I've been in New York, Ceecee smiles. "Cool." Sure, she smiles down at her hands, but it's still something.

I may not have wanted to be here before, but at that small response, I want to be here now. I smile down at her. "Let's see if we can get some chunky monkey while we're down there too."

Ceecee looks up at me in awe, eyes wide. "I love chunky monkey."

I'm so shocked at this change of behavior that I balk. I recover quickly with, "I think we just became best friends."

Her smile is so wide, so beautiful, that I want to cry. I'm getting through to her.

And somehow, Max knew I would.

MAX

Nuh uh. I don't like this. Not one bit.

Why does she have to be so damn beautiful? I'm having a hard time controlling myself around her. When I saw her bent over in front of the fridge, I couldn't stop myself. I had to feel her body against mine. So I did what I did. Worse decision I've ever made in my life. As soon as my front pressed into her back, images of Helena moaning and gasping as I hold her long brown hair in my fisted palm and drive into her assaulted me. Of course I started to get hard. I had to back away.

I want her. What's worse is she's not here for me. She's here for Ceecee. So I'll do what I've been doing for years, doing what I do best.

I'll hold back.

Helena

Ceecee and I walk out the front door to the fancy black SUV parked out front. The car flashes its lights then chirps, letting us know it's unlocked. Ceecee wheels ahead. My brows narrow as she wheels to the side of the vehicle and opens the sliding door. She presses a button on the inside, and a ramp is lowered.

I can't help myself. "Holy crap, this is awesome!"

Max opens the front door and slides into the driver's seat. "Yeah, we like it."

This is the coolest, most sporty looking wheelchair-accessible vehicle I've ever seen. "What is this?"

As Ceecee makes her way up the ramp and secures herself, Max explains, "It's called an MV-1."

I shake my head. "Never heard of it."

He nods. "It's only been out a month or so. Thankfully, I signed up early and we got one of the first sixty made. The manufacturer is here in New York, so that probably made it easier. That, and the fact I was willing to pay in cash."

Looking around the vehicle, I whisper, "I love it." Then I say out loud, "I am so glad you're not one of those tools who owns a fast car."

Max stiffens, and then stutters, "W-why?"

I shrug. "I don't know. I just don't like 'em. They're stupid, and so unnecessary."

Ceecee giggles from the backseat. "Daddy has a Jag."

I turn in my seat. "A what?"

She giggles some more. "A Jaguar."

I look back at her and groan. She giggles louder. I look over at Max and bite my lip to hold in my laugh. "Not that you're a tool, Max. I only meant all the *other* tool-ish people who have stupid cars for no good reason."

He pulls out of the driveway and he looks to be pouting. We drive in silence for a few minutes before he explodes in a rush of words, "A Jag isn't just a car, okay? It's power under your feet. It's speed and sheer excellence, all right? It's—"

I cut in with, "A crappy way to spend a hundred grand."

And Ceecee loses it again. She laughs so hard I fear she may wet herself. So she likes her dad being made fun of? I hate myself a little right now that I like Max being made fun of as long as she's smiling. I'll have to apologize to him later.

Max sighs. "You're a girl. You don't get it. If I were having this conversation with a guy, he'd get it. You need testicles for this conversation. Do you have testicles, cupcake?"

I fight my smile. "I don't thin—"

But he cuts me off by placing his hand up. "I asked you a question. Do you have testicles, Helena?"

My lips thin. *Ass*. "No. I do not have testicles, Max."

He nods. "Firstly, thank fuck for that." Ceecee accidentally lets out a giggle at her dad's silliness and we both still, side-eyeing each other in shock. He quickly adds, "Secondly, because of your lack of male parts, what you say doesn't count, babe." He shrugs. "That's just the way it is."

Sugar Rush

I discreetly reach over and squeeze his thigh in a secret hi-five. His hand covers mine and squeezes back in what I'm sure would be a cheer. We finally pull up to the grocery store and step out of the car. Ceecee does everything she needs to lower herself out of the down the ramp. As I move to help her out, Max holds me back and mutters under his breath, "Yeah, no. That's a great way to piss her off. Let her do it."

We wait a minute longer and I watch Ceecee closely. Steel determination is worn apparent on her face.

Hmmm. Interesting.

An idea strikes me, and I suddenly can't wait to get back to the house. I have to talk to my client in private.

Max moves to stand next to Ceecee, but wraps an arm around me. "So what's for dinner, guys? We can order in or I can cook."

Ceecee mumbles defiantly, "I don't want you to cook."

And for no reason whatsoever, I butt in where I'm not needed, making a spectacle of myself, when I usually prefer to blend into the background. Go me! "I can cook."

Max starts to protest, when Ceecee asks curiously, "What can you cook?"

My shoulder jumps. "Just about anything, really. I was always in the kitchen with my mom, even when I didn't want to be. She just pulled us girls in there and hoped something would stick. Lucky for her, all of us like cooking. Mostly because we love eating." Ceecee wheels herself forward, brows creased in concentration.

She looks to be thinking hard when I ask, "What do you want to eat, honey?"

"I don't really care." Darn. And I thought I was onto something there. Then she asks quietly, "But can I help you cook?"

Bingo!

I narrow my eyes at her. "Can you chop?" She nods, wide-eyed. "Can you grate?" She nods once more. I finally ask, "Can you add seasoning?" Her heads jerks up and down. I move from Max's hold to stand in between them and place a hand on Ceecee's shoulder. "Then I guess you're making Nachos tonight. From scratch."

She looks up at me in shock. "Me?"

I nod as if it's no big deal. "Sure. Of course, I'll be supervising, but you're making dinner tonight. On your own." I wait a moment before I ask, "Is that okay with you?"

We enter the store when she utters, "I just don't want to ruin it."

At the very same time, Max and I both respond with complete confidence, "You won't."

She nods then, and I feel relief flow through my body with a breath I hadn't known I was holding. She looks around the store. "What do I need?"

I look over at Max and raise my brows. "If your dad doesn't mind, you can go get two packets of Taco seasoning while I get the vegetables and meat organized."

Max says, "I don't mind," but she's already off, getting things on her own like a grown-up.

As soon as she's out of sight, my shoulders droop in relief. "Holy shitballs, that was like pulling teeth."

I squeak when I'm swooped off my feet, both literally and figuratively. Max lifts me as if I weigh nothing at all. I grip his shoulders tightly as he spins me around, laughing. "You're amazing. That was amazing. You..." he places me back on my feet, still holding me around the waist, "are amazing."

"Okay," I mutter, kind of confused.

He looks me in the eye, grinning from ear to ear, dimple cutting into his cheek. "I'm going to kiss you now."

What? No!

I shake my head. "No, don't do that!"

He makes a *duh* face. "I have to kiss you. Those are the rules."

"Max! Don't!"

He pulls me close. "What's a little kiss between friends? I've kissed Nat a hundred times before. Now it's your turn. Don't be such a baby."

Heart racing, I swallow hard and state weakly, "I'm not kissing you."

Lowering his face to mine, he orders, "Pucker up, cupcake. I'm coming in."

I open my mouth to argue, but my argument dies in my throat as Max's lips cover mine in a warm, sweet, tame kiss.

Damn it to heck. So this is what this feels like, huh?

My eyes flutter closed and my foot lifts off the ground, toes curling. I feel this kiss. I feel it from head to toe. Warmth spreads throughout my suddenly weak body, and this kiss is nothing. I know the difference between this kiss and a hot kiss, and my insides die a little at the simple fact that if this were a tame kiss, his real kisses would be explosive.

It lasts no more than a few seconds, although from the way my head becomes woozy, it feels like hours. When he pulls away smiling, I have to hold his tank tight to stop myself from falling over. He wraps an arm around my waist and walks me forward, sighing as though the kiss was no big deal. "It's a good day to be alive, cupcake. I told you you'd be perfect."

Mouth drier than the Sahara, I mutter a hoarse, "I need water."

He walks me along. "Whatever you want, it's yours. Hell, I'd just about give you whatever you asked for right now. I owe you big time."

My mind still offline, I lift my fingertips to my mouth, absently muttering, "You shouldn't have kissed me."

His arm tightens around my waist, pulling me flush against his side. Lips to my temple, he states, "You better get used to affection, Lena. I'm an affectionate guy, and when I want to give it, I give it good." His warm lips gently kiss my temple, and without meaning to, I lean into it. He adds, "We're friends now. I'm going to hug you and I'm going to kiss you. Don't worry," he utters confidently. "You'll get used to it."

That's what I'm afraid of, dipshit.

Suddenly, Max stops mid-step. "Oh shit."

His arms go rigid around me. I lift a hand to his chest. "What's wrong?"

Wrapping me in a bear hug, he whispers into my ear, "See that chick over there, in the red?" When I go to move my entire body, he whispers a rushed, "Don't look!"

I hiss, "You told me to look!"

I feel the panic come off him. "Okay. Look discreetly."

So I do, from the very corner of my eye. A tall, slim redhead stands there in the fruit and vegetable section, holding a stick of celery. She's glaring at us.

Uh oh. My body droops into his. "Max, she's pissed."

He pulls me closer, hands roaming over my body. His face falls into my neck. "I know. I told her I didn't want to go out with her and she got mad."

My body stiffens. "Are you using me right now to put on a show?"

He presses his nose to my throat and breathes me in. *The dirtbag.* "You smell good."

Not in the mood for games, I turn and bite his earlobe. He yelps then sighs, "Okay, okay. She may have said I led her on."

I lift my head and bark a humorless laugh. "Let me guess. The flirting?"

He pulls back and his golden eyes flash as he fiercely glares down at me. "I'm single. I'm allowed to flirt, so sue me. I like to flirt."

Rolling my eyes, I mutter under my breath, "With everyone but me."

His large hands grip my waist tightly, his eyes now pleading. "Help. Please."

In my peripheral vision, I see the redhead come closer. I whisper, "She's coming."

His lips hit my cheek. His sweet, minty breath warms me as he whispers against my skin, "Please, please, please, please, please."

I rush out, "Okay, but I swear, if you kiss me again, I will bite off your tongue."

Max smiles down at me with a smile that would be worthy of dental advertisements, his dimple out for the world to see, and I wonder what the hell I'm doing.

CHAPTER TWENTY-ONE

Helena

The redhead saunters over to us, saucily swaying her hips from side to side. And my mind rolls its eyes. I already know what type of woman this is. I hate these types of women. This is the type of woman I assumed Felicity was when we first met. I'm suddenly reminded I was wrong about Felicity. I should probably give this woman a chance before I judge her.

Max keeps his arm around me as he turns, smiling coolly at the woman. "Hey, Portia, how you doin'?"

Without even looking at him, she looks me up and down. "Fine, Max. I didn't know you have a girlfriend."

Oh, yeah. I was not wrong this time. She's a flaming bitch.

Not stooping to her level, I introduce myself. "Hi, I'm Helena." She looks over to Max with her brows raised and mouth set in a firm line before holding out a hand to me. I normally would not have an issue with this. The fact is, she's holding out her hand as if I'm going to kiss the back of it. The asshole. Bitchiness not being one to stop me, I take hold of her awkwardly presented fingertips and shake 'em like a man. Portia almost loses her balance and I stifle my laugh. "Nice to meet you."

She doesn't bother making nice. "I haven't seen you at the club before."

I eye her good. "I was there last weekend. And I'll be there this weekend too." Wanting to play the part, I snuggle deeper into Max, wrapping an arm around his stomach. I look up at him. "But I don't need to be there every weekend. We see each other all the time." Standing on my tiptoes, I kiss the side of his jaw in a very real display of affection.

Portia suddenly looks behind me, eyes wide. "Hello," she bristles, "little one."

Ceecee stops by my side. My heart races.

Shit. We're so totally busted.

My arm falls from Max's stomach and I expect him to come clean, but he doesn't. I move to back away, but he holds me tight. "Portia, this is my daughter, Ceecee."

Her eyes widen. "Really? I had no idea." *No shit, Sherlock.* My mind scoffs and laughs humorlessly. If she had spent a single moment getting to know Max, it would have been the first thing he'd have told her. I don't like this woman. Portia bends at the waist, into Ceecee's face. "Oh my." She lifts a hand and touches her hair as if she has the right. "You are a pretty one."

My jaw set, my stomach coils violently. Did I mention I don't like this woman?

It's not your place. It's not your place. It's not your place.

Fuck it. "I'm sorry, Portia, but we need to get going. It was nice meeting you. We might see you this weekend." Her eyes flash. She knows what I'm doing. I'm dismissing her.

And she doesn't like it. "Nice meeting you too, Helen."

My mouth opens to correct her when Max and Ceecee both utter icily, "It's Helen*a*."

My heart smiles while my mind pokes its tongue out at her. The arm I have around Max tightens, and I lower my other hand by the free side, palm open. I feel Ceecee place her hand in mine. I like that. I like it so much that I stupidly feel like this is where I'm meant to be. So I want to slap a bitch when she leans into Max and kisses his cheek with her red-glossed lips.

As she pulls away, she utters quietly, almost as if she's telling him a secret, "See you Saturday night." Then she laughs softly, lifting a hand to his cheek, wiping at it. "Oops. These lips of mine." Her eyes focus on me. "They leave a mark." A challenge.

Bring it, bitch.

We linger a moment. Max clears his throat. "I'm hungry. You guys hungry?"

Ceecee nods, but keeps her eyes firmly on Portia's retreating back. "Yeah."

"Me too," I add in a much-too-chipper way. "I'm just going to grab a couple of things. Why don't you guys head over to the checkout? I'll just be a minute." Ignoring Portia's presence in the fruit and veggie section, I move around the store in record time, grabbing the last of what we need before meeting Max and Ceecee at the checkout. Max buys the groceries in silence.

We exit the store and drive home with only the radio providing a break from the thick silence in the car. Finally, when we reach the house, Max parks the car. As I unbuckle my belt, he speaks up. "Ceecee, you know Helena isn't really my girlfriend, right?"

She looks over at me and it almost looks as if her eyes turn sad. "I know."

He looks across to me and smiles. "But we are friends. So Helena will be here a lot more, if that's okay with you."

She answers immediately without a trace of uncertainty in her voice. "That's okay with me."

I quell my sudden need to smile. Ceecee likes me.

Yay, me!

We exit the car and head inside. As soon as we're in, I start barking orders, "Ceecee, I need you to take two carrots out of the bag and grate them. Max, I need you to find a pan and colander. I'll start chopping the onion," I look over to Ceecee and smile, but then it's all on you, young grasshopper."

Uncertainty shines bright in her eyes. I step toward her and take her small hands in mine. "I will be here every second. If you need help, all you need to do is ask. And I hope you will ask, or this won't work."

Max puts a pan on the stove, a colander on the counter, and comes up behind us. "You guys good? I need to catch up on some paperwork."

I turn and shoo him away. "Away with you! Now, it's girl time." I turn back to Ceecee and wink. When I'm rewarded with a wide smile, for a split second, I think I would do just about anything to see that smile, and I pray I see it again and again.

With my hands to his back, I push him out of the kitchen while he utters, "I'll be at the dining table if you need me."

I make a *pffft* sound. "We don't need you. We're golden."

While Ceecee grates the carrots, I strain a can of lentils, chop an onion, and take the ground beef out of the plastic. As soon as she's done, I point to her then crook my finger at her. She wheels herself over to my place at the stove and I'm suddenly aware that this kitchen has been designed around Ceecee and her chair. The stove is shorter than it would be for anyone else, and has a gap underneath so Ceecee can wheel herself right in there, as does the sink. The countertops are just the right height for her.

I use the very tip of my finger to tap in front of the stove and she gets my drift. As soon as she's in position, I turn on the cooktop and bring over the ingredients for our dinner. I hand her a wooden spoon and ask, "Do you cook a lot?"

She shakes her head. "I can cook scrambled eggs. That's about it."

My hip leaning on the counter, I cross my arms over my chest. My mind shouts, *What are you doing?* when I ask, "Would you like to learn?"

Her eyes meet mine. She speaks a hushed, "Aunt Tina used to let me help, but now with Tatiana and Ava, it's..." She drifts off. And my heart pangs. Something tells me Ceecee is not just angry with her dad. Something tells me Ceecee is angry at the world.

I respond softly, "Yeah. That happens. When kids come along, it's hard to make time for anything else. Especially when they're little, you know? 'Cause babies get sick, and they need to eat almost all the time, and sometimes they just want to cuddle. It takes a long time before parents can make time to do the things they used to." I hand her the olive oil and jerk my chin to the pan. "Give it a good swirl. It doesn't matter if you don't measure it out, just make sure there's enough to coat the onion."

She adds the perfect amount then slides in the onion, and I grin. "Are you sure you don't know what you're doing? You're doing awesome so far." Her blush is small, but I see it. I add, "Like I was saying, being a parent makes people busy. But if you like, I can come over a few times a week and we can cook together." She doesn't give me an indication on how she feels about this, so I nudge her shoulder and add, "I don't know a lot of people in New York, so if you want to give me something to do during the week, I'd like that very much."

You're getting too involved.

Oh hush, brain. What could possibly go wrong?

Using the wooden spoon, she stirs the onion and doesn't look up at me when she says, "I'd like that."

Tell her. Tell her now.

"Would you still want to learn if it came with a catch?" I ask hesitantly while wringing my fingers together.

Not skipping a beat, she utters, "You want me to start exercising again."

My eyes round in shock. Ceecee is by no means a silly girl. "Yes, I would. If we could just get you doing three sessions a week, you'd likely stop cramping, honey."

Her hand stops stirring a moment as she thinks about this. "You'd be exercising with me? You'd be here three times a week?"

I nod. "Yes and yes. I'd be doing it with you. Of course, you'll be doing three more days with Whit during the week, but I'll come here after work on the days you're not at the center. We'll cook together, then do a light session. And I promise, Ceecee," I place my hand on her shoulder, drawing her attention, "I promise if we do something you don't like, we'll try something else. There's plenty out there, and we'll find something you like."

She stirs and asks, "So, this is my choice? You won't force me?"

My heart sinks. She's going to say no. "No, sweetie. No one's going to force you. And if you decide you don't want to do this anymore, we can still cook together and hang out." And I mean that. I'm starting to think I was wrong about refusing this position in the first place.

I tap my finger on the bowl of ground beef and watch Ceecee add it to the pan. While she works out the lumps, I add the carrot and lentils. She concentrates hard at the task at hand and I smile. She might be hardheaded, but she's determined; that's for sure.

We cook in silence for a long while before Ceecee speaks again. "Okay. I'll start exercising again."

A breath I hadn't known I was holding leaves me in a whoosh. I'm *shocked*. "Really?"

"Yeah," she mutters then goes on, "but only if you come to Sunday morning breakfasts with us."

My mind sobs. *Sunday morning? Oh, hell no!*

Sunday is the only day I get to sleep in, and I love sleep. At home, when it was all us girls in one house, if someone dared make noise before eleven am on a weekend, I would calmly get out of bed, beat the shit out of them, and then fall back into a coma until I felt I was recharged enough to face the day.

Grin and bear it, Lena.

Forcing a smile, I grit my teeth and chirp, "Sure. I love breakfast." Ceecee smiles at the pan, and I narrow my eyes at her. I can't help but think she's up to something, the little scamp.

Before I know it, I'm switching off the stove and bringing over an oven-proof dish to where Ceecee's parked by the counter. I open the bag of corn chips and dump them into the dish. Ceecee tops the chips with the ground beef mixture. I tell her to top it with cheese and she sprinkles it on. When she's done, I pop the dish into the oven and set the time for fifteen minutes.

I quickly put Ceecee to work by helping me clean the mess we've made in the kitchen. Soon enough, the timer beeps. Ceecee suddenly looks worried. I open the oven and the smell hits me. "Oh, dear God, Ceecee."

She panics, "*What?*"

Grinning, I turn and whisper loudly, "It smells amazing!" I carefully remove the dish from the oven. As I place it on the stove, I tell her, "Do not touch that. It's hotter than hel—" *In the presence of a minor!* Oops. "It's hotter than Ian Somerhalder."

She smiles. "It's okay. I've heard worse."

Of course she has. She's grown up with Max, Nik, Ash, and Trick. It's a miracle her ears aren't constantly bleeding, the poor dear. "Right. I'm going to tell your dad to clear up the dining table so we can eat."

As soon as I walk out of the kitchen and into the hall, I jump up and down on the spot, silently cheering at the fact that I'm doing something right. Ceecee agreed to exercise without me having to bribe her. I made it her choice.

Wait a minute. My bouncing body stills. I made it her choice. My eyes widen. Oh, my God. I made it *her* choice! A smile spreads across my face. That's *it*! I look into the dining room and my vagina jumps off a trapeze, freefalling with her arms spread wide by her sides.

Max sits at the dining table in front of an open laptop, one leg stretched out in front of him, the other bent at the knee, his foot on the base of the chair. Chewing on a pen and looking into the screen distractedly, his glasses are perched on top of his nose.

He has glasses. Not just any glasses. Trendy, geek chic, rectangular reading glasses. Jesus, Mary, and Joseph. A frown tips my lips. I raise my head and mentally pray.

This isn't fair, God. I'm not allowed to touch him. Why are you playing with my emotions like this? Is it because I asked Jacob Schmidt to show me his thing in the first grade? I was young and curious! Give me a break!

Lowering my face, I glance over at Max and swallow through my thick throat.

Let me tell you something about myself. Men with glasses…they do it for me. Something about a good-looking man changes when he puts on glasses. He becomes someone else, a gorgeous version of himself. While women were swooning over Superman, I was swooning over Clark Kent. Oh, yeah. Give me a man with glasses any day of the week.

I clear my throat and he looks up at me with a lazy smile. "Hey."

I motion to his laptop. "You almost done? Dinner's ready."

"Yeah, I'm done." He removes his glasses, placing them down on the table.

My feet move of their own accord until I'm right in front of him. I pick the glasses up off the table, lift them, and gently place them back on his head. I state softly, "Don't take them off. They look good on you."

I turn to walk away, but he snags my wrist and yanks. I land on his lap and his long, muscular arms wrap around me, holding me in place. I don't fight him this time. I've seen him with the other girls. I know this is how he is. It doesn't seem right for me to ask him to be someone else around me. He's right. I'm just going to have to get used to it. He asks quietly, "How'd it go?"

I feign boredom. "Oh, you know. We cooked. We talked. We had fun. Girls stuff." My eyes smile down at him. "She agreed to cooking lessons and exercise sessions three times a week. But only if I come to Sunday breakfasts with you guys, so please tell me that's after ten am, because otherwise, I might just cry."

I expect something. A smile. A laugh. A victorious hi-five. I get nothing. Instead, his arms tighten around me. He closes his eyes and drops his forehead to my shoulder. He holds me for a long while and I lift my hand to rub his forearm. I'm not sure why, but it feels as though he needs comfort right now.

I give him his moment before gently removing his hands and standing. I make my way to the kitchen to find Ceecee has already put together plates and cutlery. She moves out of the kitchen, and as she passes me, I can't help myself. I lean down and kiss her head. "You did good, sweetie."

She smiles up at me. "I had a good teacher."

If there ever was a compliment to receive from a child, that would be the one. My stupid nose tingles, and before I start blubbering like a loon, I quickly take the dish of nachos off the stove and move it into the dining room. Max sits while Ceecee places the plates down. He looks to the dish I place in the middle of the table and grins. When she passes him the next time, he quickly grabs a handle and pulls her chair backward. He wraps an arm around her shoulders and utters, "This looks good, baby girl. My mouth's watering. Feed me."

When she mutters an unsure, "Thanks, Daddy," he kisses her cheek and lets her go.

Heart fluttering, I sit at the table and look around me. A small smile graces my lips. I quickly realize there is no place I'd rather be.

CHAPTER TWENTY-TWO

Helena

I'm pissed.

Stupid brain.

After last night's dinner, I decided it was too late to do a session with Ceecee. Not only that, but we'd eaten our weight in nachos. Ceecee had done such a great job with cooking that I'd gone back for seconds. And it wasn't even sympathy seconds. The nachos were *good*.

Watching Max eat was something else. I had seen him eat before, but I never really noticed the little noises he makes when he's eating something he enjoys. His small murmurs of approval, his discreet nods, and furrowed brows of concentration—it was almost as if he was having a conversation with his dinner. And, of course, it was completely adorable. The ass.

We showered compliments to the chef, and from her shy smile and neon pink blush, I think she liked that. When I asked her what days she'd like me to come over, she looked at her dad, then back to me and responded,

"You can come any day after five pm." She suddenly looked nervous, but added quietly, "And you don't have to come just three days. If you don't have anything to do or whatever, you can come here."

My body stilled in stunned disbelief. Was this Ceecee's way of telling me we are friends? I believed it was. Not being able to stop myself and craving the affections of this little creature, I leaned down, wrapped my arms around her, and told her, "I will definitely keep that in mind, sweetie." As I pulled away, I added, "I'd hate for you to get sick of me though."

She lowered her eyes and mumbled, "That won't happen." And my heart soared.

Max told Ceecee to get her things then, and confusion settled over me. Then I remembered what Max had told me the other night about Ceecee not wanting to be at home, about her avoiding him. She was likely going to sleep at Nik and Tina's. Ceecee looked up at her dad. She didn't move. When she spoke softly, I melted on the floor in a big puddle of sap. "Actually, Daddy, I think I might stay here tonight."

To say Max looked surprised was a complete understatement. He looked like he might just break into interpretive dance. They dropped me off at home and I thanked them for dinner. When I made my way inside, I couldn't stop smiling. And as soon as I turned on the light, glancing around my very empty apartment, I couldn't help but feel a loss.

I didn't understand it. I had always been the type of person who was able to entertain myself, and do it happily. I liked my alone-time. So why did being alone right now feel so...lonely?

I avoided being attacked by Tedwood by catching him mid-attack and dropping him out into the hall. I made my way to the bathroom and showered before bed. As my soapy hands roamed over my body, I imagined another set of hands on me. A large, masculine set of hands that would explore me, a pair of golden eyes looking *in*to me, and a sexy dimple I wanted to lick taunting me. My palms glanced over my nipples and my body convulsed.

I was panting. My stomach dipped. I was already *there*. My hand slid down my belly, down further, lower to my spread legs. My fingers glided over my clit, and my legs became weak. Leaning my head on the tiled wall of the shower, my touch firmed. I rubbed harder over my swollen bud, images of sex assaulting my mind. Max's mouth on me, all over. His hands gripping me tight. His cock deep inside of me, thrusting hard enough to make me whimper.

Holy shit.

My body jerked. I felt it happening. A sweet numbness swept over me. Gentle tingles hit my core. I tipped my head back, mouth parted in a delicious wave of pleasure. My fingers worked harder, harder, the tingles intensifying, and then I was there. A long moan was torn from deep in my throat as my pussy convulsed, over and over. I cupped myself. My body jerked uncontrollably. Then suddenly, I was tired.

I stayed in the shower longer than I should have, glued to the spot. After I rinsed myself a second time, I stepped out, got dressed feeling like a tramp, and went to bed, my loneliness eating away at me.

There was only one place I wanted to be, and it wasn't home.

And that's why I've spent most of my night awake making three trays of breakfast muffins, eating whatever I had in the house, and getting angry with myself. Sure, it's not my fault I was forced into a friendship with Ceecee. It's Max's. So, really, I should be angry at Max. My face softens.

Who could ever be angry at Max?

I stomp my foot on the ground, ball my hands into fists, and growl. Damn him. I have never been so befuddled before. Part of me is ecstatic that I'm breaking through Ceecee's wall, the other part of me is pissed that Max is breaking through mine. How was I ever meant to keep my heart safe?

Max is a good guy, down to his core. He's a great dad, and the type of friend any person would count herself lucky to have. Let's be honest here. I never stood a chance. Shaking my head in frustration, I take the three full containers of muffins and place one in my freezer. I open my apartment door, write on my little portable whiteboard, and make my way across the hall. My finger presses the button at the side of the door. A few seconds pass before it opens.

Mrs. Crandle looks up at me through her coke-bottle glasses. Smiling, I hand her a container full of muffins and hold the board up for her to read. 'Good morning, Mrs. Crandle. I made these for you. I'm on my way to work, so I can't stay and chat, but I promise to come over for tea again!'

Her eyes follow my words. She looks up at me and smiles softly, taking the container. "Why, thank you, dear." Her smile turns sad. "You're a good egg, Helena."

Walking backward, I quickly write, 'I'll come by soon.'

She answers quietly, "That would be lovely, dear."

I turn, raise my hand, and knock on Nat's door. No one answers. I lift my hand to knock again when guilt assaults me. She and Ash wouldn't need to wake up so early if it weren't for me. If I had a car, they'd be able to sleep in, and lord knows when the babies get here they won't be doing much of that anymore. Guilt seeps from my pores. I'm a shitty sister. I lower my hand, walk down the stairs, and lift my cell to my ear. He answers immediately, "Hey, everything okay?"

I silently cringe. "You wouldn't happen to be going past my place, would you?"

He doesn't hesitate. "I'm about three minutes away. Meet you in the parking lot."

I let out a relived breath. "Thank you."

A few minutes later, he pulls up and rolls down the window to tease, "Hey, I'm not going to get roughed up again, am I?"

I snort. "James Whittaker, you bite your tongue. As if I would let that happen. Besides, the bear is still asleep."

My muffins and I slide inside and we drive on. I look over at him and smile to myself. Reaching over, I scratch at his bald head with my nails and he leans into it. "You need luck?"

Chuckling, I scratch harder. "Bucket loads of it." I pull away and utter, "Thanks for the ride. I really need to get a car."

He looks over at me, eyes searching my face. He frowns a little. "You look a little off today. Everything okay?"

James. He doesn't skip a beat. I open the container of muffins and break one in half. Nibbling at one half, I shrug. "I don't know. I mean, I thought I was fine...until last night. I think," I sigh, "this is going to sounds stupid, but I think..." *God, I'm such a loser.* "...I think I'm lonely."

As we stop at a traffic light, James turns to me. Without asking, he takes a muffin out of the container and bites into it. His eyes glaze over. "Man, that's good." He makes another noise of pleasure before stating, "That's not unusual. Remember, I told you I moved here myself?" I nod. The traffic lights change and he looks to the road before adding, "Same thing happened to me. It's a mixture of things though, isn't it? It's being homesick and away from your friends. It's not being able to step outside and visit people, because you barely know anyone. It's being single too, right?"

My eyes widen. "Wow. You really do know what I'm talking about."

His lips thin. "Yep, I do. I never told you this, but I wouldn't have stayed long if my mom and brother hadn't moved down here. It's hard being away from people you love. Luckily, you've got your sister and her extended family here. Can I ask you something?"

Looking over at him, I tell him, "You can ask me anything." And I mean it.

"Why are you single?"

It takes me a moment to answer, because regardless of how many times I've justified staying out of a relationship, putting it into words is always harder. "When I love someone, I love them with everything I have inside of me. And when I love someone, I put their needs above my own." I look at the road ahead. My chest pangs as I explain, "I can't afford to do that. I worked so hard to get here, James. I remember while all my friends were going out, I was home studying my ass off. While my sisters were celebrating the end of the year with drinks and clubs, I was home studying my ass off. When people were meeting the people they would spend the rest of their lives with, I was home studying my ass off." I take in a deep breath and add on an exhale, "I won't give up what I'm doing, not for anyone. *That's* why I'm single."

"Sounds like a lonely life," he mutters sadly.

Leaning my head against the window, I whisper, "It is, James. It really is."

We drive on in silence, and I'm thankful for it.

MAX

"What's going on with you and Helena?" Ash asks as he walks into the chill out room.

I tilt my head and think about this for a moment before I state with a nod, "I like her."

Ash pulls out a chair and turns it around before sitting on it and rolling his eyes. "You *like* yogurt. You don't *like* Helena."

I look down at my now-empty container of yogurt on the table. I smile in agreement. "I do like yogurt."

"He does," Trick cuts in from reading the paper on the sofa. I turn to find him smiling up at Ash like a fool. "He likes yogurt."

My body shakes in silent laughter. Ash shakes his head in frustration. "Whatever." He looks me in the eye. "Stay away from her."

I lift my hands in the air. "I can't do that, Ghost."

His jaw tics. "What do you mean, you can't? You can, and you will, if you like your teeth."

Standing, I pick up my empty container and dump it in the trash. "Seriously, dude, I can't. She's agreed to private sessions with Ceecee." I shrug. "No can do."

His eyes turn deadly. "Keep your hands off her."

I tilt my head and think about this a moment before answering, "No."

I walk out the door as he calls out in disbelief, "What did you say?"

Smirking, and knowing it's killing him inside, I call back, "I said no." I walk down to my office, chuckling all the way.

Suck on them apples, *Asher*.

Helena

"So when I told him we wouldn't be having relations anymore until he left his wife, he got all kinds of pissed with me. What? Like I'm the asshole, because I want to be some guy's everything? *Puh-leeze,*" mutters Felicity.

Holy shitballs, this girl is my hero. She knows what she wants, and she makes no excuses about what she's got to do to get it. Her life is a *D*-grade soap opera. Mouth gaping, I nudge her hand. "Then what happened?"

Her eyes round comically. She blinks prettily. "*Somehow,* his wife found about his sleazy ways. She got photos in the mail. Anonymously, of course." She closely examines her nails, then murmurs, "I mean, the tall blonde just happened to be blurred out, but she got the picture loud and clear. Pun intended." She winks. "His orgasm face is so ugly he couldn't be confused for anyone else."

A choked sound escapes me. Laughter bubbles up my throat 'til it bursts out of me, loud and uninhibited. Patrons of the café turn around to stare at me, and normally, I'd care, but this is just too funny for me to give half a damn. Wiping at stray tears that roll down my cheeks, I tell Felicity, "You're amazing, you know that? And to think I thought you were some du—"

Warning! Warning! Foot meeting mouth at rapid speed!

Felicity narrows her eyes at me. "Some *what*?"

Uh oh. I have no doubt in my mind that Felicity could beat the ever-loving crap out of me if she needed to. But she is my friend, and friends tell each other the truth. Wincing, I mumble, "Might've thought you were a bit of a bimbo. Sorry, babe."

Tipping her head back, she laughs at my obvious discomfort. "Oh, man, the look on your face. I know what I look like, Lena," she thickens her New York accent dramatically, flicks her bleached-blonde hair, and puts on her best duck-face impression, "but I'm glad ya realized I ain't got shit for brains."

Smiling, I tell her honestly, "You're one of the most kickass women I know, Flick."

She bunches her nose. "Nawww, I love you, too...*cupcake*."

My body stills as my eyes widen. Leaning over to her, I hiss, "Where did you hear that?"

She grins. "I might've heard Max say it to you." My head lands on the table with a thud and she chuckles. "Why does he call you that anyways?"

I lift my head from the table and mumble, "He says I smell like cupcakes."

Her face softens. She lifts a hand to her chest and sighs. "Wow. That is so adorably Max."

I mutter a disgruntled, "I know."

She grins. "I gotta tell ya; I tried to catch that man." My eyes widen. *Really?* She shakes her head sadly. "He did not want to be caught. Such a shame."

I blink at her shoulder and murmur, "Oh, yeah, such a shame."

She lifts her glass and sips at her ice water. "So how long you been crushing on him?"

Lifting my own glass to my lips, I pause midway. "What?"

"Max," she prompts, "how long you been gaga for him?"

I could lie. I could tell her I don't like him. That I never noticed his strong jaw and golden eyes, or his magic dimple. But I cave. Sipping my iced tea, I confess, "For forever. The first time I met him at Tina's wedding, I thought I'd died and gone to heaven." A soft sigh escapes me. "We were introduced and I stuck out my hand." A small smile tips my lips. "He looked down at my outstretched hand and shoved it aside. He swept me up in a bear hug and swung me from side to side. I remember breathing in his scent. It wasn't even cologne. It was just *him*. When he set me down, he kissed my cheek and told me I looked beautiful."

I breathe, "I honestly thought I had fallen in love. I thought I had met the man of my dreams." I straighten as my smile falls. "But then I saw him do the same thing when he met my older sister, Nina, and it didn't feel so special anymore. Plus, I threw myself at him at Nat's wedding." I smile sadly and shrug. "He didn't even look up from his phone. He dismissed me, and to top it off, he called me Helen."

Felicity winces. "Ouch."

I use my straw to mix my drink. "He didn't even see me."

"Well, then," a slow smile spreads across Felicity's face, "we'll just have to open his eyes."

Say what now?

"Oh no. Whatever you're thinking, you can just stop it, girl. Max and I will never be a thing. I'm good with that. I've come to terms with it. Don't you be getting involved. We don't need interference, thank you very much." I end on a regal nod.

But her smile turns into a grin. "Who said anything about interfering? I was thinking more of showing him what's been in his face the entire time."

I grunt and roll my eyes. "He doesn't care. That's the point. He doesn't want me, Flick."

Her smile doesn't falter as she utters, "We'll see about that."

If the sinking feeling in my gut is anything to go by, I'm in serious trouble.

CHAPTER TWENTY-THREE

Helena

"Okay," I huff and puff alongside Ceecee, "tug-of-war is a hardcore workout." Wiping sweat from my brow, I mutter, "We'll only do it every now and again."

Ceecee slumps in her chair, equally as sweaty as I am. "I thought you said we were doing light sessions?"

I place my fingers on my pulse to measure out my heart rate and pant, "This *was* light."

She mock-sobs. "I feel like I'm dying."

How adorable is this child? A laugh is forced from my throat as I throw her a towel and hand her a bottle of water. "You know why it feels like you're dying, young grasshopper?"

Opening her water, she mumbles an annoyed, "Why?"

Needing to make a point, I kneel in front of her, hold out my hands, and near-yell, "*Because you stopped exercising!*" As she pouts, I explain, "Your body is in shock right now, because you haven't done this for months. Do you remember how you used to feel after you exercised? I'll bet you barely broke a sweat."

Looking at my face, she eyes my sweatiness and retorts, "Oh, yeah? What's your excuse?"

Secretly loving the smartass side of her, I don't skip a beat. "A love of cupcakes and a sofa that is way too comfy for my own good." Standing, I smile down at her and hold out my hand. She slaps her hand over mine in a weak high-five and I gloat, "I'm proud of you. You pushed yourself today. I saw it. I *felt* it. You're ready to get back into this." As we walk side-by-side, I warn her, "Just so you know, you're going to be sore tomorrow." She groans, but I speak over her, "Which is why we're doing another session tomorrow. Lighter than today, but we have to push past that barrier." She looks up at me like I have to be joking, but I shake my head. "Sorry, angel face. You can give me those pretty eyes as much as you like, but this is happening. We made a deal."

She wheels herself along and mutters under her breath, "Is it too late to take it back?"

Smiling, I wrap an arm around her shoulders and pull her close. "Sure is, honey pie. We're in this for the long haul."

I am.

I definitely am.

Helena

I knew I was in trouble the second Felicity invited herself over to my place to get ready for our Saturday night out. So when she showed up with a suitcase, I probably shouldn't have been surprised.

I mean, I was. But I shouldn't have been.

With Tedwood attacking my ankle, I held the door open for her. As she made her way in, she looked around my apartment and whistled long and low. "Shit. You've been holding out on me, girl. I didn't know you had money."

Looking around my apartment in confusion, I asked, "I'm broke as a joke. Why the heck would you think I've got money?"

Eyes narrowed, she asked, "How'd you get this place?"

"My sister and her husband own the building."

An *ah-now-I-get-it* expression hits her face. Eyeing my bookcase, she asked cautiously, "How much are you paying rent?"

I shrugged. "A thousand a month."

She gasped. "Seriously?" I could only stare blankly at her. She shook her head in disbelief and uttered, "You have no idea how much rent is in this city, do you, cupcake?"

My throat thickened. Oh no. What had Nat and Ash done now? No louder than a whisper, I asked, wide-eyed, "How much?"

Her lip tilted up in the corner as she thought about it. "For a decent place like this, I'd say between two and a half to three grand a month. Maybe even more with the tight security."

No shit.

I whispered, *"No shit."*

She nudged my shoulder with her arm and smiled down at me. "You're lucky to have a family who loves you so much."

Still shaken by the onslaught of information, I muttered to nobody in particular, "I'm beginning to see that."

Nat had called me in emotional hysterics the day she and Ash had accidentally slept in, not being able to take me to work. The devious part of my mind told me to milk it for all it was worth, to lay on a guilt trip so thick that Nat would forever do what I asked. But then I realized that not only during my time here had she been wonderful, supportive, and loving, but that she and Ash had undergone serious changes in their lives without complaint. I soon remembered I would forever be in their debt for making my transition to New York as painless as it could be.

Also, I loved them.

James had happily accepted the duty of taking me to work and home again, if it wasn't too weird for me—his words. I was totally okay with this. Not only did it mean my sister and her husband would be able to sleep in, taking some of my guilt away, but I would be able to spend a little time with James, one-on-one. Nat wasn't too sure about that. I argued I needed to make friends here. She returned that the only friend I needed was her. The turd. To my utter shock, it was Ash who had talked Nat into letting this happen. He told Nat it was natural to feel protective of me, but James seemed like 'an okay guy'.

I could've kissed him then.

Okay, okay. I did kiss him. A big fat smooch he had no chance in hell of escaping, right on the lips. He screwed up his face and cringed. I winked and blew him another kiss. He rolled his eyes at me, but I felt the love. So I guess it shouldn't have shocked me that Ash would give me a bogus rent figure. But I was kind of pissed about it. More sore about it than pissed, I guess.

Covering my face with my hands, I groaned out loud. "Oh God, is that what I am? The *poor* sister? Ugh. That sucks assholes."

Felicity just laughed. "Don't sweat it. I'm sure they're going to ask you to babysit when they have kids, and they'll do it knowing you can't say no."

I sobered in an instant. "Wow, do you *know* my sister? Because I think you spiritually channeled her there for a second." Staring down at her offending suitcase, I ask carefully, "So, what you got in there? A severed head?"

Smiling like the Cheshire cat, she simply raised her brows, knelt down, and unzipped the bag. She peeled back the lid to unveil a portable salon. "I told you we'd make Max see you, didn't I? I'm making good on that."

Already shaking my head, I objected. Strongly. "No, no, no, no, no. N-O. *No*."

Felicity smiled at me. Her bazillion dollar grin. And a smiling Felicity was something to be reckoned with. She was so damn pretty I felt I would change teams for her. "Listen, I'm not asking you to do anything you're uncomfortable with, just to let me do your makeup and dress you tonight, is all. How bad could that be? You won't even have to pick your underwear. I'll make it easy for you."

I could see there was no fighting this. She had that look in her eyes. I let out a long, agonizing breath. "No short skirts. No short shorts. Nothing that'll show my legs."

A confused look crossed her face. She looked down at my uncovered legs and bunched her nose. "Why the hell not? You've got killer legs. I mean, they're not tall, but they're shapely and firm." She reached down to pinch the skin of my thigh, unable to get a grip. "They're tight, bitch. What gives?"

How to explain without sounding nuts? "Okay. This was the way it worked back home. Nina showed leg. Nat showed leg *and* boob. I, however, only showed a bit of cleavage. I never really liked my legs, but I like my rack. Not wanting to show too much, I always chose to expose rack, rather than leg. *Capisce*?"

She looked at me dumbfounded for half a minute before gaping. "You're dumb as shit, baby. You're lucky you're cute to boot." With that sentence, she showed me why I liked her. She reminded me of the relationship I have with my sisters. I loved that.

Saying that, we barely agreed on clothing. We almost got into fisticuffs over it. Finally, I decided on a multicolored green leaf-print chiffon number. The dress was long, but draped and sheer, requiring a miniskirt underneath, and showing a healthy amount of boobage. After having tried it on and examining it under every possible light source, I deemed it okay. When I gave in, Felicity almost collapsed with gratitude. "Thank fuck for that! Moving on!"

She spent a good part of the next hour doing my hair and makeup, lightly curling my dark hair, leaving it in long tresses down my back, and making my eyes dark-rimmed and smoky.

I had to admit...I liked the way she did it. It looked hot, and that's not a word I would use to describe myself.

We argued *again* over shoes. I didn't like heels, never did. I liked strappy sandals or low-heeled wedges. This was simply a comfort thing. I tried on eight pairs of shoes before Felicity let me off wearing nude strappy sandals. Thank the Lord. With myself done, Felicity got to work on herself. If I hadn't have seen it myself, I wouldn't have believed it. She managed to get herself looking supermodel-runway-ready in forty minutes. And I secretly hated her for it.

She decided on a white button-up dress. Who knew she could make something so wholesome look so sexy. Undoing the top three buttons to let her black bra show, she wrapped a black belt tightly around her waist and slid on a pair of black strappy sandals. Looking down at her shoes, I scowled at her.

She rolled her eyes. "Oh, please. If you were as tall as I am, you'd get it. Try meeting a guy looking like an

Amazon. Guys don't like chicks being taller than them. Sad, but true." Running her fingers through her hair, she put on a ton of mascara and glossed her lips, then folded up the short sleeves of her dress and turned to me, grinning from ear to ear. "We look good, baby, but I swear to God, if Max doesn't notice you tonight, looking the way you do, I'll buy you a dozen of those cupcakes you like in consolation."

Already salivating, I almost yelled, "Deal!"

This was going to be interesting.

Helena

The moment we arrive at The White Rabbit, something feels different. For the first time since I've been in New York, I feel happy to be out amongst the people, without feeling tired. I guess everything was coming together in its own way. And I'm happy for this. Felicity and I stroll up to the entry, where B-Rock, the massive, bald-headed African-American security guard, makes us kiss his head before getting in. He is a sweet guy and tells us his wife, Honey, had just given birth to their fifth child the previous week. He gets double kisses for that.

Felicity and I hold hands as we sweep through the crowd over to the stairs, where a new Alice is manning the out-of-bounds, family-only, VIP area. Having been here a few times before, I know the protocol. Smiling, I start, "Hi. We're on the list. Helena Kovac and friend."

The Alice doesn't lift her eyes to us. With her head down, she checks the list and lets us in without a word spoken. Most people would have thought that bitchy, but I can see immediately the girl is just shy and probably not used to working with people.

We make our way up the stairs, and before I hit the top step, I see them. Nat, Mimi, Lola, and Tina sit on one side of the booth, while Nik and Trick sit on the opposite side. They're all smiling and laughing, already having a good time. I can't help but feel my stomach coil at not seeing Max sitting there. I mean, I know the guy has to work, but I was still hoping to see him. I mentally hang my head in shame.

Okay, okay. I'll be honest. I really just came here to see him. Ugh. I know. *Pathetic.*

I paste on a smile, link my arm through Felicity's, and walk us over to the booth. "Hi, guys," I call as we approach the side. The women turn to me smiling, but quickly gape.

Nat is the first to speak. "Holy shit."

Tina blinks, and then adds, "Yeah, I second that."

Lola whistles. "Damn, Lena."

Mimi ogles me appreciatively. "Oh yeah, I'm liking that dress."

A blush heats my cheeks. I mumble, "Ah, thanks. I don't think you've met Felicity before," then I pull her with a jerk, throwing her in the line of fire. Felicity handles it like a pro, greeting everyone with smiles, handshakes, and compliments on what they're wearing. It's like she was made to be around people.

I slide in next to Nik, and Felicity sits by my side, already talking away at the girls. I hear conversations going on around me, but I don't hear much of anything being said. I'm too busy looking around. Looking for someone.

"He's downstairs, in the security room with Ash," is whispered into my ear.

My cheeks flame. I look up at Nik, and stammer, "I don't know...I mean, I wasn't look—" He raises a brow as he looks down at me, and I know I'm busted. I slump. "Was I that obvious?"

He lowers his voice a notch. "Not to anyone but me. I see all."

I sit and smile with no feeling, pretending to listen to the conversation as I sip my drink. I should get up and dance. I should ask Felicity to dance with me. That's what people do when they go to clubs, don't they? They dance...I think. Nudging Felicity, she takes the hint and steps out of the booth. I tell everyone, "We're going downstairs to dance," but we somehow end up at the bar, talking to Sheriff and downing shots of tequila.

After four shots, I know I'm starting to become intoxicated. How do I know this? Firstly, I'm starting to think everything is hilarious. Secondly, I'm beginning to lose function of my legs. Felicity pulls me to stand. "Come on; let's dance!"

As I stand, I wobble on my feet and we both burst into laughter. Sitting back on my stool, I utter, "I might sit this one out. You go ahead. I'll watch."

Not needing any more prompting, she heads out into the sea of people, and soon enough, she's bumping and grinding with a very attractive guy. And this guy is taller than Flick. Bonus.

Felicity: Would you be totally pissed if I went home with this guy?

I focus hard on my cell's screen before laughing. Finding her in the crowd with my eyes, she pouts, and I respond to her text smiling.

Me: No way! I'll only be pissed if you don't get an orgasm out of it. Have fun!

I look up at her, and the random dude is sucking on her neck. Reading the text I just sent her, she lifts her thumbs high in the air. I blow her a kiss and turn to the bar. Someone occupies the stool next to mine, but I don't look over. I yell out over the music, "Sheriff, I need another shot over here."

But the person next to me reaches over the bar and gets two shot glasses and a bottle of tequila. He places a shot glass down in front of me and I gape. "I don't think you're allowed to do that," I tell him.

I look up, and smiling, golden eyes meet mine. "Sure I can."

And my heart swells. Smiling like a loon, I lean forward and wrap my arms around his neck, squeezing him to me. "Max! I was just thinking about you! I missed you!"

I feel his body still. "You missed me?"

"Duh!" *Oh, man, I must be completely hammered.* "I've been looking for you!" *Make that obliterated.*

His arms wrap around me. He gives me a gentle squeeze before releasing me. His golden eyes look down into mine as he says in all seriousness, "I've been looking for you too."

Not quite wanting to let go of him, I place my hand on his thigh and smile up at him. "I dressed up." I thank the gods above for leaving out 'for you'.

His eyes sweep my see-through dress and flash a moment before they hood. He mutters hoarsely, "I can see that. You're stunning."

That's about the time I ramble. "My friend Felicity helped me. I don't really like all the girly things. I mean, you've seen my undies. I don't really know how to make myself appealing to the opposite sex. I must've missed that class."

Max makes a choked sound before downing his shot, then my own. Coughing, he wheezes, "You're looking for a man tonight?"

My mind suddenly sobers. I smile softly, but it's forced. "Sure. I mean, I'm only human, right? I have needs like anyone else."

He eyes me good before saying, "You want to know how to be appealing to the opposite sex, Lena?" My eyes widen. Max is about to impart his wisdom on me. He'll give me the key to his heart. I need to listen, and listen I will! Lifting a hand, he gently pushes stray hairs away from my face, lowers his lips to the shell of my ear, and whispers, "Just breathe, baby."

My breath leaves me in a whoosh. Then I say the stupidest thing I could ever say right now, "Please kiss me."

CHAPTER TWENTY-FOUR

Helena

"Please," I beg through a shaky breath. "Please kiss me."

Max groans, running a hand down his face. "C'mon, sweetheart. You don't even like me. Now I know you're drunk."

Reaching up, I take his hands down from his face and hold them tightly. "I'm not drunk." But he eyes me in a way that I know he knows I've been drinking, so I adjust my last statement. "I'm not *that* drunk. I'm tipsy at most. I'm Croatian, dude. It'll take a lot of booze to take me down."

He hesitates, but right now, I'm willing to do anything to have those lips on mine. Anything. Even play dirty. I play with his fingers and look down at his manly hands. They're nice hands. "Do you know the last time I was with a guy was four years ago? Seriously, Max. *Four years ago*! And it's building up inside of me, you know, that feeling? I just...I just really want to feel that again." I fight a sigh. "I sound like a crazy person, don't I?"

When I lift my face, we're nose to nose. His eyes search mine a long moment before he gently presses his lips to mine. My stomach dips. He keeps his eyes on mine, watching for my reaction. The kiss lasts a few seconds and it's nice, but as he pulls away, I feel myself pout.

That was it?

Lifting his hand, he runs his thumb over my bottom lip and utters, "Okay?" Blinking, speech evades me. I simply nod. His gaze moves down to my lips, and without meaning to, they part slightly. Max closes his eyes tightly and mutters, "I'm trying to be good here, Lena. Stop doing that."

I'm confused. "Doing what?"

Lifting his hand, he pinches the bridge of his nose. "Stop being sexy."

And my vagina floods.

When I discreetly press my thighs together, Max spots it. His eyes flash. "Fuck. Now you've done it." His warm lips connect with mine, harder than before. One arm goes around me while the other hand fists in my hair. And it *hurts*. I whimper. Oh, God, it hurts so *good*. It's like he knows exactly what I need.

My eyes close. I moan into his mouth. I pull away only a second to pant, "More." My hands roam his broad chest a moment before he slips his cool tongue into my mouth. He tastes like icy, sweet mint. In a moment of sheer bliss, I gasp into him and clutch his shirt.

Tilting his head to the side, he deepens the kiss, pulling me impossibly close. His lips leave mine. He pecks kisses onto my lips before trailing down my jaw, further down my throat, kissing a line down to the valley between my breasts.

My nipples become taut; I feel them rubbing through the sheer material of my dress. Damn. I can't stop. I want this too much. Lowering my head, I place my lips by his ear and whisper, "Take me somewhere."

His lips still and he pulls away, covering his eyes with his hands, almost looking ashamed. "You got me fucked up." Only loud enough for me to hear, he mutters through a sigh, "You got me seriously fucked up, cupcake."

He moves to stand, but I snag his wrist and ask in shock, "Wh-where are you going?"

Avoiding my gaze, he places his hands in his pockets and looks down to the floor. Taking in a deep breath, he responds on an exhale, "You don't want me. Don't worry; I'm not judging. I get it. You miss it." He puffs out a long breath. "I do too." Looking pained, he closes his eyes. "And looking like you do, smelling like you do, with my cock aching just from you standing a foot away from me, it's hard to turn you down." He steps away from me, adding, "But you deserve better." He turns and walks away from me.

Oh, hell no.

I might have put up with this once, but I am not putting up with it again. I stand so hard that my stool wobbles as I stomp after him. Gaining on him, I reach his side and grab hold of his arm. He looks down at me in confusion, but I cut him off, pissed as hell. "Don't you do that. Don't you tell me you think you know what's best for me." Going out on a limb here, I pause, and then ask cautiously, "Do you want me?"

He shakes his head. "That's not the point."

My heart aches. "That is exactly the point. Tell me. Do you want me or not?" Because if he doesn't, I'll walk away and pretend none of this ever happened. I'll do what I can to maintain a relationship with Ceecee and help her whenever she needs. Max and I will go back to being friends.

He steps closer to me, his hand cupping my waist. "I want you. I want you more than anyone I've ever wanted in my life."

I can't believe this. Did he really just say that? Oh lawdy lawd, he *did*. What am I meant to do with this? Slowly, so as not to spook him, I wrap my arms around his neck and pull his face down to mine. A hair's breadth away from his lips, I utter, "Then take me home."

Reaching up, he takes my hands and lowers them. "I can't give you anything. I don't want a relationship, Lena."

And angels sing in my ear. I smile from ear to ear, and then chuckle. "Me either."

His brows furrow. "What? I'm not kidding, cupcake. I don't want a relationship."

My hands clap together in front of my chest, and I murmur, "Dear God, you're perfect." Grinning, I tell him, "Same here. I don't want a relationship. I worked my ass off to get where I am. I don't need a man to make my life complete. I just want to have some fun."

He straightens, thinking about what I've just said. He points to me. "Then what exactly would this be?"

I shrug. "No strings. Friendship. Sex. Affection. Whatever."

His eyes widen marginally. "That sounds pretty good, actually." But his face falls. "What about Ceecee?"

"I love Ceecee. I'll continue to work out with her, and I'll make sure she doesn't know about us."

He scratches at the back of his head. "I don't keep things from my daughter. I'd have to tell her."

Huh? "Tell her what, Max?" I lean forward and whisper loudly, "That we're *fucking*?"

His face turns serious. "No, but I'd have to tell her I like you and that we're more than friends. I'd tell her you're my girlfriend, for as long as we want to do this. Then, when you get sick of me, I'll just tell her we broke up."

His *girlfriend*? My heart starts to palpitate. I swallow hard. "But we'd just be friends that are bumping uglies, right? I wouldn't *actually* be your girlfriend. Right?"

"I don't share you. If you want to sleep with someone else, this all stops, yeah?"

My nose bunches. "I wasn't planning on sleeping with anyone else, Max."

A small smirk appears on his face. "Friends that share affection and sleep together. I think that would make you my girlfriend, baby."

My stomach and heart flutter in unison. I like that he called me baby. Maybe it wouldn't be so bad if he called me his girlfriend. Even though I know this term is a fabrication of what would really be happening. "What would we tell everyone else?" I ask quietly.

He wraps his arms around my waist, pulling me into his torso. "Exactly what we tell Ceecee." He leans down to peck at my lips. "I won't keep you a secret, Lena."

I look off into the distance, mind working a mile a minute. "I'd have to tell James then. He might tell me I can't work with Ceecee anymore. Now it's a definite conflict of interest."

"Let me talk to him. I'll take you home tonight, sleep at yours, and then we'll tell Ceecee tomorrow over breakfast, yeah?"

Oh, my God. This is really happening.

"Okay." I smile up at him. "Yeah, okay. So we're really doing this?"

His nose touches the tip of mine then captures my lips in a sweet but firm kiss, leaving me breathless. He pulls away and my eyelids flutter as he utters through a smile, "Fuck yeah. We're doing this."

The kissing started as soon as we got out of the car. I threw my door open, stepped out, and went to rush up the stairs to my apartment, but Max showed me he had other plans. As soon as my feet hit the sidewalk, arms circle my waist from behind, holding my body still. I turn in his arms, and as soon as I see his smiling eyes, I melt. It's not fair for someone to be that good looking. It just isn't.

"Hey," he mutters.

I smile. How can I not? "Hi." He pulls me close, cupping my cheek as his lips hit mine. I grip his sides tightly, trying my hardest not to fall over, although I'm sure he would catch me. He kisses my mouth then runs his lips over my bottom one, nipping then soothing the sting with gentle, warm pecks. My heart aches from the tenderness his mouth rains upon mine. The leisurely kiss is intoxicating. Soon, I feel light and happy knowing we'll be in my apartment tearing clothes from each other.

My vagina twerks in approval.

Against my lips, he mutters, "I don't think we should have sex tonight."

Shock hums through my body, killing my buzz. My jaw drops and I ask on a whisper, "*What*?"

Lifting a hand, he searches my face and tugs at the ends of my hair. "Listen, you've been drinking, and I need to be sure you want this as much as I do, or we're gonna have problems."

Oh, brother.

The alcohol in my body hangs its head in shame while my mind shakes its head at it, and my vagina puts its hands on its hips and glares at it.

I reach up and grip the lapels of his shirt, smiling hard. "I'm fine. I swear." My smile falls. "Please don't withhold sex from me." I laugh nervously. "It's been too long and I might just go crazy."

His lips hit my forehead. His breath warms me as he speaks softly, "What's another day on four years?"

He has a point. I guess. But I pout and whine, "But I want sex *now*."

Reaching behind me, his large hands grip my ass. *Hello!* He pulls me into his body and my stomach dips violently as something hot, thick, and hard pushes into the softness of my belly. He replies hoarsely, "Me too. And I want it bad, but I want to wait. Just until tomorrow."

His hands grip my behind harder. His eyes close as he pushes deeper into my belly. With a pained groan, he pulls away, and I bite my lip to stop my smile. It pleases me knowing I'm not the only one suffering. And because I'm as classy as an elephant in a tutu, I look right down at his erection and gasp, "Oh my," while touching my fingertips to my mouth. If the outline of his bulge is anything to go by, I'm going to be very sore tomorrow night. And I'm so looking forward to it.

Holla!

Not taking my eyes off the groin of his jeans, I sigh. "Okay. We'll wait."

Holding his hand out to me, I take it and bask in the warmth of his body. He entwines our fingers and we walk to my apartment in comfortable silence. Somewhere between there and here, it hits me. I'm standing in front of my apartment, hand-in-hand with the guy I've been crushing on, and he wants me as much as I want him. Happiness warms me. I let out a content sigh. I don't feel lonely anymore.

Taking my key, I unlock my apartment and open the door. The second I walk in, Tedwood lunges for me. At the last second, he notices I have company, and instead of latching onto my leg, he flies past it, purring and rubbing himself up against Max's calf.

The little worm!

Anger bubbles through me. Without thinking, I kneel down then lower my face to the small cat's, point at his nose, and whisper, "I know what you're doing...and I don't like it."

Blinking up at me, Teddy steps forward and licks the tip of my finger. Anyone else would see this as a sweet gesture. They would *oooh* and *aaah* and tell me how sweet my little kitty is. But I know what this is.

This is Tedwood mocking me. I'm being mocked by a freaking kitten.

I stand, remove my shoes, and throw out my hand while walking into the kitchen. "That's Tedwood. Teddy for short. He hates me, but pretends he likes me when I have company. He likes to mock me by letting me pat him for approximately four pats and not a pat more, or he turns my hand into minced meat. He also shows his love by shredding my clothes. Oh, and yesterday, he did a giant cat turd in my favorite sneakers."

Filling a glass with water, I sip from it and watch as Max picks up Tedwood, holding him in front of his face with a stern glare. "Listen here, little man. You upset your mom, you upset me. So if I were you, I'd stop with the stooge antics, all right?"

He takes his finger and scratches behind his ear. Holding Teddy under his arm, he smiles over at me. "There. You have any more issues, you let me know. I'll put him in line."

My heart smiles. Sweet, silly Max. Max walks over to where I am and takes the glass of water from my hands, taking a big gulp. "So are you just gonna stand there stroking my pussy all night?"

Water sprays all over the counter, and I smirk as Max coughs and sputters, "Jesus, cupcake." He coughs some more. "You're killin' me."

I plant my palm on his chest and taunt him with a grin. "Your rule, not mine, remember?" He places Teddy on the counter, looks over at me with a sly smile, and then reaches down, grips the bottom of his shirt, and pulls it right up, over his head. I take a step away and gulp. "You said no sex."

Reaching for me, he pulls the thin string around my waist and my dress loosens. "I said no sex. I didn't say I wouldn't be touching you tonight."

My dress falls off one shoulder, revealing my black lace bra. Another step back, and the other shoulder falls, the dress pooling at my feet, leaving me in my bra, a black mini skirt, and my tan sandals. Thank God almighty for the low lighting. You can't hide from much, dressed like this.

Max takes a step toward me and I take him in. His lean, muscular body taunts me. My soft belly protrudes a little, and I lift my hand to cover it. He shakes his head. "Don't do that. I want to see you. I've imagined this a thousand times, so really, it's nothing I haven't already seen."

My cheeks heat. "I'm not perfect."

He holds out his arms by his sides. "Neither am I."

Before my mind can think, my mouth opens wide and sings, "Yes, you are." He eyes me. With his hands balled by his sides, I see the veins in his arms bulge. His body tight, his pecks jut and jump about. I could be wrong, but I think I've said something to upset him. I whisper, "What's wrong?"

Jaw steeled, he mutters through gritted teeth, "Just trying not to pull up that tiny skirt and fuck you over the counter, is all."

Sweet lord of mercy. I swallow hard, then stutter, "I-uh...I-I wouldn't mind."

He walks over to me slowly, his eyes never leaving mine. On the way, he undoes his belt, unthreads it, and drops it on the floor. The clank echoes throughout the apartment. He toes off his shoes and socks, leaving a trail of clothing behind him. Then he's dressed only in dark jeans, his torso and feet free.

And it's the sexiest thing I've ever seen in my life.

My heart races and my palms sweat.

The only thing sexier would be if he were wearing his glasses. The mental visual gives me goose bumps. He stops a foot away from me, the moonlight streaking across his face. His golden eyes flash as his eyes trail my exposed body. "You're even more beautiful than I imagined."

My brain sneezes and causes a short somewhere. I blurt out, "I have a fat ass."

His lips twitch and he scratches at his chin. "I gotta be honest here." He takes a small step forward, leaning down until his lips touch the shell of my ear. "Your ass makes me harder than hell, baby." I shudder, and involuntarily, my eyes close. I breathe out a sigh as his hand cups my butt. He squeezes. "This ass." He squeezes harder, borderline painfully. "This ass has kept me awake at night," he sighs then lowers his voice to a whisper, "and I never even missed the sleep."

That. Is. It.

I groan then growl, "*Ugh!* You can't just say things like that, Max!"

His lips tilt up at the side. "Sure I can. I just did."

I roll my eyes. "Not when you're planning to keep your cock in your pants, you're not!"

His hands slide up from my ass to grip my hips. He looks me in the eye and says slowly, meaningfully, "Who said anything about keeping it in my pants?"

And my vagina swoons in a cold, dead faint.

CHAPTER TWENTY-FIVE

MAX

I look down into those gorgeous, bright green eyes and a small part of the bitterness inside of me dies. She doesn't just look at me. She sees more of me than most people, and I don't know why I'm letting that happen.

This is not going to end well. It's not going to end well for *me*.

As she's standing there in nothing but a lacy black bra and a mini skirt that's so mini it's basically microscopic, I grip her hips tightly. If I don't, I'll throw her on the ground, tear her clothes off, and fuck her like an animal. And Helena doesn't deserve that. She's a lady. She deserves something good.

My heart pounds in time with the pulsing of my cock.

I want to give her something good. I want to give her me.

My eyes trail the length of her body and I can't believe how lucky I am. This tiny woman has porcelain smooth skin, long, dark, wavy hair, tits that all but spill out of her bra, a soft belly, tight legs, and an ass any man would be proud to say is his, not to mention her sexy-ass bee-stung lips.

But there's more. There's more, and I don't want to admit it. I'm starting to feel something for her. Something more than friends. And I know if I let this happen, I'm going to pay for it with my heart.

Again.

Helena

Dragging him behind me, I pull him into my bedroom and move to turn on the bedside lamp, bathing the room in soft light. I make my way to the foot of the bed, where I left him standing. When I reach him, I look up at him while my fingers tug at the button of his jeans. It's harder than it looks. I yank at it 'til it decides to cooperate. When it's finally free, I slump in relief. He cups my cheek and I lean into it as I slowly pull on his zipper. And, at long last, he's open to me.

Turning my head, I breathe into his palm, planting a wet kiss right in the center of it. Carefully, I reach inside the open flap of his jeans. My fingers wrap around his boxer-covered length, my core clenches at his sudden intake of breath, and I'm mildly alarmed.

He's got a bratwurst down there.

It's thick and long, and burning up. I want to feel skin-on-skin, but I know I need to make this last. My fingers tighten around him and move up and down slowly. Up and down, pulling and squeezing as I do. His hand still at my cheek, I turn, part my lips, and take his thumb into my mouth all the way, sucking in time with my tugs. A low groan is torn from him, and by the sound of it, he's in pain.

"Sit." This comes out so huskily it doesn't even sound like me. He does what I ask, sitting on the edge of the bed, and I have yet to remove my hand from him, fearing if I do, he'll change his mind.

Stupid moral man!

As soon as he's seated, I release my hold on him, reach up, and pull down his jeans. They come off easily. I don't remove the boxers. They're black and silky, and he looks amazing in them. With his back to the lamp, the front of his body is shadowed. I kneel in front of him, undo the button on the front of his boxers, and look into his eyes. "I've missed this," I whisper. Reaching inside the slit, I take hold of his hot, hard length and he hisses. Rather than shy away, I grip him tighter and pull him through the opening.

All I can do is blink.

It's magnificent. The skin feels soft, but in the dim light, I see his cock and swallow hard. It's angry looking. The length is rock-hard, veined, and the tip is red. A single pearl of precum spills out from his slit. I repeat myself, quieter this time, "I've missed this." Then, I lower my head and gently lick up the stray drop. The sweet saltiness hits me like a shot of adrenalin. I open my mouth as wide as I can and take him into my mouth.

I moan around him. He groans in unison. We're a symphony of sex, and it's making me hotter than hell. I suck him as deep as I can, then slide back up to the tip. The next time I suck him in, I hollow my cheeks. His growl fuels me. "Fuck, baby. That's it. Suck me hard."

Running my hands up his thighs, I scratch them lightly on the way down as I bob my head, reveling in the clean taste of him. Suddenly, I'm knocked back as he stands, quick as lightning. Sitting flat on my ass, I blink up at him, and then glower, "What the fuckity fuck?"

Eyes closed, teeth gritted, squeezing his cock tighter than I've ever seen a man squeeze one before, he mutters, "Shut up. Shut up. Shut up. Please, shut up."

Oh.

It hits me.

He's going to come.

My pride smiles and puffs out its chest while strutting around like a peacock. Panting, he squeezes himself tighter, groans, and then tips his head back, mumbling, "Sorry, baby. Gonna come. Shit. Sorry."

He drops his head, eyes apologetic. I quickly move to kneel in front of him once more. There's no need to explain my intentions when I reach up to pull down the cups of my bra, exposing my breasts. Biting my lip, my fingertips glide over the smooth skin of one breast while I tweak the nipple of the other. I watch through hooded eyes as his taut stomach contracts as he tries to remain in control. Suddenly, his gorgeous face turns blissful. He replaces the firm hold on his cock with a looser grip. His lips part, his breathing heavies, and his entire body stills and then shakes as a low growl escapes him.

Wet warmth hits my chest. Once, twice, three then four times. The wetness slides down, over my breasts, in-between my breasts, over one nipple. My pussy convulses. I'm deliciously wet.

Shit.

I'm already there.

As in *there*.

My spine tingles and I clamp my legs together as my mouth rounds in an *O*.

Max starts, "Shit, I'm so sorry, Lena. I—" When he spots my expression, he stills. "What's happening here?"

My eyes roll into the back of my head as pleasure gently pulses through me. "Shut up. Shut up. Shut up. *Please,* shut up."

Eyes closed, I feel him step closer to me. "Are you—?"

Gritting my teeth, I hiss out, "Yes," as I reach down to cup myself. I breathe out, "Oh shit. No. This wasn't meant to happen."

Hands under my arms lift me onto my bed. As soon as my back hits the bed, a large, hard body covers me. He reaches down and lifts my skirt around my waist. In record time, he pulls my panties down my legs 'til I'm free. Roughly, he grips my legs and parts them, lying between them and placing the tip of his cock at my bud of happiness. He rocks against me and sparks fly. "Damn. You're so wet. I got you, baby. Let go."

My breath hitches. I grip his waist so hard that my nails mark him. I wrap my legs around his thighs and grind against him, hard and uninhibited. Chest to cum-covered chest, there is apparently no place for inhibitions in my bedroom right now. My soft breasts pressing against his broad chest does something to me. I whimper. Taking my lead, he watches me closely through hooded eyes, but thrusts against me faster and firmer. Every time his hot, hard length slides over me, my clit sings.

It takes thirty seconds for him to take me there.

Thirty *life-altering* seconds.

My lower back prickles as my core begins to pulse. Max lowers himself to take my mouth in a demanding kiss, and I moan into it. Reaching up, I wrap my arms around his neck, deepening the kiss. His tongue dances with mine. Ecstasy pours through my body. Heart racing, I clamp my legs around him, tilt my head back, and cry out, "Oh, God. *Yes!*" My body jerks uncontrollably, and fifteen seconds later, it's over.

Something wet on my lower stomach drips down my hip, onto my bed. Max pants at my cheek. It takes me a minute to get my shit together. I open my eyes to find Max looking down at me, eyes smiling. I can't help it. I cover my eyes with a hand and burst into laughter. "Well, that kinda sucked." I remove my hand to find him grinning down at me, dimple out for the world to see. Without thinking, I reach up and poke it gently. "I like this."

"I like you."

I trail my fingertip from his jaw, down to the slight dip in his chin. "You're just saying that because you came." I look down at the wetness on my stomach, and then back up at him. "Twice."

He just continues to grin. "I'm not even sorry."

"Not even a little?"

He pecks my lips and the light look in his eyes turns intense. "Not even a little." Flipping onto his back, his cock still out, he pulls me into his side, bare-assed. "Wow. Dry humping. I don't think I've had that much fun since I was sixteen."

I cuddle into him, my nose wedged under his jaw, breathing in his woodsy scent. "It was ridiculous. Although I'm feeling pretty good right now. How about you?"

"Phenomenal." And I feel the vibrations through his chest.

"Then that's all that matters." My eyes feel heavy. "We should probably shower."

Sounding as sleepy as I am, he pulls me closer and utters drowsily, "Yeah. Shower. Sure."

And that's the last thing I hear before everything fades to black.

The sound of the front door closing wakes me. Blinking sleepily, I sit up to glance over at the clock. It reads ten past seven in the morning. Looking down at the empty space next to me, my heart heavies. It looks like sleeping next to Max is too much for him. I should've known he isn't as into me as I am with him. It's the story of my life, really.

First, there was my first high school boyfriend, Jonathon. I was sixteen. He dated me for three weeks, stealing my first kiss then asking me if I thought my sister, Nat, was into him. When I told her about it, she showed him just how much she liked him. The next day at school, she told everyone he had a teenie weenie winkie. His new nickname from that day on was Midget Digit.

Then, there was Denver. Yes, his name was Denver. My mind chuckles, sighs, and then shakes its head. Just from his name, I should've known he was a douche nugget. We dated senior year for a whole eight months. I was just about to turn eighteen. He did all the right things, said all the right things, he was on the basketball team, and was tall.

I like tall guys, so sue me.

After six months of dating, and five months of being discreetly—or not so discreetly—pressured, I gave it up to him. He was my first. He told me I ruined it, because I cried. But the thing was, it *hurt*, and he did nothing to prepare me for that. I know we were young, but he knew better; he was just a selfish lover. I figured maybe he was just excited and forgot to warm me up...but with two more months of this, I went to talk to my sisters. Something just didn't feel right.

My sisters were appalled that I put up with this for a whole two months. They told me about the female orgasm and about how real men treat a woman with care. Nina bought me my first vibrator. She told me to practice masturbating with and without it. She told me my hands are a major factor in sex. This was weird, but I trusted my sisters more than anyone.

My first orgasm happened with a vibrator, and it was so intense that it felt like I was being electrically shocked. Hell, it probably *looked* like I was being shocked. I also threw the vibrator mid-orgasm against the wall. Hard.

When Nina and Nat asked me how it went, I blushed, showed them the now-broken vibrator, and had to listen as they cried from laughter. I covered my face to hide my smile. Damn them. Nat explained through her laughter, "You don't have to have it on high, Lena. There are different settings. Try somewhere in the middle next time. We'll get you another, Bazooka Jane."

The next night, I tried with just my hand. But it was completely frustrating. I didn't do it long before I stopped. I was rubbing myself raw. I definitely wasn't turned on. I didn't know what I was doing wrong. So I went to my sisters for guidance. The answer was simple, yet so effective.

Nina shrugged. "I usually just think about someone hot doing things to me." She turned to Nat. "What about you?"

Nat smirked. "Playgirl magazine. Under my mattress. Works every time." Nat offered to lend me her magazine, but I shuddered. The same hands she used to pleasure herself were used to handle that magazine. So my sisters put me to task. We went down to our local newsstand. They made me, an eighteen-year-old girl, go and ask Giuseppe, a vendor I have known all my damn life, for the latest issue of Playgirl magazine.

Thankfully, the elderly vendor didn't even flinch. Although, Nat and Nina stood behind me snickering.

With a shaking hand, I held out the money. He took it with a smile before handing it to me. Just as I was walking away, he called out to me. We all turned to see him coming toward me with a brown paper bag. Slumping in relief, I hid my shameful whore magazine in the depths of that bag and thanked him again.

That night, I tried again, using my reinforcements. It happened. It took longer and it wasn't as intense, but it happened. And, boy, was I proud! I told my sisters and we high-fived after, of course, Nat asked me ten times if I had washed my hands. The asshole.

That was when my sisters told me to start implicating what I had learned into the not-so-great sex I was having with Denver. I wasn't sure about this. I knew Denver well enough to know he didn't like change, but I figured if I were the one making the change while he was able to continue doing his own thing, it wouldn't be an issue.

I was wrong.

It was the following Friday night when Denver and I were able to have some alone time. His parents were going to be at a neighbor's house for a barbecue, and these were normally adult-only events that ran late into the night. We'd have the entire night to ourselves.

Denver was a sweet guy. He could be oblivious, but he treated me well and showered me with affection. The only issue in our relationship was the sex. We made it to his bed, undressed, and started fooling around. When he finally was inside of me, I hesitated, but decided to go for it. My hand slid down my breast to my belly, lower to where I needed it, and Denver stopped thrusting. "What are you doing?"

I whispered, "Keep going. It's okay; just keep going."

But he didn't keep going. "Where did you learn that?"

I tried to reassure him once more. "Please, honey. Keep going."

That's when I felt him deflate inside of me. My cheeks flushed. This was the *opposite* of what should have happened! Denver stayed quiet for a long time. I didn't know what to do. He was on top of me. I was being held down. Finally, he sat up, releasing me. I covered my bare breasts, feeling suddenly uncomfortable. When he spoke again, fury lined his voice. "I asked you a question, Helena. Where did you learn that?"

I don't know why, but I lied. Panic makes you say and do stupid things. The lie sounded weak, even to me. "I-um...I read it somewhere in a magazine."

He wasn't buying it. Not that I was selling it well. He hissed, "You're cheating on me."

"What?" Then I was really panicked. "No! No, I'm not!"

He stood and paced in front of the bed, naked. "You're lying. You're cheating on me. How else would you know to do that? You'd never been with anyone before me. You're cheating on me." He paused mid-step then turned to me. "And you thought I wouldn't find out." By this point, I was crying my poor little heart out.

He didn't care. He pointed at me, furious. "Get out of my bed. Take your clothes, and get out. We're over."

As a teenaged blubbering mess, I knelt on the bed and begged. "Don't say that. I'm not a cheater, I swear! I was just trying to make it good for me!"

And that's where I fucked up. I took a teenaged boy's already bruised pride and rubbed salt into the wound by telling him he wasn't a good lover. He stilled, a look of shock crossing his face. A moment passed. The look of shock morphed into one of pure derision. "Fucking whore." He walked out of the room. I heard the front door open then close. The sound of his car starting made my heart skip a beat.

He'd left me there, naked and alone, crying my eyes out, with no way to get home.

I dressed as quickly as I could, went downstairs, and called Nina to come get me. Of course, she called Nat and told her I was a mess. Nat left the party she was at and came with Nina to pick me up. They took me to a movie theater. We watched a sappy romantic comedy. They tried to mend my broken heart with junk food and affection. They made me laugh when I wanted to cry, and when I did cry, they held me tight, whispering words of reassurance. They told me Denver was just a boy, and when I met a real man, he would appreciate me for who I was, not what he wanted me to be. That he would never be ashamed of me.

There are many reason I love my sisters, but that memory is one I will always cherish.

I had hoped Max would be that man.

I guess I was wrong.

BELLE AURORA

CHAPTER TWENTY-SIX

Helena

"Wake up, cupcake," is whispered into my ear. Groaning, I turn away from the voice and try to go back to sleep. My bed shakes as he chuckles quietly. "Come on, baby. Wake up. Seeing you in bed makes me want to play with you, but we don't have time. Wake up."

I turn back around and peek up at him. I mutter roughly, "You left." Max smiles down at me. I ask quietly, "Why did you leave?"

With gentle fingers, he moves hair off my forehead and explains quietly, "Well, we got a little crazy last night. My pants were covered in cum." He looks down at me pointedly. "My *own* cum."

Oh. So he wasn't trying to sneak out. I can't help but laugh. "Ah. I see."

As I hug my pillow tightly, he runs a hand over my shoulder and down my arm. "Yeah, I needed clothes and I was awake, so I went home to shower and change." He jerks his head to the door. I turn to see a black duffle bag by my closet. He adds, "I brought spares."

He brought spares.

He brought *spares*? Next thing you know, he'll have his own toothbrush here!

Holy hell, this is moving too fast.

He stands and walks over to the bathroom. "Bought a toothbrush on the way."

My eyes snap open. Panic fills me. Okay. I'm officially freaking out here. Sitting up in my bed, I ask, "Really? You think you'll need one? I mean, do you think you'll be staying here a lot?"

Not at all sensing my alarm, he calls back from the bathroom, "Uh, yeah, I think so. I mean, you'll be coming to the club every Saturday. We'll go home together, sleep here, and then we'll go get Ceecee and do breakfast on Sundays." He walks back into the room and sits next to me on the bed. "Oh, and my mom wants you to come to dinner tomorrow night."

His what now?

It's too much. I forfeit. "Whoa, whoa, whoa. No one said anything about family dinners, Max! What the hell? How does your mother know about me? What did you tell her?"

A slow grin spreads across his face. "You're freakin' out."

I sputter indignantly, "What? No. No, I'm not. I'm just curious as to why your mother is asking me to dinner when we barely just saw each other naked, and sorry, but I don't know why you need a toothbrush here, 'cause we said we were just going to be having sex, you know? Sex and friendship sounded fun, but not when it comes with a blue toothbrush in my bathroom! And-and-and I think I need a paper bag." I pant, breathless. "Give me a paper bag!"

The stupid man just laughs. "You're a trip." As I continue to hyperventilate, he utters, "Mom called this morning to see if I wanted to do breakfast there, but I told her I couldn't, because Ceecee and I were doing breakfast with you. She asked about you. I told her we were seeing each other. I told her that it was sudden, but it was happening. She got excited 'cause she's my mom." He leans over, taking my chin between his fingers. "I haven't dated in a really long time. I told you I wouldn't keep you a secret, cupcake. I don't regret what happened last night. Sure, it didn't go exactly as planned, but it was still amazing, because it was with you. And I want more of you."

Wow. Talk about putting it out there. That was awesome. I'm totally okay with that.

Heat blooms in my middle. I suddenly want to rip off his sweats.

His face falls. "Unless...I mean, unless you're having second thoughts." He holds up his hands and blurts out, "Which it's okay if you are. I don't want to pressure you or anything." He nods as if reassuring himself. "If you don't want to do this, just say so and I'll back off."

I smile, because we both know that's a lie. Max doesn't know how to back off. Shaking my head, I admit, "This is happening so fast. I panicked, but I'm okay now." Lifting my head, I look him in the eye. "I want to do this."

He throws himself face down on the bed. I hear a muffled, "Thank fuck for that," and I chuckle, running a hand through the back of his hair in consolation.

Standing, he checks his cell phone. "Okay. You're good, I'm good, and we're good. Let's go get Ceecee."

I look up at him in confusion. "You said ten am."

He looks like he wants to laugh. Much to his credit, he doesn't. "It's ten-thirty, babe."

My eyes widen. Jumping up, I rush to the bathroom. As soon as I look in the mirror, I'm surprised it doesn't explode from the offence my appearance is causing. My hair is knotted, my face is a mess from last night's makeup, and the tank I threw on sometime during the night reads 'Sexy Beast'.

I groan knowing Max has officially seen me at my worst. "Oh, my God, Max, you have to give a woman sufficient time to get ready for things. Breakfast takes a good half-hour to get ready for. Dinner takes a decent hour and a half. Now you're here and waiting, the pressure's on! You can't do that to a woman!"

His tall, muscular frame blocks the bathroom door. "Sure I can." At my murderous glare, he puts his hands in the air and retreats, "Okay, okay. Take your time. We're not in a hurry. I'll be watching TV."

It takes me thirty-five minutes to scrub my face free of makeup, brush my teeth, wash and dry my hair, change my sheets, apply light makeup and gloss, and change into my favorite faded and ripped jeans, a white tee, my flip-flops, and a pair of Ray-Ban aviators.

As I walk into the kitchen, I grab my cell from its charger and call out to Max. "Let's go, bonehead."

He switches off the TV and walks behind me to the front door. As I move to open the door, I'm pulled back with a swift yank. One arm moves around my waist, holding me prisoner, while the other palms my ass. He utters roughly, "Looking good, Lena. I like you in jeans."

Mouth suddenly dry, I prepare to snap back a sassy retort, but all that comes out is a breathy, "*Oooooohh.*"

He turns me, trapping me between the front door and him. His golden eyes hood and my nipples bead involuntarily. Leaning down, he brings his face down to mine. Dear God, he smells like the tears of a unicorn. His lips barely touching mine, he utters, "You look beautiful", and then he smacks a light kiss to my lips. Standing tall, he takes my small hand in his, cocooning it. "C'mon, I'm hungry."

I barely have time to shut the door behind us as I'm dragged down to his truck.

MAX

I smile to myself as I drive hand-in-hand with Helena.
Oh, man.
She is going to kill me.

Helena

I hum along with the radio, smiling to myself. I discreetly look down at our entwined hands resting on the center console. It's been a long time since I've just held hands with a man. And it feels nice. A little too nice. Nicer than I remember it. Or maybe that's just because it's with Max.

We pull up to a nice big house in the suburbs. Max turns off the car and turns to me. "Come inside with me."

Umm… no.

I smile and suggest, "Shouldn't I just wait here while you get Ceecee? We'll be late for breakfast."

He shrugs. "So we'll catch lunch. C'mon, cupcake. My mom will be upset if you don't come in."

My smile falls. "Yeah, I guess she would be." But I don't move to exit the car.

He stares me down. "Were you born in a barn?"

I try hard not to laugh at that. Instead, I cross my arms over my chest and return, "Jesus was born in a barn."

Max makes a *pffft* noise. "Look at where it got him." At that, I laugh. He pleads, "Just a minute, that's all. Please?"

Who could refuse a begging Max? I sigh exaggeratedly long. "Okay, okay. One minute. That's all."

He opens the passenger door for me, takes my hand, and walks me down the drive to the front door. He opens it without knocking and I hear the sounds of multiple women chattering in the kitchen. I suddenly want to disappear.

I try to dig my flip-flop-covered heels into the floorboards, but Max drags me along, completely oblivious. As soon as we come into view, a pretty, short, mature woman rushes over to us. She chatters away in a language that sounds to be Spanish. Reaching up, she takes Max's cheeks in her hands and pulls him down to her. She kisses his cheeks and forehead while still talking in rapid speeds, and then pats his cheek adoringly.

And Max just stands there, no fight in him. It's the sweetest thing I have ever seen. Then she looks over at me. She gasps, placing a hand to her heart. She looks back at Max and tells him, "She is beautiful."

My cheeks heat.

He adds, "I know. I told you so. Gorgeous."

My cheeks flame.

Taking a step toward me, the woman reaches out and takes my hand in hers. "Hello, Helena. I am Cecilia. I have seen you before, but never so close. You are a beautiful woman, and my son is a lucky man." She speaks with a slight accent and I warm to her immediately.

Smiling, I squeeze her hand and respond, "Thank you, but he's not as lucky as I am."

I know Max must think I'm saying this for show, but I'm not, and I see the pride shine in her eyes. With that short sentence, I've won her heart. She stands taller and nods. "Come. Let's eat."

Eat? What?

I look over at Max and he mouths, "Sorry," not looking at all apologetic.

My blood boils. I've been had.

He takes a step toward me and wraps an arm around my shoulders. He whispers into my ear, "I'm sorry. I knew you'd panic, so I didn't tell you. It's just us and my sisters. Relax."

Just as I open my mouth to hurl whispered-abuse at the man-child, Ceecee appears in the hall. Face of stone, she approaches. "So, is it true? Are you dating?"

Turds of fury, she doesn't look happy. I shrug lightly. "Yes, honey, we are."

Max doesn't say a thing, just squeezes his arm around my shoulders in silent support. When Ceecee lowers her gaze in thought, Max asks her, "What are you thinking, baby?"

She looks up at us. "I think I'm okay with that."

I'm so surprised that I don't realize I've blurted out, "Really?" until it's already out.

She smiles up at me. "You're cool, Helena. I like you." Suddenly, her face turns cautious. "But you're still going to be doing sessions with me, right? And teach me how to cook?"

I'm not sure about what James will have to say about this, but rather than tell her that, I state confidently, "Nothing could stop me." And I mean it.

Smiling shyly, she answers a hushed, "Cool."

Max pulls me into the kitchen, where Leti, Maria, and Isa are cooking up something that smells delicious. Walking right into the fray, Max puckers up as they take turns kissing his cheek. Feeling like an intruder, I raise my hand and utter a nervous, "Hey, guys."

Isa is the first to pounce on me. Literally. She wraps her arms around me and squeezes me tight. "Thank God, it's *you*! When mom told me Max was dating someone, I thought she'd be some ditzy blonde moron!"

When she releases me, Maria steps in to take her place. Hugging me, she utters into my hair, "I know, right? I thought she'd be some club floozy, but when Mom said it was someone we knew, I thought maybe Mimi had swapped teams." She kissed my cheek as she pulls away, smiling. "I'm happy for you two." A sudden bubble of emotion hits me hard, tightening my throat.

Leti, the oldest sister, steps forward, arms extended. I walk into them and she wraps me up in a warm, sisterly hug. She whispers into my ear, "He's been lonely too long. Thank you, Lena. Welcome to the family."

I close my eyes tightly, begging the tears to retreat, but one strays, trailing down my cheek. As I pull away and swipe at my cheek, I force a laugh. "Well, shit. Go ahead and make me cry, why don't you?" The sisters smile at me in a way that says '*you're welcome*'.

Arms snake around my middle. Max places his lips at my cheek and reprimands his sisters. "Hey, this is our first official date. No making my woman cry."

His woman. Ugh. Too many feelings.

The front door opens, and a familiar deep voice calls out, "We're here."

Oh, no.

Max stiffens. I pinch his arm and he flinches, "Ouch! Hey, what was that for?"

I step out of his arms and whisper in a very deep and exaggerated Max voice, *"Don't worry; it'll just be us and my sisters!"*

He shakes his head. "I didn't know about this." When I eye him, his eyes widen and he throws up his hands. "I swear!" He seems genuinely surprised to hear Nik's voice. When his mother comes back into the kitchen, he asks a hushed, "Mama, what's happening? I thought I said only the girls."

She walks past him and shrugs. "There is too much food for just the girls. When I cook for the family, I call the *family*." She heads back into the pantry and Max stands there looking stunned.

He turns to me, outraged, then points to the pantry. "She set me up!"

Nik and Tina walk into the kitchen, Tatiana and Ava in their arms. Tina beams when she spots me. "Oh yay! I'm so glad you're here!"

She puts Ava on the ground then hugs me tightly, rubbing my back, poking me with her protruding belly. "I've missed you. We never get time to talk."

Nik leans down and kisses the top my head. "Sweetheart."

I open my mouth to speak, when the front door opens again. These voices, I know. I cringe. Nat walks into the hall and sees us standing around. "'Sup, guys?" She glares at me. "You wanna tell me why you don't answer your phone?"

I mutter acidly, "I didn't answer, 'cause *you* were calling."

She swoops me up into a hug. "You know what? I don't even care you're a whoresaurus to me. It's too nice of a day to be pissy." She releases me then punches my arm. Hard. When I wince, she smirks. "Yeah, as if I'd let you get away unharmed."

While I rub the sting out of my arm, Trick and Lola come in from the back of the house. Trick shrugs, looking mildly annoyed. "What's goin' on here? I thought we were gettin' our eats on?"

Lola rolls her eyes, taking turns hugging us all. I reach out to hug her, and she mutters, "It's always about food with these men."

Someone squeezes my bottom. I turn quickly to find Mimi smiling down at me. "Hey, babe."

Smiling, I wrap my arm around her super tall, reed-thin body and lean my head on her. "Hey, yourself."

Trick walks by and kisses my cheek, then calls out to Lola, "I was promised food, woman!"

No one even seems to think it's remotely weird I'm here. Thank God. Cecelia makes her way out of the pantry. She spots the new arrivals and takes turns kissing them all and shooing them out onto the back porch. When I step outside, I take in the beautiful backyard. Under the covered porch is a long outdoor setting that will seat all us adults and children quite comfortably. Nat was right. It is a nice day. The sun is shining and there is barely a cloud in sight. I close my eyes and let the light breeze flow over me. I feel at home here.

Leti steps outside with a large tray of bacon in her hands. "Sit, everyone. The food's ready."

I step forward and ask, "Can I help with anything?"

She smiles over at me. "Yeah, you can actually. Park your ass and eat before these greedy men scarf it all."

I smile and roll my eyes, taking a seat in the very middle of the closest side of the table. Max takes the seat on my left side and moves it away, and then sits on my right side. Ceecee wheels herself into the now-open spot on my left, and smiling, I reach down and squeeze her hand. "You've been exercising, young grasshopper?"

Wide eyes, she looks up at me and nods enthusiastically. "Yeah, I have. And Dad doesn't even need to remind me."

"That's awesome, honey. I am so proud of you. Any cramping?"

She smiles softly down at her lap. "Nope. None."

My heart soars. You couldn't wipe the smile off my face. "That's because you're a champ."

When everyone is seated and chatting away, Maria places the last of the dishes on the table and announces, "Let's eat!"

The men dig in first. I'm not surprised to see Nik handed the plate he has just filled to Tina. He's always been too sweet for his own good. No wonder women love him. He's sexy *and* attentive. I sit there, waiting for the hungry males to get their fill before I stack my plate.

There is so much food. There's pancakes, eggs cooked two ways, bacon, sausage, paella, buttered flatbread, spicy baked beans, tortillas, baked tomatoes, pan-fried garlic mushrooms, cubes of potato sautéed in butter, freshly made salsa, and quiche.

Oh, my Gods. Secretly, I'm ecstatic to be here.

I turn to Ceecee, stand, and take her plate. "What are you having, honey?"

She looks down at the plate, and then back up to me. I suddenly realize that Ceecee may not like people getting her food anymore. So when she responds, I slump in relief. "Scrambled eggs, bacon, and a pancake for now."

I set her plate down in front of her then run my hand over her pretty auburn hair, leaning down to kiss her forehead. "*Bon appétit.*"

The men have stacked their plates, but I turn to see Max's plate empty. I look up at him in concern. "You okay? Why aren't you eating?"

He smiles down at me, talking in a hush. "Have I told you that you look beautiful today?"

My chest aches from the sweetness. Responding just as quietly, I smile softly and tell him, "Yes, you have, but I don't think I've told you how handsome you look today. Which you do, by the way."

His smile deepens. "Well, now I have to kiss you."

My eyes widen in panic. I whisper hiss, "Max, don't. Please don't."

He leans closer to me. "Those are the rules."

I let out an exasperated noise. "Who makes these rules? Max, please don't."

A hair's breadth away from my lips, he utters, "They're going to find out anyway." Then his lips touch mine in a soft but deep kiss, and suddenly, I'm glad to be facing away from Ceecee. No one wants to see their dad kissing some chick. I hate my heart for racing. I hate myself for not pulling away. But I just can't. I'm powerless against this man.

The kiss lasts a short while, but long enough to show everyone the line of friendship has been crossed. As he pulls away from me, he pecks my lips, once, twice, then three times. Leaning back in his chair, he rests his arm at the back of my chair and looks around the table. Everyone but Nat, Ceecee, Max's sisters, and his Mom are gaping. In fact, those not gaping are grinning from ear to ear.

I hear Nat mutter excitedly, "I knew it."

Max looks around at the people gaping and stands before reaching for my plate. "C'mon, guys. Breakfast is getting cold."

He piles my plate with all my favorite breakfast foods and some I haven't tried, when Nik's shock morphs into a beaming smile. He turns to a scowling Asher and utters, "Told ya. You owe me ten bucks." Digging into his pocket, a sulking Ash pulls out a note and slaps it into Nik's hand. Nik winks at me. I lower my face to hide my smile and shake my head slowly.

Ash glowers up at Max. "I'm gonna kick your ass."

Max places my plate in front of me, lifting his own, filling it with food. As he sits, he returns a bored, "Quiet your sass, Ghost." Wrapping his arm around my shoulders, he kisses my temple, turns back to a now-fuming Asher, and mutters an amused, "You'll upset my girl."

Placing a hand over my face, my body shakes in silent laughter.

Sweet, funny Max.

CHAPTER TWENTY-SEVEN

Helena

After what happened to be the best breakfast I've ever eaten in my entire life, Max and I took Ceecee home. This was where I thought the two would drop me off home and have some father/ daughter time.

I was wrong.

As soon as we walked through the door, Ceecee stated, "Sundays are so boring."

Why did I feel the need to open my mouth? Because that was just me. I responded, "They don't have to be."

She slumped in her chair. "No. They are. It's like a rule or something."

I eyed her, then Max. "I don't know who is making these rules you two claim are law..."

Then something spectacular happened. Ceecee looked over at her dad, and at the same time, he looked over at her. They exchanged a secret glance before bursting into laughter. She giggled. "Daddy makes the rules."

He chuckled back. "Oh, hell no, little woman. *You* are in charge of the rules."

A smile I could not help lit my face. "Are either of you going to tell me about the rule thing, or are you just going to laugh behind my back and make me suffer?"

Max narrowed his eyes at me then nudged Ceecee. "Should we tell her?"

She side-eyed her dad. "I don't know. What do you think?"

He shrugged. "Up to you, baby girl, but I think she's okay."

Ceecee smiled at me, nodding. "Yeah, I guess. She *is* family now."

And at the very same time, my heart ached with pure joy, then burned from sheer terror. It hit me like a brick to the face. I did not want to lose this. So what happened when Max got sick of me because he thought our non-relationship had gone far enough? I would just have to wait for that day and hope it would be later rather than sooner. I would also have to pray I had it in me to nurse my wounded heart once I lost not only sweet Ceecee, but also sweet, moronic Max. Worst-case scenario, I would go home to California to lick my wounds in private.

Ceecee explained, "Daddy has a rule about rules." I tilted my head in confusion as she went on. "If you see that you're in a no-win situation, you make a rule to help you get there."

I chuckled. "Isn't that...? Hmmm. What is the word I'm looking for? Oh, yeah, I got it." I looked pointedly at Max and accused, "That would be *lying*."

But Max shook his head. "Strictly embellishment. And it works."

I peeked over to Ceecee. "Does it really?"

She smiled. "It does."

I sighed and threw up my hands. "Well, okay. Now that I know about this, I'm going to have to try it myself."

Max plucked at his tank and toed off his shoes. "I'm going to have a quick shower. You girls good?"

I looked over at Ceecee. We smiled and said in unison, "Fine."

As Max disappeared, I called Ceecee into the kitchen, where we spent some time baking cookies and making a mess of ourselves. As I used to do with my sisters back home, I dipped my finger into the butter and painted Ceecee's face, then flicked flour on it to make it stick. Leaning over the counter, I encouraged her to do the same to me. I closed my eyes and let her go to work on my face. When Max popped into the kitchen, he looked at us, threw up his hands, and backed out of the door slowly.

The man can read between the lines.

As soon as our cookies were done, I got a paper towel, wet it, and cleaned my face. I handed Ceecee another wet towel and let her clean her own messed up face. We made our way to the living area, where Max had his feet up watching a college sports match. Ceecee transferred herself onto the pink single-seater I could see was hers, while I parked myself next to Max.

Ceecee looked over at the DVD shelf. "Want to watch a movie?"

I had no reason to decline, not that I wanted to. "Sounds great. Max, get up and choose."

He mock-glared at me. "We've been dating a whole day and you're already making demands?" He stood and walked over to the shelf. "Sheesh. Talk about high maintenance."

We watched *How to Train Your Dragon,* and I actually really enjoyed it. Actually, I'm not sure whether I liked the movie, or being snuggled up to Max with his arms around me. I was becoming surprisingly comfortable with his open affection. When the movie finished, I stood and stretched. "Sorry to put you out, guys, but I think I should go. I've got work tomorrow."

Max turned to his daughter. "You gonna be okay if I take her?"

She nodded with a slight roll of her eyes. "Yes, I'll be fine. Take your time."

My face flushed.

Did she know her dad was trying to be sly about having dirty deeds with me?

Ugh. That would suck.

But Max, being Max, was cool as a cucumber. "Okay, baby. I'll be an hour or two at most. You make sure you have your cell on you at all times, and if there's an emergency—"

She cut him off with, "Yeah, Dad. I know. If there's an emergency, go across the street to Uncle Nik's."

He sighed and leaned down to kiss her forehead. "You're a good girl."

Ceecee smiled softly then wheeled herself over to me, wrapping an arm around my waist. "Thanks for showing me how to make cookies."

I smiled down at her. "Anytime, honey. You're a fast learner."

We said our goodbyes and the second I sat in the truck, Max turned to me, eyeing my body. "You know the second we get to your apartment, your ass is mine."

Well, darn it. I liked the sound of that.

Speaking on a whisper, I closed my eyes and told him, "You are not to speak to me for the duration of this car ride. Trust me, it's for your own good." We drove in silence, but Max had a hold of my hand, playing with my fingers, and the closer we came to my apartment, the harder I had to squeeze my legs together. It had been too long.

We exited the car and walked up the stairs leisurely, like a normal couple, but as soon as I opened the door to my apartment, I was pushed inside and the door was slammed shut. Panting, I looked up at him in shock. "Holy Jesus, if you're going to push me around, you better be prepared to fuck me like you own me."

He stared at me wide-eyed. After a moment, he breathed, "*Dios mío*, you're fucking perfect." Then, he looked over at the kitchen counter and hesitated. "Next time. The first time you take my cock, I want to see your face."

Oh, snap.

I was starting to like bossy Max. He moved toward me, and as if it were choreographed, he dipped his face to mine the moment I lifted mine to his. We kissed slowly, savoring each other's taste. He ate at my lips, growling, and I gasped in delight. This was a side of Max I had yet to see.

He pulled at my tee, slipping it over my head, leaving me in a white cotton bra. I scraped my nails at the bottom of his black tee and he pulled it off one-handed. With his lips on mine, I worked at the rest of his clothing in a daze. Somehow, I managed to pull his sweats down his hips. He must've already removed his shoes, but I don't remember him doing it. Max reached down to unbutton my jeans, but I beat him to it.

He walked me backward to my room, pushing me back onto the soft, clean covers of my bed. As I lay there, breathing heavily, he slid my jeans down my legs. Then it was just us, nothing in-between.

With white cotton panties to match my white cotton bra, I leaned up on my elbows to find Max staring down at my body, palming himself through his silver silky boxers. I moaned as my pussy convulsed. Hard. Unintentionally, my body jerked and I cupped myself to stop a premature orgasm.

A choked noise escaped Max. I peeked through one eye to look at him. Gripping himself tight through the thin material, he closed his eyes and muttered a tormented, "Not again."

No, no, no. This session was going to last, by thunder!

Reaching up to the front of my bra, I unhooked myself and held the two cups firmly in my grasp. "Max." He opened his eyes as I let the bra fall down my arms, freeing my breasts.

He took a step forward, pulled me up, and then lifted me up, into him. I wrapped my legs around his hips and wound my arms around his neck. He turned and sat on my bed, leaving me in his lap. The moment I loosened my hold on him, he lowered his mouth and captured one taut bud between his lips, sucking while groaning. I gasped and raked my hands through his hair, tangling my fingers through it. I hadn't even noticed myself rubbing against him 'til he swapped sides, showering the other nipple with much needed affection.

I was soaked. As in, *soaked*. My panties were officially a write-off. He gently bit my nipple then laved it with his tongue, knowing the perfect amount of pain to inflict to make it feel good. I was beginning to feel spoiled. With his arms around me, he pulled me deeper into his mouth as he sucked and bit and licked me. The pressure was starting to build. I didn't want it to end so quickly. Leaning back slightly, I cupped his cheeks, bringing his face back to mine for a deep, tender kisses, and he took them like a starving man needing those kisses to survive.

My cheeks flushed pink and my body burning up, I needed more.

Sliding off his lap, I stood in front of him, taking his hands and placing them on the elastic of my panties. He got the hint. He got it real quick. His fingers gripped the hem of the small panties and tugged them down my legs.

I was naked. And I loved it. I felt powerful. And that was rare. The way Max looked at me made me feel sexy. The man had no poker face. He liked what he saw.

His twitching erection also liked what it saw. It was his turn to stand and he stood tall. His olive skin looked good enough to lick, so I did.

Leaning forward, my lips hovered at his nipple a split second before I placed my lips around it, biting it gently. His stomach jerked and a low growl sounded in his throat. I wanted to show him what he had done for me. Clearly, I had.

I rested my fingertips on the elastic of his boxers. This was it. This was where it got serious. I mentally prepared myself. I was ready for it. Hooking my fingers through the elastic, I slid the silky boxers down, slowly. As the material passed his hips, his erection sprang free and my lips parted. I wanted it in my mouth again, but there would be no time today. I needed Max, and I needed all of him.

He gently laid me down in the center of my bed and covered my naked body with his, warming me. My hands roamed his body as his lips searched mine. He was such a contrast to me. I was soft. He was hard, everywhere. I was pale. He was bronzed.

As his hand trailed the length of my leg, he grasped behind my knee, lifting my leg up onto his hip. Gently nudging my other leg, I spread enough for him to fit in the space between them. He lowered himself onto me a second time, but this time, it felt different. His hot, hard length rested between my wet folds and it was incredible.

He peered down into my face, shallowly thrusting against my wet flesh. He knew what he was doing, and I was grateful for it. I would not be faking an orgasm today! Yay, me!

Lowering his face to mine, he bit my bottom lip gently, then muttered, "I'm going to fuck you now."

My nipples hardened against his chest, and I know he felt it, because he pressed his chest firmer to mine with a content sigh. Reaching down, he fisted himself. He brought the hot tip of his cock to my wet entrance and gently worked my arousal onto him. He didn't thrust like a mad man. He pushed the head of his thick length into me, precise and controlled.

A gasp tore from my throat. I frantically reached up to grip his shoulders as my eyelids fluttered closed. Panting, I begged, "More."

Max had a hard time holding onto control. The muscles in his arms and stomach jumped and jutted about as he let out a strained, "Fuck me, you're tight."

He pushed further into me, an inch at a time, and it was equal amounts pleasure and pain. But I felt his worry as his body stiffened over me. "Am I hurting you?"

The truth was it did hurt a little, but I knew it would pass. I didn't want him to stop, so I said the only thing I could to fuel him on. "Oh, God, it hurts so good. *More*. Don't stop."

A light thrust pushed him past the halfway point and I moaned at the delicious friction. He worked himself in further with shallow thrusts until I was almost completely impaled. "I'm gonna stop there. I don't want to hurt you, baby."

Lifting my eyes to his, I glared at him. "I want it all."

He smiled softly down at me. "Next time, baby. You haven't been touched for a long time, and I—"

Gripping his shoulders tightly, I lifted my hips then thrust downward, his entire length spearing me. We moaned and groaned in unison. My heart raced. My breathing hollowed. He felt amazing. And he was inside of me. All of him. Breathless, I looked up, his golden eyes hooded and intense. I breathed, "Fuck me."

And he did. He started thrusting, and a delicious throbbing started in my core. I thought I'd faint dead away from the intense pleasure of it. Max thrust harder, the sounds of our flesh connecting echoing throughout the room. I lifted my face and he met me halfway, taking my lips in deep, wet kisses reserved for the type of passionate sex we were having.

He gripped my hips, pulling me up into his thrusts, and the world around me faded away. My eyes closed for a single second before an unexpected orgasm shook me. My eyes shot open as my body went numb with pure, unadulterated pleasure. Gasping, my lips parted. A low guttural moan was torn from me. My core contracted, hard, and I began to pulse around him.

I watched Max bite the inside of his cheek, his jaw ticking as his thrusts turned animalistic. He pounded into me, as if unable to stop himself. Basking in the delicious glow of my orgasm, I lifted myself up onto my elbows and kissed his mouth, my tongue trailing his bottom lip.

He growled, face pained, and I knew he was close. Reaching up, I wrapped my arms around his neck, pressing my breasts against him as he thrust into me.

His arms tightened around my back, pulling me impossibly close. Panting into his ear, I whispered a hoarse, "You feel so good inside me."

His body shuddered violently. He stilled, tipped his head back, and roared, pulling out a split second before he spilled warm cum onto my stomach.

No condom. Shit.

I'm sure we'd discuss our carelessness later on, but right now, we were both semi-comatose. Eyes closed, his chest heaved as if he'd run a marathon. Sounding tired, he mumbled, "So good. So fucking good." His sleepy eyes opened to peer down at me. "You're incredible. And on a completely unrelated note, I think I love you."

I chuckled. "You can't declare love during sex." Grinning up at him, I added, "Those are the rules."

He laughed long and rough. With his cock resting on my pubic bone, he lifted his hand, palm up. I lifted my own hand and we high-fived, both laughing at the ridiculousness of it. Sighing serenely, he stood and walked out of my room. I admired his taut butt for only a moment before he came back with tissue. Then I admired his front. He wiped me down with a gentle hand before throwing the tissue into my bedside trashcan and climbing into my bed, molding himself to my back.

We were spooning.

I was spooning with Max Leokov. And he was naked.

Could life possibly get any better?

One arm snaked around my waist while his free hand gently massaged my breast. "So that was pretty much the best sex of my life," he admitted, pressing soft kisses to my shoulder. I made a non-committal sound in my throat. He pushed, suddenly sounding nervous, "It was good...right?" I made another non-committal sound, knowing he was near freaking out. I yelped when he bit my shoulder and boasted, "I know what you're doing! I know you came, woman!"

I burst into laughter. "Okay, okay. I was trying to freak you out." I turned in his arm to face him. His smiling eyes held me captive. "I've never had better." I snuggled into him, pressing my lips to his throat, speaking against it. "I loved it. Every second."

The vibrations from his throat tickled my lips. "Good, 'cause we're doing it again. Forever and ever, amen."

Forever.

If only.

This morning, I felt lighter and happier than I had been in a long time. Longer than I can remember. So when I came to work cheery as cheery is, you can imagine my shock when a grim looking James called me into his office and started the conversation with, "I'm sorry, Helena. This isn't going to work."

CHAPTER TWENTY-EIGHT

Helena

"What?" I ask, mouth suddenly parched.

James taps his pen on his desk, avoiding my eyes. "Max called me last night. You're dating. It's officially a conflict of interest. The center can't support your work with Ceecee anymore."

I'm surprised at the disappointment I feel. Dread forms a cold, hard stone in my gut. I reach up and rub absently at my temple. "I'm so sorry, James. I didn't plan this thing with Max; it just happened."

James finally looks up at me. "He's the guy, isn't he?" When I don't respond, he adds, "The one who didn't *see* you. It was Max, wasn't it?" I smile sadly, but don't say a word. James sighs. "Ceecee's doing good now. She's motivated, and I think she'll be okay without you."

Bitterness runs cold in my veins.

She's only better because of me, and given time, I would've helped her be great.

Wow. I have no idea where that thought came from. I know James works hard with her. I guess I'm just jealous of the working relationship he still has with her that I'll no longer be allowed to have.

He raises a brow in question. "What? You're not even going to fight me?"

I let out a tired sigh. "Would it help?"

Shaking his head, he utters, "Not even a little."

Pissed, I stand. "I'm sorry, James. Like I said, I didn't see this coming myself." As I take a step toward the door, something holds me back. I turn and add, "But as Max's girlfriend, I'm going to be seeing Ceecee on a regular basis. I'm teaching her to cook. I promised her. I'll also be supervising her home sessions. Tell me if you have a problem with this, James." My blood boils. "Tell me you have a problem with this, so I can break promises to a thirteen-year-old girl with abandonment issues."

Sometime during my rant, a small smile has broken through James's disappointment. "The center doesn't have anything against client/PT relationships, and based on her current enthusiasm, I can't see an issue with you maintaining a close friendship with Ceecee." He stands and walks over to the window, looking out. "And if you, I don't know, decided to exercise in the same place and at the same time Ceecee should happen to exercise, I can't stop that." He turns to me and says pointedly, "I just don't have that kind of power, unfortunately."

I still. Is he saying what I think he's saying?

Blinking down at the ground, I confirm, "So if I were to, say, do cardio in the park at the same time Ceecee decided to do cardio at the same park, and we happened to bump into each other, I wouldn't be risking my job."

James nods slowly. "Like I said, I just don't have that kind of power."

It's times like this when I really wish I hadn't agreed to not hug James. I move to step out of his office, but as I do, I mutter a hushed, "Thank you, James."

His, "You're welcome," is just as quiet.

I shuffle over to my desk and take a seat, staring into my computer screen. When it hits me that I can still train with Ceecee, a beaming smile spreads across my face. Felicity skips over and sits on my desk. I look up to see her smiling down at me. "I told you he'd notice you. He just needed to see you at a different angle." She stands and starts skipping away. "White Rabbit this Saturday?"

Typing in my computer password, I call out, "I'm there."

I don't see her, but I hear her singsong response. "*Holla!*"

MAX

When the elevator opens, I walk down the hall wearing a smile I thought was buried deep inside of me. Turns out, Helena found it and dug it out against my will. I lift my coffee to my lips as I walk into my office. Just as I move to sip, I still. An angry looking Asher and a stern-faced Nat are standing by my desk, obviously waiting for me. My eyes widen. I don't like this. I greet them hesitantly, "Hey, guys. What's up?"

Nat steps forward, crossing her arms over her chest. She stands tall and asks firmly, "What are your intentions with my sister?"

Well, shit. And I thought it would be a good morning.

Ash takes two steps forward to stand by his wife. He looks down at her and says, "I'll handle this." He lifts his face to mine and narrows his brows. "What are your intentions with my sister?"

Asher can be a scary guy, if you haven't grown up with him. I place my coffee cup on the edge of my desk and respond on a smile, "I like her."

Nat's harsh face crumbles to reveal her beautiful smile. "You do?"

I smile harder and sigh dreamily. "She's incredible." I really mean it.

But Ash isn't having any of it. His jaw stiffens and I know he wants to punch me in the gut. Nat throws her hands up in the air a moment before jumping at me. I catch her at the last second. Her soft laugher tinkles in my ear. "Oh, my God, this is so great! You'll come to California with us for vacation and stay at my parents' house, and when you get married, we'll be family! Not like the family we are now, but *real* family!" Nat pulls back, fixing my collar and grinning. "She'll be a great mom. She always wanted kids." She gasps dramatically then turns to Ash. "Can you imagine little MaLena babies running around?"

A look of confusion crossed Ash's face. "MaLena?"

Nat rolls her eyes at him as though he's stupid. "Max and Helena. Get with the program, babe."

Helena and me married? Little baby Helena's and Max Juniors? My heart starts to race. *Hell* to the *no*. Just as I lift my hand to argue the point, Nik arrives at my office door and jerks his chin toward Nat. "What's the crazy lady gasping about?"

I open my mouth to answer, but Nat cuts me off with a happy, "Max and Helena are getting married and having babies!"

Nik's eyes widen comically. "She's *pregnant*? Already?" He shakes his head. "Jesus, man. You sure don't fuck around."

That's it. I raise a hand and begin, "Whoa, man. She isn't pregnant." I turn to Nat. "And we aren't getting married." I face Ash. "But I like her, and we're taking it slow. All we're doing is dating. Everyone needs to relax."

I hate myself for thinking of Maddy right now. I remember how I felt when she left us. We never heard from her again, but I dug. I sincerely wished I hadn't when I found out she remarried and had two little boys of her own.

How can she do that? How can she live her life like we don't exist? Like we *never* existed?

This is why I don't normally date. I can't go through that again. It near killed me the first time around. I wonder how long it'll take Helena to realize a man with a disabled teenage child isn't what she's looking for.

Luckily, this thing with Helena isn't serious.

Yeah, right.

Luckily, we're keeping emotions out of this relationship.

Keep telling yourself that.

Luckily, there's no risk of losing my heart again.

She's already in there, man.

Nat's face falls. She opens her mouth to speak, but closes it quickly. She takes a moment then tries again. When she speaks, it's quiet and cautious. "The last real boyfriend Helena had was senior year, and he hurt her, Max. He hurt her in a way that she was scared off dating." Hearing some douche hurt Helena makes me want to punch a hole in the wall. "'Til *now*. She really likes you, Max. She might deny how much she does, but I can see it. She likes you a lot." She breathes deep then replies on a whispered exhale, "Please don't hurt her."

Hurt *her*? Why can't anyone see it? *She* has the power to hurt *me*. And she will, when she's had enough of me. And even knowing that, I can't let her go. I'll be around for as long as she wants me. Helena can't love a guy like me.

Who wants a person with half a heart?

I wrap my hand around Nat and hug her. "I won't hurt her. I promise."

Smiling softly as she pulls away, she utters, "That's all I ask." She straightens. "Right. I have to get to work, but I'll see you all later."

She kisses Ash on the mouth, and kisses my cheek then Nik's as she leaves.

Ash turns to me. "I swear to God, man. I love that woman more than my own life, and she loves Helena more than her own. You hurt her," he looks me in the eye to show me how serious he is, "I will fuck you up."

Without a backward glance, he leaves me office, and I call out, "Noted."

Nik stands by the door, leaning against the frame. "Gotta admit I was surprised about Helena, but not *that* surprised."

Huh? "What do you mean?"

He tilts his head, brows raised. "She's gorgeous. She's funny. She's got experience working with kids like Ceecee, and she's got a good heart." My heart clenches painfully when he adds, "She's everything you deserve and more." He stands, then shrugs lightly. "So tell me why you're scared."

My brother. He sees all.

I sit on the edge of my desk, thinking about my answer. "I'm not scared."

Nik walks over to my desk and sits by my side. He nods lightly. "You're scared." I don't know what to say, because he's right. I am scared. The silence lasts only a moment before Nik utters, "Remember how miserable I was before Tina came along?"

Before Tina came along, Nik was a moody bastard who only used women for sex. But Tina didn't want sex. She wanted friendship. Up until then, Nik had never had a friend who also happened to be a girl. We gave him shit about it, but I'm grateful for Tina. She gave Nik something I never thought I'd see in my life. She gave him a reason to live. "Yeah, I remember."

He nudges my shoulder with his. "Don't you want something like we have? Because you can have it. You've got a woman who could give you that, and she's right in front of you."

My throat thickens with emotion, and I hate myself for showing weakness. I dip my chin and whisper a strained, "I can't do it again, Nik."

He assures adamantly, "Yes, you can. A woman like that won't let you down. A woman like that will catch you if you happen to fall. A woman like Helena is hard to find, but easy to keep if you treat her well." He pauses a moment before stating, "She isn't Maddy."

I mutter, "Yeah, well I thought Maddy was all those things you just said, so I guess I'm not the best judge of character."

A sound of aggravation escapes him. "Dude, I know you don't remember things the way I do, so here it goes. I'm laying it out there, whether you want to hear it or not." He slides off the desk to stand in front of me. "Maddy was a whiny bitch. She always was."

My head snaps up in shock. "What?"

Nik sighs. "I know when you're in love you see the best in a person, but *I* wasn't in love with her. Fuck, I barely liked her on the best of days. So I'm going to tell you, now after thirteen years, why Maddy was never good enough for you." Sitting there in shock, all I can do is listen as he starts, "When you first told me you were in love, I was rooting for you. I mean, it's not every day a young man comes to his brother to tell him he's met the one. I spent all night talking to you, telling you to bring her over so we could meet her. I remember how excited you were about it. The next day, you came home looking like someone shit in your cereal, because Maddy wasn't ready to tell people about you." He looks down into my eyes. "That was her first strike. She acted like she was ashamed of you."

My brows furrow. "It wasn't like that. She wanted to make sure I was into her before she told her parents about us."

Nik rolls his eyes. "Oh, yeah? What was stopping her from telling her friends? Fuck knows you would've told everyone about her if she hadn't told you not to. I mean, *c'mon*. You spoke on the phone for months and declared your love for her on hundreds of occasions."

I never saw it like that. "Well, I guess. It was a long time ago."

He holds up a hand. "Secondly, when you guys were dating and she'd come to mom's, she'd always make a point to explain how she couldn't eat there because she'd already eaten, and she did this knowing Mom would be cooking. She was rude like that. So she'd sit there like an asshole watching everyone eat, and then complain to you about needing to get home, when really, she just didn't want to be around us. She didn't like us, and you'd always stick up for her."

I shake my head. "It's not that she didn't like you guys; it's just that her family was different from ours, you know? They weren't loud like we are. They were proper folk."

Nik's mouth gapes before he booms, *"You're still sticking up for her!"*

I wince as soon as I realize I totally am. "Sorry, bro. I guess old habits die hard."

His face turns soft. "The last thing I remember, and I'll never forgive her for this, was when she got pregnant..." his eyes close sadly, "...and she blamed you for it. She told you that you were trying to trap her, to keep her from leaving you, and that you never wanted her to go to college. She hated you for it. She resented you. But you were so damn in love with her, you couldn't see through the sunshine shining out of her ass."

I remain quiet. Everything he just said is true. She did blame me for getting her pregnant. She blamed me for missing her pill. She didn't want Ceecee. She never did.

Nik utters softly, "I'm sorry, bro, but that's the truth." He places a hand on my shoulder in a brotherly gesture of support. "According to Maddy, you were never good enough for her." He squeezes my shoulder then walks out, closing the door behind him.

I don't react for a long time. A long minute passes before I reach across the table with a shaking hand and pick up my coffee mug. I grit my teeth and grip it tight before hurling it across the room. I watch as it hits the wall, smashing into pieces and splattering coffee across the white surface.

Breathing hard, my body shakes with uncontrollable rage.

Panting, I whisper a shaky, "I hate you, Maddy."

Helena

My body itches. I scratch absently at my chest as my leg bounces under the desk. I'm having withdrawals. Reaching across the table, I pick up my cell and type quickly.

Me: Excuse me, oh bringer of many an orgasm, you need to call Icing on the Cake and have me UNBANNED! I need cupcakes...stat!

His response comes immediately.

Max: Cupcake, I thought I was all the sugar you needed.

I can't help but snicker. The ass.

Me: Although you are magically delicious, this is not a joke. I'm having withdrawals. I'm itchy and red, and I'm grouchy. You don't want me to be grouchy to my clients, do you?

A minute later, my phone pings.

Max: I definitely do not want you grouchy, sweetheart. I'll make the call. Give me half hour.

My heart swells at his calling me sweetheart. Then I stomp, clap, and silently squeal.

Me: I could kiss you right now!

A moment later, my phone vibrates in my hand.

Max: Baby, I want more than your lips.

In a mock-swoon, my head hits my desk with a thud. After the throbbing between my legs subsides, I lift my head and type a response.

Me: I'm at work! You can't be sexy to me while I'm at work!

I should've guessed his response before I got it.

Max: Sure I can. X

I go about typing out my client reports with a smile on my face. Time passes quickly, and before I know it, I'm done. Sitting up in my chair, I reach behind me and rub my stiff shoulder. I guess having sex after such a long time is hard on the muscles. A pair of manly hands land on my shoulders and start kneading. A low moan escapes me. "Oh, *yeah*."

Lips hit my ear and whisper, "I think I've heard you say that before." My eyes snap open, but the whispers continue, "But it was more like '*Oh, yeah, more*' and '*Oh, yeah, just like that*'."

Relaxing back into him, I ask through a smile, "What are you doing here?"

I try not to pout at the loss of his hands on me, then stand and turn to face him. Max grins down at me, looking good enough to eat in dark denim, a grey long-sleeved tee bunched up to the elbows, and white sneakers. He also holds a box in his hand.

A large pink and white box.

My heart skips a beat. I ask in shock, "You didn't?" Snatching the box out of his hands, I set it on my desk and open it to find a dozen pretty cupcakes sitting there, waiting to be sampled. I spin around and sputter, "B-but why?"

He lifts his hand and runs his thumb down my cheek. "Because you're amazing. Because you're funny and sweet. And because you deserve a sugar rush."

My heart implodes from all the feelings. I don't even care I'm at work. I take the three steps over to him, lift my hands to cup his cheeks, and pull his face down to mine, planting soft, wet kisses onto his full lips. "Thank you, honey."

He reaches up to my hands on his cheeks and gently takes them into his own, stepping away. He lifts my hands to his mouth and takes turns kissing at the knuckles of each hand. "I have to get back to work." Walking backward, he asks, "You're coming to cook with Ceecee tomorrow, yeah?"

I shrug, knowing I could never deny him. "Of course."

He winks at me before turning and jogging out the door. I sit back at my desk, smiling, and eye the open box of cupcakes, my sudden hunger for cake dissipating.

My smile fades. Max was right.

He's all the sugar I need.

And that scares the living shit out of me.

CHAPTER TWENTY-NINE

Helena

With Felicity pulling at my hair to make a thin side-braid, my face bunches and one of my eyes closes from the pain. "*Ow*, turdette." I hiss in a breath through my teeth. "That hurts."

The tall blonde simply smiles cruelly. "Beauty is pain, assface."

Today is Saturday, and we're getting ready for The White Rabbit. The week passed pretty quickly, what with me working during the day then four out of the five nights I'd been at Max's, hanging out, cooking with Ceecee, and eating like a piglet. I didn't go last night, even though he asked. I felt Max and Ceecee needed time to themselves, so I set Max on a task. I told him to buy all the things to make ice-cream sundaes and have Ceecee make them both banana splits.

Later that night, I received a photo text message of Max and Ceecee smiling into the camera, both faces covered with ice cream and chocolate sauce. It was adorable, and I suddenly wished I was there.

My phone vibrates in my hand and I lift it, checking the display.

Max: Three hours 'til I see your beautiful smile.

A giant smile breaks out on my face, so giant that my cheeks hurt. I've been getting these for five hours now. Every hour on the hour. The first said, "Seven hours 'til I kiss your honey mouth." The second said, "Six hours 'til I see your pretty green eyes." The third said, "Five hours 'til I squeeze your sexy ass." And the fourth said, "Four hours 'til I wrap my arms around you. And when I do, I'm not letting go."

It's safe to say the man knows how to make a woman feel special. It's also safe to say my heart is not safe when it comes to Max. He's becoming far more of a distraction than I imagined. He doesn't want to see me every now and again. He wants to see me *every day*. And when I tell him I can't see him, he pouts.

It's so freaking cute that my heart aches.

I'm not sure what's going on between us, but it feels real. Like a real relationship. It's not even about the sex. The last three nights I'd been there, all we did was kiss, cuddle, and talk on the sofa after Ceecee had gone to sleep.

I'm so confused about the role I'm supposed to be playing. It doesn't really seem like a role anymore. Max was the one to tell me he couldn't give me all of him, but it feels like he's giving me every last piece of him. He's burrowing a place into my heart, right next to the place reserved for Ceecee, and what's more alarming is that I want them there.

Felicity pulls at my hair again and my mouth rounds in time with my eyes. "*Ow, bitch!* You did that on purpose!"

Her reflection eyes me hard in the mirror. "I've lived here my whole life and I can't find a man who wants a serious relationship. You've been here a month—a freakin' month!—and you get pick of the litter." She pouts into the mirror. "It's not fair."

I scoff. "Max and I are taking it slow. We might not even work out, Flick."

He's counting on it, actually.

She rolls her eyes at me. "He's been sending you messages all day long about how much he can't wait to see you. He brings you cupcakes at work and wants his daughter to know you. I think this is more serious than you both realize. He's super sweet to you, and he doesn't even flirt anymore!"

He doesn't? I ask, surprised, "He doesn't?"

Her brows rise and she shakes her head slowly. "Nope. Well, not with me anyways. I haven't seen him flirt with Willa either. Hell, I haven't seen him flirt with anyone." Her brows narrow. "You know what? Maybe we'll watch him for a while tonight on the floor. See what he does. Because I swear to God, the woman who makes Max Leokov lose his flirt..." she tilts her head to the side, "...she's the one."

My heart perks up at the same moment my brain blows a big raspberry. I sigh. "You're delusional. Clinically insane. You should see someone about that."

Felicity chuckles. "You're lucky I like you." A wry smile follows her laughter. "Also, I bought you a dress to wear tonight, and," my loud groan of disapproval is ignored as she speaks louder, over me, "and you *are* wearing it tonight."

And here comes the whining. "I already told you I don't like wearing dresses." Straightening in my chair, I cross my arms over myself. "Nope, I'm not wearing it."

Felicity leaves the room, calling back, "I think you might just change your mind," when she reenters my bedroom, I can't contain my gasp as she adds, "when you see it."

In her hands is one of the most spectacular dresses I have ever seen in my life. It's completely black, sleeveless with a jewel neckline, comes mid-thigh, and has a small frilled skirt around the waist, making it easy to hide a little pooch if you have one. The stitching on the entire dress is a yellowish mustard color.

I love it immediately. But I still can't wear it. "It's gorgeous, Felicity. And I love it. Really, I do. But—" I look into her eyes, pleadingly, "but I can't wear it."

Her face falls. "Okay. That's okay." She sighs, running her hand down the dress. "I mean, who cares if I went downtown to find you a hot dress to wear for your new man. You don't do dresses. I should've been more thoughtful. But you could've at least tried it on, you know? For me?" She gives me puppy dog eyes and bats her ridiculously long lashes.

I roll my eyes at her antics and snatch the dress from her hands. "Fine, but just for you. And once I try it on, it's coming off."

Felicity claps and smiles. "Yay! Okay! Get your butt in there."

Once in the bathroom, I change out of my yoga pants and tee, and slip into the dress. I gape at my reflection.

It's perfect.

It looks perfect on me.

I have never wanted to wear a dress as much as I want to wear this one. Stepping out of the bathroom, I walk back into my room and Felicity squeals, "Oh, my *gawd*! It's gorgeous. I mean, you're gorgeous in it. I love it. You're totally wearing it."

She stands behind me, zipping me up. I mutter, "I-um...I don't know. You don't think I look a little too fancy?"

"You look just the right amount of fancy. I swear it's like it was made for you. As soon as I saw it, I knew. It cost me a bit, but I knew I had to get it for you. It was in the window of a store called Lena." She shrugs lightly. "It was, like, a sign or something."

Suddenly feeling naked, I hold myself. "I'm still not sure."

Felicity lets out an exasperated sigh. "I'm getting a second opinion." Then she walks away. I hear the front door open, and then she returns with Nat in tow.

Nat gapes openly, walking around me, sputtering, "B-but how?" She turns to Felicity. "How on earth did you get her to wear this?"

Felicity wears a smug smile. "Guilt."

Nat's eyes widen as she snaps her fingers and hisses, "*Guilt!* Of course!" She mutters, "I used to threaten her with grievous bodily harm." She shakes her head. "Never worked."

I ask Nat cautiously, "How do I look?"

She suddenly looks bored and sniffs, "You look a'ight."

I know my sister well enough to know that if she's teasing, I look smoking hot. Smiling, I turn to Flick and state, "Okay. I'm wearing it."

Nat smirks, then snickers, "Dear God, Max is going to have a fit."

My smile falls as my stomach knots. "You don't think he'll like it?"

She makes a noise of annoyance. "No, dipshit, he'll love it." She walks out of my apartment, but adds on a shout, "Unfortunately for him, so will all the other guys there." Before she enters her own apartment, she cackles maniacally.

Oh.

Felicity grins, nodding at me knowingly. "Oh, yeah. Time Flirtzilla got his."

I roll my eyes at them, but I do it smiling. A jealous Max? I'd kill to see that.

My phone buzzes on the dresser.

Max: Two hours 'til I hear your sweet laugh.

My heart beats faster as serene warmth flows through me.

Oh, brother.

I'm fucking doomed.

Helena

As soon as we arrive at the club, my stomach dips in excitement. I'm pretty sure I'm not meant to feel like this. B-rock greets us and lets us in. We hold hands, swimming through the crowd of people. It's pretty darn full already, and it's only nine forty-five. Normally, the place would be dead until past ten. As soon as we arrive at the bottom of the stairs to the VIP area, the new, shy Alice stands there, eyes firmly fixed to the ground. Felicity speaks first. "Hi there. Helena Kovac and friend."

Shy Alice stutters, "Of c-c-course. P-p-please, go right up." She reaches over and undoes the velvet rope, but as she does this, I get a good glimpse of her face. And I still as shock washes over me. "Willa?"

Shy Alice cringes. "No. Sorry."

Felicity watches me with curiosity in her eyes. She steps closer to the new Alice and bends down to look in her eyes. Flick's eyes widen in surprise as she all but yells at our co-worker, "Holy shit, girl! You got some 'splainin' to do!"

Willa cringes once more, turning her face up to look at us. Her eyes dart from side-to-side. "Please, you can't tell anyone I'm working here. Please." She's in a serious panic.

Placing an arm on hers in comfort, I utter, "Hey, we're not going to tell anyone. Right, Flick?"

Felicity smiles softly. "It's not my business to tell, Willa."

Willa visibly slumps. "Oh, thank goodness. I don't want Whit to know. I don't..." she lowers her voice, "...I don't want him to see me dressed like this."

I look down at the sexed-up Alice in Wonderland costume she wears. The skirt is shorter than a mini, with white lace fishnets and garters underneath. Her feet are adorned by ridiculously high white Mary-Jane heels. She wears a white-blonde wig with a light blue bow, and bright red lipstick. And she looks sexy.

I grin up at her. "Willa, have you seen yourself? Did you take a good look in the mirror before you came?"

She looks uncomfortable. "Of course I did. I know what I look like." I'm confused until she adds, "I look like a tramp. It's unseemly for a lady to dress like this. But I'm desperate. I need the money."

Felicity chokes on a laugh before asking, "Do you think Helena looks like a tramp tonight?"

Willa's face turns pale. "Oh, heavens no!"

Felicity turns on the spot. "What about me?"

She suddenly looks wistful. "No. You look beautiful. Both of you."

I take a step up the stairs. As I do, I tell her, "You look sexy wearing that, and if James saw you in it, I don't think he'd be able to keep his hands off you." I continue up the stairs, but hear Felicity add, "I've never seen you look better, honey. Have fun tonight. And don't worry, we'll keep it quiet."

Reaching the top of the stairs, I look down to find Willa biting down a shy smile.

Mission accomplished.

We reach the booth to find poor, pregnant, massive Tina sitting with her shoes already off, resting them on a stool one of the guys must've brought over for her. She's talking to Nat, Isa, and Leti while rubbing her belly. Mimi, Lola, and Maria talk over drinks at the VIP bar. The only guys in sight are Nik and Trick, standing by the booth.

Saturday nights are normally much more relaxed for them. Ash will be busy in the security room, while Max works the floor, making sure the patrons are kept happy.

"Hi, guys," I greet as Felicity and I sit across from Tina.

She doesn't look happy. "Hi."

My brow furrows. Whoever made Tina upset will be getting bitch-slapped. It takes a lot to upset Tina. You just don't do it. "What's wrong?"

Nik sighs. "Tina was using the downstairs bathroom and saw women doing drugs in there. She's upset someone brought that stuff into the club."

That's understandable. I look up at Nik. "Can't you do something about it?"

He shrugs. "I can't go into the girls bathrooms. I'd need to hire a female staff member to man the area. And I'm not sure if it would pay to do that."

Felicity bunches her face in thought. "Can't Max do it? Just stand by the door?"

Nik shakes his head. "He does a lot on the actual floor. We'd miss him there. Besides, what could he do standing by the door? It'd be a waste of his talents."

Because I'm special, I raise my hand. "I'll do it."

Tina blinks. "You'd do that?"

My shoulder jerks up lightly. "Sure."

Nik eyes me for a moment, looking to be thinking hard. "I don't know. Sorry, babe. You just don't look aggressive enough."

Nat grins. "Oh, she's aggressive all right." She clears her throat. "For instance, I could tell you about a little poster she keeps in—"

Before she's even finishes the sentence, I throw myself across the table, tackling Nat to the ground. I grit my teeth as I wrap her in a headlock. "You say one more word and you're dead!"

A laughing Nat chokes out, "See!" I tighten my hold on her a wee bit harder and she cackles. "Get the fuck off me, bitch!"

From somewhere behind me, Lola singsongs, "Helena, I can see your undies!"

Trick mumbles in a daze, "You don't see a lot of women wearing those types of undies."

Then I hear *him*. "Dude, I said the same thing."

I hear Ash grumble, "When'd you see her undies?"

Max responds without thought, "I've seen 'em a few times now."

As Nat pushes me off her, I look up in time to see Ash pounce on Max, catching him in a headlock. Ash hisses, "I'm gonna kick your ass!"

But Max chokes out an amused, "*It was worth it!*"

Ash releases Max and pushes him away. "You're not worth ten-to-life."

Nat stands then helps me up. Nik asks, "You serious about working here?"

Max cuts in with a surprised, "What?"

I nod, panting from exertion. Choking your sister is hard work. "Yeah, I need the money."

Max asks a confused, "You need the money?"

Nik nods, smiling. "You're hired." He takes his black badge from around his neck and places it around mine. "I don't think you need an orientation. Your pay is thirty-six an hour and you'll work four hours a night, Saturdays only, for now. How'd you like that?"

I'm astounded. "I dig it."

Max stands in front of me, looking pissed. "You need money and you didn't tell me?"

I roll my eyes. "Of course I need money. I'm a human living in New York." I narrow my brows at him. "What's all this attitude about? I thought I was going to be kissed and hugged and squeezed and all that jazz."

His face softens. "Come here." I walk into his open arms, sliding my arms around him, and he wraps me up tight, running a hand up and down my back. Burying his nose into my neck, he mutters, "This dress."

I grin, asking innocently, "What about it?"

He nips my neck. "You're killing me, cupcake. I have to work while you're wearing this. Fucking torture."

Mimi snorts. "First, you don't like him, and now you can't keep your hands off him!"

Max lifts his head from my neck, catching my mouth in a firm kiss before turning me in his arms so I can face the crowd. Lola smiles at us and coos. "You *guys*! Adorable, I swear." Playing with her straw, she asks curiously, "C'mon, Helena. Tell us why you didn't like Max. I'm dying to know."

Max grunts, "You're not the only one," and I elbow him in the gut. He flinches then lets out an outraged, "What?"

I open my mouth to refuse them, but Felicity's already there. She laughs out loud. "Oh, man. It's a doozy."

Nat gasps. "You know?" She turns to me. "Why does she know? You never told me."

I open my mouth to speak a second time, but it's too late. Felicity utters, "Well, it all happened at your wedding. I'm surprised you don't know."

I lean over to Flick and hiss, "Shut. *Up!*"

Max covers my mouth with his hand, urging her on. "No, no! Don't stop. I want to know!"

So she begins, "Well, Helena had her eye on Max from the very first time she saw him."

My cheeks heat, and I dip my chin to fight my embarrassment. Max asks me quietly, "Is that true?"

I shrug lightly, not willing to answer. Felicity continues, "And it's a wedding. C'mon, you girls know what I'm talkin' about, right?"

All the women wear a knowing look on their faces, nodding and smiling slyly. We're women. Weddings make us emotional. Emotional and horny. I don't know why, but those are the rules. My mind flinches.

Now you're even talking like him!

Before I can stop her, Felicity takes it there. "So Helena's ready to make a move on our handsome Max. She's been watching him all night as he flirts with everything with a heartbeat, and she's built up the courage to ask him to have a drink with her. And she does." She turns to Max, shaking her head at him. "And he doesn't even look up from his phone. In fact, he completely ignores her."

The women's mouths gape. Max's arms tighten around me.

Tina looks sad. "Max, you didn't."

But before Max can say anything, she finishes up, "Oh, he did. And that's not the worst part. After he ignored her, he dismissed her." She pauses for effect before adding, "Then he called her *Helen*!"

The women gasp in disgust while the men let out low sounds of discomfiture.

Oh, yeah.

Tonight sucks assholes.

CHAPTER THIRTY

MAX

My gut sinks. I didn't do that! ...did I?

I let out a long sigh. Chances are I did. I hurt Helena. *Fuck me.*

But, damn it, I'm gonna make up for it somehow.

Helena

Nat leans over looking pissed and smacks at Max's leg, muttering, "Dickhead."

At the very same time, Nik slaps Max across the back of the head, mumbling angrily, "Asshole."

Max squeezes me tightly, defending himself. "I don't remember that! I swear!" He looks over at Nik. "You think if Helena threw herself at me, I'd say no?" Nik makes a noncommittal noise in his throat, looking down at his brother in contempt.

I bunch my nose. "You calling me a liar?"

Max turns me in his arms. "No, I'm not, baby. I'm just saying I don't remember that happening." He dips his head, shaking it lightly. "No wonder you hated me. I'd hate me too." He looks up, his golden eyes sincere. "I'm sorry, cupcake. Never meant to hurt you."

And just like that, it's forgotten. He looks truly ashamed. I reach up to cup his cheek. "I know that. Now. And it's done. We're good. I promise."

He leans into my touch, eyes closed. After a moment, he groans, "Are you fucking kidding me?" When his eyes open, he looks pained. "I could've had you all those months ago and I fucking choked?" He groans again, mock-sobbing. "God, I *am* an asshole."

Chuckling, I stand on my tiptoes, pecking at his lips. "Yeah, well, suffer." I turn to face Nik. "I'm going downstairs to check out the women's bathroom. What do I do if there are people in there doing nasty things?"

Nik takes his two-way off his belt and hands it to me. "Just call it in. Security will be right outside the door waiting for you. Don't lay a hand on 'em. You're not trained for that, and as an employee, you could get us sued. If you find you're liking the job, I'll get Ghost to take you on a short security and crowd control course."

I nod, smiling. "Cool. And noted. No touchies."

Felicity walks down with me, hitting up the bar as I walk into the bathroom. It's empty, and I'm fine with that, because I really need to take a whiz. I head into the stall and do my business, flushing the toilet and moving to open the door, but as I do, three women walk in. I peek out of the crack in the door. I can't see everything, but I can see enough.

"The pickings are slim tonight," mutters a short brunette.

The taller brunette whines, "Where are all the hotties? I really need to get laid."

When the third woman speaks, I perk up. I perk up, because I know that voice. The tall, slender redhead utters, "Oh, please. None of the men here are good enough to even look at me."

The redhead is Portia. I shake my head at her comment. She said *me*, not *us*. Her poor friends.

The shorter brunette smirks, "You're just sore because that guy who works here gave you the brush-off."

The taller brunette asks, "Who cares if he has a girlfriend? I'd still hit that."

Portia sneers, "The girlfriend shows his taste. I don't want him if he chooses to be with a woman like that. He obviously has low standards."

The fucking mole! I bite my tongue and ball my fist in an effort to not go out there and show her a thing or two about manners.

The short brunette grins. "But he *is* rich."

Portia pauses. "Well, there is that. And he would be nice to look at, for a while at least. But to deal with him, I'd have to deal with his kid too."

My heart races as my anger singes my insides.

The tall brunette asks, "What's wrong with that?"

Portia makes a face, her lip curling. "I don't know. She's retarded or some shit."

I don't know how it happens, but the stall door opens and suddenly I'm on top of Portia, clawing at her face while pulling her hair. As she squeals, I hiss out, "You fucking bitch! You goddamn whore! *She's just a little girl!*"

Portia shrieks out, "Get security!"

Then, we're alone. I throw her to the ground, standing. Panting, my body shakes with rage. The inside of my mouth tastes of metallic rust and I know I'm bleeding. I look down at a shocked Portia's red-marked face and utter a hushed, "You're disgusting. You're nothing but a pig."

The doors to the bathroom burst open. Nik, Max, and Asher all rush in to see me looming over Portia.

Max looks at me in confusion. "What the fuck?"

Portia looks over at them and shrieks, "*She attacked me!*"

I can't tell him. If I tell him, he'll be devastated.

Nik sighs. "Are you kidding me? A bitch fight? *Fuckin' hell, Helena.*"

Ash looks over my shaking body and states, "Something happened."

He always knows.

I look over at Max then Nik. "I'm sorry." I walk out of the bathroom and somehow end up back upstairs.

When Nat looks over at me, smiling, her face turns shocked. She jumps up and rushes over to me, searching my body. "What happened? Lena, tell me what happened!"

But I can't. She walks me over the bar, sitting me down on a stool, and a glass of waters appears in front of me. Nik stalks over to us, looking pissed with a capital P. He booms, "I don't believe this. You hit her! After I specifically told you not to touch anyone!"

Max comes up behind him. "Shut up, Nik." He kneels in front of me, looking up into my eyes. "What happened, cupcake?" I don't answer, so he asks, "Did she bait you? What happened?"

Nik rolls his eyes. "She baited you and you fell for it. You realize she's planning to take us to court, right?" He grits his teeth and roars, "*Fuck!*"

Nat glowers at Nik. "Don't you fucking *dare*, Nikolai! My sister would not have touched anyone unless it were necessary!" God bless Nat for sticking up for me. Unfortunately, in this case, she's wrong.

Asher adds calmly, "I think we should give her some room and shut the fuck up."

Max sounds frustrated. "I can't help you if you won't tell me what happened. What did she do, Helena? *Talk to me.*"

Tina appears by our sides. "What's going on here?" She peers over at me, stunned. "Lena, honey. Your lip is bleeding." I know it is. It's throbbing like a bitch.

Mimi speaks from the sideline. "I think Ash is right. Give her some room."

But Nik is too pissed to hear any of it. "I'll tell you what. How about Helena tells me what the fuck happened, and then I'll leave her alone?"

Max stands and gets in his brother's face, jaw set. "Shut the fuck up, Nik. You're not my boss. You better remember that."

Nik's face distorts with anger. "Your girl causes shit not ten minutes after I put my faith in her. Her fuck-up is your fuck-up."

Nat, Tina, Mimi, and Lola all bite out, "*Hey!*" at Nik's rude comment. I've never seen him so angry.

Tina approaches him and speaks softly. "Honey, calm down. She'll talk when she's ready."

Nik straightens and looks up into my eyes. "She'll talk now. What happened?" Nik can be a seriously intimidating guy.

Nat cuts in, "Fuck you, Nik!"

Nik turns on her. "Of course you're sticking up for her. I need to know what happened." My gut coils.

Mimi steps in front of Nik. "We're all friends here, remember?"

Nik sniffs, "Some more than others."

That was a cheap shot. My blood boils. I close my eyes as my chest heaves. Tina gasps in astonishment. "Nik! What has gotten into you?"

He steps closer to me, angry eyes trained on mine. "What happened?"

I open my mouth, but all that comes out is, "I-uh—"

Nik grits his teeth and asks again, "What happened, Helena?"

Max growls in threat, "Take one more step toward her, Nik. I fuckin' dare ya."

I close my eyes. My body thrums. My chest heaves.

Nik asks again, near yelling, "What the fuck happened in there?"

I stand so fast my stool hits the bar with a bang. Hands shaking, I stand a foot away from Nik, looking up into his rage-filled eyes, and thunder, "*She called Ceecee a retard!*" I'm mortified as the angry tears trail down my cheeks, my body shaking with fury. I lower my face into my hands to hide my weakness and whisper, "She called Ceecee retarded."

The silence is so thick you could carve it with a knife. Lowering my hands, I swipe furiously at the tears. I reach out with a shaking hand to take the glass of water into my hands. I sip at it, wishing I could disappear into the darkness, but I know that's not a choice.

Breathing in carefully, I stand as tall as I can and speak softly through an exhale, "I'm sorry for the trouble, Nik." I remove the two-way from my side and badge from around my neck, placing them on the stool. "No need to fire me. I resign. Sorry for spoiling everyone's night. I'm going home. Goodnight."

Tina and Lola both plead, "Helena, no!" and "Stay!" while Nat orders, "Don't you go anywhere. Not 'til he apologizes!"

I turn and walk away with what dignity I have left before I hear Nat scream to who I'm sure is Nik, "You asshole!"

I half-expect that Max will come after me, but he doesn't.

And once again, I'm left feeling how I felt when I first came to New York.

Completely and utterly alone.

MAX

Immobilized by blind fury, I blink as I watch Helena walk away, head held high. I've never seen her look more beautiful, fat lip and all. But as she walks down the stairs, out of sight, my gut churns. I swallow hard knowing that this might be it. This might be where Helena realizes it's too much work being with a man like me. But seeing her stand over Portia after she handed her ass to her, defending my baby girl...*shit.*

I think I'm falling in love, but I don't remember it happening like this the first time round. Did love make a person feel like they'd hit the highest high and lowest low at the very same time? I never wanted this to happen. But knowing Helena as I do now, how could I have ever stopped it?

I should be used to people's offensive and rude comments. But at least when it comes from children, they don't know any better. When I hear adults using the word retard, it just makes me want to smack a bitch. My daughter is not slow or stupid. She is an exceptionally smart and able person, regardless of her injury.

Nik stands there, hands on his hips, looking down at the floor. I feel the guilt come off him in waves. Nat yells at him. "You asshole!"

Tina gives Nat a pleading look. "Nat, stop." She steps closer to him, placing a hand on his chest. "Honey, you didn't know." But he steps back. I've never seen him step away from Tina. Not ever.

He doesn't look up. Instead, he takes the discarded badge and two-way, and makes his way to the door by the bar, leading to the office. He walks out, leaving us standing here. But he doesn't get away that easily. I follow him.

Tina stops me by gripping my wrist. "Max, don't, please. Just let him go."

I look down at my sister-in-law and kiss her forehead in reassurance. "I'm not going to yell at him, Tina, even though he'd deserve it if I did. I just need to talk to him."

I walk over to the door by the bar and scan my way in. I keep walking and don't stop until I make it to Nik's office. He sits at the desk in the throne he calls an office chair with his eyes closed, rubbing at his temple. I clear my throat and he raises his head, looking haggard. He looks to have aged ten years in ten minutes. He shakes his head and mutters roughly, "I fucked up."

He looks as if he wants to say more, so I don't bother speaking. Sometimes, all you need to do for someone to feel better is just listen. Sitting up, he stands and paces behind his desk. "I spoke to you the other day about how great your girl is, and I just tore her down. And I did it in front of everyone." He puffs out a breath. "What the fuck is wrong with me?"

I utter quietly, "No one's perfect. People screw up."

Nik laughs humorlessly. "Yeah, they do. I know that better than anyone, so what the fuck *was* that?" He groans. "Oh, God, she's gonna hate me." Then he sighs dejectedly. "The one girl I like for you and I bully her to tears. And all she was doing was sticking up for my niece."

"Helena's surprising like that."

Nik eyes me a moment before his brows narrow. "What? You're not gonna tear me a new asshole?"

I lean against the doorframe. "You're doing a good job of that yourself. Doesn't look like you need help."

He looks up at me, his eyes apologetic. "I'm sorry, man."

I nod, knowing full-well he is, but say, "I'm not the one you should be apologizing to."

He sits on the edge of his desk, head lowered. "I know." He looks up at me and promises, "I'll make it right. First thing."

"Good." I cock my thumb and point to the door. "You mind if I go save my ass from getting dumped?"

His lip tilts up at the side. "Sure thing."

And with that, I walk out of the office and make my way to the parking lot.

Helena

"I'm fine. Just a little shaken up is all. I haven't lost control like that ever," I mutter into my cell phone as I walk into my apartment. My phone has been ringing off the hook since I left the club.

Nat sniffs. "Yeah, well, the whore got what was coming to her." I agree, but I still made a mess of things, and I don't know how to make it better.

I sent a quick text to Felicity when I left, claiming a sudden illness. She responded with, "You poor little whore! Get well soon. Love ya!"

Nat asks, "You want me to come over? We can watch movies and eat all the junk food."

I chuckle. "All the junk food?"

She responds cheerily, "Yep. All of it!"

Smiling, I force a yawn. "Nah, I'm just going to have a shower and get into bed." I ask cautiously, "How's Max doing after all of that?"

She asks a surprised, "You haven't talked to him?" She hesitates, and then replies, "He went to talk to Nik, but he never came back out of the office." She adds an annoyed, "I'm not talking to Nik, by the way. Not until he apologizes to you."

I sigh. "Don't do that, please? For God's sake, let's just let it go and move on. I don't want to think about it anymore."

She pouts, "But he was so rude to you. I've never seen him be like that before. I can't just get over it. Sorry, the only person who's allowed to be rude to my sisters is me."

Stupid Nat, making me laugh when I want to feel sorry for myself. I say lightly, "Whatever, ho. I'm getting into the shower now. Peace."

"Peace out, sistah!"

I feel something soft and warm at my ankle. I'm surprised to find Tedwood purring up at me. I lean down and scratch him behind the ear. "Oh, I bet you know Mommy's had a bad night." Cats sense shit like that, don't they? "You're a good boy when you want to be."

Unzipping my dress, I work it down my body, stepping out of it and throwing it into my bedroom, and then make my way down the hall and step into the bathroom. I start the shower, step in, and wash away the shitty night I've had.

After a good, unnecessary half-hour in the shower—unnecessary, because I didn't wash my hair—I wrapped a towel around me and walked into my room. As I make my way into my room, I come to a halt in the doorway.

Max sits on the edge of my bed, facing me. "Hey."

My gut sinks. He's here to break up with me. I tighten my grip on the towel and respond weakly, "Hey."

He stands, taking the four steps toward me. "Don't ever do that again."

I lower my head, ashamed. "I'm sorry. I know I shouldn't have done it. She just said it and I don't know what happened." I look up into his eyes, pleading for him to understand. "I just lost it."

He makes a face. "Not *that*." He takes a step closer, looking down at me menacingly. "Don't ever leave me again without giving me your mouth."

Huh? I ask confused, "You're not upset with me?"

He lifts a hand to my lips, outlining them, following his finger with his eyes. "Why would I be?"

I mutter against his fingers, "I attacked a female club patron."

He leans down, gently placing a kiss at the swollen side of my mouth, then nods. "You're passionate."

I close my eyes and murmur, "I let her words get to me when I know better."

He shrugs. "Because she insulted Ceecee. An insult to her is an insult to you." He catches my chin between his thumb and forefinger, forcing my gaze up to his. "How could I ever be mad at you for loving my daughter?"

I like that. Oh, boy. I *really* like that. Bottom lip quivering, I squeak out, "So you're not breaking up with me?" He sighs, yanking at my towel. It falls and I'm left naked. Max wraps an arm around my back and the other under my ass as he lifts me. "What are you doing?" I ask in disbelief as I cinch my arms around his shoulders, holding on tightly.

He carries me over to the bed, laying me down in the middle. Undressing himself, he mutters, "I'm gonna fuck you until you stop being stupid."

Leaning up on my elbows, I gulp at the sight of his bare chest. "Might take a while."

As he pulls down his boxers and climbs over me, he grins and utters, "Challenge accepted."

His body covers me in hard warmth and his mouth devours mine with such passion that I moan out loud. Relief pours through me as I realize Max is still mine.

For now, anyways.

CHAPTER THIRTY-ONE

Helena

Knocking at my front door wakes me, but before I can get up to answer it, Max leans over me and kisses my forehead, slipping out of bed. I hear low murmurs of conversation before Max tiptoes back into the bedroom. Half-asleep and deliciously sore from last night's sexathon, I ask a hushed, "Who is it?"

As he dresses himself, he looks over at me and responds cautiously, "It's Nik. I told him I'd give you guys a minute." My palms sweat, and reaching down, I slowly pull the covers up to my nose. Max smiles softly at the action. "This isn't round two, all right? He just wants to apologize."

I don't want to admit it, but after seeing Nik like he was last night, I'm a little scared to be alone with him. However, I do trust Max. I whisper through my covers, "Okay."

He smiles down at me, climbing over my body to bury his face in the crook of my neck. "You want coffee?"

With his mouth on me, it's hard to concentrate. "Is a frog's ass watertight?"

His breath warms my throat as he chuckles. "Two sugars with a splash of milk, right?"

My eyes snap open. *He knows how I take my coffee?* My heart beams. Whelp, shit got serious and someone forgot to inform me. I lift my arms out of my cocoon of safety and wrap them around his shoulders as I breathe into his ear, "Yeah, honey."

Lifting his head, he kisses the tip of my nose before standing. I ask through narrowed eyes, "You've still got your key, don't you? That's how you got in last night."

Max grins so hard his dimple cuts deep into his cheek. "You're so pretty."

When I roll my eyes, he chuckles and calls out to Nik, "Don't kill each other, okay? I like this one." I smile to myself. But my smile falls to the ground with a plop, when Max tells Nik, "And I plan to keep her."

Does he mean that? I can never work out whether the means the things he says or if they're just for show.

The front door opens then closes, and I close my eyes and sigh knowing I have to face him sooner or later, and the later I wait, the more awkward this will become. Gaining what little courage I have left in me, I slide out of bed and dress in my pajama shorts and loose pink *Cupcakeinator* tee and walk out of my room, into the living-slash-kitchen area.

Nik stands at the open fridge door, rubbing absently at his belly, looking somewhat disappointed. "What are you living on? There's nothing in here."

A shocked laugh bursts out of me. "Your brother says the same thing only all the freaking time."

Nik closes the fridge door and turns to me, a strained smile on his face. "We're alike, him and me. My sisters are a little different. They don't need food every hour to live." I smile, but it's as strained as his. He steps forward and starts, "Listen, Helena, I'm sorr—"

But I cut him off with a shake of my head. "Please, don't apologize. You were right. I screwed up, and I'm the one who's sorry."

He pulls out a stool from the counter and sits, staying quiet for a while before he utters, "I've always been protective of Max. I don't think anyone would blame me for it after what happened with Maddy."

I know about Maddy, but not from Max. I haven't ventured there, but I've been told by Nat it just isn't something Max likes to talk about. With good reason. As far as I know, he only has bad memories of the woman. Nik adds, "But when he told me you were dating, I was happy for him," he looks up into my eyes and utters sincerely, "because you're a good woman."

As long as he's buttering me up, we're going to be just fine. I walk over and pull another stool out, parking my butt on it. "Well, if it isn't the famous Leokov silver tongue."

Nik chuckles. "I'm not just saying that to say it. I'm saying it, because it's true, and I should've known you wouldn't have touched that asshole without a good reason. But for a split second, I thought—stupidly, I might add—that maybe you were gonna be a troublemaker. Like *she* was. And me, being me, I freaked out, not only because I don't want to see him go through that shit again, but because I know this is something he *can't* go through again." He tilts his head, a sheepish smile crossing his face. "So I pushed when I should've reigned it in, and I'm sorry."

I look down at the counter before I push my luck. "I know I'm meant to feel sorry for what I did, but I don't. Not even a little. I'd probably do it all over again. The bitch deserved it."

Nik's rough laugh washes over me. "Yeah, I figured you'd say something like that. And secretly, I'm glad she got hers."

I peek up at him and wince. "So about the lawsuit—"

But he cuts me off with a gentle shake of his head. "Didn't you hear? We have witnesses to say she hit you first."

My mouth gapes. "But she didn't—"

He speaks over me, lip twitching. "And wouldn't you know it? There isn't CCTV in the bathrooms. We reported her before she managed to report us." He shrugs. "Good to have friends at the NYPD."

I smile. "Sure is."

He smiles down at me, stands, and opens his arms wide. "Come here."

Without a second thought, I stand and walk into his embrace. He wraps me up into a bear hug and sways me from side-to-side. "I'm so sorry. I promise I won't ever talk to you like that again."

Squeezing him tightly, I lay on the guilt-trip I know I'm entitled to. "You were so mean."

As he lets out a sore groan, I chuckle and he kisses my temple. "You're all right, kid."

We separate, and being a smartass, I ask, "So you don't mind my dating Max?"

He scoffs, "Dating? Shit, I hope you marry his lame ass."

"Oh, my God, don't say things like that! You'll scare him off," I mutter, only half-joking.

Nik raises his brows and states in earnest, "You couldn't chase that fear away." He reaches over and squeezes my hand. "You make him happy."

The front door opens and Max walks in with two coffees in a cardboard holder. He looks down at Nik's hand over mine and accuses, "You stealin' my girl, homes?" Then he looks over at me and asks, "You good, cupcake?"

His concern and consideration warms me. "Yeah."

Nik looks down at the coffees. "You didn't get me one?"

Max grins. "Nope, but I got Mrs. Crandle a tea." He did? This *man*. Sweet Jesus, he's killing me! "Now take the hint and go home."

Nik shakes his head, but walks to the door. "Shut up, bonehead."

Max scowls. "You shut up."

Nik turns back to me and utters, "Helena. Always a pleasure, sweetheart." Then he tells Max, "Make sure you bring her to dinner tomorrow night."

Max opens the door for Nik. "I will. Smell ya later, bro."

Nik lifts his hand high in a wave and Max closes the door on him. I can't help but laugh. "You're so rude to him."

Max smiles and says, "He knows I love him. Besides, it's fun pissing him off." He checks his watch. "Should we pick up Ceecee soon and have a real breakfast? You know, before midday?"

My smile falls. I'm really not feeling up to seeing anyone today. In fact, I was hoping to have a day in. Alone. "Would you be totally peeved if I skipped breakfast this morning?"

His face turns apprehensive. "Everything okay?"

I force a cheerful smile. "Of course. I'm just feeling a little...tired today."

His face falls further. However, he clears his throat and nods. "Uh, yeah. Okay. That's cool. I'll tell Ceecee we'll see you tomorrow."

No argument? No questions? No guilt? Who *is* this man?

Walking over to him, I snake my arms around his middle, rest my chin on his chest, and look up at him. "Thank you for understanding."

But how he responds tears me apart inside. "I know I can be too much sometimes."

Pulling back, I frown. "Anyone who's ever told you you're *too much* doesn't know you at all." I run my hand down the side of his cheek and state, "You're the perfect amount of *much*. I just don't think I'd be the best company today, and I don't want Ceecee to feel like I don't want to be there."

He smiles then, and it's a real Max smile. I immediately relax. He bends down to kiss the top of my head. "You know, if something's bothering you, you can talk to me."

I squeeze him a second time and admit, "Thanks. I think I'm just homesick. I miss the beach." Pulling back, I gasp. "Why don't the three of us go to Coney Island next weekend? I mean, I know it's not exactly summer, but that would be fun, right? Do you think Ceecee would like it?"

Max chuckles. "Whoa, there. Hold up. Firstly, sure. Secondly, yes, that would be fun. Thirdly, she'd love it."

Now I'm excited. I grip his forearms and rush out, "I heard people at work talking about how Coney Island's wheelchair access has tripled over the last few years, and they've got these cool things called *Mobi-Mats* that they've set down on the sand so people with wheelchair's can make it almost all the way to the water! Maybe if it's warm enough, we can take her all the way down to the beach, you can lift her out of her chair, and she can dip her feet in the water?"

Although he smiles, his brows crease. He looks like he wants to say something, but instead shakes his head. "We can do anything you like, Lena. Anything."

My brain snorts coke and blacks out, leading me to blurt out, "You're turning out to be the best boyfriend ever, and that scares the crap out of me." After I say this, I bend at the waist, reach up with a shaking hand to hold my now-sweating forehead, and hyperventilate.

Wow. That was just...bravo.

But Max just laughs. When I right myself, I smile up at him so weakly that it feels like a cringe. He walks to the door, opens it, and confides, "You keep saying things like that and I'm gonna go ahead and fall in love with you." At the shocked look on my face, he grins. "Don't say I didn't warn ya." Then he walks out, closing the door behind him.

Close to three hours later, I sit on my bed so bored out of my brains that I think I might just stub my toe.

You know? For fun.

Tedwood sleeps curled in a ball on my side of the bed, and as I stroke his feather-soft fur, I stare at my phone.

Just call him.

No. He'll think I'm needy.

Send him a text.

Then he'll think I'm sending mixed messages.

Tell him you need to talk to Ceecee.

I smile. I *do* want to speak to Ceecee. I want to know what she did over the weekend. I want to ask her about her exercises and tell her I hope she's doing better. God. Is it pathetic for one for your best friends to be thirteen?

Reaching next to me, I grip my pillow, hold it to my chest, and throw myself back onto the bed. As soon as my back hits the mattress, my phone chimes. I reach over and check the display.

Max calling.

Happiness flows through me and I answer with, "Hey. I was just thinking about you."

I'm surprised when Ceecee giggles. "Uh…it's me."

The sound of her giggle makes my heart sing. "Well, I was thinking about you too, young grasshopper. How was breakfast?"

She makes a noise. "It was okay. Because you couldn't come, we just stayed at Grandma's." She asks, "Are you feeling better?"

I hug my pillow and nod, even though she can't see it. "Sure am, honey pie. Turns out, all I needed was a nap." Then I beat around the bush. "What are you guys doing now?"

She states, "Coming over."

I sit up and blink. "Coming over where?"

She giggles again. "To your apartment."

A beaming smile crosses my face. "Really?"

I hear the smile in her voice. "Well, Daddy asked me to check if that was okay. He said we won't stay long. I just wanted to bring you some chicken soup, because you weren't feeling well."

I'm surprised as emotion flows through me, clogging my throat. "You made me soup?"

She suddenly turns shy, mumbling, "Yeah, but Grandma helped." She pauses a moment, then asks quietly, "Is that okay?"

I bark out a laugh. "Yes, it's okay! Just tell your dad to pick up some ice cream and popcorn. We'll watch a movie."

"Really?"

"Yes, really." I decide to go full truths. "Honey, I'm so glad you called. I was bored out of my brains."

I hear the happiness leak out of her as she rushes out, "Okay! We'll see you soon! Bye!"

She hangs up in a hurry and I laugh as I throw my cell down on my bed. I turn to Tedwood and he peeks open one eye. I ask him, "You feel like a cupcake?" I stand and walk into the kitchen, yelling back at him, "I feel like a cupcake."

Twenty minutes later, they arrive, but Max doesn't bother knocking on the door. He uses his key. And I like that in a way that most people would find weird. Ceecee wheels herself in first, holding a dishtowel-covered Tupperware container. She smiles up at me. "Careful, it's hot."

Dressed in black yoga pants, a hoodie, and white socks, I lean down and hug her tightly. As I pull away, I kiss her cheek and utter, "Thank you so much, C. I'm starved." I take the container and place it on the counter as I watch Max struggle with two full grocery bags as he walks into my kitchen.

I also like that super weirdly. I walk over to him and take one. He catches my lips in a quick kiss, pulls back looking apologetic, and mouths, "Sorry." Then whispers, "We won't stay long."

Placing the bags on the counter, I shake my head and utter, "Don't be silly. I want you here."

Ceecee gasps and reaches down. When she turns around, Tedwood sits in her lap and she whisper-hisses wide-eyed, *"You have a kitty!"*

I smile down at him. Ever since Max gave him that pep talk, he's been acting semi-normal. The worm. Walking behind Max, I open a cupboard and take out a white packet. I hand it to Ceecee and tell her, "His name is Tedwood, Teddy for short. And if you give him a few of his smelly fish treats, he'll let you love him."

She smiles so hard her cheeks are at risk of exploding. I make my way back to the kitchen, where Max stands watching Ceecee. I reach over and place my hand in his, entwining our fingers. He looks over at me, smiling. I smile in return before looking back at Ceecee. I whisper sincerely, "I want you here."

Letting go of my hand, he wraps an arm around me, pulling me into him. I reach up, placing my hand on his chest, mildly terrified of how right this feels. Standing on my tiptoes, I lay a gentle kiss on his jaw before taking my container of soup and moving to the sofa, where Ceecee plays with Teddy. "So, what junk did you get us?"

Max works at putting thing in the fridge and freezer, calling out, "We got everything we need for a banana split, chips, dip, popcorn, and—"

A beaming Ceecee cuts him off with, "We got cupcakes!"

Making a sound of mock-disgust, I raise my hand to Ceecee's and as she giggles, we high-five. Shaking my head, I mutter solemnly, "And may God have mercy on our souls."

"Amen," comes from both Max and Ceecee.

I blink up over at them a moment before I whisper in admiration, "That was awesome."

I turn on the TV, open the container of soup, and spoon some into my mouth. "Oh, God," I moan out. I smack my lips together and praise the chef. "Damn, girlie. I'm not even sure you need lessons anymore. You're turning out to be a regular Jamie Oliver."

Her face falls momentarily. "But I like cooking with you."

My heart swells and I reach over to stroke her reddish-brown hair. "You can cook with me whenever you like. Soon enough, you'll be teaching me new things." I eat my soup in record time then stand and take it into the kitchen, where Max opens bags of chips and dumps them into bowls. I steal a handful then sit back down, sharing my loot with Ceecee. "What are we watching?"

Max joins us, bringing the chips and sodas, and then hands me a DVD case. I gasp dramatically. "*How did you know?*" I turn to Ceecee and beam. "I love *Pirates of the Caribbean*. In fact, I love anything Johnny Depp. I still have a poster of him in my clos—"

Max's face takes on a look that reminds me of when you suddenly smell someone's fart. "Johnny who?"

Biting the inside of my cheek to hide my grin, I mumble, "Nothing." I slip the DVD into the player and sit back on the sofa. Max lifts my feet onto his lap and starts massaging them.

Talk about spoiled.

Sitting one bowl of chips on the armrest between the sofa and Ceecee's chair, Max takes the remote, looks me in the eye, and asks, "Ready?"

No. I don't think I am ready for what he's offering.

But I'll sure as shit try to hold on and ride the rollercoaster.

I smile softly. "As I'll ever be."

CHAPTER THIRTY-TWO

MAX

Walking into Nik's office, I pull up a chair and state, "I need next Sunday off."

Sunday nights aren't usually busy, so I'm not surprised when he doesn't look up from typing at his computer when he responds, "Okay. I'll make sure Trick can work it." This part comes a little harder. It comes harder, because I've never asked for this, and I'm not sure what his answer will be. As if just noticing I haven't left yet, Nik raises his head and narrows his eyes at me, "What do you want now?"

"Next Saturday off too."

He leans back in his chair and looks at me, hard. "Why?"

I shrug and try not to sound like a pussy when I mumble, "I want to take Helena home for the day. She's homesick, misses the beach."

Nik's brows rise and he puffs out a laugh. He shakes his head and grins knowingly. "When are you going to tell her you're in love with her?"

I scoff. "It's only been three and a half weeks since we got together. I'm not in I—"

He cuts me off with a firm, "Yes, you are."

Frustration wells in me. Leaning back in the chair, I sputter angrily, "That wasn't meant to happen. It wasn't part of the plan."

Nik raises a brow in question. "What exactly was your plan?"

I stand and emphasize every word with quick pauses in between, "To *not* fall in love." Nik tips his head back and bursts into laughter. My lip curls. "What are you laughing at, *Dik*?"

Still chuckling, he utters, "Do you think I wanted to fall in love with Tina? Hell *no*. It wasn't the right time for me. I had a plan too. The plan I had to settle down was set to commence next year." He grins. "It don't work that way, Maxie-boy. Put it this way. If Helena called you today and told you she wanted to see other people, what would you do?"

I roll my eyes. "I'd say fuck no and that wouldn't be happening."

He smirks. "'Cause the thought of some other guys hands on her makes you want to draw blood, right? Because she's your woman, and she loves your daughter. She makes you smile for real, not the one you learned to put on for the sake of other people. And because when she holds your hand, she does it for the world to see, and she cares about small shit like that. Or maybe it's because she truly cares about you, heart and soul."

The fight successfully knocked out of me, I puff out, "Yeah."

Nik looks up in thought. "Take Friday off too. I don't think you've taken her out on a real date before, have you, you cheap bastard?"

My brows narrow in thought. "No, I haven't."

Nik sighs, "Do I gotta do everything for you?"

As I step back out of his office, I flip him the bird. Walking down the hall, I hear him call out, "Sure you don't want me to wipe your ass too?"

I puff out a laugh.

Asshole.

Helena

God, I'm missing home. A lot. Today more than yesterday. As I wait for my three pm session with Sam, a Marine vet and amputee, I reach across my desk, pick up my phone, and type out a text.

Me: You are the reason doves cry.

With a calmed sigh, I place my phone where it was and print out exercise sheets to give Sam. As I hit print, my phone vibrates.

Nina: Oh my God, you whore. I spat my coffee out everywhere.

I smile down at the screen, but it's a sad smile.

Me: I miss your fat ass.

Nina: I miss your cellulite and weird eye.

I squint down at the screen.

Me: When are you going to tell our middle, balder, fatter sister about you know what?

She doesn't respond for a very long time, and I know she knows I know, so I send her another quick statement.

Me: I love you. There. I said it. Happy?

A moment later, my phone vibrates.

Nina: Soon...ish. I'll visit soon. Love you too. X

I still have twenty minutes before the next session, and I'm up to date with all my file entries, so I pick up my phone and dial.

He answers almost immediately, sounding happy to hear from me. "Cupcake, why are you reading my mind? I was just thinking about you."

I smile into the receiver. "Oh, yeah, well guess what?"

"What?"

I quell down my excitement and singsong, "I managed to get Ceecee a place in a wheelchair basketball game." As I chuckle at my triumph, I explain, "The kids are just like Ceecee. They've all struggled with being different, and they have a really positive feedback system. It's a social media network where the kids can talk to each other about whatever's bothering them, but don't worry. Parents are encouraged to go on there too. Nothing is private or hidden, so she won't be talking to any creepers. I made sure of that. But what it is, really, is a support network for Ceecee with kids her own age. What do you think?"

Silence. Then, "I think you put a lot of thought into this, into helping Ceecee."

I admit, "I have. I really have, and I think I know why she ended up rebelling. I think it was because she started to feel lonely in her own family. And before you say anything, it happens. So many of my clients feel like they can't talk to their family about their problems, because able-bodied people can listen, but they can never truly understand how they're feeling, you know?"

He responds thoughtfully, "Yeah, I guess I never thought about it like that."

"Well, that's kind of the point, honey. You wouldn't. So the game is this Saturday at ten am. It's not far from the house either. I'll send you the address and I'll meet you there."

He hesitates. "This Saturday?"

My face falls. "Yeah, this Saturday. Is that going to be a problem?"

"I sort of…" he pauses, "…had something planned for you. A surprise."

I smile. "A surprise? For me? Max, you don't need to give me surprises." I lower my voice and utter, "I'm a sure thing."

He chuckles, then utters, "I know I don't need to, but I wanted to. But if Ceecee's game is Saturday, then we can't do it."

I shrug to no one in particular. "That's okay. I think it's really important for Ceecee to meet people with similar injuries that are her own age."

He pauses. "So you'd just put your own surprise on hold for Ceecee? Just like that?"

My brows rise. Why the hell does he sound panicked? "Uh, yeah. Yes, I would."

He covers the phone for a second, and although it's not very clear, I hear him utter a pained, "*Damn you, Nik. Damn you.*"

I ask cautiously, "Everything okay?"

Rustling, then he's back. "Yep. Everything's peachy. Okay, surprise is on hold. Ceecee has basketball Saturday. And you and I are going on a date Friday night. Dinner, movie, the whole shebang. No excuses."

I grin. "We are?"

He states adamantly, "No exceptions."

My smile turns soft. Max wants to take me out. Out where people will see us together as a couple. Warmth blooms in my middle. "Okay. It's a date."

He utters confidently, "Damn right it is." He kisses the phone then hangs up, leaving me smiling like a loon.

Helena

The week passed slowly, but with my session times filling up, at least the workdays will be moving along at a quicker pace as the weeks pass. Felicity and I exchanged knowing smiles with Willa, and even talked her into having lunch with us on Thursday. As soon as we sat down to eat, I asked gingerly, "So how long have you been in love with Whit?"

James Whittaker was one manly man. He was also stupidly sexy. But he was our boss, and he claimed that employer/employee relationships were a no-go at the center. This confused me, because I checked the office intranet. There was absolutely nothing in there about interoffice relationships or the banning of them.

Willa went ghost white and licked at her lips. She looked like she was about to deny having any such feelings for him, but as she lifted her sandwich to her lips, she muttered, "Since forever," before she took a bite.

Felicity was in shock. She turned to me and asked in awe, "How did you do that?

I shrugged at her. I've always made people feel comfortable with talking to me. Instead of responding, I dug further, "And why have you done nothing about this?"

I was almost surprised when her pretty hazel eyes glared at me from across the table. Almost, but not. "And what on earth would I say, Lena? Hi, James, mind if we step into your office to discuss a matter that's been bothering me for a while? What matter, you ask? Oh, the one where I almost swoon when you smile at me." She rolled her eyes. "Please. I know I'm not his type." Her face fell. "I'm not anyone's type."

Felicity pushed her shoulder and grinned, "Oh, my Lord, there's so much attitude hiding behind that sweet face. I am going to have so much fun with you."

Swallowing my mouthful, I asked, "How can you be sure if you've never given him the signs?"

Felicity nodded in agreement while Willa's face turned guarded. "What signs?"

"The subtle ones." I shrugged as I thought. "You know? Light touches. Eye contact. Smiles that are just for him."

Felicity gasped. "I have a great idea!" Willa groaned and threw her head down onto the table, forcing a laugh out of me. Felicity rubbed her back, chuckling, and uttered, "This afternoon, we'll run an experiment. Willa, you're going to flirt with Whit. Today."

Lifting her face, mouth gaping, Willa sputtered, "I am not!" Felicity nodded slowly, smiling larger every second. Willa shook her head. "You're crazy."

Felicity admitted on a shrug, "It's my best quality."

I asked sagely, "What do you have to lose?"

Later that afternoon, Felicity and I instructed Willa on what to do. First, we had her approach James and talk to him about a client. She did this, but it didn't work out as we hoped. Instead of approaching him, he came to her to talk about something, and when he did, she was seated at her desk. Not a lot of opportunities to discreetly touch him there.

But mid-conversation, James came up behind her to show her something on her computer, and he did this all up in her grill. I mean, his chin was almost resting on her shoulder. It looked like Willa wasn't going to be playing this game one-sided.

Next, we planned a run in. Yes, exactly as it sounded. They would run into each other. So when James came walking down the hall, looking down at his papers and not paying attention to what he was doing, Felicity and I mouthed, "Go!" shooing her away. She stood in his path, and that was that.

Next thing, James had his arms around her, holding her up a moment before she hit the ground from the impact of collision. He looked into her eyes and muttered, "Are you okay?"

They were close. Closer than they should've been. She whispered, "Yes."

But his brows narrowed as he stood her up, placing his hands on her shoulders. "Are you sure? I'm so sorry. I didn't see you there."

Willa shrugged, smiling sadly. "A lot of people don't."

Then something miraculous happened. James placed his hands on his hips, looking down to the ground. After a moment's hesitation, he muttered, "Then they're missing out," before walking away.

Willa turned to us, dumbstruck. Felicity and I silently danced and cheered. James Whittaker was totally into Willa, and Felicity and I were going to make it happen. Somehow.

Then came Friday, and Willa was still a nervous mess around James. But during our lunch break, we dragged Willa out of the office and swore blind that James liked her. However, Willa, being the shy little violet, wasn't having it. "He's just being nice."

We were becoming exasperated. There was one thing left to do. I asked, "Do you have a tank under that shirt?" Willa nodded. "Good," I uttered a moment before I reached forward and tugged at her shirt so hard that the buttons went flying. Felicity gaped a moment before she burst into laughter.

Willa looked down at her ruined shirt and whispered, "I can't believe you did that." She turned to a still laughing Felicity. "I can't believe she did that."

I put on my best embarrassed expression. "Oops."

This left Willa dressed in short athletic shorts and a skin-tight white tank, showing enough skin to make any man stop and stare. When we arrived back at the office, talking and laughing, we bumped into James on the way to our desks. I pointed back at Willa, who was now hugging herself, and stated, "Don't be hard on her. I accidentally ripped her shirt."

James frowned down at me. "How did you accidentally rip her shirt?"

I shrugged. "The Hulk doesn't know his own strength."

When Willa went to move by James, he blocked her path and not on purpose. He was eyeing her body, getting his fill, and I'd guess he didn't even know he was doing it. When she swallowed hard, blushed, and muttered, "Excuse me," James moved. A little. As she walked by him, she brushed against him.

My brain smiled smugly, and just as she passed me, I flicked my pen off my desk. Willa immediately bent down to pick it up, giving James a front view seat to her firm ass. James looked down, gripped the side of my desk, then turned and walked away. Fast.

Oh, yeah. He was totally into her. If only he could see what was right in front of him.

It was sad.

Really.

CHAPTER THIRTY-THREE

Helena

"Turkey on white okay?" I call out to Asher as he works on my leaking showerhead.

He calls back from the bathroom, "What the fuck *ever*." His New York accent thickens when he spouts, "I'm starving' here."

Nat laughs at something on TV, sitting on my sofa, eating chips from the bag, while I go ahead and work on feeding her apparently famished husband. How famished he is, I couldn't tell. It seems Max, Ash, Nik, and Trick eat almost all day long. I'm not even sure how Mama Leokov wasn't eaten out of house and home.

As I grab the Turkey and mayo from the refrigerator, I side-eye Nat, biting the inside of my cheek. I know I shouldn't say anything, that it isn't my business to tell, but the longer I think about it, the faster my heart beats. It beats faster and faster, when suddenly I blurt out, "I need to tell you something and it's important, but you're likely to overreact, and I'm sure she would just tell you if she was sure you wouldn't overreact and blab to Mom and Dad, but we *know you,* and you have a tendency to overreact, dammit."

Nat turns to me slowly, searching my face. "What the hell are you talking about, Cheech?"

I slap the bread on top of the sandwich and growl, "You're so slow. I actually can't believe you don't know this already. Granted, I shouldn't know, but I did some detective work and found out, because I fucking care." I glare at her. "Don't you care?"

Her brows rise to her hairline before she calls out to the bathroom, "Ash, baby, I think we need to take Helena to the hospital or some shit."

He calls back, "She bleeding?"

Nat looks over me. "No, but she's talking crazy."

He grunts, "She *is* crazy."

I glower at the bathroom door. "Crazy like a fox!"

Nat chuckles before asking, "What are you talking about, Lena?"

I make a sound of exasperation. "Nina." Nat's face tells me she clearly doesn't know what the eff I'm talking about. I roll my eyes, throw my arms out by my sides, and boom, "She's gay!"

Her eyes widen in disbelief a moment before she bursts into laughter. She laughs and laughs and coughs then laughs some more. But I'm not laughing. I look at her with a firm eye, and slowly, her laughter dies. After a moment, she sputters, "Are you joking? You're not joking, are you?" She chuckles humorlessly. "Why do you think she's gay?"

I look her in the eye and utter, "The simple fact she has a girlfriend."

Nat's eyes widen comically a moment before she jumps up from the sofa and paces, clearly shocked. "A girlfriend? What the fuck? How do you know this?"

I tip my head to the side. "Like I said, I did my research."

She turns to face me with her hands on her hips, looking more hurt than I've ever seen. "And she would hide this from me? Like I'd give a flying fuck if she preferred tuna to a hot beef injection? Why would she hide this?"

Leaning my hip against the counter, I purse my lips. "I think she'd hide this, because of Mom and Dad."

Nat looks up at me, determined, but her voice is small and unsure. "Mom and Dad wouldn't care. They love her. They love us."

My mom and dad are from Eastern Europe, one of the only places left in the world that is still ridiculously homophobic. I love my mom and dad, but on this issue, I'm not sure they would be okay with it. I raise my brow. "You so confident that you would put money on that?"

At that moment, Ash walks out of the bathroom, wiping his hands on a rag. "Done. Now feed me, woman."

Smiling, I hand him his plate. "Thank you, best brother-in-law ever."

Taking a bite out of his sandwich, he raises it in the air in acknowledgement and jerks his chin at me, but Nat stands there looking more confused by the minute. She turns to Ash and asks, "Did you know about this?"

He swallows before scratching his brow. "That Nina's a rug-muncher?" He nods, completely oblivious. "Yeah. So?"

Oh, my godfather, Ash. Has no one taught you anything about women? Deny, deny, *deny*!

Nat's turns to her husband in false calm. "You didn't think I should know about this?"

Sitting on the sofa, he reaches into the bag of chips and shoves some into his mouth, then garbles, "If she wanted you to know, she'd have told you, baby."

Face turning a nice shade of pissed-the-hell-off, she reaches into her back pocket, pulls out her cell, presses a few buttons, and then holds the phone to her ear. My eyes widen.

Uh oh.

After a few seconds, she screams into the phone, "You like taco and you never told me?"

As Nat continues to hurl weirdly supportive abuse at Nina through the power of telecommunication, Ash chuckles at me. "Oh, now you've done it."

I wince. *Yikes.* Reaching for my own cell, I type out a quick message, hoping she won't be pissed.

Me: Um...surprise?

A moment later, my display lights up and I mope.

Nina: You are so fucking dead, bro.

Nat paces, flailing her arms animatedly and rambling, "...because, hey, I know lesbians! I'm totally cool with lesbians! What I'm not cool with is my *lesbian* sister hiding her sexuality from me like I'm a goddamn anti-lesbite!" She pauses in her tracks, listening, before her brows narrow dangerously and she fires back, "*It totally is a word!* Google it!"

I look over at Ash and mutter, "You think she really didn't know?"

He looks over at me, brows raised, before looking at the scene his wife is making, then looks back to the TV, reaching for more chips. "She really didn't know."

Nat sighs. "I'm not going to tell them. Relax, Max. But it would've been nice for you to tell me yourself and for me not to have found out through the youngest Kovac spawn." She smiles softly and I know Nina is apologizing to her, probably by calling her a moron for not working it out sooner. "So I hear you've got yourself a girl, huh? What's her name?" Nat laughs. "Amelia. Nice. Sounds like she's a real lady." She grins. "So does that make you the man in the relationship?" Her smile falls. "Hello? Nina?" She holds up her cell, looking irate. "Bitch hung up on me!"

I shrug and tip my head slightly. "Calling a woman a man will do that."

Nat stares down at the phone as if it offends her, and even though she's acting like a turd, I know she's happy to be in the know. Maybe Nat finding out isn't so bad. Pushing her cell back into her pocket, she mumbles through a pout, "Sensitive beaver-eating mole."

Uh, yeah. Okay. Maybe not.

Helena

When Max told me he and I were going out on a date, I prepared myself for the best date ever. That was my first mistake. My second mistake was building it up in my head. And when I say I built it up, I mean I made it into the freaking Eiffel tower. Then he came to pick me up dressed in dark jeans, a black button-up shirt untucked, his white sneakers, and his too-long-to-be-tamed hair carefully tousled, and my heart let out a long, dreamy sigh.

By that point, my engine was already revving. I sashayed over to him, smiling innocently, like a wolf in sheep's clothing, hoping for a taste of what was to come later in the night. His bright smile faltered when I pressed myself against him, leaning up to kiss under his jaw, letting my hand linger on the silver belt buckle at the waist of his jeans.

He cleared his throat before he rasped, "What are you doing, cupcake?"

Of course he could see right through me. I wasn't hiding what I wanted from him. Not in the slightest. My light jeans a contrast to his dark ones, I pushed my breasts into his chest (thank the lord for high heels), my silky tan tank brushing deliciously over my stomach, spurring me further, and breathed, "Having dessert."

His arms went around me then, one firmly wrapped around my back, pulling me devastatingly close, while the other hand slid down my body, over the curve of my hip to cup my butt. He made a low noise of arousal in his throat, and the hand splayed on my cheek squeezed. "We're gonna be late for dinner."

I pouted, looking up at him with what Nat calls my Bambi eyes. I had practiced this look growing up. The time spent practicing clearly paid off. There was little I would ask for that my parents would say no to when I pulled these babies out. I lifted my fingers, spacing them an inch apart. "Not even a little play?"

He looked down at me with those liquid golden eyes and I knew I had him. He sighed dramatically before kissing my mouth, and he didn't do it half-assed. He never did. He kissed me deep, taking his time, tasting me. "How can I say no to you?" Grinning, I lowered myself, slow and sexy, 'til I knelt in front of him. He looked down at me questioningly, and then I reached up to undo his belt. His eyes widened a moment before he broke into a grin. "Rock'n'roll, baby."

He lifted his shirt a little to help me out. It took no time at all to unbutton him and lower his zipper, and then with a swift yank, his jeans and boxer were around his knees. He was only semi-erect, but still looking too big and much too thick to fit entirely in my mouth. I wrapped my fingers around him, ignoring Max's hiss, then looked up into his eyes.

I knew men liked that. I had been friends with a guy in college, a total horn-dog, who once told me that guys loved when a woman was on her knees, looking up at them innocently. Even more so when the woman was wearing lipstick, apparently any color would do. He also told me that men loved when a woman maintained eye contact during a blowjob. I was about to test that theory.

Max looked down at me, eyes hooded, mouth slightly parted. It was always like this with him. He had no poker face. He wore his heart on his sleeve, and I loved that.

I loved him.

This was still not something I was willing to put out there. Hell, I didn't know if I *ever* wanted to put it out there. I knew it was too soon. I knew it would freak the fuck out of Max. I decided to work on him slowly. If I spooked him, he'd run. I couldn't lose him. He was already part of me. So was Ceecee. I was done fighting it.

Max was my one exception. He was likely one of the only men out there who would not only support my work choice, but also be proud of me for doing it. And if long hours and weekends were shot, I know he would understand. After all, his work at the club was not during the most convenient hours either. But I was willing to deal.

I was happy keeping my secret, and would do whatever it took for it to remain that way. The only person I would have to careful around was Nik. The man saw everything.

Max gently reached down, cupping my cheek with one hand, while lifting my long hair over my shoulder with the other. I looked up once more, holding his heavy cock, gently kissing the head. Blinking, I whispered, "So big."

He gripped my chin, his lips twisting into a small, sexy smile as he rumbled, "You like it, baby? Say you like my cock."

It wasn't really a request. It was a demand. My core clenched and I licked the sensitive underside. Speaking against his throbbing length, I sighed softly, "I love it." *I love you.*

My lips parted, and with him guiding me by his hold on my chin, I took in what I could of him. But it wasn't easy. For the amount of smart-assing and shit-talking we manage, my sisters and I have quite the small mouths. Curse it to heck.

Opening my mouth wide, I took in a little more, sucking him deep. Max threw his head back, one hand at my chin, the other now fisting the hair at my nape. At the slight pain, I moaned around him, and his fingers tightened around the loose strands of my hair as he gently thrust in and out of my mouth.

At one point, he thrust a little too hard without meaning to and I gagged. Imagine my shock when that only fueled Max's fire. *The dirty fucker.*

I knew the exact moment he lost control. His hooded eyes trained on where my mouth wrapped around his cock and he growled, a low, animalistic sound I was starting to love to hear, and I heard it every time I put my hands on him. I was wetter than I should have been. Giving head shouldn't be that much of a turn on, right? Regardless, I was soaked, and even though I wanted him inside me, I would settle for watching Max lose control, because watching Max lose control was becoming my most favorite thing to witness.

The hand in my hair loosened before both of his hands cupped my cheeks. He made low rumbling noises in his throat as he quickened his thrusts, his brows furrowed in concentration, watching me closely. He was almost there. He stopped his thrusting and I began stroking him as I kept sucking as deep as I could. Breathing heavily, he cursed. "Fuck, baby, I'm gonna come."

When he tried to pull out, I tightened my fingers around him and sucked harder, willing him to understand I wouldn't be letting him go this time. His eyes snapped open. "Are you sure?"

Jeez, Max. I'm kinda busy here. You mind saving the questions 'til after?

Not willing to take my mouth off him, I sucked deeper, faster. His chest heaved with every breath he took, groaning in pure pleasure. It almost sounded like a purr. He released my cheeks to run his thumb over my bottom lip as I bobbed my head onto him. He muttered, "So pretty. You're so fuckin' pretty."

That was that. When he came, he came fluidly. This was not hot, harsh sex. This was pure intimacy, made more intimate as I swallowed every spurt of the warm saltiness of my reward. His pleasure was my reward. We stayed that way for a long while. His throbbing cock now softening, I gently released him, running my tongue along his still impressive length. He shuddered, blinking down at me drowsily.

I had to smile. I'd done that to him. I loved that so damn much. So when Max opened his mouth, I'd expected something just as intimate as my act to follow.

I was wrong.

He helped me up, pulling me to him, then he squeezed me tight.

This is nice, I thought. I buried my nose into his neck and breathed in the subtle scent of his cologne. Pulling back, he kissed my cheek before tucking himself back in and smiling down at me. "Thanks, cupcake." He sighed, contently. "I needed that."

My face fell. I blinked. It took a moment to register what he'd just said. Obviously I had misread what this was. This date was not a step forward in our non-relationship. This was nothing to him. This was the reason I needed to hide my feelings. This was the reason I'd likely be single forever.

And that fucking sucked.

Pun intended.

The moment I said what I said, I saw the look on her face. The disappointment, the sadness and hurt. Did I really just *thank her* for one of the best blowjobs in my life?

This is why I'm going to be single forever.

I'm a coward, and a royal fuck-up.

CHAPTER THIRTY-FOUR

Helena

I manage to paste on a smile and quell down my stupid emotions enough to fake my happy, take Max's hand, and walk down to his car with him. As we drive, he holds my hand. I look down at our entwined fingers and my chest pangs. What that simple gesture means to him and what it means to me are two different things. It means everything to me. To him, it's just a sure sign he's getting laid later. I clench my teeth and roll my eyes as I turn back to look out the window.

You're so stupid. He doesn't care about you. He cares about Ceecee. You're being used.

Am not.

Hello? Dignity? Where the hell are you?

We made a deal. I knew what I was getting into. I shouldn't be so shocked, and truthfully, I'm not. Max never promised me anything. I was the one who let herself get lost in false hope. I knew better than to do such a thing. I'd never have the sweet love that Tina and

Nik have, or even the passionate love that Nat and Asher have. And maybe it wouldn't be so bad. Maybe I'd be content without it.

Then why is your heart aching just thinking about it?

I look over at Max, and as if he senses it, he turns to me. He searches my face, eyes narrowed before asking softly, "You okay, babe?"

"Of course," I lie easily.

His fingers squeeze mine. "If you don't want to do dinner, it's okay. We can just get something to go and take it back to your apartment. Mom's got Ceecee for the night." His dimple pops out with his smile. "I can undress you and rub lotion into you. You know, give you a massage."

I smile at that. Why does he have to be so clueless in some ways, make me angry, then say something sweet. It's almost impossible to stay mad at him, damn it right to hell. I hide my smile by biting my lip. "Rub lotion into me? Massage me? Whoa. I wouldn't dream of putting you through something like that."

Max sighs, bringing my hand to his mouth, kissing my knuckles. "I admit it would be a trial, but I know together, we'll get through it."

Together.

My playful mood is gone with the use of that one word.

How long will we be *together*?

We arrive at the restaurant and Max manages a parking spot right out front. He warned me it wouldn't be fancy, but I didn't expect this. My mood picks up as he opens the passenger door for me like a gentleman. I ask in surprise, "Mexican?"

He shrugs, and I could be wrong, but I swear he blushes. "I wanted to take you someplace I love." He stills. "You do like Mexican, right?"

I narrow my eyes at him. "You don't think you should've asked that beforehand?"

His face falls dramatically before he lifts a hand and pinches the bridge of his nose. "*Fuck, Lena*. I'm so sor—"

"I love Mexican," I chuckle then tease, "dumbass."

He breathes deep then lets out a long exhale. I take his hand, still chuckling, and he shoots daggers at me. He walks by my side, imitating me in a ridiculously high-pitched voice. "I love Mexican, *dumbass*." His voice turns normal again and he mutters a low, "I would remind you that as soon as we leave, your ass is mine. I'd remember that if I were you."

I round my mouth in mock-horror and stand on the spot, shaking my legs with enthusiasm. "Oh, no. The bad man's gonna get me."

His palm connects with my ass hard, ripping a shocked yelp from my throat. He stands toe-to-toe with me, looking down into my face. "How'd you like that?"

I swallow hard and my nethers tingle. Honesty is the best policy, I've always said (when it suits me, of course). I respond a hushed, "I liked it enough to want to push my luck again, and again, and again."

He lowers a hand to my collarbone, stroking his thumb over the sensitive skin there. His mouth hovers over mine. "Stop it."

I run my bottom lip across his and mutter, "Stop what?"

He kisses me hard on the mouth. Pulling back a hairs-breadth, he bites my bottom lip, gently tugging at it before responding, "Stop being sexy."

My grin is small, but it's there. "Sorry, but you started it."

He returns, "You started it."

I scoff, "You so totally started it!"

He mock-glares at me. "Real mature, Lena." We walk hand-in-hand, grinning like a couple of fools. He holds open the door for me, and as I walk into the restaurant, he whispers by my ear, "*You started it*," and I burst into laughter. I love this silly side of Max.

We're shown to our table in this quaint restaurant, and although it's small, it's beautifully decorated with red-and-white-checkered tablecloths, stools instead of chairs, and candles on the tables. It makes for an intimate setting, and I secretly love that Max brought me here and not some fancy restaurant where the meals are served on plates the size of car tires with meals the size of my palm. When the server arrives by our table, Max looks over at me and asks, "Mind if I order?"

I smile sweetly. "Not if you know what's good."

He grins at me. "I know what's good, baby."

I reach for my glass of water and sip, when a soft voice by the side of the table utters, "Max?"

Max and I both look up at the server, but Max is the only one who pales. "Oh, um, hey, Kate. How you doin'?"

Kate, the young Hispanic-looking server with olive skin, long black curls, and soft eyes responds in a hurt tone, "You never called."

My eyes leave the server, and wide-eyed, I turn to stare at Max. "You have got to be kidding me right now, Max." Did he seriously bring me to a restaurant where he shtupped one of the wait staff?

But Max blinks up at Kate, silently cursing her before stating the obvious. "I'm on a date here, Kate."

Kate turns to me still looking hurt, and I feel for her. I know what it's like to be rejected by Max. It seriously blows. With a sigh, I tell her, "Honey, trust me. He's completely oblivious when it comes to the opposite sex. You need neon signs and flashing lights for this one."

Max utters an offended, "Hey," while Kate smiles and admits, "I thought it was just me."

I shake my head. "Nope. It's all him. Believe me."

Max repeats his insulted, "Hey!"

I'm curious now. I jerk my chin up at her. "What did he do?"

Max starts, "I don't think we need to be discussing tha—"

But Kate cuts him off. "He took me out for lunch and we made out." She turns to look down at him, placing a hand on her hip. "Never to be seen again."

Max squirms in his chair, then forces a laugh. "Kate, babe, it was just a kiss."

Well, I hate to admit it, but I'm glad he hasn't fucked her. But still. I shake my head at him. "Oh, Max. You're such a turd."

Kate jerks her chin at me, mirroring my previous gesture. "You his girl?"

Max tries to break into the conversation with, "So this is kind of funny, right?" but as we speak over him, he fades out and continues to squirm.

I sigh dramatically. "Sadly, yes."

Her eyes narrow at me before she declares, "I like you. You're getting the house nachos on the house."

Smiling at her, I reach out to her. "I'm Helena. Sorry Max is a big, stupid baby."

She grins, taking my hand. "Kate. Nice to meet you, and don't worry about it." She glances at him before whispering, "He's kind of flighty."

Max is one of the most reliable men I know. He's not flighty at all, but I know what she's doing, so I don't correct her. Instead, I play along. I wink at her. "You're lucky you got away when you did."

She chuckles, then steps away. "I'll be right back."

As she does, I smile over at Max. "I like her."

He stares me down, clearly not amused. "Glad I could make introductions. I'm sure you'll be best friends forever."

Silently gloating in his discomfort, I reach across the table and snatch up a handful of corn chips, crunching away through a sly smirk. Mouth semi-full, I speak around my chips, "C'mon, Max. Admit it. It's kinda funny."

Kate returns with a plate full of nachos, piled with ground beef, oozing cheese, and chopped tomatoes. It looks amazing, and the smell of the spices has me salivating. She places it down in front of me with a smile. "Enjoy. Call me when you're ready to order."

Max starts, "We're ready to—" And I laugh as she turns, swishing her hair, and walks away, obviously ignoring him. Max eyes my plate, licking his lips. "Can I get in on that?"

Lifting a corn chip stacked with goodies, I shake my head. "Nope. Consider it your punishment," I tease, then I shove it in my mouth.

A pathetic look crosses Max's face. He rubs absently at his belly. "But I'm hungry."

Adorable.

No. Scratch that.

Adorably *pathetic*.

I reach across the small table to cup his pathetic cheek. He leans into my touch and I purse my lips, muttering, "Nawww, my big, stupid baby." He pouts, nodding in agreement, and although this is the worst date I've ever been on in my life, I'm having so much fun. And I don't know why! Something pushes that thought to air. I tell him, "This has been the worst date ever," but I do it with a smile. A real smile.

Max leans further into my cheek, eyes apologetic, and mouths, "Sorry."

Pulling my hand away, I admit, "But I'm having so much fun," I throw him a shy smile, "with you."

He smiles then, his billion-dollar, GQ magazine smile. "Naw, shucks, lady." But his smile falters. "You sure you're not pissed about that girl?"

"Am I going home with you tonight?" I ask.

His brows narrow. "Damn straight."

I shrug. "Then I don't care." Smiling, I nibble at a corn chip. "I win."

Something about my answer affects him, and I'm not sure how to read it. His eyes widen a little before they hood. He looks to be biting the inside of his cheek, as if trying to keep his mouth shut. Shaking his head, he mutters, "You are somethin' else."

When Kate returns, she takes our order from Max, glowering at him the entire time, but sparing a sweet smile for me as she leaves. She brings our meals and places the plates down in front of me gently, using as much care as possible, but when she places plates down in front of Max, she releases them an inch above the table, making them clash and clatter before turning and swishing her hair as she walks away. And I chuckle to myself. He must've really pissed her off. *Meh*. Serves him right.

I place the nachos in the middle of the table and reach over to his plate to snatch one of the most perfect looking chicken enchiladas I have ever seen. Max watches in shock as I steal from his plate. Bunching his nose, he reaches over to my plate and steals one of my steak fajitas in retaliation.

I smile over at him and wink. Little does he know, I am not Nat. Sharing food makes me happy. Nat would cut a bitch for stealing off her plate. I cut a piece of enchilada and pop it into my mouth. The fresh, spiced flavor is amazing. I moan and close my eyes. It's only when my eyes flutter open that I realize Max is talking.

"I'm sorry. What?"

He grins. "I asked you if you left a guy back home."

He's asking me if I had a boyfriend back home? Why the sudden interest? *Don't read too much into it, numbskull.* Shaking my head slowly, I cut at the enchilada for a second bite. "No. I didn't have time to date back home, and I never planned on dating here. I suppose I could have dated back home, but then where would that leave the guy? Probably in a corner." *Like Baby in Dirty Dancing.* "My job comes first, and as long as I'm building up my hours, I think it would be unfair to commit to someone, knowing they'd have little to no time with me."

Max looks down at his plate, confusion written all over his face. I ask a long, drawn out, "What?"

Lifting his face, brows still furrowed, he replies softly, "I think whatever amount of your time you could give a guy, he'd be grateful for." He holds my eyes. "He'd be a lucky man to have you, cupcake. Even for a minute."

Oh, shit. That was deep and sweet and freaking adorable. My heart pounds in time with my head. I'm in trouble. *Stop it, Max! I'm not meant to love you!*

If he's venturing into deep water, I feel as I thought I should be meeting him halfway. "Tell me about Ceecee's mom."

He immediately stiffens. "No."

My brows rise at the hatred in his voice. "Uh, okay."

We eat in silence for a little while as I give him the few minutes to calm down before I notice him deflate. His shoulders slump and jaw tight, he mutters, "Sorry. She's a sore subject."

I nod. "Understandable." The silence between us is so thick it's becoming awkward. And I've not had an awkward moment with Max since we've been dating. I don't like it. Reaching over the table, I rest my hand on his forearm. "We don't have to talk about anything you don't want to. But if you need someone to talk to, I'm here with open ears."

His eyes dart from the hand on his arm then up to my face, searching. He looks suspiciously toward me. "That's it? No '*I asked you, so you gotta tell me*' or '*Fine, we're done*' bullshit?"

I'm sure the expression on my face screams affronted. "I prefer you happy, and I can see talking about this is having the opposite effect. So, no."

His eyes close, once again pained as he mutters under his breath. "She prefers me happy. She cancels her own surprise for wheelchair basketball. She doesn't care about the waitress." He lifts his eyes heavenward. "Why are you doing this to me?"

Um, okay then. "What are you talking about?"

Max smiles. It's forced. I know this, because it doesn't reach his eyes. "Nothing." He holds out a hand and I place my own in it. He lifts it to his mouth and kisses it. "Just glad I'm here. With you." He kisses my knuckles a second time. "No place I'd rather be."

I smile softly. "Ditto."

Dinner only gets better from that point. Max and I eat, talk, and laugh most of the night, and when it comes time to leave, he leaves a more than decent tip for poor, sweet Kate. I'd like to say my sympathy runs deep, but I'd be lying. I am more than happy to be the one going home with Max. Ecstatic, really.

Like a gentleman, he opens the car door for me and sees me inside. We drive back to my apartment, and from the moment we step outside of the car, we can't keep our hands off each other. Reaching up, he hooks a hand behind my neck, pulling me closer, and then his lips come down to mine.

And I melt into him. The kiss is deep and sweet. My knees turn to jelly and my core clenches tighter than ever. His lips are soft, softer than I imagined, and the smell of his cologne makes my head swim.

My mouth waters. *God, he's delicious.*

A total DILF.

We can't keep our lips to ourselves the entire way upstairs. When we reach my apartment, I unlock the door, lips firmly attached to his, and we step inside, closing the door behind us. His arms wind around me, holding me tightly, leading me toward my bedroom, when something comes to mind.

Separating from him, I step back, delighted in the small growl that escapes him. I walk backward to the kitchen, unbuttoning my jeans as I do, smiling sexily. I slowly lower my zipper, hook my thumbs into the waistband, and push my jeans down my legs. Stepping out of them, I move to the counter.

I see the exact moment he understands. Fire lights in his eyes, and suddenly, he rips at his clothes. I chuckle softly as he fights with his belt buckle. In the sudden excitement, he's become clumsy. He kicks his shoes off, leaning down and hopping on the spot to remove his socks. He lowers his jeans halfway, then takes a step, tripping over them. He rights himself, pulling his shirt over his head, forgetting the buttons and having it get stuck around his neck. He pulls, tugs, and yanks until he's finally free and nearly naked.

My silky tan tank is easily removed, and then I'm only in my cream lace bra and matching French-cut panties. Which is fine, because Max is dressed only in black and white checkered boxers. He palms his erection as he walks over to me. Eyes hooded with lust, he admits, "I don't think I can hold back."

Reaching behind me, I undo my bra, letting it fall down my arms. "I don't want you to."

He squeezes his cock tight through his boxers. "It might be rough."

Making a show of it, I slide my panties down my thighs, letting them go at the knee. They fall to the ground. "I love rough."

He eyes my body appreciatively, then mutters unconsciously, "You make me crazy."

I love the way he looks at me. "You make my body burn."

One more step and he's in front of me, looking down at me. He leans down, pushing my back into the side of the counter, and takes my lips in a feral kiss before spinning me around and pushing his front into my back.

The hard warmth of his body gives me goose bumps. Reaching around, he takes my hands and places them on the counter. "Don't move."

My stomach clenches. Oh, my. Gentle hands roam my body and I ache. One hand squeezes my nape in such a dominant way, I press my thighs together and bite my lip to stop myself from crying out. The other hand caresses my shoulders, back, lower still, the curve of my ass, squeezing gently before he steps back.

I fight a mewl. His fingertips graze the skin of my bottom a moment before he slides them down between my legs.

Eeeek! Yay!

My eyes close in delight as he hisses out, "Fuck. Jesus, Lena, I—*fuck*." He presses into me from behind, his hard heat pushing into my ass, a finger sliding back and forth through my heat. He puts his lips to my ear and whispers, "You always gonna be this wet for me?"

Not even a moment's hesitation. "Always, baby." I haven't even noticed he's removed his boxers 'til the head of him seeks entrance. Arching my back, I hold the counter tight and mutter, "For as long as you want me."

He stills at my back, and my eyes snap open as I think hard about what I've said wrong. Moving my hair over my shoulder, a gentle kiss at the base of my neck eases my tension. With his lips against me, he utters, "When are you gonna understand, woman?" His cock slides through my wet heat, teasing. I moan weakly. He places himself at my entrance before stating harshly, "I am *never* letting you go."

With one severe thrust, he's inside of me, stretching me, all the way. And I see stars. I gasp, "Oh, God!" at the same time Max lets out a guttural, "Jesus. *Fuck.*"

Bending at the waist, I lower my face to the counter, resting my cheek to the cool surface as he pounds into me angrily. Every single thrust pulls a pant from me. My breasts bounce in time with my body. Max snakes a hand around my stomach, pulling me deeper into him as he drives into me. He's so deep he hits places of me I didn't know existed. It's amazing. Breathtaking.

Slamming into me, he whispers, "Shit. Perfect. Tell me what you need, baby."

Shame long out the window, I cry out, "Pull my hair." Never stopping his violent pace, he reaches up and wraps his fingers into my hair, pulling lightly. But it's not enough. When I wheeze out, "Harder," his grip and pace turn cruel.

He hisses out, "Fuck, you're amazing."

More painful than expected, I moan loudly as my core contracts suddenly. The pressure builds higher and higher. My core squeezes tighter and tighter. Sweat streams down my forehead and neck as I grit my teeth expectantly, waiting for the impact of the delicious torture I'm being assaulted with.

My body goes numb with perfect warmth as the stars behind my eyes explode, shattering into a million pieces like a mosaic of multicolored glass. Beautiful and painful at the same time. I come around him, moaning, milking him with every pull, and he growls, "Right behind ya, babe."

His thrusts turn erratic, uncontrollable, and in the state of bliss I'm in, I squeeze him internally, wanting his release. Releasing my hair, he grips my hips and drives into me balls deep once more before his fingers dig into me. A low, guttural sound is forced out of his throat as his cock explodes inside of me, jerking. As he comes down from his high, he slowly pulls out then pushes back in. He does this a number of times and our combined arousal runs down my thighs.

No condom.

At my uncharacteristically calm thought, he states, "Didn't use a condom."

I nod, turning back to him, looking over my shoulder, his cock still inside me. "I'm on birth control. I have an implant in my arm. And I'm clean."

His eyes soften. "Get tested every year at my physical. I'm good."

I smile a small smile. "Well, all right then."

Pulling out, he turns me, pressing me back into the counter, his hard, naked body on mine. "Never fucked like that before."

My smile turns shy. "Me either."

Max leans down, placing a soft kiss on my lips. "Never wanted to before you." He pulls back, placing a loose strand of hair behind my ear. "I wasn't lying, Lena. You drive me crazy."

I swallow hard. "Crazy can be good."

His eyes dance. "With you, anything's good."

He's *killing* me. I must save myself from the sweet! Slipping out from under his arm, I rush toward the shower. "Last one in's a rotten egg!"

He chuckles behind me and I start the shower, wondering what it would take for Max to love me like I do him.

CHAPTER THIRTY-FIVE

Helena

Max and I woke early, cuddling and exchanging sweet kisses before we had to pick up Ceecee from Tina's, where Mama Leokov had been watching all the children the night before. Time kept creeping up on us, but we didn't care. We'd both showered the night before, and thanks to Max's overnight bag, he'd packed everything he needed, from clothes, an electric shaver and hair wax, to deodorant and cologne.

If you asked me if I had dug into that bag when he wasn't there just to smell his cologne, I would tell you to mind you own freaking business...but I wouldn't deny it. In fact, the second pillow on my bed smelled an awful lot like that cologne. Funny, as I use that pillow as my snuggle pillow.

When it came time to go, I slid on navy sweats, a white tank, a black zip-up sports jacket, and slipped on my sneakers, putting my hair up in a high ponytail, and not a stitch of makeup. Max walked out of the bathroom and I almost died.

By God, he is magnificent.

He strolled out of my bathroom wearing black sweats, white Chucks, and nothing else. I eyed the lean, hard ridges of his stomach, my mouth parting in appreciation. When a tight black tee covered those ridges, I felt myself pout. Max strolled over to me, stopping only an inch away. He took my chin between his thumb and forefinger, and lifted my face to his. He pressed a firm, meaningful kiss on my pouting lips before pulling away, his golden eyes searching mine. "You keep looking at me like that and we'll never get going."

I breathed, "Right," but my eyes went to his lips.

He stepped away and groaned, "*Lena!* Fuck. Now look at what you've done." He grasped his growing erection and I laughed softly, covering my blush with my hand. He glared at me. "Yeah. Laugh it up. I'm gonna scare the fuckin' kids with this shit! So, *stop*."

But I couldn't. I walked over to him and pressed myself into his body, smiling up at him. Placing a hand on his chest, I teased, "You get moody when you're horny."

His muttered response was fuel for my ego. "Never been this horny before in my life, not even when I was a teenager." He reached back to the counter for his black *NY* baseball cap, placed it on his head, and then glowered down at me. "You got pussy voodoo or some shit, I swear."

He took my hand and led me to the door, grabbing a hoodie on the way. "Let's go, cupcake." He paused at the door, looking back at me with that familiar tender gleam in his eyes. "Have I told you how beautiful you look today?"

Ugh. Swoon.

I give Max the name of the park, and luckily, he knows where it is. I turn in my seat to chat to a nervous looking Ceecee. Her golden eyes bright with excitement, her auburn hair pulled into two sweet looking pigtails, dressed in a pink velour tracksuit, and white tee, she looks gorgeous this morning. "How're you doing back there, young grasshopper?"

She looks up at me with wide eyes and whispers, "I don't know if I can do this."

My eyes narrow at her. Sergeant Lena, coming through! "Don't give me that BS. Look at what you've done all by yourself in the last month. It's short of a miracle. Your fitness is past what I planned for. If you can do that, you can do this."

She raises her brows. "I didn't do that alone. You helped."

I roll my eyes. "Semantics. I didn't force you; you agreed to do it and you kept your promise." It's true that I still have a light session with Ceecee three times a week before our cooking lessons, as well as the three sessions she has with James. And she does it without complaint.

The kid is a little socially awkward. She has friends at school, but she doesn't like for them to come over, or for her to go to their houses, mainly because those houses aren't access-friendly for people in wheelchairs. Ceecee told me how once she went to a school friend's house and it was awkward. So awkward that Ceecee decided having friends at school was okay, but that was as far as it went. There would be no friend communication outside of school.

I told her that she must be lonely. My heart broke when she responded with a light shrug, saying she was used to it. I'm feeling all too protective of this girl. I can see it and realize this could be an issue, but, God help me, I can't stop myself from trying to help. This isn't just another child. This is *Max's* child. And she is a sweet, smart, self-conscious girl who I want the best for. I love Max. And I love Ceecee just as much. Maybe more, because she needs it more. As long as I'm around, Ceecee will never feel lonely. I swear it.

When she swallows hard, face pale, I start to sweat. "Hey," she looks up at me, near panting, and I utter quietly, "if you really think you can't do this, we'll go home." She blinks up at me in surprise and I feel the need to reiterate, "This is your choice, honey. One hundred percent."

And just as I knew she would, she responds a hushed, "Maybe I'll just go and see how I feel."

A beaming smile crosses my face. "That's my girl."

Max squeezes my knee in gratitude. He knows better than to cut into our girl-talk. Never taking his eyes off the road, he talks back to Ceecee over his shoulder. "Baby girl, how would you feel about going to Coney Island tomorrow?"

Her eyes widen. "Really?"

Max smiles. "No shit."

A shy smile spreads across her face. "Okay, but only if Helena comes."

I make a *pffft* noise. "As if you could stop me, honey."

He squeezes my knee again. "Then we're all set." He looks over to me, grinning. Not being able to help myself, I lean forward and press a hard kiss on his mouth.

Ceecee breaks into a fit of giggles. "Ew, gross."

On a sigh, I tell her honestly, "Girlie, one day, you're gonna look at a certain man and wonder what you ever found gross about boys."

Max's brows furrow as he adds hastily, "But not for, like, another thirty years." He looks back at her in the mirror. "Maybe forty."

Ceecee breaks into another fit of giggles, and looking over at Max, I join her. He winks at me, and taking his hand in mine, I sigh dreamily.

I am so in love with you.

We arrive at the park, and when Ceecee extracts herself from the car, Max takes my hand and we walk over to the basketball court. I can already see some kids in wheelchairs, as well as some adults, but I can't make them out. As we get closer, I see Felicity, Willa, and James. Smiling like a loon, I call out, "What are you guys doing here?"

Willa smiles sheepishly. "I heard you enquire about the game, so I figured we'd come to cheer Ceecee on."

Felicity grins. "Check it out." She opens her jacket to reveal a white tee she has decorated with colored Sharpies. It reads, "Ceecee's number one!" Ceecee giggles, and stepping forward, Felicity holds her hand up to her and they high-five.

James finishes up speaking to a young man with a prosthetic leg before jogging over. He holds his hand out to Max and they do a little bro-shake-slash-back-slap. "How you doin', Max?"

To my surprise, Max lets go of my hand and pulls me into the side of his body, uttering meaningfully, "Better than I've been in a long time."

James watches him closely, searching his face a moment before dipping his chin in silent conversation. *What the hell was all that about?* James looks over at me, eyes smiling. "You look good, Lena."

I bat my lashes. "Why, thank you, kind sir. You don't look so bad yourself." I wink and feel Max's fingers dig into my hip. I look up into his suddenly stormy eyes and mouth, '*Ow.*' In response, he narrows his eyes to slits and pecks my lips.

James kneels down in front of Ceecee. "You ready for this, C?" At her hesitation, he adds, "It's not like a real game or anything. It's just a lot of fun. We mess around with the ball and joke and laugh. Sometimes, people switch teams midgame, and then other times, there is no team at all. I promise you'll like it." She doesn't say a word and he smiles knowingly. "You need luck?"

She covers her mouth with a hand to suppress a giggle and nods. He sighs melodramatically. "The things I do for you people." Then he lowers his bald head. Ceecee reaches up with both hands and rubs it for luck, giggling all the while.

James wishes her luck, then jogs back to the young amputee, helping him remove his prosthetic leg and sit in a wheelchair. When the young man turns to us, Ceecee gasps. It's quiet, but I hear it loud and clear. I look down at her to find her eyes wide, mouth parted, and a small blush on her cheeks. Lifting my head, I look back at the boy. He looks a little older than her, maybe fifteen. When he spots her, he stills. His face becomes void of expression as he watches her watching him. I peek behind me to find Willa and Felicity chatting and laughing with Max.

Glad for the girls' distraction, I lean down to Ceecee and say, "Why don't you go say hi? Make friends? Isn't that why we're here?"

Ceecee nods, never taking her eyes off the boy. A small smile plays at his lips, and I can't help but notice how handsome he is for a young man. Chances are, he's going to be gorgeous when he grows up. Standing, he was tall, and sitting, he still looks tall. With messy brown hair, light eyes, and tanned skin, the harsh angles of his face make him look like a young version of Matt Bomer.

As she starts to wheel herself over to him, my heart smiles with pride as the boy wheels himself to meet her halfway. They simply eye each other carefully before the boy smiles and says something to Ceecee, holding out his hand. She takes it reluctantly, her blush now a blazing inferno, shaking it and mumbling her own greeting.

He talks to her as they stroll around the court. He points out things and laughs while he chats to her, completely comfortable in her near silence. When he nudges her with his elbow, smiling, she laughs. And it's such a sight that my heart swells. I also think I might cry. The boy leads her to a group of kids in wheelchairs, both boys and girls, and introduces her to them. They all smile and talk to her, and to my absolute shock, she smiles and talks back. This was a great idea.

Felicity breaks my thoughts with, "Let's take a seat; they're about to start." We all move to sit, but I notice Willa's missing. I spy her at the side of the court, fingers hooked into the wire fence, watching James like a love-sick puppy as he instructs the kids.

He calls out, "You know what to do, guys." He points to Ceecee's new friend and says, "Sam, I'm leaving Ceecee in your charge. Show her how things go, but take it easy on her. You've got ten minutes of free ball time before I blow the whistle," he grins, "then it's on!"

The kids cheer and clap before they disband, grabbing basketballs and playing with each other. I'm not even a little surprised when Sam leads Ceecee to the other side of the court, bouncing the ball to her and explaining how things go, watching her all the while. I am, however, surprised when Felicity gasps, "Oh, my *God*! Look, look, look!"

James joins Willa on the opposite side of the fence. His fingers linked into the fence, dangerously close to hers. My eyes widen. "*I told her he liked her!*"

Max looks over at the fence. "Who likes who?"

Felicity fills him in. "We've been pushing Willa and Whit together for a week solid. She loves him and he likes her. He's just fighting it, like men do." She bunches her nose and looks at Max. "Why do men do that?"

He swallows hard, looking away, letting out a strained, "No idea." He shakes his head and looks to me. "But I thought he liked you."

I raise a brow at him and scrunch my face in my famous *are-you-crazy* look. "What? We're friends; that's all. We flirt a little," I look back to him meaningfully and bat my lashes, "but there's no harm in a little flirting. Is there, Max?"

Felicity immediately gets my jab, tipping her head back and roaring with laughter. "Ooh, she got you good."

He looks down at our entwined hands and murmurs, "I don't flirt any more."

I snort. "Yeah, I know. Not even with me!" I side-eye him and ask quietly, "Why don't you ever flirt with me? You never did, right from the beginning."

He plays with my fingers a moment before looking up and stating, "Because I think you deserve better than that." He leans forward and kisses my temple. "A woman like you deserves real words, not pretty words that don't mean nothin'." He says this so sincerely that my heart skips a beat.

Crap. I wasn't expecting an answer like that. I lean into lips and he presses another soft kiss to my temple.

Felicity watches us closely, her face crumbling. "Oh, my God. It's finally happened." She fans her face, blinking rapidly. "Someone took the flirt out of Max Leokov," she sniffles, "and it was my friend who did it." She blinks away tears. "I'm so proud."

I reach over and shove at her shoulder. "Shut up, Flick."

Watching Ceecee, I mutter to no one in particular, "Would you look at how happy she is? I don't think I've seen her smile this much since I got here."

Max puts his arm around my shoulder and agrees, "She's loving it. And it's all because of you. You're the best thing that's happened to her." He places his lips at my ear and whispers, "To me, too."

My chest pangs. Lip curling, I turn and smack at his chest. "Stop it. Just don't."

The look of shock on his face is adorable. *The asshole.* He holds his arms out and shrugs, "What'd I say now?"

I shake my head, anger easing out of me, leaning into him once more. He just gave me a speech on not using words for fun. It's not fair for him to say something like that to me when he doesn't mean it. Both of his arms come around me, squeezing me tight, and I bask in the warmth of him.

Lord knows, I won't have it forever.

Watching Ceecee squeal with laughter and smile so much is the highlight of year. My own cheeks hurt from smiling while watching her during the basketball game—if a basketball game is what you'd call it. It was more forty-five minutes of kids in wheelchairs steal the ball from each other and speed away from the others while they tried to catch the person who had the ball. Every now and again, James would run onto the court, snatch the ball, and run around, laughing as they made chase.

He was right. Ceecee loved it. And she made friends. I saw her exchanging phone numbers with her new friends, but I saw the special light she had in her eyes for Sam. True, he isn't in a wheelchair full-time, but I'm guessing whatever caused his injury meant he was in a wheelchair for a long while before he walked again. And as much as Ceecee had eyes for him, he had eyes for her. I saw how his face fell watching her go. I believed Ceecee might've been experiencing her first crush.

On the way home, I turned in my seat and asked Ceecee a long, drawn out, "*So*?"

She smiled. "It was okay." She shrugged nonchalantly. "I guess."

The little sneak. Nodding, I turned, facing the road, and asked a bored, "What do you think about going again next Saturday?"

She hesitated a moment before responding, "That might be cool."

That might be cool. *Awesome!*

I peeked over at Max and squeezed his knee lightly. "Can we go out for ice cream?"

He looked back in the mirror to his daughter and winked. "Anything for my girls."

At the very same time, Ceecee and I uttered excitedly, "*Chunky Monkey!*"

I turned and we both blinked at each other before I started to laugh. Ceecee giggled, and before I knew it, I was laughing so hard that tears streamed down my face.

I swiped at my eyes and spotted Max shaking his head at the both of us. But he did it smiling. "Knuckleheads."

CHAPTER THIRTY-SIX

Helena

I make my way downstairs on a mission to find Max. That's my main objective right now. The White Rabbit is jumping tonight. As the weather gets warmer, the more people decide making the trip out on a Saturday night is worth it. I glance over the crowd and spot him by the bar, talking to a couple of pretty ladies. His smile is warm and engaging, but I don't care. The smiles they get doesn't compare to the ones he gives me.

Moving through the crowd, my deep purple maxi dress swishing around my ankles, my strappy flat-covered feet tread lightly across the dance floor, only seeing him. How can I see anything else when Max is in the room? Warmth spreads through me. I've never met anyone like him before. He's sincerely the most caring, thoughtful man I have ever had the pleasure of knowing.

At the end of the dance floor, I walk up the stairs toward him. When he spots me, he says a few words to the women before stepping closer to me, smiling wide. I beam at him, picking up my pace. My feet carry me faster and faster toward him. Finally, close enough, I leap into his arms. With no effort at all, he catches me easily.

I love you.

I press my mouth to his, hungry for his kisses, needing to show him how I feel.

I love you.

His mouth opens and I stroke his tongue with my own, snaking my arms around his neck, pulling him close.

I love you.

Pressing deeper into the kiss, I pull my lips away from Max's to whisper against them, "I'm in love with you."

When I try to kiss him again, he pulls back, hands tightly gripping my hips, looking down at me in confusion. "What did you just say?"

I'm done. I can't play this game anymore. I've not been playing for a long time. This just got real. "I'm in love with you." I smile warmly up at him and shrug. "I love you." His eyes darken a shade before he crashes his mouth to mine, taking my lips in a fierce, animalistic kiss. His fingers dig into my skin, and although it hurts a little, I feel the passion radiating from him. Closing my eyes, I tangle my fingers into the hair at his nape and give as good as I get. Pulling back, I rest my forehead on his and breathe, "I love you, Max."

Today, after Max took us ladies out for an ice cream, it was with a heavy heart I asked to be dropped off at home. When Ceecee asked me to come watch a movie with them, I declined, even though I wanted to more than I wanted to take my next breath. As I stepped out of the car, Ceecee asked, "Helena, can we go back to the park tomorrow morning?"

Max looked back at his daughter, then over to me. He shrugged. "We're skipping breakfast anyways. I promised Nik I'd help him out with painting the girls' rooms before Coney."

I smiled back at her. A small part of me grinned knowing she likely wanted to see Sam again. "Sure thing. Same time?"

She nodded excitedly.

Max stated, "Then tonight, you'll sleep at the house and take the van to the park while I'm at Nik's. When you're done, we'll meet at home and head to Coney from there." He made everything seem so easy. I agreed, and with tension in my gut, I left my two favorite people in the world.

Felicity came by, and with what was quickly becoming a routine, we got ready together and caught a cab to the club. B-Rock accepted our hugs and kisses before letting us inside, and when we approached the VIP section, Willa—dressed as a sexy Alice in Wonderland—waved us over with a huge smile. She hugged us and announced, "I'm doing it. Tonight."

Felicity and I glanced at each other, confused. Flick asked, "Doing what exactly?"

A sweet smile crossed Willa's face. "I'm going to kiss Whit tonight."

My jaw dropped. I shook my head to clear it. "Have you been drinking?"

She giggled, and I hadn't heard anything so sweet in my life. Covering her face with her hands, she uttered, "No, but he's giving me all the signs, like you said. And I'm done with waiting for him to make a move." She stood taller. "Tonight is the night."

Felicity took her hands in her own and beamed, "You'll have to find us and tell us how it went."

I scoffed and touched her arm. "Girl, if he kisses you right, we won't see you 'til Monday. And you'll be walking bowlegged."

We made our way upstairs and found Nat, Lola, and Tina sitting at the usual booth. Tina lifted her swollen feet onto a stool, while Nat rubbed them. As I approached, I smiled down at her and patted her belly lovingly. "You taking care of my nieces or nephews?"

She smiled sweetly. "I am, but they're not taking care of me. My back is killing me."

"Why didn't you stay home?"

Suddenly, Tina blurted out, "I needed to get away from my heathen children!" My brows hit my hairline. I'd never heard Tina say anything but good things about being a parent. She laughed. "Don't misunderstand me. I love my babies to bits, but I need time away from them. You know? To talk to adults."

Nat muttered, "And to get your fat feet rubbed," then winked at Tina.

I looked down at her belly and asked, "How much longer?"

She shrugged. "I don't know. The doctors say from next week it could be any day." A serene look crossed Nat's face and I knew deep inside me that she'd be a great mother. She couldn't wait to hold her babies.

Lola looked up at me, squinting. "Aren't you supposed to be in California?"

I bunched my nose. What kind of crack was Lola taking? "No. Why would I be?"

She shook her head, distracted. "I could've sworn I heard Trick say Max was taking you home for the day. Something about missing the beach."

It was then that I remembered.

"I sort of...had something planned for you. A surprise."

He wanted to take me home, to California, for the *day*, because I missed the beach? *Sweet baby Jesus.*

I muttered absently, "Excuse me," as I walk toward the edge of the staircase.

I had to find him. And I had to find him now.

Gripping my ass tightly, he groans into my mouth as he leads me away from the bar. Taking my hand, he pulls me up a flight of stairs I haven't seen before. When we reach the top, he swipes his keycard at the side of a door and it unlocks. I've never been here before. "Where are we?"

Gripping my hand so tight I think it might fall off, he mutters a short, "The office."

He opens an office door and turns on the light, pulling me inside and shutting the door behind us. I stand in the middle of the room, eyes darting left to right. I spot the photo of Ceecee and I realize we're not just in any office. We're in Max's office. My heart stutters when I notice the photo next to Ceecee's.

It's me. Fast asleep. And I'm snuggled deep into Max's throat as his eyes smile into the camera, kissing my forehead. *When the heck did he take that?* Drawn to the photo, I move toward it and ask a small, "When did you take this?"

He locks the door and states, "The first night we slept together." My gut coils. Why would he do that? I look over at him questioningly, and he says reluctantly, "Knew you were special."

My throat thickens with emotion. "But…"

"You told me the last guy you slept with was four years ago." He blinks up at me. "Know how long it's been since I last fucked a woman?" I shake my head slowly. He steps closer to me, accentuating every word with a step. "Nine. Long. Years."

How is that possible?

"How is that *possible*?" I ask, perplexed.

Toe-to-toe, he cups my face gently, running his thumbs over the apples of my cheeks. "Got bored. Having sex without emotion wasn't doing it for me."

I close my eyes to stop the sting behind them. "And me?"

His breath warms my lips. He presses a whisper of a kiss to them before repeating, "Special." He kisses me once more before uttering a soft, "You're my cupcake." Another kiss. "You're my sugar rush."

Damn. Did he really just say that? I blink back tears. I'm in bad shape over here. I sniffle. "That's the sweetest thing anyone's ever said to me."

He kisses my cheek and his lips linger. I feel his smile there. "Don't cry, baby. You're killin' me here. I want you happy. Always happy."

Even though I close my eyes tightly, a tear escapes as I promise a choked, "I am happy. The happiest." I open my eyes to look into his. "I can't remember when I've ever been this happy before." His eyes soften on me, his thumbs still at my cheeks, wiping away stray tears. I lean forward, pressing a lingering kiss to his mouth. "So, does this mean you want me around on a semi-permanent basis?"

A small smile plays at his mouth. "Helena, baby, didn't you hear me last night?" His eyes bore into mine. "I am never letting you go. Not ever."

My breath leaves me in a whoosh. I thought that was just sex talk! Unable to catch my breath, I whisper a shaky, "Don't say that if you don't mean it. I—" I swallow hard and tell him honestly, "My heart couldn't take it."

His smile deepens and he presses into me, forcing me back a step. My calves hit his desk, making me sit. Eyes wide, I ask softly, "What are you doing?"

As if it's an everyday occurrence, he lifts his shirt to unbuckle his belt. "Making love to you on my desk." He unbuttons his jeans. "Whenever I'm in here, I'm thinkin' of you." He lowers the zipper. "I don't want some made-up fantasy." He lifts the hem of my dress up over my knees. "I want the real thing..." I lift my butt, helping him to lift my dress higher still, to my waist. He hooks his forefingers through the sides of my panties and lowers them down past my ankles, "...'cause nothing compares to you."

Holy hotness.

His hands slide up my thighs, reaching under me to cup my ass. He lifts me and places me closer to the very edge of his desk. It feels like I'll fall, but I don't stress about it. I know if I slip, Max will catch me. Lifting his hand to my mouth, he presses two fingers at my lips. It takes me a moment to understand, but when I do, I part my lips and he slides his fingers into my mouth. I suck at them, enjoying the pained look on his face. His erection twitches through the gap in his jeans and it fuels me. Reaching up, I grip his hand and suck his fingers harder, wetting them well. I release them with a pop and he smirks, lowering his hand between my legs.

He slides in a finger, testing how aroused I am. When he quickly realizes I'm already there, he slips in the second finger, gently fucking me with them. My face flushes as I gasp. This has never felt great for me, but when Max does it, it's amazing. My core clenches, milking his fingers, and he looks down between my thighs in wonder. "Never wanted anyone like I want you."

Tilting my head back in pleasure, I sigh softly and pledge myself to him. "You have me." He wastes no time. He gently pulls his fingers out, places the head of himself at my entrance, and slides in all the way. My eyes shoot open as electricity flows through me. Every nerve in my body has been awakened.

He lifts my arm, wrapping it around his neck as he pulls me close, our lips a hair's breadth away from one another. But he doesn't kiss me. Instead, he thrusts into me, eyes open, watching me as though he needs it. We breathe into each other as our bodies rock, working as a team. I clench my internal muscles, and closing his eyes, he hisses.

My nipples become taut. His hand comes up to cup my cheek, and when his eyes open once more, they're hooded with desire. My legs wrap around his thighs as I feel myself lose control. I need him close. Closer than close. I feel the telltale tingles in my bottom, working all the way up my spine. My stomach clenches and my eyes flutter closed as I mutter, "I'm coming."

He speeds up his thrusts. "Open your eyes, cupcake. See me."

Panting, I whisper a hoarse, "You're all I see."

It hits me like a shockwave. My pussy clenches around his thick cock. A moment after my release, he stills, pushing in to the hilt. He groans through gritted teeth and I feel every warm spurt of his climax inside of me. It feels like heaven. Dropping his forehead to mine, he presses a small kiss to the tip of my nose before smiling like the cat who got the cream. "Well, work will never be the same."

I blink up at him a second before I burst into laughter. Max lowers his nose to my neck, his silent laughter coming out in short, hot puffs against my skin, and all I can think about is how great it feels to hold this man.

After we clean up, we walk back out to the bar hand-in-hand, wrapped up in each other. Nothing could burst my bubble of happiness. The second we walk out the door, we're almost bowled over by a couple of horny patrons sucking face and groping each other like there's no tomorrow.

It takes me a moment to realize that the horny patrons are actually Willa and Whit.

Helena

Waking up next to Max should be illegal. No man should look that good in the mornings. Even though we got to the house after three, we managed to somehow go to bed well past four. I don't know how that happened.

Okay. I lie. It might've had something to do with the fact Max wanted me in the middle of his bed, on all fours, and he wanted to ride me slow. Who would I have been to decline such an offer?

He set his alarm for seven—torture, I know—and when his alarm trilled, he woke with ease, showered, and kissed me goodbye. He whispered, "I gotta go, babe. I left the car keys on the bedside cabinet. Come home when you girls are ready to go."

Blindly reaching out for him, he allowed me to snuggle him a minute more before he placed a kiss to my forehead and left. I set my alarm the night before for nine, but it felt like I had just snuggled Max before my alarm was violently vibrating on the bedside cabinet.

I roughly remembered the front door opening and Ceecee calling out, "Helena? Are you up?"

That about did it. My feet found the floor and I stumbled out into the hall, half asleep, with my hair everywhere. As soon as I saw Ceecee, her smile was as bright as a pure ray of sunshine. "You didn't forget about the park, did you?"

My voice rough from sleep, I uttered, "No way, Jose. Let me grab a shower and we're outta here." Before I walked over to the bathroom, I kissed the top of her head, loving the sweet smell of her.

In no time at all, I showered and dressed in jeans ripped in all the right places, flip-flops, a slouchy sweater, and my aviator sunglasses before piling my hair onto the top of my head and tying it in a messy bun. Ceecee was waiting for me in the hall dressed in faded jeans and a sweet floral top, her hair brushed and let down to fall at her shoulders. I smiled to myself. My little girl indeed has a crush. No one dresses up to go to the park. She made a good choice. Sam won't know what hit him.

We drove to the park, chatting about nothing in particular. When we arrived, Ceecee let herself out and I asked, "When is Sam meeting you?"

Ceecee's brow furrowed in confusion. "Sam? I'm not meeting Sam."

I felt my own brows furrow to match hers. "Then who are you meeting?"

Ceecee opened her mouth to respond, but something in the distance caught her attention. She smiled then, bigger than I'd ever seen her smile, and wheeled herself off in the direction behind me. I turned, and with the sun in my eyes, I removed my sunglasses, holding a hand up to shield myself from the distracting rays. Ceecee approached a woman sitting at a bench. A slender, pretty woman with shining auburn hair, falling in waves down her back, and with one look at this woman, my entire world shattered.

There was no mistaking it.

The woman was Ceecee's mother.

CHAPTER THIRTY-SEVEN

CeeCee

I know it's her the second I see her. The photos in the box were old, but she hasn't changed that much. She looks like me. Well, I guess *I* look like *her*. The only difference is that I have my dad's eyes. My heart pounds as I move closer to her. As soon as she sees me, a sad smile crosses her face and she stands.

She's pretty. I mean, *really* pretty. Her long reddish-brown hair is wavy and sits just at her waist. I immediately decide to grow my hair to that length. Maybe she'd like that. I'll have to ask her. What do I call her? Mom? I guess she is my mom, even though I can't ever remember her being around.

She eyes my chair and asks hesitantly, "Cecelia?"

I nod, unable to speak. She waves an arm out to the bench. "Take a seat." As soon as she says it, she winces. "I'm sorry; I meant—"

I decide to put her out of her misery and cut in with a quiet, "It's okay. I know what you meant." I wheel my chair beside the bench and she sits once again, shifting away from me. She's probably as nervous as I am.

She plays with her fingers, looking away from me. "Why did you contact me, Ceecee?"

My heart sinks at her tone. "Because I wanted to meet my mom."

At the word *mom*, her eyes widen. "Please, call me Madeline." My cheeks flush. She sounds so stiff, so formal, as if I'm nothing to her. Shaking her head, she asks, "Does your dad know you're here?"

I shake my head and force a smile. "No, he doesn't."

He just doesn't get it. Every time I ask about my mother, he stops the conversation before it even begins. Then I found the box. It was like a sign. I don't need his permission. After all, this woman is my mother. She looks so classy dressed like she is, in black pants and a white shirt, the type you see in expensive magazines. Maybe she'll take me clothes shopping sometime. I'd really like that.

Madeline clears her throat. "Ceecee, the only reason I agreed to meet you today was to have a serious chat with you."

My gut clenches. *What kind of chat?*

Before I can ask, she states, "I have a husband and two young sons." Her eyes meet mine and they're cold as ice. "I'm sorry. I know this might sound harsh, but I don't have room for you in my life."

Helena

I stand there, in the place she left me, waiting for the moment she needs me. And I spot it before it comes. The woman doesn't even look at Ceecee; she talks to her hands, the arrogant bitch. My feet already moving toward them, protectiveness surges through me, burning through me like fire in my veins. Ceecee's face crumbles and she cries hard.

My pace quickens, and soon, I'm running across the park as fast as I can to protect my grasshopper from this hard looking woman. As soon as I approach them, I kneel down and wrap my arms around Ceecee. The woman stands, looking down at Ceecee in shock. I wrap my girl up tight, and bark, "What did you say to her?"

Ceecee looks up at her mom and sobs, "Why don't you want me? What did I do? Was I a bad baby?" Ceecee pleads, "Tell me what to do and I'll do it! Please, don't leave!"

The woman's eyes fill with tears, but she doesn't speak.

Oh, my God. Rage fills me. I stand from my kneeling position, eyes blazing. Placing a hand at Ceecee's shoulder, listening to the saddest cry I have ever heard in my life, I repeat a severe, "What did you say to her?"

The woman stutters, "I-I-I-I...shouldn't have come here."

Watching this pitiful excuse for a mother look at her child as though she's offensive, I whisper, "Then why did you?"

She steps away. "I'm sorry. I shouldn't have come." Without another word, the woman turns her back and walks away, leaving behind a completely devastated child.

Kneeling once more, I wrap my arms around Ceecee and hold her tightly as she wails, heartbroken, weeping from pure agony. *How could she just walk away? Again?* I don't even realize I'm crying until I feel wetness trail down my cheeks. I pull out my phone and text Max.

Me: Come home. Now.

I just hope I can get her home in one piece.

It takes a while to get Ceecee back into the car. She's quiet. Way too quiet. And I don't like it. Not that I blame her. The stupid bitch she called Mom really did a number on her. From her brokenhearted rambling, I manage to find out the mother has a new family and doesn't want Ceecee to be part of it. I tried to ask how she found her, but all she said was something about a box. It was hard to make out.

As soon as we arrive at the house, Max is waiting for us. Looking about as worried as a father should be, he rushes over to the van. "What happened?" Before I can answer, he spots Ceecee's blotchy, tear-stained face, and without waiting, he grips the sides of the wheelchair and pulls her down to the ground. Kneeling, he brushes a hand over her hair. "Baby girl, what happened?" When she doesn't answer, he looks back up at me, eyes wild. "What the fuck happened?"

That's when Ceecee croaks, "She doesn't want me," tears trailing her cheeks.

My heart silently breaks. Max looks confused. "Who? Who doesn't want you, baby?"

Her sad eyes peer into his. "Mom."

Max stands then, as rigid as a pole. Gritting his teeth, he turns to me and hisses, "What the fuck did you do?" My mouth gapes. *Me?* "Ceecee, go on into your room for a while, baby. I need to talk to Helena."

I look down at the pretty little angel, and face void, she does as her father says. As soon as she walks through the front door, he sucker-punches me with words. "Maddy was at the park? That's who you met?" I nod and open my mouth to speak, but I'm cut off. He booms, "You had no right! You should've come to me. I would have never let that bitch near her. How could you go behind my back?"

Shock turns my body rigid. I had expected a thank you for protecting his daughter, not a third degree. "Max, I thought—"

He paces. "No! You didn't think!" He jabs at his temple, eyes cold and uncharacteristically narrowed. "You didn't fucking think, Lena."

I step away, not from fear, but from hurt. "I didn't do anything wrong."

He forces a venomous laugh. "Oh, you didn't?" He points toward the house and shouts, "How the fuck do I fix this, Lena? What do I say to her now? 'Sorry, baby, but surprise! Your mom, the woman who left you before you were a year old, is responsible for your injuries, and she doesn't give a flying fuck about you'?"

I have never heard Max talk this way. I have never seen Max angry, or talk hatefully, or look at anyone the way he's looking at me right now. I want to walk away from this, just turn and walk out, but I can't. If I could only explain it to him, surely he'd understand. "This is all a big mistake."

His nostrils flare. "No. The only mistake I made was dating you."

I stumble back, hit by the force of his statement. I blink up at him, stunned at the hurt he's trying to inflict. Trying and succeeding. His eyes shut tight, his knuckles turning white. His breathing heavies. I know panic when I see it, and Max is overcome right now. I try to reason with him and utter gently, "You don't understand, Max. It wasn't like you think."

All of a sudden, his eyes shoot open, he leans into my face, and he roars, "You are *not* her mother! You aren't a parent; you don't know what it's like. I will do whatever I need to do to protect her, because I love her. You don't get to make calls about *my* daughter. *You are not her mother!*"

A thick silence cocoons us. We stand in it a long while, trapped before I find my voice. "Thank God for that."

The look of fury on his face tells me he misunderstands me. I immediately continue. I need to explain, but my voice sounds weak, even to me, "There is no way I could ever be her mom." I take a step back as my eyes begin to burn. "If I were her mom," I breathe in a ragged breath, "nothing could keep me from her."

Max's face morphs from angry to empty. I take another step back. My voice, quieter than before, says, "If she were mine, I would spend my life protecting her." Another step back. "I would do anything to see her sweet, crooked smile." One more step. Tears blur my vision; my voice cracks. "I would die before I hurt her. I would die *for* her."

I turn to walk away, but stop mid-step. Not looking back, I utter, "If she were mine, I'd spend my life letting her know how grateful I was for her. She would never be forgotten," I pause a moment, "but you're right. She's not mine. I'm not her mother," my feet carry me away slowly, "but sometimes, I wish I were."

He doesn't stop me when I leave. He doesn't chase me down, or apologize. As I reach the street, I tuck my hands into my pockets and just walk. My heart stutters with the realization that things have changed.

And not all change is good.

MAX

I watch her walk away, and even though I want to stop her and ask her what she meant by what she just said, I can't. I can't, because my daughter is inside, and she's hurting. Deep.

Maddy.

She saw Maddy.

God. *Fuck!* Jaw tight, I make my way into the house and search for Ceecee. I find her in her room, staring out the window. My chest aches. She looks so small. So lost. I don't know how to fix this. If Helena had just told me Ceecee wanted to meet her mom, I could've explained why that wasn't going to happen. But no, she went behind my back and organized a meeting with the heartless woman who gave birth to my daughter, and look at what she's done. All the progress Ceecee's made in the past month...gone.

I knock on the doorframe and move to sit on her bed. She doesn't acknowledge me. Resting my elbows on my knees, I utter gently, "So, you met your mom." She doesn't move. "I bet it makes sense now why I don't like talking about her, huh?"

Her bottom lip quivers and she takes in a shaky breath. She doesn't respond, but nods to the window. I can't help but ask, "Why didn't you just ask me if you wanted to meet her?"

Ceecee turns to me; her tear-stained face makes my gut burn. "Would you have let me meet her?"

I shake my head. "Hell no."

"That's why," she explains weakly.

I sigh. "She tell you she's got a family?" Ceecee nods. "And I'm guessing she wasn't as excited to see you as you were to see her." Ceecee shakes her head softly. I ball my hands into fists to spot myself from losing my shit. "You don't need her, baby. You never did. You got me, and I love you enough for a hundred people."

Chin trembling, tears fall from her eyes and she nods in agreement. "I know, Daddy. I love you, too."

My heart races. I'm close to the breaking point, but I keep my calm enough to ask, "How'd Helena find her? She hire someone? Took me close to a year to track her down."

Ceecee looks over at me, confused. "Helena didn't find her. I did."

My body stiffens. "What?" I ask, numb.

Ceecee wheels herself over to her closet. She opens the door and pulls out...

My heart beats even faster. My body hums. *You have got to be kidding me.* As she pulls out the box I've kept hidden all her life, I ask on a whisper, "Where'd you find that?"

Rather than answering the question, she mutters, "Her address was in here. Photos too. I sent her a letter weeks ago asking her to meet me this morning. She sent one back saying she would." Her eyes find mine. "Helena didn't know. She thought I was meeting my new friends." She opens her mouth to speak, but closes it. Finally, she says a hushed, "I didn't tell anyone."

Dread fills me as the realization hits me. Helena didn't know.

"I didn't do anything wrong."

"This is all a big mistake."

"You don't understand, Max. It wasn't like you think."

My heart stop beating altogether. What have I done? I close my eyes, trying to swallow, but my mouth is suddenly as dry as the Sahara Desert.

Jesus fucking Christ, what have I done?

"You're right. She's not mine. I'm not her mother. But sometimes, I wish I were."

I feel the blood drain from my face. My palms sweat.

"Are you okay, Daddy?" I swallow hard, the pressure in my ears building as she whispers, "I'm sorry, Daddy. So sorry."

I turn to my daughter. "I'm fine." *No, I'm not.* "As long as you are."

Ceecee smiles sadly. "I always thought meeting my mom would be a happy memory."

I shake my head and sigh an apologetic, "Cricket."

She shrugs. "Helena told me it didn't matter, that mom didn't matter." She smiles a small smile. "She got angry and said all that matters is I have a family who loves me, and Mom isn't cool enough to join our family, because she has a giant stick up her ass."

Helena. Of course she did.

Our family.

Our family.

My stomach turns as my head pounds. I think I might just throw up. I stand and move toward my baby girl, hugging her tightly and placing a kiss to her head. "I'm glad you're okay."

Ceecee straightens and states, "I can't imagine you with her." Unknowingly stabbing me in the heart, she mutters, "She's not like Helena, and I sort of thought she would be. I thought she'd be cool, and funny, and loving." Her eyes narrow in thought, likely pulling a memory from this morning. "She was just…cold."

I rub absently at the pang in my chest. Ceecee looks up at me, grinning. "You should've seen Helena yell at Mom. She wasn't even scared."

I'll bet she wasn't.

I clear my throat. "I think maybe we should do Coney Island next week, don't you think? We've already had a lot of excitement for one day. Maybe we can just sit around, watch movies, and eat junk today, yeah?"

She reaches up and takes my hand. "I'd like that, Daddy." Stroking her hair, I smile down at her before moving away. As I walk out of her room, she calls out, "Can you call Helena to come too?"

Somehow, I think she'll kindly decline. Not that I'd blame her. I'm an asshole. Rather than telling Ceecee that, I call back, "I'll call her." And call her, I do.

But she doesn't answer.

Not any of the eighteen times I call.

CHAPTER THIRTY-EIGHT

Helena

It takes me over an hour of walking for me to realize I have no idea where I am. Luckily, my cell, which rings in my pocket every minute or so, is in my pocket. I call for a cab and wait patiently for it, sitting on the stone fence of a fancy house. A woman comes outside the property, pretending to get the mail, but I see her eye me good.

A wave of irritation flows through me, but I squash it. Standing from my sitting position, I turn to the woman and smile. "I'm sorry. I didn't mean to sit there. My feet are a little sore."

The woman walks over to me. She looks to be in her fifties, with kind eyes. "That's okay. You sit if you need to, doll."

My throat thickens and I choke out, "I've been walking a long time."

My phone chirps in my pocket. I pull it out.

Max calling.

I stare down at the display, devastated.

The woman steps closer. "Are you okay, sweetie?"

The simple question causes my emotions to erupt. With my phone vibrating in my hand, tears flooding my vision, I sob out, "I'm pretty sure my boyfriend just broke up with me."

The woman makes a knowing sound in her throat before taking a seat next to me on the fence. "Ah. Young love." She pats my hand, her light pink fingernails flawless. "I'm sure it'll work out. If not, there are plenty of other fish in the sea."

Forcing down another sob, I sniffle, "Not like Max, there isn't." I look up at her. "He's it. My sugar rush."

My phone chirps again and again, and the woman nods down at the cell in my hands. "Seems like someone's trying awful hard to get ahold of you."

My voice lowered to a hush, I tell her, "I don't feel much like talking to him right now."

She sits by me in silence, her mere presence a pillar of support I hadn't know I needed, this woman I don't even know. "You know, when we were younger, my Stan had a knack for saying things in anger. Things he didn't mean, but things that hurt me regardless."

I use my sleeve to wipe at my face, and ask, "What did you do?"

She smiles at me, her eyes full of wisdom. "I forgave him. Every time."

My nose bunches. "I don't know if I could do that."

She shrugs lightly. "You ever said something you wish you didn't? Something that hurt someone without meaning to?"

Had I? Yes, I had. More than once. I nod, and she asks, "How did it make you feel?"

"Like shit," I whisper.

She puffs out a small laugh. "Exactly. Now, if your beau, Max, your sugar rush, is feeling like that right now, would you want to make him feel worse about it?"

I shake my head. "Now I'm not saying to run at him with open arms, honey." She winks, the string of pearls around her neck gleaming in the sunlight. "Nothing wrong with a little guilt trip. Sometimes, silence is the best punishment a woman can show a man."

A cab pulls up in front of the house and we both stand. I turn to her. "Are you and Stan still together?"

"In my heart, yes." She smiles sadly. "He passed nine months ago and I miss him dearly." A sincere look crosses her face. "And I'd give anything to hear his voice again, even if it were those hurtful words, because I'd forgive him again, and again, and again. I guess you could say that Stan was my very own sugar rush."

A wise woman. I hold out my hand. "I'm Helena."

She smiles sweetly, placing a gentle hand in my own. "I'm Martha Mae. But, please, call me Mae."

I squeeze her hand. "Thank you for the talk."

As I walk over to the cab, she calls out, "Helena, love isn't proud." When I turn, she adds with a light tilt of her head, "Sometimes, you have to put away your pride for the sake of love. But those times, with the right person, are completely worth it. Remember that, honey."

Smiling gently, I step into the cab and relay the address of my apartment. When the cab takes off, Mae waves, smiling back at me. I take in the words of the intelligent woman.

"Love isn't proud."

Nik stares at me hard, his jaw ticking. "Maddy? As in Ceecee's mom. *That* Maddy?"

I nod, nursing my beer. I lift it to my lips and utter, "The very same," before I sip. When I wasn't able to get ahold of Helena, I asked Ceecee if she wanted to go play with the girls. Of course, I had ulterior motives. I needed to talk to my brother. I needed advice, and if anyone knows better about how to fix what you've fucked up, it's Nik.

As Tina, Ceecee, and the little ones laze around on the sofas, watching a kid's movie, Nik and I sit on the back patio, away from little ears. My brother narrows his brows at me. "Why are you so calm about this?"

I'm not calm. I'm hurting, real bad, but not as much as I imagine Helena is. "Ceecee met her mom. It's done. The bitch doesn't want anything to do with her. I'd bet her family doesn't even know about Ceecee." I shake my head. "She was distraught, man. Never seen my baby so upset before."

He sips his beer. "I can imagine. I'd have lost my shit."

"I did," I admit. "I said some pretty fuckin' nasty things to Helena." I turn to see Nik watching me closely. I utter, "I fucked up."

Nik smirks. "Welcome to the club. I was wondering when you'd join us."

I glare at him. "Not funny, dude."

His smile falls. "You're right; it isn't, but it's probably not that bad. What did you say to her?"

I breathe deeply, and exhale slowly. "That dating her was a mistake. That she wasn't Ceecee's mom. That she had no right to do things she didn't even do." I pause a second before I tell him, "She told me she loves me, man. Just last night."

Nik remains silent, and I know it's bad. If it weren't, he would be teasing me. His non-response tells me how serious this is. How badly I fucked up. After a while, he asks, "You call her?"

I scoff. "Only thirty times."

"You text her?"

"I am not apologizing to her over a fuckin' text." I sip my beer and mutter, "She deserves better than that."

"You go over there?"

I shake my head. "Got Ash to make sure she got home okay." I tap the side of the bottle. "After he threatened to cut my balls off and feed 'em to me, he called later and said she got home around two. That was a couple of hours after she left."

Nik narrows his eyes at me. "You love her?"

No hesitation. "With all my heart."

He sits up in his chair. "Then why are you here, moping around like a fucking pussy?"

I open my mouth to respond, but nothing comes out. I try again and hate the weak state of my voice, "Because I don't know how to fix this. What if she doesn't forgive me?"

"Women like Helena don't need grand gestures. I know, because she's more like Tina than she is like Nat. You want to know how you fix this?" I look up at him and nod once. He rolls his eyes. "You get off your ass, go over there, and make a fuckin' effort."

My gut clenches. "I don't know."

Nik states, "I do." He pushes at my shoulder, jolting me. "You gonna let her go without a fight?"

Fuck no.

I know what I have to do. Not saying another word, I stand and stride over to the door.

Nik calls out, "'Atta boy, Max. Go get her."

Helena

"Don't wanna be...all by myself..." Here it comes. The big one. Mouthful of ice cream, I belt out a garbled, "*Anymooorrrrreeee.*"

My phone chirps. *Nat calling.* I slide the screen and answer around my ice cream, "Yeah, what?"

Her small chuckle sounds in my ear as she whispers, "Dude, the walls are super thin."

Oh. Seems my private performance has unknowingly become a concert. Eyes wide, I whisper back, "Oh. Right. Noted."

The amusement now gone from her voice, she asks a careful, "You okay, ho-bag?"

When I finally got home and Asher was waiting for me, he asked if I wanted him to make Max a permanent soprano. With a smile, I told him no, but kissed his cheek and thanked him for the offer. I asked him not to tell Nat what happened, that I'd tell her when I was ready. He wrapped an arm around me and I walked him to the door.

He looked like he wanted to say something, but also wanted to keep quiet. After a moment, he blurted out, "Men fuck up. And we do it a lot. Thank God, we got women who love us; otherwise, we'd be lonely sacks of shit." He rolled his eyes and grunted, "I don't think Max is good enough for you, but that's not because Max isn't a good guy. Max is one of the best guys I know. The reason I don't think he's good enough for you is the same reason I don't think I'm good enough for Nat. It's because you deserve better than the best. I know it's your choice who you date, but chances are I won't like any of 'em. And I'll like 'em a whole lot less than I like Max." Without waiting for a response, he kissed my forehead and went home.

I smile at the concern in Nat's voice. "I'm fine. I think I'm just missing home."

She hesitates. "You're not thinking of leaving, are you?"

"No, I'm not," I answer, even though I was earlier in the day. I thought about it, but it was a silly thought. "As long as the work is good, this is the place for me."

She lets out a humorless laugh. "Thank God. I love having you here. If you went home, I'd be shattered."

Wow. Nat never puts herself out there. I'm touched. I smile. "I wouldn't leave you. Who would keep you out of trouble?"

She laughs then. "You're almost as much trouble as I am."

"Am not."

"Are too."

A knock at my door sounds and I roll my eyes at her need to take this argument face-to-face. "Am not times a hundred."

I walk over to the door as she says smartly, "Are too times infinity."

Shit. What beats infinity?

Unlatching the door, I pull it open and grin. "Am not!"

But it's not Nat. It's Max.

My heart races.

He looks almost as bad as I feel. Nat calls out, "So I'm guessing by your silence that I've won this round."

I shake my head and speak into the cell, "Sorry, I gotta go. Max is here."

She purrs into the phone. "Ah, I get ya." Then sings, *"Let me lick you up and down 'til you say stop."*

I fight my hysterical laugh and mumble, "Yeah, like I said, I gotta go."

But she ignores me, singing louder, *"Let me play with your body, baby, make you real hot."*

I hang up and swallow hard. "Hi."

Max opens his mouth to speak, but Nat is not to be ignored. She shouts through the wall, *"Let me do all the things you want me to do."* I cover my mouth with a hand, flushing as she finishes her solo. *"'Cause tonight, baby, I wanna get freaky with you."* A moment later, she yells a huffy, *"You shut up, ASSer!"*

My face beet red, I bite the insides of my cheeks to stop myself from smiling, and look up at Max to ask quietly, "What are you doing here?"

He looks down at his feet and crosses his arms over his chest in a most defensive posture. "Can I come in?" He looks up at me then, asking gently, "Please?"

I push open the door and step aside as he enters, looking awkward and out of place. I close the door behind us and walk into the kitchen. Just because he yelled at me, blaming me for what happened this morning, doesn't mean I can't be polite. "Something to drink?" He shakes his head. I open the fridge. He's always hungry. "Something to eat?'

He sighs, his brow pinched. "No. Thanks."

I'm probably just delaying the inevitable, but it's somewhat of a defense mechanism. "Are you sure?" I ask as I move to close the fridge, and he loses whatever patience he has.

"Jesus, stop. Please. I just want to talk to you!"

Here it comes. The official break-up. Avoiding his eyes, I walk over to the sofa and sit. I play with my fingers, still not willing to look up into those gorgeous golden eyes. I feel the cushion depress, and his leg presses against mine. "Helena, look at me."

I do. Only because if I don't, I won't believe this actually happened, and I don't want to live in denial. He reaches over and takes my hand. I fight an eye roll. *Oh, great, he's holding my hand. Never a good sign. Just do it already. Put me out of my misery.*

"Ceecee told me what happened. I know you didn't have anything to do with Maddy showing up." Vindicated. Well, at least that's something. He adds, "I said some things to you in the heat of the moment. Things I didn't mean, and I need to apologize for them."

If I look him in the eye while he apologizes, I'll cry. I dip my chin. His fingers grip my chin, lifting 'til we're eye-to-eye. He searches my face a long moment before he utters sincerely, "I'm sorry, cupcake." His voice turns rough. "I am *so* sorry."

My eyes fill with tears, but I refuse to let them fall. Instead, I whisper, "It's okay."

His eyes blaze. "It's not okay. If anyone else spoke to you the way I did, I would fuckin' murder them."

My eyes close of their own accord. I repeat, "It's okay. I forgive you. I know you were put in a stressful situation. Not only was your daughter hurt in the fray, but you thought I betrayed you after you told me Ceecee's mom was a sore spot." I stress the conviction by steadying my voice. "I get it. I do." I open my eyes and take in a shaky breath. "But I never would. Betray you, that is."

His face turns pained. "I know you wouldn't, baby."

Well. That's that. I stand and head to my room. Taking out what I'd prepared when I got home earlier, I bring it out and hand him his overnight bag. He looks at it in confusion before he stands, towering over me, eyes blazing. He takes the bag from my fingers and throws it aside. It hits the ground with a dull thud. His eyes wide, he places his hands gently at the base of my neck, gets in my face, and states, "I'm not letting you break up with me. So you can go ahead and put that back in your closet."

A record screeches somewhere in my mind. *What? Me* break up with *him*?

Before I can get a word in, his eyes plead. "Baby, please, forgive me. I swear to you I didn't mean what I said. I said those things because I was hurting. You were never a mistake. You're the best thing to come into my life since Ceecee. And I know you're not her mom, but," he speaks so softly, I wonder if I imagine it, "you're the closest thing she's got right now. She loves you." He hesitates before admitting on a small voice, "I love you."

'Love isn't proud.'

My insides stir. Placing my hands over his, I lean my forehead onto his chin and whisper, "Say it again."

He kisses my forehead and mutters against it, "I'm so sorry, baby."

I look up at him, eyes glittering. "Not that. The part where you said you love me."

His smile is small. "I love you."

"Really?"

His dimple cuts into his cheek as he leans down to place a wet kiss on my mouth. "Been fighting it. Didn't want it. But I'll be damned if you try to take it away from me. We've got somethin' good now, but we can have something incredible." His lips cover mine. "I love you, Helena. Really, really."

Suddenly, his body stills and he pulls away looking unsure of himself. "You still love me, cupcake?"

I roll my eyes, reach up, and punch him in the arm hard. He winces and I scoff. "Yes, I still love you. *Asshole*."

He nods solemnly, but smiles, rubbing his arm. "Okay. I deserved that." We stand, smiling up at each other. "So, now what?"

I shrug. "Now, nothing."

He raises a brow. "We have our first major fight, pronounce our love to each other," he chuckles, rubbing the back of his neck, "and then we go home and do nothing about it?" He shakes his head. "Something seems off about that."

I blink up at him. "I hear make-up sex is all the rage."

He looks over my shoulder, staring at the wall in thought, rubbing at his chin. "Make-up sex, you say?" After a moment, he straightens and stalks forward. "I'm willing to give it a shot."

Turns out, make-up sex is indeed all it's said to be. In fact, as we lie on my bed naked, panting, and sweaty, I know I'll be willing to cause a few arguments in our relationship just to apologize.

With my mouth.

CHAPTER THIRTY-NINE

Helena

If you had asked me three months ago if I wanted a relationship, I would've laughed boisterously and patted your sweet little head. But now I see it's not the relationship to fear. It's being in a relationship with the wrong person. As I sit on Max's lap, his arm resting across my thighs as he presses kisses to my shoulder, I realize a relationship with the right person is not scary. It's amazing.

Being yourself and having someone love you for it is *amazing*. If I knew it would be this way, I would never have fought it. I would've embraced it. But that's the catch, isn't it? You need to risk to gain. I took my leap of faith and it paid off. I got the best reward I could ask for. I got Max, and in turn, I got Ceecee too.

Turning on his lap, I lower my face to his, pressing light kisses on his mouth. As always, butterflies flutter in my belly.

Will it always be like this? Secretly, I hope so.

His eyes flicker down to my neck. Reaching up, he takes the necklace in his hands, eyeing the ring dangling from it. "You don't always have to wear it, baby."

Max's ring. As if I'd ever take it off. It wasn't a proposal, exactly. More of a promise of what's to come. "I'm never taking it off," I vow openly.

After Max told me he loved me that night, four weeks ago, we've been inseparable. The very next day, he gave me his ring. With a flush, he muttered, "You don't have to wear it or anything. I just want you to have it."

It was adorable. And thoughtful. And I loved him even more for the sentiment. Of course, being that Max has giant fingers, it was never an option to wear it the traditional way. I found a white gold chain, put the platinum ring on it, and I haven't taken it off. Not once. When Ceecee spotted the ring, she looked a little too happy about it. Eyes darting from me to Max, she uttered, "Are you going to marry my dad?"

Seriously. She did that on purpose, the little sneak. Before I had a chance to answer, Max wrapped an arm around me. "When I ask, she'll say yes."

The confidence of the statement oozed off him, and I wanted to hit him. But it hit *me*. What he had just said.

When he asks. Not *if* he asks.

My heart squealed and my mind swooned. Ceecee looked down at the table, her mind calculating. "So when you get married, that would make you my stepmom, right?"

Heart warm, I smiled down at her. "Yes, honey, it would."

She breathed, "Cool," and it sucker-punched me right in the gut. She wanted me to be her stepmom. Truth is, I was ready for it, even then. And one day, maybe we'd add another baby to the mix. When it came to Max and Ceecee, it came naturally. I trusted my gut and knew that whatever difficulties we faced, we'd do it together as a team. As a family.

Eyes smiling, Max's arms tighten around my waist. "Never taking it off? Really? Never *ever*?"

I press a soft kiss to his cheek and promise, "Never ever."

MAX

Three months later...

This fuckin' ring is burning a hole in my pocket. Proposing at a family dinner is probably not the way I should be doing this. Helena walks around my mother's kitchen counter, holding two bowls of salad. As she passes me, she leans up, and instinctively, I lower my lips to hers for a quick kiss. When we separate, she winks at me. And I feel it in my cock. I can't do this any longer. I can't wait. I need to ask her to marry me. I need her to say yes. I need to make sure she'll be with me forever.

I just need her.

Mama steps out of the pantry and calls out, "Dinner's ready! Everyone out!" She finds my eyes as everyone moves out, and winks at me. Of course I had to tell my mom. She'd box my ears if I didn't. To say she's excited about Helena becoming a real member of our family is an understatement. There was a moment there when I thought Mom wanted to propose on my behalf.

Hell, I even called Helena's family to ask permission. It seems it wasn't just her dad's permission I needed to get. I needed permission from them all. Including Asher. After a half-hour over-the-phone presentation on why I would make a good son-in-law, Helena's dad gave me his blessing and I was good to go.

I take a deep breath and make my way outside to find Nat sitting on one side of Lena, and Ceecee sitting on the other side, while Lena and Nat feed Nat and Asher's new babies, Willow and Daniel, AKA Low and Danny.

My brow bunches. That wasn't part of the plan. I need to be sitting next to her to propose. I find an empty seat beside Nik and my mom. I sit there with a pout.

Now what?

Watching Lena feed Willow is something else. She looks down at the baby girl like she's the most precious thing in the world. A vision of Lena holding a bundle with dark brown hair, her pouting lips, and my golden eyes flashes before me. I smile to myself.

Everyone works around me, filling their plates, but I can't take my eyes off her. When Ash steals Willow from her clutches, she sulks. My smile deepens. She stands, filling Ceecee's plate, and when she's done, she places the plate in front of Ceecee, smooths down my baby girl's hair, and kisses her head. My smile turns into a grin.

Lifting her own plate, she starts piling food on it, and before I realize what I'm doing, I stand, reaching into my pocket. From across the table, I open the ring box and hold it out. Helena continues to fill her plate. Smiling like a damn fool, I ask loudly, "Helena, will you marry me?"

A few feminine gasps, then silence surrounds us. Pausing mid-salad-scoop, she looks over the table at me, stunned. Looking down at the ring, she recovers quickly. With a small shrug, she utters, "Uh, sure." Then she smiles up at me. "Pass the potato salad, babe?"

I smile so hard my cheeks hurt. "Of course, cupcake." Placing the open ring box on the table, I pick up the bowl of potato salad and hand it to her. She takes it, biting her lip to hide her smile. A small round of applause, some cheers, and then everyone continues what they were doing. We take our seats on opposite sides of the table, smiling at each other like a couple of clowns.

She mouths, 'Love you.'

I mouth back, 'Love you more.'

And I do.

I really do.

Later that night, Ceecee and I lounge around on the sofa, while Helena makes our celebratory banana splits. I turn to my daughter and watch her a moment before asking, "You happy, baby?"

Ceecee turns to me, smiling. "Yeah, I am."

I nod. "That's all I need to hear."

We continue to watch in silence before Ceecee asks a hushed, "Am I going to have brothers and sisters?"

My brows rise. Not a question I was expecting. "You want brothers and sisters?" She nods. Hiding my smile, I call out, "Yo, cupcake."

A few seconds and Helena pops her head into the living room. "Yeah?"

Taking a handful of popcorn, I ask, "You want kids?"

She stands there, dumbstruck. Her eyes dart from me to Ceecee, then back again. Then she smiles. "Yeah, I do." Without waiting for a response, she heads back into the kitchen. I look back at the TV, but hold up my hand. When Ceecee high-fives me, I grin.

Everything's looking up.

EPILOGUE

Helena

I walk out of the store, flicking through the photos, smiling and chuckling to myself. Six months after our engagement, Max and I got married. It wasn't a lavish affair. It was quaint. We had all the people we wanted there and did it all our way. For instance, even though he wore a three-piece tux, Max wore his black Chucks instead of dress shoes. And even though I shouldn't have been wearing white, I did, just because I wanted to.

Nik insisted we have the reception at The White Rabbit, and considering it was the place of our first real kiss, I was all for it. Nina decided she would be my maid of honor, because she didn't live in New York; therefore, she felt she deserved the position as I'd be seeing Nat all the time. Nat and I both agreed, and she and Ceecee were my bridesmaids.

Max asked Trick to be his best man, with Nik and Ash as his groomsmen. My dad cried the entire ceremony, my mom handing him tissues all the while. Mama Leokov dabbed at her eyes, and overall, it was a happy occasion.

Max looked at me like I was the most valued woman in the world, stopping every half-hour to ask, "Have I told you how beautiful you look today, sweetheart?" We ate and danced into the wee hours of the morning, and I smiled all damn night. Even now, a week later, as I look down at my wedding ring, I ache with happiness.

I spot the florist a few stores down and head inside.

Mae

As I place the cookies into the oven, the doorbell rings. I open the door, and a delivery man stands there holding an outrageously large bunch of flowers. "Martha Mae..." He glances down at the delivery slip before looking up at me, "I'm sorry; there isn't a last name here."

I'm stunned. "That's me."

He hands me the flowers with a smile. "Looks like someone is thinking of you. Have a nice day, ma'am."

I struggle to see over the top of the colorful bunch, pausing to place them on the table in the hall. I take the card and open it.

Dear Mae,

A wise woman once told me love isn't proud.

Thank you. For everything.

Thinking of you,

Helena Leokov.

Oh my. Inside the envelope is a photograph. I smile when I realize it's a picture of young Helena on her wedding day. The handsome man by her side with eyes the color of melted honey smiles, looking down at her with pure love. Helena holds hands with a pretty young girl in a wheelchair.

I can't help but notice the small bump at her belly. The bridge of my nose tingles as I look up at the portrait of my late husband. "Well, how do you like that, Stan?"

I smile up at him, tears filling my eyes. Happiness warms me.

She did it.

She got her sugar rush.

A message from the author

Hi guys,
Thank you for reading *Sugar Rush*. I hope you enjoyed reading it as much as I enjoyed writing it!
You can help me an awful lot by leaving a review on Amazon and Goodreads.
Thanks again.
Your love and support mean everything to me.

Belle xx